SOUL OF SERPENTS

JONATHAN MOELLER

THE DEMONSOULED SERIES #3

SOUL OF SERPENTS
Jonathan Moeller

LEGAL

1

WARBAND

Mazael Cravenlock awoke from a dream of a great black wolf.

For a moment the wolf's howls echoed in his ears.

He sat up in bed, blinking.

Yet the howls continued.

Those weren't howls, he realized, but a blast from the horns carried by the night guards upon the castle's walls.

Castle Cravenlock was under attack.

Mazael surged to his feet, and his bedroom door burst open. A boy of twelve years stood in the doorway, clad in the black-and-silvery livery of the Cravenlocks. Usually the boy wore an expression of chilly arrogance, but now his eyes bulged with fear.

"My lord," said Rufus Highgate, "my lord, the sentries..."

"I know," said Mazael. "Find one of the pages, send him to Sir Hagen. Tell Hagen to rouse the garrison. Then get back here and assist with my armor. Go!"

Rufus sprinted off. Mazael paced around his bed, bare feet sinking into the carpet. His rooms atop the King's Tower held only a bed, a desk for writing, a wardrobe for his clothing, and racks for his armor and weapons. A thick carpet to guard against the winter chill was the only concession to comfort.

That, and the rooms had a superb view of the castle and the surrounding countryside.

Mazael hurried onto the balcony, seventy feet above the courtyard. The night guards stood upon the curtain wall, crossbows in their hands. Torchlight blazed in the courtyard as men raced back and forth. Sergeants bellowed commands to armsmen, while knights ran for the stables, followed by their squires. Good - Sir Hagen had already roused the garrison. Yet where was the attack?

Beyond the curtain wall, light flashed in the darkness. Cravenlock Town, an overgrown village of four thousand people, stood a half-mile in that direction. Mazael saw firelight from the town, and heard the distant sound of steel on steel, the shouts and screams of men and women.

The town was under attack.

His hands curled into fists. These were his people, his lands. And someone dared to attack them? He would make these attackers pay, he would make them suffer...

Mazael closed his eyes, forced himself to calm.

Fury was not a luxury that a child of the Old Demon could afford.

For a moment he remembered a blue-eyed woman lying on a cold stone floor, black hair pooled around her head.

He knew where the rage of the Demonsouled ended.

Rufus sprinted into the room, breathing hard.

"My lord," he said, "I've sent the message..."

"Good," said. "Help me with my armor."

He'd worn the same armor for years, but it had been destroyed last year during the great battle below the walls of Tumblestone. So Lord Malden had made Mazael a gift of a new set. A chain mail hauberk with a steel cuirass, and gauntlets backed with steel plates and armored boots, all crafted by Knightcastle's finest smiths. Mazael pulled on the armor with Rufus's help. The boy was nervous, but he worked quickly and without error. That was good. He would make a capable knight.

Assuming he lived through this attack.

Mazael tugged on a black surcoat adored with the sigil of three crossed swords, the symbol of the Cravenlocks. Rufus fetched his sword belt, and Mazael buckled it around his waist. A dagger hung on his left hip, and a longsword on his right. The longsword's pommel was a golden's lion head, glittering rubies in its eyes. Lion, Mazael called the sword, and it was worth more than his castle and everything in it.

Older than his castle, too.

He took one last thing. A silver coin, the size of his thumb joint, threaded with a fine chain. Mazael tucked it into his belt.

"Come," said Mazael, and he left his rooms, Rufus following, and hurried from the King's Tower. Chaos still reined in the courtyard, but it was an ordered chaos. Mazael's knights sat atop their horses, lances and shields in hand, armor flashing in the torchlight. His armsmen had also been mounted, sword and mace ready at their belts.

Two hundred men. Mazael hoped it was enough.

"My lord!"

A grim-faced man with the shoulders and chest of an ox strode to Mazael's side. He wore a Cravenlock surcoat and a mail hauberk, eyes glinting over a close-cropped black beard. One hand rested on his sword hilt, and the other bore a shield adorned with the sigil of a burning bridge.

"Sir Hagen," said Mazael. "What news?"

"Someone lit the alarm beacon in the town's church tower," said Sir Hagen Bridgebane, Mazael's armsmaster. "The night guards saw it and summoned me." He scowled, shaking his head. "It's too dark. We can't see anything. But I think the town militia is holding. For now."

"Who is attacking?" said Mazael. "Bandits?" It would indeed take a daring band of bandits to attack a walled town. But who else? The Elderborn tribes? One of Mazael's vassals? Some of Mazael's knights and vassals hated him, but none were bold enough to stage such a raid.

Lord Richard Mandragon, perhaps? Mazael remained in his liege lord's good graces. But Lord Richard the Dragonslayer was feared with reason. If he decided that Mazael was an enemy, he would not hesitate to strike.

"I don't know, my lord," said Hagen. "But they've no horses, I'm sure of that. We're ready to ride when you give the command." He grimaced. "But the wizards want to speak with you first."

"Good work," said Mazael. "We'll ride when I give the word. Leave the squires here. I don't want any of them killed fighting in the dark."

Hagen hurried to his horse, shouting commands.

Rufus brought out Mazael's war horse, a vicious-tempered destrier named Challenger. The huge horse looked as eager for blood as any knight. Mazael swung into the saddle and accepted a lance and a shield marked with the Cravenlock sigil from Rufus.

"I should accompany you, my lord," said Rufus. "It is only honorable."

"No," said Mazael. "Stay here with the other squires. I'll not explain to your father why I got you killed in a night battle."

Rufus scowled, but obeyed. Mazael urged Challenger to a walk, steering the beast with his knees. Sir Hagen waited near the barbican, along with three other men. The first was old and tough as an ancient oak tree, clad in mail and leather. The hilt of a greatsword jutted over his shoulder, and a mace and war axe waited at his belt. Sir Nathan Greatheart claimed to have retired, but the old knight still fought with the prowess of a much younger man.

The other two men wore black cloaks and long black coats adorned with metal badges. The older of the two was nearing forty, with tousled hair and a pointed brown beard. The second was barely over twenty, face shadowed beneath his cowl. A black metal staff rested across his saddle's pommel.

None of Mazael's men went close to the two wizards. Especially the younger one.

"Lord Mazael," said Timothy deBlanc, the older wizard. "My war spells are at your command."

The younger wizard looked up, black eyes glittering in the depths of his cowl.

"And you'll need them," said Lucan Mandragon. He was younger than Timothy, but far more powerful. Men called him the Dragon's Shadow, and dared not meet his eye as he passed. "My wards were triggered. At least one of the attackers is using magic. Possibly more."

"Can you take them?" said Mazael.

"We shall do our best, my lord," said Timothy.

Lucan's contemptuous sneer expressed more confidence than words.

"Good," said Mazael. "Sir Hagen!"

The armsmaster spurred his destrier forward, lance and shield ready. "My lord?"

"Tell the armsmen to keep watch," said Mazael. "They're to close the gate after we leave, and leave it closed until we return. The knights and mounted armsmen will stay in formation. Any fool rides off on his own, I'll have his hide." Hagen nodded and bellowed the orders to the sergeants. "Sir Nathan!"

The old knight turned his horse. "Lord?"

"Take command of the knights," said Mazael.

Nathan frowned. "I am no longer armsmaster of Castle Cravenlock, and I..."

"Yes, yes, I know," said Mazael. "Do it anyway."

A flicker of a smile went over Nathan's seamed face. "As you bid, my lord."

"Sir Hagen!" said Mazael. "We ride."

Hagen gave the orders. Chains rattled, and the portcullis slid open with a metallic groan. Mazael kicked Challenger to a trot and rode through the gate, the knights and armsmen falling in around him. Sir Aulus Hirdan, Mazael's herald, rose at his side, the Cravenlock banner fluttering from his lance. Though Mazael doubted anyone could see it in the dark.

The road to Cravenlock Town sloped alongside the side of the castle's crag. The sounds of fighting grew closer, accompanied by strange, bestial roars. Had the attackers brought war dogs? Timothy shifted in his saddle, fumbling with a fist-sized chunk of wired-wrapped crystal. Mazael had seen him use that spell before. It bestowed a sort of limited clairvoyance, letting Timothy sense the presence of enemies. Timothy held up his hand, and the crystal flashed with a pale white light.

"Timothy!" said Mazael. "How many?"

"I...I do not know, my lord," said Timothy, shouting over the drumming of the hooves. His eyes darted back and forth, tracking things unseen. "At least...two hundred. Probably three hundred. They're at the town gates for now. But...my lord..."

"What is it?" said Mazael. "Are they in the town already?" Gods, he hoped not. House to house fighting would negate the advantage of his horsemen.

"No," said Timothy. "But...I've never sensed anything like them before. It's as if...it's as if they're not human..."

Lucan gave Timothy a sharp look, hand tightening around his black staff.

"The San-keth?" said Mazael. "Or the changelings?"

"No," said Timothy. "No, I know how they feel to my arcane senses. This is...different. Darker, considerably."

Demonsouled, then? The thought of three hundred Demonsouled gathered made Mazael's blood run cold. But Mazael doubted that any number of Demonsouled could cooperate for any length of time.

He knew very well the sort of homicidal madness carried by Demonsouled blood.

"Whatever they are," said Mazael, "they're still flesh and blood, and we'll sweep them away. They're massed near the town gates?"

Timothy gave a sharp nod, eyes still twitching.

"Then we'll hit them there," said Mazael. "Sir Hagen! Get the men in line. Once the enemy is in sight, we'll charge and ride them down." With luck, the gate held the attackers' attention, and they would not spot Mazael's horsemen until it was too late.

Hagen and Nathan bellowed orders, the knights and armsmen forming a wide line. The horses moved forward at a trot, ready to leap into a gallop. Cravenlock Town came into sight, the rooftops rising above the thick stone wall surrounding the town. Lord Mitor, Mazael's predecessor and elder brother, had let the wall fall into disrepair. Mazael had ordered it rebuilt, despite the expense. He also insisted that the town men's form a militia, training regularly, despite their grumbling.

He doubted anyone would grumble after this.

Torches blazed atop the stone wall. Militiamen fought from the ramparts, wielding crossbows and spears. A dozen ladders rested against the wall, and Mazael saw dark-armored shapes scrambling up the rungs, spears and axes in hand.

The invaders.

Mazael took a look at them, a good look, and blinked in disbelief.

The invaders were not bandits. Nor were they were Mazael's vassals, or Lord Richard's men.

They weren't even human.

Mazael had never seen creatures like them before.

They looked almost like men, albeit men with leathery gray skin and long, pointed ears. Their eyes were colorless, milky white, yet they seemed to have no difficulty seeing. The creatures wore greasy leathers, ragged furs, and black chain mail. Dozens of them lay dead below the gate, covered in black blood. Yet the creatures showed neither fear nor pain, and flung themselves at the defenders with abandon, roaring and howling like beasts.

Lucan swore, very softly.

"What are they?" said Mazael.

"I had never thought to see them," said Lucan.

"Damn it, what are they?" said Mazael.

Lucan looked at Mazael, his eyes reflecting the firelight. "Malrags."

"Malrags?" said Mazael. "Malrags are a legend, like..."

"Like the Elderborn?" said Lucan. "Like the San-keth?"

Mazael growled. "Legend or not, they are still flesh and blood. Sir Hagen! Sir Aulus! Sound the charge..."

The air crackled, and a bolt of green lighting screamed out of the cloudless sky, so bright that it filled the plains with ghostly light. It struck the arch over the gates with terrific force, blasting stone and wood to glowing shreds. Smoking debris rained over the Malrags and the town militia alike, knocking them to the ground, and the horses whinnied and stamped in terror.

For a moment the battlefield remained motionless, the echoes from the lightning blast rumbling into silence.

Then the Malrags raced for the ruined gate.

"The charge!" said Mazael, raising his lance. "Now!"

Sir Aulus lifted a horn to his lips and loosed a long blast, a thunder of a different sort rolling over the plain. Mazael put his boots to Challenger's sides, and the big horse surged forward with an excited snort. Behind him the knights' and armsmen's horses exploded into motion, the earth rumbling beneath steel-shod hooves.

The Malrags near the gate turned, forming a line of spears, but it was too late. Mazael caught a brief glimpse of a Malrag at the forefront of the mob. The hands gripping the spear had six fingers, black veins throbbing and pulsing beneath the leathery gray skin. Then the Malrag disappeared beneath Challenger's hooves in a flash of black blood, even as Mazael drove his war lance through the face of another Malrag. He ripped the lance free and struck again as Challenger thundered forward, the horsemen crashing into the Malrags. Horses screamed and stamped, men shouted, and the Malrags bellowed their battle cries.

Mazael stabbed his lance into a Malrag, the heavy blade crunching past armor and sinking into the creature's neck. Yet the Malrag showed no fear, no sign of pain, even pulling itself up the shaft to claw at Mazael's arm. Mazael plunged the lance into the creature's chest again, and the Malrag toppled, wrenching the weapon from Mazael's hand.

Challenger galloped through the Malrag mob, breaking free on the other side. Mazael wheeled the big horse around, drawing Lion from its scabbard with a metallic hiss. The ancient steel blade glimmered in the torchlight, seeming to flash and flicker.

And then Lion jolted in Mazael's hand. Power flowed up Mazael's arm, and the light reflecting in the sword's blade turned blue. A halo of sapphire radiance crackled around the sword, and then the blade burst into raging azure flame. Lion had been forged long ago by the great wizard-smiths of ancient Tristafel, created to destroy things of dark magic.

It seemed that the Malrags, whatever else they were, were also creatures of dark magic.

Mazael shouted, kicked Challenger into motion, and rode back into the fray, striking right and left. The Malrags had shown no fear of steel weapons, even of wounds and death, yet they flinched away from Lion's raging blue flame. Mazael struck the arm from one Malrag, and the head from another, Lion blazing like an inferno in his fist. The Malrags reeled back, and Mazael's knights and armsmen fell upon them.

The enemy broke and ran. The creatures did care about pain or injury, but they feared Lion's flame, and Mazael's men were more numerous and better armed. Dozens of Malrags sprinted into the darkness around the town. But others raced through the ruined gate, vanishing into the streets of the town.

Damnation. They could go from house to house, killing. Or hide themselves in the cellars and attics to attack later. For that matter, the ones fleeing from the town could band together and raid some of the smaller villages.

"Sir Hagen!" said Mazael. Hagen rode to Mazael's side, his sword and armor splattered with black Malrag blood. "Take seventy men. Hunt down as many of those devils as you can. I'll deal with things here." Hagen nodded. "Sir Nathan!" The old knight turned, greatsword in one hand. How he managed to use such a massive sword so effectively from horseback, Mazael had no idea. "Get the rest of the men together. We'll have to go from street to street, finish off the Malrags."

Sir Nathan shouted the commands, and Lucan rode to Mazael's side, that strange black staff laid across his saddle.

"My lord," said Lucan. "Listen to me. I've read the ancient records. Every Malrag warband has two leaders. A shaman, a spell caster. Probably the one that cast that lightning bolt upon the gate. And a chieftain, a war leader...a 'balekhan', in the Malrag tongue. The Malrags will not give up until both of them are dead."

"Then we'll simply have to kill them both," said Mazael. "You and Timothy can deal with the shaman, I trust?"

Lucan sneered. "Please."

Mazael turned Challenger toward the ruined gates. He rode into the town, his men following after. Some of the militiamen hurried from the walls, while Mazael ordered others to stand guard over the ruined gates. Hooves rang against the cobblestones, but Mazael saw no sign of any Malrags. Where had they all gone? At least a hundred had made their way into the town.

He heard the sounds of fighting coming from the town square. The square held two large buildings. The Three Swords Inn, four stories of mortared stone and trimmed beams. And the town's church, a massive domed structure, dating from the old kingdom of Dracaryl. When the town was under attack, the women and children fled to the church...

The women and children.

The sounds of fighting grew louder.

Mazael cursed and kicked Challenger to a gallop, his knights and armsmen following.

2

BALEKHAN

Five Malrags lunged out of a narrow alley, brandishing their weapons. Lion's flame burst to fresh life, and Mazael swung, the blade ripping into a Malrag's neck. Around him the other horsemen crashed into the Malrags, trampling them to the ground.

Then the street was clear of enemies, and Mazael's men flooded into the town square.

Forty or fifty of the town's militia stood in ranks before the church's doors, forming a line of spears and shields. Perhaps a hundred Malrags charged at them, howling and roaring, black axes and spears in hand. Yet the militiamen held, and did not run, even as the Malrags ripped into them. They were fighting to defend their wives, their children, their homes.

They were Mazael's people, and he would make the Malrags regret ever having set foot in the Grim Marches.

"At them!" he bellowed, lifting Lion high as he kicked Challenger to a gallop. The horsemen thundered forward, and a cheer went up from the beleaguered militia. The Malrags spun, turning to face the new threat, but too late. The horsemen ripped into them, Malrags dying beneath stamping hooves and flashing weapons. Mazael brought Lion down in a massive overhead blow, splitting a Malrag skull,. He spun Challenger in a circle, looking for any sign of the shaman or the balekhan.

The air tingled. It was Mazael's only warning before a bolt of emerald lightning screamed from the sky, painting the church and the struggling men with ghostly light. The bolt exploded into the square's center, throwing chunks of molten stone into the air, the blast knocking men and horses to the ground. Challenger whinnied in alarm, rearing up on his hind legs. The big horse had been trained withstand the sight of blood and violence, but not lightning bolts raining from the sky. Mazael lost his balance and fell, his armor clattering against the cobblestones.

He scrambled back to his feet, ignoring the ache, and looked around for the source of the lighting bolt.

He spotted the Malrag shaman. The creature perched on the rooftop of the inn. It was thinner and smaller than the other Malrags, almost spindly. It wore a ragged robe of black leather, sparks of green light crackling around its clawed fingertips.

And unlike the other Malrags, a third eye, blazing with cold emerald light, rested in the center of its forehead.

"Lucan!" shouted Mazael, running towards the inn.

LUCAN MANDRAGON FLUNG OUT A HAND, muttering an incantation under his breath. Power welled up within him, and his magical senses reached out, searching for the source of the spell that had summoned the lightning.

He found the source atop the inn, crouching over the battle, ragged robes blowing in the nighttime wind.

So. A Malrag shaman. Such a creature had not been seen in the Grim Marches for over a century. Lucan wondered why the Malrag warband had attacked Cravenlock Town, of all places. The Malrags must have crossed Great Mountains to enter the Grim Marches, and Castle Cravenlock was six days' march from the nearest foothills.

Which suggested the unpleasant possibility that other Malrag warbands had crossed the mountains, and roamed the Grim Marches even now.

But Lucan could worry about that later, after he had crushed the Malrag shaman.

He knew quite a few spells to destroy things. Places. People.

It wasn't by choice. His master, Marstan, had been a respected master wizard. He'd also been a necromancer, and tried to use his spells to steal Lucan's body for his own. Lucan had fought him off, killing him in the process...but not before he had received Marstan's powers. His knowledge.

His memories, full of blood and death and torture and misery.

Well. Lucan would put that knowledge to good use now.

He lifted a hand, gathering more power, and muttered a spell. Magical force gathered, and Lucan clenched his fist, loosing a psychokinetic blast that would hurl the Malrag shaman from the rooftop and smash it against the street below.

The shaman spun, the glowing third eye in its forehead narrowing, and worked a spell of its own, clawed hands flickering through intricate gestures. The air around the creature shimmed, and Lucan's spell shattered against the power of the creature's ward.

His eyes widened in astonishment. That spell should have killed the shaman. There were master wizards who lacked the power to block Lucan's strike.

And even as Lucan drew in power for another spell, the shaman gestured. Green lightning fell from the sky, swallowing Lucan.

MAZAEL SPRINTED towards the inn's door, Lion in hand. He had to kill the Malrag shaman, before the creature could rain more spells upon his men. Could Lucan defeat the shaman? But even if Lucan distracted the creature, that might be enough for Mazael to reach the roof and plunge Lion into the shaman's back.

The shaman gestured, its third eye narrowed, and another bolt of lightning thundered out of the black sky. Lucan and his horse vanished in the green flash, and the shockwave knocked Mazael off balance. He staggered several steps and crashed into a Malrag. The creature snarled, exposing jagged yellow fangs beneath its gray lips, and drew back its spear for a stab.

Mazael was faster. He bashed the Malrag across its face with his shield. Black blood and yellowed fangs flew from its jaw. He twisted, and ripped Lion through the Malrag's throat with a single powerful blow. The Malrag fell, choking on its own blood. Mazael stepped past the falling corpse, looking around.

There was no sign of Lucan Mandragon.

Mazael struck down another Malrag and started for the inn.

And then he froze.

A Malrag was staring at him.

But this Malrag was different than the others, different from the shaman. It stood eight feet tall. Instead of black chain mail, it wore elaborate black plate, the armor adorned with scenes of dismembered men and women. White eyes glimmered behind its masked helm, and it carried massive serrated sword in its left hand.

The first Malrag he had seen, Mazael realized, carrying a sword.

Which meant that this was the Malrag war leader, their chieftain.

The balekhan raised its sword in a black blur and sprang at Mazael, roaring.

LUCAN STAGGERED TO ONE KNEE, leaning hard upon the black metal staff in his left hand.

His wards, his defensive spells, had turned the worst of the Malrag shaman's lightning strike. They had not saved his horse, which lay in pile of smoldering char a few feet away. Around him the fight raged, militiamen and knights struggling against Malrag warriors. One of the Malrags looked at Lucan and grinned, hefting a black axe.

Lucan snarled, muttered a spell, and made a hooking motion with his right hand. A patch of gray mist swirled before him, and a creature sprang out of nothingness. It looked like a deformed hybrid of a tiger and an octopus, and was even more hideous than the Malrag. It was a predator of the spirit world, bound and summed by Lucan's will.

The Malrag hesitated for just a moment, which was long enough for the deformed thing to loose a hideous shriek and spring upon the Malrag, fangs and talons tearing. The Malrag collapsed, the spirit creature's barbed tentacles glistening with black blood.

"Guard me," commanded Lucan, climbing back to his feet.

He turned his attention back to the Malrag shaman, gathering his magical strength for another strike.

And no sooner had he done so than another blast of lighting ripped out of the sky. Lucan changed his spell, casting a ward instead, and flung out his hands. The lightning bolt snarled around him, sparking and spitting, and leapt back to strike the shaman.

But the Malrag shaman cast a spell of its own. The lightning bolt rebounded from its outstretched hands and ripped into the inn, blasting away half of the roof in a spray of burning splinters. Lucan made a slashing motion, and loosed invisible force to hammer at the shaman. Some of the remaining shingles shattered into dust, but the Malrag shaman cast another ward, absorbing the Lucan's attack.

And the shaman loosed still another lightning bolt. Again Lucan raised a ward, the lightning shattering against his spell to splinter against the ground in crawling emerald fingers. This time Lucan lacked the strength fling back the bolt at the shaman.

Yet the lightning was just as strong as the first strike. If anything, it was stronger.

Lucan reeled, dizziness washing through him, head spinning with the effort. The shaman was stronger, he realized. Thanks to Marstan's memories, Lucan had the greater skill. But a man with a scalpel would not win in a fight against a man with a hammer, and Lucan's subtle skill simply could not stand against the shaman's raw power.

Not for very long, anyway.

The shaman flung another lightning bolt, and this time it took all of Lucan's skill and strength to stop it from devouring him.

~

THE BALEKHAN LEAPT AT MAZAEL, the black sword falling like an avalanche.

Mazael got his shield up just in time.

He almost died anyway. The blow struck with terrible force, tearing a chunk from the shield, and Mazael stumbled back several steps. The balekhan leapt forward with catlike grace , sword looping for Mazael's head. He ducked the blow, sidestepped, and brought Lion around in a backhanded swing, the blade crunching into the armor plates across the balekhan's side. The balekhan snarled and jerked away, black sword coming up in guard.

Mazael lifted his shield and took a cautious step forward, Lion ready in his fist.

The balekhan regarded him for a moment, and then began to speak, the first Malrag Mazael had heard use words. The creature's voice was a snarling growl, its language strange to his ears.

And yet...and yet the meaning of the words echoed in his mind. As if the creature spoke directly to his thoughts.

-So you are the one-

Mazael circled to the side, the balekhan following his movement. Again the creature spoke.

-We have heard of you. Child of the Great Demon. I see the power blazing in your soul. Had you claimed your birthright, I would kneel before you and name you the Destroyer, as is only proper. But instead you have made yourself weak and pitiful-

"I have heard such boastings before, creature," said Mazael, "and from the lips of those more powerful than you. Weak or not, you dared to attack my lands, and you will die for it."

The balekhan laughed.

-Mortal fool! A worthy warrior you are, but still a fool. I have died many times before, and I shall die again, ere the Great Demon is reborn. But you shall not be there to see it-

The balekhan surged forward, black sword leading. Mazael dodged the attack and swung Lion, the burning blade connecting

with the Malrag's armored shoulder. The balekhan roared in fury and brought its fist around in a massive backhand for Mazael's face. He got his shield up in time but the punch rocked him, splinters flying from the shield. The balekhan whipped the massive sword around, and this time the strike ripped the top third from Mazael's shield.

He paced back several steps, moving out of the balekhan's range. The creature was strong – stronger than any man he had ever fought, stronger than Mazael himself.

And Mazael was Demonsouled. His arm and shoulder ached from the pounding they had taken, but he already felt the pain lessen as the demon power in his soul healed his wounds, restoring his bruised flesh.

But he doubted even his Demonsouled nature could heal him if the balekhan cut him in half.

The Malrag leader roared, sword whipping over its head, even as more green lightning fell from the sky.

~

LUCAN'S CLOAK and coat smoldered, wisps of smoke rising from their edges. He had only just turned the last lightning strike aside. Two or three more, he realized, and he would be finished.

And yet the Malrag shaman showed no signs of tiring. Crude its skill might have been, but the creature had a vast reservoir of magical power.

Power that Lucan could not match.

The summoned spirit creature kept the lesser Malrags at bay. For an moment he thought about summoning more creatures to attack the shaman, but dismissed the idea. He barely had enough to magic left to maintain the binding over the first creature, let alone to summon additional ones.

His hand tightened around the black staff, its sigils digging into his palm. Did he dare to...

Then he saw Timothy.

The older wizard sat atop his horse, hands flying through a spell. Timothy could not match Lucan's skill and power, but the other wizard did not lack for courage. Timothy flung out a hand, and a fist-sized blue spark leapt from his fingers to smash against the shaman's defensive wards. The wards turned the spell aside with ease, and the shaman spun to face Timothy, claws flashing with green lighting.

But Timothy kicked his horse into motion, and the lightning blast missed him by a dozen yards. His horse whinnied and screamed, but Timothy kept the beast under control, and even managed to fling another blue spark at the shaman.

It gave Lucan all the opening he needed.

He drew in his remaining strength, muttering a spell, and loosed a blast of invisible force at the Malrag shaman. Its defensive wards screamed beneath the strain, and for a moment Lucan thought he had the creature.

But the wards held. Barely, but they held. The shaman turned to face Lucan, beginning the spell to summon lightning once more.

And Lucan was left with no other choice.

He poured his will into the black staff , bending all his thought upon it. The staff shivered beneath his skin, like something alive, and grew cold against his fingers. Crimson light flickered in the depths of the carved sigils, as if the staff had been filled with burning blood.

And then power flooded into Lucan, power beyond anything he had ever used on his own, sweet and intoxicating. His weariness and pain fell away, as if his veins had filled with fire.

Was this, he wondered, what Mazael Cravenlock felt all the time?

Lucan had learned about Mazael's Demonsouled heritage a year ago. The blood of the Demonsouled held great power, but the blood of a child of the Old Demon held even greater might. Lucan had stolen a vial of that blood, and only its strength, its power, had allowed him to survive the brutal fight with Morebeth Galbraith in the Kings' Chapel of Knightcastle.

But the power of that blood had burned away in moments.

So Lucan had created this staff with a vial of Mazael's blood, stolen as the Lord of Castle Cravenlock slept. Then Lucan forged the staff in his secret workshop below Castle Cravenlock, imbuing it with the power of Mazael's Demonsouled blood.

Power that Lucan could now draw upon at will. He had not told Mazael. Mazael recognized the need to fight dark powers, but not the necessity to use any tool available in that fight.

Lucan screamed out a spell and thrust the staff, the carved sigils ablaze with crimson light. His spell struck the Malrag shaman and hammered through its wards with overpowering force. The top off the inn exploded, the remaining tiles and most of the roof beams shattering. Lucan's will seized the Malrag shaman, flung it from the roof, and hurled it against the cobblestones of the square like an insect beneath a boot.

Bones shattered, black blood splattering against the inn's walls, and the light of the shaman's third eye went out.

Lucan bellowed in triumph and turned, the staff blazing in his hand. He would crush the Malrags, first, destroy them one by one. None of them could stand against his power! And then he would kill Lord Mazael and his men, seize control of Castle Cravenlock. And from there, Lucan would destroy his father and his brother, make them pay for all they had done to him. The Grim Marches were his! The world was his! He would...

The crimson light winked out, smoke rising from the staff's carvings.

And the power drained away from Lucan, along with the madness inspired by Demonsouled magic.

He fell to his knees as pain wracked him. His stomach twisted, and Lucan empted his guts onto the cobblestones. It got worse, every time. Every time he drew upon the staff's power, the madness grew more violent, the aftereffects more painful.

Using the staff could kill him, Lucan knew.

Yet he could not stop using it, could not stop craving it. It was just as well the staff only sustained short bursts of power. If it did not, he would use the Demonsouled power until it drove him insane and he killed everyone in sight. Or until the Cravenlock armsmen overwhelmed him and killed him.

Not for the first time, Lucan wondered how Mazael managed to live with such dark power in his mind.

Mazael and the balekhan spun in their mad dance.

He held Lion's hilt in both hands. The balekhan's great black sword had long since smashed Mazael's shield to kindling, the torn leather straps still dangling from his armored forearm. The balekhan was far stronger than Mazael, far stronger than any human, but Mazael was faster, even in his armor. He danced around the balekhan's armored form, Lion stabbing and thrusting at the weak points in the black plate . He scored three hits on the balekhan, minor wounds that sizzled beneath Lion's azure flame, wounds that had slowed the huge Malrag.

Yet the creature remained as strong as ever.

The battle rage filled Mazael, making him stronger, faster. But he dared not give into it. He knew that if he surrendered to the Demonsouled rage, it would consume him, make him into a monster. A woman he loved had died to save him from his darker half.

He would not let her death be in vain. Not now, not ever.

But he would take down this damned Malrag for daring to attack his people and his lands.

Mazael caught the descending black sword in a high parry, arms trembling with the strain. There was no way he could hold a parry against the balekhan's strength. So he rolled his wrists and sidestepped, Lion's blade licking at the gap in the balekhan's shoulder plates. The huge Malrag reeled in pain, yellowed fangs bared in a snarl. It might have been stronger, but Lion's azure flame seemed to hurt the balekhan far more than the physical wounds. He thrust at the balekhan's face before it could react, and the Malrag flinched back, eyes narrowed against the sword's fire. If Mazael could get close enough, he could drive Lion through the helm's eye slit and end the fight.

And then the inn exploded.

The thunderclap rang over the square. For a brief instant the battle paused as the struggling knights, militiamen, and Malrags looked at the Three Swords Inn. Mazael glimpsed Lucan, standing in a halo of blood-colored light, a burning staff clenched in his fists. He saw the inn's roof rip apart, as if torn by invisible hands, saw the Malrag shaman driven to the ground with terrific, bone-crushing force.

That blood-colored light shining from Lucan's staff. Something about it called to Mazael, made his tainted blood rise, as if in recognition...

The balekhan recognized Mazael's distraction and surged forward.

Mazael just got Lion up in time to beat aside the thrust aimed for his heart, but the sword banged off his shoulder, denting the armor. Mazael rocked back on his heels as the balekhan came at him, its sword a storm of flickering black metal. Mazael retreated, working Lion left and right to beat aside the attacks.

Then the balekhan's sword came around in a massive sideways cut, and Mazael could not dodge in time. The blow bounced off his cuirass with a scream of tortured metal, and the force sent Mazael falling hard to the ground. He scrambled backwards, trying to get out of reach, but the balekhan loomed over him, sword raised for the killing blow.

A dark shape sprang past Mazael, snarling.

The balekhan hesitated, turning to meet the new threat, and the dark shape leapt upon the Malrag leader. Mazael had a brief glimpse of black fur, of flashing white fangs and teeth. The balekhan fell to one knee with a cry of rage, greatsword blurring, but the dark shape twisted to the side, and avoided the blow.

It was Mazael's opening.

He surged to his feet, ignoring the ache in his chest, all his strength and weight behind Lion's point. The blade drove through the slit in the masked helm, plunging deep into the Malrag's left eye. Fire exploded from Lion, erupting out the balekhan's nostrils and fanged mouth.

The balekhan fell at Mazael's feet with a clatter of black armor. He wrenched Lion free from the smoking helm and looked for the dark shape that had assisted him.

A great black wolf stood a few paces away, watching him. It was the biggest wolf Mazael had ever seen, almost the size of a small horse. Its claws and fangs were like ivory daggers, and its jaws looked as if they could bite through steel plate. The wolf's eyes were blue, like polished sapphire mirrors.

And in every way, the wolf was identical to the one Mazael had seen in his dream.

He gazed at the wolf in astonishment. Was he hallucinating? Had he gone mad? But no - some of the nearby militiamen gazed at the wolf with unease.

Mazael took a step towards the wolf.

It turned and fled, moving with terrific speed, and vanished into the darkness.

3

THE WOLVES GATHER

The battle was over by dawn.

With the balekhan and shaman slain, the Malrags lost both their leadership and the advantage of the shaman's magical power. Caught between the militiamen and the knights, the Malrags fell one by one. Some groups of Malrags broke and ran, escaping down the town's streets or vanishing through the ruined gate.

Bands of militia hunted the Malrags in the streets, while those who escaped through the gate found Sir Hagen and his knights.

As the sun rose over the carnage in the town square, Mazael stood on the church steps. Sir Hagen, Sir Nathan, and Timothy stood with him, along with a short, lean man in leather armor splattered with Malrag blood. Neville was the mayor of the town, and the captain of the militia.

There was no sign of Lucan.

"How many?" said Mazael.

He heard singing coming from within the church, as the priests gave thanks for their deliverance. And weeping, as well.

Not everyone had been delivered.

"The lads are counting," said Neville. "Three hundred Malrags, we think. Maybe three hundred and twenty-five."

"How the devil did three hundred damned Malrags get so close to the town without anyone noticing?" said Hagen, scowling. He had come through the fight unscathed, his sword and armor dark with Malrag blood. "We send out patrols every day."

"Odds are those men are dead," said Nathan, voice quiet. "The Malrags may look like beasts or devils, but they are cunning. Undoubtedly they slew the scouts to mask their approach." He shook his head. "Some of the Malrags had heads dangling from their belts. Our scouts, I fear."

"The legends say Malrags live in mountain holes," said Hagen. "We're six days' march from the Great Mountains, my lord. If three hundred Malrags made it all the way to Cravenlock Town...there are undoubtedly other warbands loose on the plains."

"An invasion, then," said Timothy.

"One problem at a time," said Mazael. "How many men did we lose?"

"Nine knights," said Hagen. "Seventeen of the armsmen."

"Thirty-five of my militiamen," said Neville. He shook his head and looked at the bodies laid out before the church steps, their faces covered by cloaks. "We've a lot of widows, this morning."

"Forty-five men wounded," said Timothy. He looked exhausted, his coat and face smudged with blood, both Malrag and human. "Perhaps thirty of them will see another sunrise."

"Damnation," said Mazael.

"It could have been much worse," said Nathan. "Sixty-one of our men slain, for three hundred of the Malrags? Devils these things might be, but one mounted man is still worth seven men, or devils, on foot."

"Aye," said Neville. "I was certain we could not hold, my lord. It is well you arrived when you did."

Mazael looked at the shrouded corpses. "Not soon enough."

"But we were victorious," said Hagen.

"For now," said Mazael. "There are undoubtedly more of those things on the plains. We'll need to prepare, at once."

"Your commands, then?" said Nathan.

"First, get the gate rebuilt," said Mazael. "If more Malrags show up, I want to be ready for them. Once the gate is done, dig a ditch around the wall. We don't have any water to flood it, but anything that slows the Malrags down will be useful."

"It shall be done, my lord," said Neville.

"Keep the militia ready," said Mazael. "Daily drill. The town must be guarded at all times. I want no more Malrags to set foot in Cravenlock Town. And if these Malrags were part of a larger host, we may need to take the field against them. The militia must be ready for that."

Neville swallowed, but bowed. "My lord."

"Sir Hagen," said Mazael. "Send patrols. Knights and mounted armsmen, well-armed and equipped. They're to scout the countryside for two days' ride in all directions and report back. I want no more surprise attacks."

"As you say," said Hagen, looking over the town with a grim eye. "If any Malrags come within five leagues of castle or town, they shall regret it sorely."

"Good," said Mazael. "Timothy, see to the wounded. You set a warding alarm over the castle against undead and San-keth." An alarm that had saved their lives last year, when the San-keth cleric Blackfang had attacked. "Can you ward the town and castle against the Malrags?"

"I can, though it shall take time," said Timothy. "And I will need Malrag blood for the spell," he looked over the square, "though it seems plenty is it hand. And I shall certainly need Lucan's assistance."

"Where the devil is Lucan, anyway?" said Mazael. "Did that shaman strike him down?"

"I don't know," said Timothy. "He...almost lost the fight, I think. But I was able to distract the shaman, draw its attention long enough for Lucan to strike back."

"Which he did with vigor," said Mazael, looking at the ruined top floor of the Three Swords Inn.

"He was still alive then," said Timothy. "After that, he disappeared." He hesitated. "Perhaps one of the Malrag warriors slew him."

"I doubt that," said Mazael. It would take more than a mere Malrag warrior to strike down Lucan Mandragon, the Dragon's Shadow. "When he is found, tell him to attend to me at once. Meanwhile, we all have a great deal of work to do."

They went about their tasks. Mazael found Challenger and rode from one end of the town to the other, from the ruined gate to the church steps and back again. He praised the militiamen, knights, and armsmen who had shown conspicuous valor during the battle. He bade the workmen laboring at the gate and moat to work hard, reminding them that the lives of their wives and children depended upon their efforts. He spoke with the women who had lost husbands and sons during the fight, promising that they would receive their share of charity from the church, and that anyone who tried to prey upon the widows and orphans of Cravenlock Town would feel his displeasure.

In truth, he had little work to do. But Mazael had led armies in battle before, and he knew that above all else, armies needed leadership. The men needed to know that their lord would look after their safety, that he appreciated and relied upon their efforts, that he had a plan for crushing their enemies.

So he rode through the town, speaking to his people.

Sometimes, when he spoke to the widows, he fingered the silver coin hanging from its chain at his belt. Romaria had carried that coin, had used it as a focus for the minor spells she knew. At least, she had carried until that terrible day when the Old Demon killed her before the altar of Castle Cravenlock's chapel.

Ah, but he wished she were here now. The people of Castle Cravenlock and its town were Mazael's - his to defend, his to protect.

His, and his alone. A burden he could share with no one.

Later that morning, the squires arrived from the castle,

summoned by Sir Hagen to tend to their knights. Rufus Highgate looked at the carnage with shocked eyes. The boy had seen blood- shed before - almost all noble-born children had - but never on such scale.

And certainly he had never seen a dead Malrag before.

Yet the boy summoned his resolve, and tended to Mazael's armor and weapons. Mazael bade him to fetch some food, and Rufus returned with a skin of wine and half a loaf of dark bread. The wounded had been laid out in the church, and the Three Swords' common room had been taken over by Neville and Sir Hagen, so Mazael circled around to the back of the church, to the graveyard, to sit and eat.

And to rest. Just for a moment.

Most of the town's dead were buried outside the walls, and so the graveyard was ancient, its monuments and crypts centuries old. Mazael sat against the low stone wall encircling the graveyard.

Just a moment to eat and rest.

He fell asleep before taking a bite.

AND AS HE SLEPT, Mazael dreamed:

He stood alone in the Grim Marches, Lion in his hand. The empty grasslands stretched away in all directions. A cold wind blew past Mazael, tugging at his cloak and setting the grasses to rustling. Storm clouds writhed and danced overhead, flashing with lightning.

Green lighting. Like the lightning the Malrag shaman had called down.

Mazael looked to the east. Far in the distance he saw the dark mass of the Great Mountains, the division between the lands of the kingdom and the barbarian realms beyond. He had seen those moun- tains dozens, hundreds of times, in his life. Yet now they crawled with dark shapes, misshapen figures beyond count.

Malrags, tens of thousands of Malrags.

They were coming. A great host of Malrags, bent upon destroying and burning everything in their path. He gritted his teeth and set himself, raising Lion. Let them come! He would carve his way through them, make them pay in blood for every step they took upon his lands...

The Malrag horde moved.

But they did not go west, towards Castle Cravenlock and the Grim Marches.

Instead they went south.

Mazael blinked. South? Why go south? There was nothing to the south. Only the Great Southern Forest, inhabited by the Elderborn tribes. And Deepforest Keep, somewhere in the Forest's vast heart. But why would Malrags go there, when the Grim Marches lay close at hand?

Mazael turned, watching the Malrag horde, and saw the great black wolf staring at him.

The wolf's blue eyes blazed like Lion's blade, its black fur ruffling in the wind.

"Who are you?" said Mazael.

The wolf made no answer.

"You aided me," said Mazael, taking a step towards the wolf, "against the balekhan."

The wolf backed away, fur bristling, white fangs bared in rage.

And in fear.

"I mean you no harm," said Mazael. "Who are you?"

A voice thundered down from the sky.

"Lord Mazael! Lord Mazael!"

MAZAEL AWOKE to Rufus's voice, the squire shaking his shoulder.

"Lord Mazael," said Rufus.

Mazael grunted, looked up at Rufus.

"Sir Nathan sends word, my lord," said Rufus. "He needs to speak with you at the inn. Letters have arrived from my father."

Mazael nodded, got to his feet with a grunt. "Aye. Go to tell Sir Nathan I'll be along presently."

Rufus nodded. His face had returned to its usual haughty mask, but there was fear in his eyes.

"Your father," said Mazael. "His letters...they hold ill news?" Castle Highgate guarded the sole pass through the Great Mountains to the lands beyond. If the Malrags had attacked, had broken into the Grim Marches...

Rufus shrugged. "My father must still be alive, to have written the letters. But these Malrags, my lord...I've never seen anything so terrible."

"I have," said Mazael. "I have seen both San-keth and Demon-souled, and faced them. Yet I am still here, am I not?"

That seemed to reassure the boy.

"Go," said Mazael, turning, "go and..."

He saw Lucan Mandragon.

The wizard stood a short distance away, shrouded in his black cloak, cowl pulled up. He leaned heavily upon the sigil-carved staff, both hands wrapped around it. He almost looked like a monument himself, a grave marker carved of black marble.

"My lord?" said Rufus. "Is something amiss?"

The squire couldn't see Lucan. Which meant Lucan was using his mindclouding spell, a kind of magic that let him move unnoticed among crowds.

Which meant he had something unpleasant to tell Mazael.

"Go," said Mazael. "I need a moment to collect myself. Tell Sir Nathan I will attend him presently."

Rufus bowed and ran off.

"That boy," said Lucan, drawing back his cowl, "reminds me of his father. Lord Robert is an arrogant bore, and the boy seems keen to follow in his footsteps."

"He'll make a capable knight one day," said Mazael. "Are you well?"

Because Lucan did not look at all well. Dark rings encircled his black eyes, and his gaunt face was paler than usual. Sweat glittered on his jaw and forehead, pasting black locks of hair to his brow. He looked like a man in the early stages of a terminal fever.

"Not particularly," said Lucan. He closed his eyes, took a deep breath, his fingers tightening against the black staff. "Defeating the Malrag shaman took...rather more that I expected. But I'm not dead yet."

"I had a dream," said Mazael.

Lucan blinked. "The Old Demon?" Mazael had told Lucan about his father's dreams, how the Old Demon sometimes sent nightmares to torment Mazael.

"No," said Mazael. "When I fought the balekhan, it almost had me. Yet a great black wolf attacked the balekhan, distracted it, gave me the opening I needed to slay it."

Lucan frowned. "A wolf?"

"I dreamed of that wolf," said Mazael. "Last night, ere the horns woke me. And again just now."

Lucan's frown deepened. "This wolf...did it seem like a dream of the Old Demon?"

"No," said Mazael. "The Old Demon's dreams were different. Full of dread and blood and death. This was different. The wolf simply...watched me. Nothing more. It was angry with me, and afraid of me. It ran when I approached it. And that was the entirety of the dream."

Lucan sighed. "I wished I had more of an explanation for you. At least you may be sure the wolf does not wish you harm. Otherwise it would not have helped you against the balekhan. Which was an impressive feat, by the way. Few have managed to slay a Malrag balekhan in single combat."

"So you know more of these Malrags, then?" said Mazael.

"Aye," said Lucan. His mouth twisted. "Or, rather, Marstan did. Which amounts to the same thing."

"Then tell me what you know," said Mazael. "My dreams mean little, compared with the danger the Malrags bring to my people."

"Little is known about their origins," said Lucan. "There are differing stories. One says that the Great Demon created them, to replace mortal men after he slew them all. Another says the Old Demon bred them, to use them as soldiers to overthrow Tristafel. Still another says they are the consequence of man's sins, wickedness given physical form to punish us." His lip curled. "I think that one unlikely, myself."

"So my father created these things?" said Mazael. The Old Demon had not forgotten about him, he knew. Had the Old Demon sent the Malrags to the Grim Marches in vengeance?

"Possibly," said Lucan. "Or possibly not. The truth isn't known. But what is known is that Malrags will follow a Demonsouled of sufficient strength. They are almost...compelled to do so. The Malrags, you see, are not mortal, not in the way we understand the term."

"Not mortal?" said Mazael. "They died easily enough upon my sword."

"But they will be reborn," said Lucan. "The Malrags are neither men nor women. They do not give birth, or lie together to make children. They are demon spirits, bound in flesh. The Malrags grow in great hives, hidden in deep caverns. When a Malrag is...born, for lack of a better word, one of these demon spirits is bound into the body. The balekhan you slew and the shaman I defeated have probably been killed dozens of times before. Should they be reborn within our lifetimes, no doubt they will try to take vengeance upon us."

"So if they are immortal, if they can be reborn again and again," said Mazael, "how can I defeat them?"

"They are immortal, in a sense, but not invincible," said Lucan. "As you saw yourself. A Malrag might wait decades to be born. And, it is true, they are all exceedingly cunning and clever. Living life after life is an excellent way to acquire new knowledge and skills. And yet, for all their knowledge, for all their skills, the Malrags are...limited."

"Limited?" said Mazael. "How?"

"They have no free will."

Mazael frowned. "Then they are like...animals? Or mindless slaves?"

"Not at all," said Lucan. "You misunderstand me. Mortal men can choose to do good or evil. Even the stupidest and weakest man can choose between good and evil...as can the strongest and cleverest. The Malrags cannot. They are incapable of choosing good. A Malrag only understands pain – the pleasure of inflicting it, and the fear of enduring it. Nothing else."

"Then how are they able to function?" said Mazael.

"Usually, they do not," said Lucan. "The Malrags form into warbands under the strongest balekhans, and fight amongst themselves, dying and being reborn over and over. Or the balekhan is slain and replaced by one of the other warriors. There is a reason the Malrags have not been seen in the Grim Marches for over a century. The only thing that can unify them is something stronger than themselves."

"A Demonsouled," said Mazael, closing his eyes.

"Aye," said Lucan. "Usually it is a powerful Demonsouled that forces the Malrag warbands to come together in an army. Not always, though. Sometimes the San-keth have done it, or even a wizard of surpassing magical power. Though it is a dangerous course. If the Malrags sense the slightest trace of weakness in their leader, they will tear him apart."

"A Demonsouled of surpassing power," said Mazael. "So someone like Amalric Galbraith is commanding the Malrags."

"Or Morebeth Galbraith," said Lucan. His hand twitched towards his stomach, where Mazael's Demonsouled half-sister had impaled him. Mazael still had no idea how Lucan had managed to survive such a dire wound. "She was, I think, more powerful than Amalric. But, yes. Almost certainly a Demonsouled of great power is commanding the Malrags. Quite possibly another child of the Old Demon."

"A dire prospect," said Mazael, hand closing into a fist. Amalric had almost killed him, and Morebeth had almost corrupted him. He did not relish the prospect of facing another child of the Old Demon in battle.

"But one that offers hope," said Lucan. "If we find and kill this Demonsouled, the Malrag army will disintegrate. The Malrag warbands shall turn upon each other, and we can hunt them down one by one."

"Assuming this really is an army," said Mazael, "and not just a lone Malrag warband."

Lucan raised an eyebrow. "A lone Malrag warband that managed to penetrate six days' ride into the Grim Marches, kill all your scouts, and attack Cravenlock Town? That is unlikely. I rather doubt those letters from Lord Robert contain good news."

"I know," said Mazael, rising to his feet and adjusting his sword belt. "And I had best attend to them."

He headed towards the graveyard's gate, stopped.

"Lucan," he said. "Could I command the Malrags?"

"Undoubtedly," said Lucan. "But only if you let your Demonsouled essence consume you. I would not recommend it. The use of Demonsouled power carries a...steep price." His hands tightened around the black staff. "As I'm sure you know better than I."

"Yes," said Mazael. "There is a line that I will not cross."

"You still carry that?" said Lucan.

Mazael looked down. His hand was curled around the silver coin on its chain.

"Yes," he said. "So I remember what my Demonsouled blood cost me."

"You don't," said Lucan, "seem likely to forget."

"Nor will I," said Mazael, turning towards the graveyard gate. "Now, come. Let us see what is in Lord Robert's letters."

THE NEWS, as it turned out, was all bad.

Lord Robert's stronghold, Castle Highgate, occupied the high pass leading from the Grim Marches to the barbarian lands beyond. Three weeks ago a force of ten thousand Malrags had appeared, burning the mountain villages and killing everything in their path. Lord Robert and his forces fell back to the castle, preparing for a siege.

And while they did, Malrags entered the pass. Thousands of them, tens of thousands. More than Robert's men had been able to count. They streamed through the high pass, descending to the Grim Marches like a storm of black-armored locusts, breaking into smaller warbands to spread more chaos. Lucan had been right. This was no mere raid, no band of Malrags looking for blood and plunder.

This was an invasion.

"The militia will remain in service, every last one of them," said Mazael to Neville and Sir Hagen after reading the letter. "Also, I want every man and boy over the age of fifteen and able to hold a weapon enrolled in the militia. Even if they cannot march in the field, we can use them to keep watch over the town."

"But what of the planting, my lord?" said Neville. "Spring is almost upon us. These Malrag devils may have no need to eat, but we do. If we do not get crops into the ground, we'll be boiling our boots for soup come winter."

"We have more arable land than hands to work it," said Mazael. "If necessary, we will put the women to work in the fields. Or we will rotate the militia in shifts."

But as it happened, such plans were unnecessary.

THE REFUGEES BEGAN ARRIVING the next day.

At first a trickle, only a few small bands. Then dozens of them, in larger and larger groups. Terrified children, weeping in fear, or silent with shock. Hollow-eyed women, faces tight with fear and strain. Ragged men, many wounded, faces streaked with dirt and blood. Their stories were all the same. The Malrags had struck in the night. Black-armored devils had forced the walls of their village, or burned their barns and houses. The Malrags had shown no mercy, cutting down men and women and children alike. One weeping man told a story of how a Malrag balekhan had run through his pregnant wife, laughing all the while. Mazael accepted some in the castle, giving them places to sleep in the halls and courtyard, while he lodged others in the town, ordering the townsmen to open their homes to the refugees. He put the refugees to work digging the moat, improving the town wall, and preparing for the sowing.

Some of the villages had held, and sent messengers to Mazael begging for aid. He dispatched what men he could spare, with orders to fortify the villages and raise militias.

And from some villages, no word came at all, whether refugees or messengers. Mazael suspected the Malrags had wiped out those villages, killing every last man, woman, and child.

He vowed to make them pay for that blood.

~

THE MALRAGS DID NOT GIVE up.

Over the next week, Mazael's scouting parties spotted no fewer than four warbands, all of them heading towards Cravenlock Town. Each time he gathered his knights and mounted armsmen, leaving the castle and town garrisoned with militia, and rode out to face them. Every time he was victorious. The Malrags, for all their ferocity in battle, had no cavalry. Which was not surprising, given how horses hated and loathed the creatures. A Malrag warband, caught in the open upon the plains, was vulnerable to a mounted force a third, even a quarter, of its size.

It was Mazael's only advantage. Each Malrag warband easily outnumbered Mazael's horsemen. If the creatures gathered together, he would have no choice but to withdraw to Castle Cravenlock and endure a siege.

~

MORE LETTERS ARRIVED, from other lords.

Every lord whose lands bordered on the Great Mountains faced Malrag attacks. Lord Astor Hawking reported that a force of three thousand Malrags had attacked his castle of Hawk's Reach and been repulsed. Lord Jonaril Mandrake had faced two thousand with his mounted men and broken them, though he had taken heavy losses.

"We have no choice," said Sir Nathan to Mazael after the last letter arrived. "The Grim Marches are under attack. You must send word to Lord Richard."

Lucan scowled at the mention of his father. Lord Richard the Dragonslayer and Lucan the Dragon's Shadow were not on good terms.

"Aye," said Mazael. "He's right, Lucan."

Lord Richard Mandragon kept order among his vassals with a mixture of open-handed generosity and utter ruthlessness. He showered his loyal men with gifts of land and gold...and crushed anyone who betrayed him. Or anyone who might betray him. Mazael had won Lord Richard's consent to marry his sister Rachel to Gerald Roland last year. But the warning had been clear. If Mazael ever thought of siding with Gerald's father, Lord Malden Roland, Lord Richard would crush him utterly.

And if Lord Richard ever learned that Mazael was Demonsouled...

"I will write the letter myself," said Mazael. "And I may need to send word to Lord Malden, as well."

Lucan raised an eyebrow. "And I know my father will not approve of that." Lord Richard Mandragon and Lord Malden Roland were mortal enemies. Lord Malden had never forgiven Lord Richard for the death of Belifane Roland seventeen years past, and Mazael doubted that the old man's hatred had waned.

"It may not matter," said Mazael. "If the Malrags come at us in sufficient numbers, we will need every man able to ride a horse and hold a blade. And Gerald Roland married my sister. The Rolands are tied to me by blood. Lord Malden will send some aid, if I ask."

"Assuming, of course," said Lucan, "that my father and Lord Malden simply do not go to war, the Malrags be damned."

Later that day a messenger in the livery of the Mandragons, black with a crimson dragon across the chest, arrived at Castle Cravenlock. Lord Richard sent word to all his vassals. The Malrags had brought sword and fire to the Grim Marches, and he commanded every lord and knight to raise every able-bodied man and assemble at Castle Cravenlock. From there the armies of the Grim Marches would march under Lord Richard's banner to destroy the Malrags.

The Grim Marches were at war.

4

THE LADY AND THE KNIGHT

Rachel, once of House Cravenlock, now of House Roland, began the morning by making love to her husband.

It had been two months since their son had been born, and it was time. Gerald had been so patient with her – he was always patient, always kind – but he still had a man's needs. And Rachel was ready. She was twenty-five, and they had been married for only a year. Most noblewomen Rachel's age had been married since the age of sixteen or seventeen, and had three or four children, if not more.

She loved her son, she loved her husband, and she wanted to make more children with him.

Afterward she lay against him, her head resting on his chest.

"That was...unexpected," said Gerald.

She smiled. "You didn't complain."

"Certainly not," said Gerald. He was a year younger than she was, tall and strong with pale blue eyes and blond hair. Their son had inherited his eyes and her black hair. "Won't Aldane be awake soon?"

She sighed and pressed tighter against him. "Not quite yet. Another half-hour, perhaps. And if he wakes up, Sarah can tend to him until I join her."

"I'm still surprised you didn't take a wet nurse," said Gerald. "Most noblewomen do."

Rachel levered up on one elbow, looked him in the eyes. "Aldane is my son. I will nurse him. I...waited so long for him, Gerald. For him, and for you."

Gerald smiled, kissed her. "Whatever pleases you, my dear."

"You should spend the day with me," said Rachel. "With me, and Aldane. That would please me. Very much."

"If only I could," said Gerald. "I'll need to meet with Father and Tobias and the Justiciar Commander this morning. They'll want to discuss the situation in Mastaria, of course."

"Why isn't the war over by now?" said Rachel. A year ago, her brother Mazael had smashed the assembled forces of the Dominiar Order below the gates of Tumblestone. With their leadership destroyed and their army broken, the Dominiar Order collapsed, and Lord Malden Roland's vassals claimed the Dominiars' lands for their own. Mastaria swore fealty to Knightcastle now. A few Dominiar remnants had tried to carry on the fight, but they had been destroyed one by one, or fled to the east and the north. "Surely the Dominiars cannot have the strength left to fight?"

"They don't," said Gerald. "In fact, the Dominiar Order, save for a few renegades, no longer exists. The church has even withdrawn its support for the Order. And the Dominiars were cruel lords - it seems the Mastarians much prefer my father's lordship. No, it's not the Dominiars. Some of our younger lords and knights are flush with conquest, and want to invade the Old Kingdoms."

"But that's foolish," said Rachel.

"It is," said Gerald. "The Old Kingdoms suffered cruelly under the Dominiars. Now that they've regained their freedom, they'll not give it up again with a sharp fight. Invading the Old Kingdoms would be folly, but some of our rasher vassals desire new lands, and the Justiciars want to wipe out the pagan faiths and bring them to the Amathavian church."

"Men," said Rachel. "No matter how much money and land you have, it's never enough. You always need more."

"Well, I can hardly fault their ambition," said Gerald. "A man needs lands and incomes to win a wife." His hand slid down her bare back. "And if the prize is so lovely as you...why, who can fault their daring?"

"Flatterer," said Rachel, closing her eyes. "And I am no prize."

She wasn't, whatever Gerald might think. She had done things in her past, things she did not like to remember. In the depths of her despair, she had prayed to Sepharivaim, the cruel god of the San-keth serpent people. She had pledged herself to marry Skhath, a San-keth cleric, and promised to let him father half human, half San-keth changelings upon her. But Mazael had saved her from all that.

Mazael, and Gerald.

"Normally I would not worry," said Gerald, "but Tobias is enamored of the idea. And Tobias has great influence with Father, ever since Father sank into his...depression. Tobias is hotheaded, true, but he can listen to reason. I will talk sense into him and the Justiciar Commander, and that will be that."

"Good," said Rachel, not opening her eyes.

They lay in silence for a moment.

"Do you remember Romaria?" said Rachel.

"Yes," said Gerald. "The woman from Deepforest Keep, the one Simonian of Briault killed. I think she was the only woman your brother ever loved, Rachel."

"She was," said Rachel.

"Why do you ask?" said Gerald.

"You mentioned the Old Kingdoms," said Rachel. "It...put something in my mind. I remembered Romaria talking to Mazael about the Old Kingdoms, how she hated what the Dominiars had done there. So keeping Tobias from invading the Old Kingdoms would have made her happy. And that will have made Mazael happy. Which will make me happy."

"That is all it takes to make you happy?" said Gerald. "Who knew it was so easy?"

She laughed and gave him a gentle punch on the shoulder. "It would make me happier if you could spend the day with us."

"I cannot, if I am to talk Tobias out of invading the Old King-doms," said Gerald. "But...after that, yes. After the midday meal. We will spend the rest of the day together. And we'll take dinner together. Just you, me, and Aldane. And the servants, of course. A daughter of House Roland cannot be expected to cook, after all."

"Of course not," said Rachel. "I am a noblewoman. I would make a dreadful cook."

"There is one other thing I need to discuss with Tobias and Father," said Gerald. "These rumors from the Grim Marches."

"Rumors?" Rachel lifted her head. "What rumors?"

"You haven't heard?" said Gerald. "If you haven't...I don't wish to disturb your mind."

"Tell me," said Rachel.

"We received word from Tristgard and the other towns along the border," said Gerald. "Some refugees have been arriving from the Grim Marches."

"Fleeing what?" said Rachel.

"We don't know," said Gerald. "There have been rumors. A plague, for one. Or that the lords of the High Plain or the Stormvales have attacked Richard Mandragon. Or that devils have taken physical form and stalk the Grim Marches."

Rachel snorted. "Who would be foolish enough to invade the Grim Marches? Mazael would destroy them. He defeated the Dominiars twice, after all."

A piercing cry cut into her words. She had moved Aldane's crib to the anteroom last night, under Sarah's watchful eye, so she could make love to Gerald in peace. But even the bedroom door, thick iron-banded oak, did little to block the baby's voice.

"Ah," said Gerald. "He sounds hungry."

"Your son," said Rachel, "will take after his father and uncle, and command armies in battle. You could hear his voice even over the clamor of a battlefield, I'm sure."

~

AFTER GERALD LEFT, Rachel dressed in a robe and fed Aldane.

It was almost spring, so Rachel sat on the balcony outside her bedroom. The rooms she shared with Gerald were in Ideliza's Tower, which rose from Knightcastle's highest tier. According to the story, the tower had been named for the doomed lover of a long-dead Roland knight, back in ancient times when the Rolands had still ruled as kings, rather than lords, over Knightcastle.

She sat on a bench, cradling Aldane as he nursed.

From the balcony she had a grand view of Knightcastle, its towers and parapets and walls, the three concentric curtain walls ringing the vast stone maze of the castle. Beyond she saw the silver ribbon of the Rivesteel, shining in its valley, and the rooftops and towers of Castle Town. Barges moved along the river, carrying cargo from Knightport, and shipping goods down the river.

It was a beautiful view. Rachel loved Knightcastle, loved its grandeur and beauty, loved the stories and legends attached to it. It was so different from the bleak walls and towers of Castle Cravenlock, looming on its crag. Rachel had grown up at Castle Cravenlock, but the castle had too many dark memories for her. Her cold father. Mitor's brutality. Skhath and the San-keth temple below the castle.

No, she didn't want to remember that.

Knightcastle was her home now. Gerald and Aldane were her family.

She looked at Aldane's red face, his eyes closed as he suckled, and smiled.

Though she did miss Mazael. Perhaps she could travel to Castle Cravenlock for a visit, once Aldane was old enough. Still, she hoped to be pregnant again soon, and the roads were no place for a pregnant woman. Perhaps she would ask Gerald to invite Mazael to visit Knightcastle. Aldane was his nephew, after all.

"My lady?"

Her maid Sarah stepped into the balcony, holding a plate. She was a young woman, younger than Rachel, with a gaunt face and black hair cut into ragged spikes. The hair and the dress hanging on her thin frame made her look slovenly, but Rachel had no cause for complaint. She had hired Sarah in the sixth month of her pregnancy, and the maid had given loyal service ever since.

"Your tea, my lady," said Sarah, setting the plate on the stone bench by Rachel's hand. "And some cheese and fruit. You should eat more. You need to keep up your strength, my lady. Nursing a baby is...hungry work."

Rachel laughed. "You worry too much, Sarah."

"Only for your son, my lady," said Sarah, lowering her eyes. "He is...he is such a handsome boy. I worry for him so."

"That is kind of you," said Rachel.

Sarah bowed. "I will leave you to your breakfast, my lady."

"No, don't go," said Rachel. "It would be nice to talk."

Sarah hesitated. "That...may not be proper, my lady. And will not Lady Rhea be visiting you this morning?"

Rachel sniffed and adjusted her hold on Aldane. "I shall speak with whom I wish." At Castle Cravenlock, Mitor had forbidden her from speaking with the servants. Now she delighted in flaunting that rule. "Besides, Lady Rhea is a most...formidable woman." Gerald's mother knew her mind, and as the chief noblewoman of Knightcastle, was not afraid to speak it. "It is difficult to simply talk to her, one woman to another."

For a moment Sarah hesitated, gazing at Aldane, her face going blank.

Then she smiled. "As you wish, my lady." She bowed once more and sat besides Rachel on the bench.

"It is a fine day, isn't it?" said Rachel.

"It is," said Sarah, looking again at Aldane. "And he is indeed a handsome boy. I...had several brothers who did not live to their first year. Aldane is so much stronger than them."

"Do you have a large family?" said Rachel.

"Oh, yes, very large," said Sarah. "I have many brothers and sisters. And many half-brothers and half-sisters." Her smile grew distant. "My father was somewhat...indiscreet, my lady."

"Perhaps you'll have many children of your own, someday," said Rachel.

Sarah sighed. "No, I fear not. I had a...pox, as a child. It left me barren."

"Oh! I didn't know. I'm so sorry to have mentioned it."

"It is all right," said Sarah, looking at Aldane again. "I made my peace with it long ago. I shall have to live to serve others, I suppose. And it will make me happy to see your son grow up strong."

"He will," said Rachel. "I'm sure of it."

"Yes," said Sarah, smiling again. "He will."

LATER THAT DAY Rachel sat in the courtyard outside Ideliza's Tower, enjoying the sun. Aldane lay sleeping in a basket at her feet, while Sarah stood nearby, humming a tune to herself. Rachel sewed, working on one of Gerald's surcoats. Mitor had encouraged her to sew, believing it ladylike, but Rachel enjoyed it anyway. It kept her fingers busy, her mind from dwelling upon the darkness of the past.

She smiled to herself.

Boots clicked against the flagstones, and Rachel looked up. Gerald walked past the barren gardens, clad all in blue, his cloak held in place with a silver brooch shaped like the greathelm sigil of the Rolands.

His was face grave.

"What is it?" said Rachel, rising and taking his hands. "Did Tobias go to war against the Old Kingdoms?"

"Tobias?" said Gerald. "No, no. It was easy to talk him and the Justiciar Commander out of the idea. We had other news by that point."

"Other news?" said Rachel. "Gerald, what happened?"

He took a deep breath. "We received a letter from Mazael."

"Mazael?" said Rachel. "Is...he safe? Is anything wrong?"

"He is well," said Gerald. "At least for now. Rachel, the stories were true. The Grim Marches are at war."

"With who?" said Rachel. "The lords of the High Plain? Or did Lord Richard turn on Mazael?" That thought filled her with fear. She knew well the ruthlessness of Richard Mandragon. If he had decided Mazael was an enemy...

"No," said Gerald. "Worse. Malrags."

Sarah looked up, frowning, and then looked away again.

For a moment Rachel did not recognize the word.

"Malrags?" she said at last. "No, no, that's...impossible. Malrags are only a story, a myth, like..."

"Like the San-keth?" said Gerald, and Rachel fell silent. "Mazael writes that Malrag warbands have been raiding the Grim Marches. One even tried to attack Cravenlock Town, though he destroyed them."

"Of course he did," said Rachel, her mind numb. Malrags? First the San-keth, and then the Demonsouled wizard Simonian of Briault. Hadn't Castle Cravenlock already suffered enough? "It will take more than Malrag devils to defeat Mazael Cravenlock."

"Undoubtedly," said Gerald. "But Mazael asks for aid. The Malrags have come down from the mountains in great numbers, and he and all the lords of the Grim Marches are hard-pressed. I am of a mind to take a thousand men and ride to his aid, if Father and Tobias approve." He sighed. "If they approve."

"Why would they not?" said Rachel. "Mazael is their kinsman by marriage now. Theirs, and yours."

"True," said Gerald. "But he is also the vassal of Richard Mandragon. Father has never forgiven Lord Richard for Belifane's death, even after all these years. I fear Father would rather watch the Grim Marches burn than to lift a finger to aid Richard Mandragon."

"How can he think that?" said Rachel with a sudden flare of temper. "He wouldn't be aiding Lord Richard, he would be aiding Mazael. Mazael, who defeated the Dominiars and conquered Tumblestone in your father's name. Mazael, who won the great tournament before our wedding, And Mazael defeated Amalric Galbraith, destroyed the Dominiars, and saved Knightcastle! How could Lord Malden refuse to aid him?"

"Father is...rather firm in his views, I fear," said Gerald. "He greatly respects Mazael, but he hates Lord Richard even more. And Lord

Richard is utterly ruthless, as you know better than I, my love. If I ride to Mazael's aid with a thousand men, Lord Richard might decide that I am a threat, or that Mazael is siding with Lord Malden against him. And if he does, he will turn against Mazael and do his utmost to kill me. Richard Mandragon is not a man to provoke."

"But Mazael needs our help," said Rachel. "He is my brother! To stand by and do nothing while he and his lands are in peril...it would be shameful, Gerald."

"I know," said Gerald. "I will speak with Father and Tobias again tomorrow. We will find a way to send aid to Mazael, I promise you. Even if I must hire mercenaries out of my own pocket and sent them to the Grim Marches, Mazael will have our help."

"Do you promise?" said Rachel, and regretted it at once. It was the plea of a querulous child, and she was a married woman with a son.

"I promise," said Gerald. "Mazael is your brother, but I was his squire. He trained me at the sword and lance and horse. I will not refuse him aid, not now, not ever." He smiled. "Besides, you said it yourself. Who better to fight the Malrags than Mazael? By the time we send him aid, he may well have defeated the Malrags utterly."

"I hope you are right," said Rachel.

But the fear gnawed at her nonetheless.

5

CALIBAH

" Sir Gerald and I will retire for the night," said Lady Rachel, turning towards the door of the bedroom she shared with Lord Malden's youngest son. "Please fetch me when Aldane wakes up. He'll be hungry."

The woman who called herself Sarah of Castle Town gripped her skirts and did a quick curtsy.

For Sarah of Castle Town was not her real name. Her true name was Sykhana, of Karag Tormeth, the high temple of the great god Sepharivaim, lord of the San-keth race. One of the San-keth arch-priests had given her that name, on the day she had survived the brutal training given to all calibah, to the changelings. How proud she had been then, how filled with zeal for Sepharivaim, how eager to win glory and power for the master race of the San-keth.

But the fire of her zeal had long ago turned to ash, and Sykhana cared nothing for Sepharivaim or the San-keth race.

"Of course, my lady," said Sykhana. "It shall be as you say."

Rachel smiled and gave Sykhana a quick hug. "You have been a great help to me, Sarah, since Aldane was born. And before, too. Why, I don't know what I should have done without you."

"You honor me, my lady," said Sykhana.

That was a lie. Sykhana detested the woman. Not because Rachel Roland was an apostate from the true faith of Sepharivaim, though that should have been the reason. No, Lady Rachel was weak and stupid and useless. A pretty flower, kept safe by the strength of her husband and father-in-law, a flower that would wilt at the first hint of frost. The first hint of pain and suffering.

Sykhana had known little else during her life.

And Lady Rachel did not recognize the gift, the wonderful gift, she had in Aldane Roland. In the ability to bear children.

Sykhana despised Rachel Roland, but she did not care about the woman.

Rachel chattered on matters of little consequence, and Sykhana feigned interest. To judge from the flush in her cheeks and her dilated pupils, Rachel no doubt planned to lie with her husband once again before she fell asleep, and Sykhana felt a surge of jealous rage. Not over Gerald Roland - she had no use for him. But if his seed quickened in his wife's womb, she could grow great with child once more. She could give birth to another son, strong and beautiful.

Something Sykhana would never know.

At last Rachel ran out of words and vanished into the bedroom to join her husband. Sykhana stalked across the sitting room and onto the balcony. All around her she saw Knightcastle in its ancient splendor, towers and parapets and spires, and the Riversteel's valley and the bustling docks of Castle Town, busy even at night.

She did not care about that, either. Let Knightcastle burn. Let the world burn. It mattered little to her.

Very little mattered to Sykhana any longer.

She looked into the sitting room, at the crib near the bedroom door. She stared at the small sleeping form, and some of the tightness drained from her jaw, her hands unclenching.

Aldane Roland mattered to her.

Before she realized it, she stood over the crib, gazing at the baby. His breathing was slow and steady, his face slack with sleep. From time to time one of his little hands twitched, or one of his feet kicked, pushing the blanket from him. Sykhana reached down and tugged the blanket back into place.

He was perfect. Beautiful, the most beautiful thing she had ever seen. Rachel and Gerald did not deserve him. They would raise him to be yet another knight, yet another brainless fool with a sword and a horse. Sykhana could give him so much more. Aldane would know power and glory beyond anything any mortal had ever known. He would live in splendor and bliss forever. His name would resound throughout the ages, and generations yet unborn would fall to their knees and worship him as a god...

"Sykhana," said a voice.

She whirled, arms and legs moving into the unarmed fighting stances taught by the priests of Karag Tormeth. Her fangs sprouted over her lips as she moved, ready to pump poison into any foe. Her inner eyelid, which gave her eyes their human appearance, slid back, and the pale moonlight suddenly became as bright as the sun.

And she saw the...shape standing in the corner of the sitting room.

It looked like a man cloaked in hooded robes, albeit a man made of darkness and pale silver light. The moonlight shone through the window, but the hooded man cast no shadow against the wall. Which made sense, since the man wasn't really there at all. It was nothing more than an image, a projection sent by a man standing hundreds of miles away.

By the wizard standing hundreds of miles away.

"Malavost," said Sykhana.

A lip lined in silver light and shadow twitched in amusement. Most men and women regarded Malavost with fear, called him "Master", lest his wrath fall upon them. But Sykhana did not care about Malavost, or his magic, or all the dark stories that swirled around the renegade wizard.

But she did care about what Malavost had promised her. She cared about that very much.

"Sykhana," said Malavost. His voice sounded tinny, as if coming through a long metal tube. "You're looking well. The dress a servant suits you better than I expected."

"How droll," said Sykhana. "You have business with me, I assume? Projecting an image over such a distance must tax a wizard of even your power."

"Less than you might think," said Malavost. "My reserves are considerable. But I'm not making this effort merely to amuse myself. The hour has come."

Sykhana blinked. "You mean..."

"Yes." A smile flickered over his shadowed face. "It is time."

Sykhana's hands started to tremble, and she forced them to remain still. "At last?"

"Need I repeat myself?" said Malavost. "It has begun,. Everything is ready. We need only one more thing. Do what you came to Knight-castle to do, and meet us in the Grim Marches as soon as possible."

"The Grim Marches?" said Sykhana. "Why there?"

Again a smile crossed Malavost's face. "Our plans have come to fruition. Meet us at a village called Gray Pillar, a day's ride east of Castle Cravenlock. Do you know it?"

"Aye," said Sykhana. She had traveled through the Grim Marches a year past, after Mazael killed Mitor Cravenlock and became Lord of Castle Cravenlock. Mitor had been a proselyte, a loyal follower of Sepharivaim, while Mazael...

Needless to say, the San-keth archpriests wanted Mazael dead, badly, and had promised a great reward to any follower of Sephari-vaim who slew him. No one had yet succeeded.

But Sykhana did not care about Mazael Cravenlock, or the wishes of the archpriests. They could not give her what she wanted.

Malavost could.

"Good," said Malavost. "Remember. The village of Gray Pillar, in the Grim Marches. Do what I have asked of you, and meet us there."

"And you'll keep your promise?" said Sykhana. "You will do what you said?"

"I shall," said Malavost. He smiled, his image rippling and flicker-ing. " Just as I have promised."

The image flickered once more and vanished into nothingness.

Sykhana left the anteroom, her heart racing with excitement. She forced herself to calm, and it came easily. She had trained in the gloomy dungeons of Karag Tormeth, under the most brutal teachers, to kill with ease, to move silently. Tonight, of course, she hoped to kill no one.

But if anyone tried to stop her, she would leave them dead upon the floor.

She had a small room behind the kitchen of Ideliza's Tower, furnished with a narrow bed, a wardrobe, and a wooden chest. Sykhana stripped out of her dress, knelt, and opened the chest, throwing aside the clothes it contained, and pressed a hand to the bottom of the chest.

The false bottom opened, and she lifted it aside to reveal her weapons.

She dressed in the garb favored by the changeling assassins of the San-keth, the Fangs of Sepharivaim. Armor of close-fitting, overlapping black leather plates, designed to emulate a serpent's scales. A lightweight black cloak, to obscure her outline and help her hide in the shadows. A pair of gauntlets, equipped with razor-edged climbing claws. A weapons belt, sheathed daggers at the ready.

She prepared her weapons. One by one she lifted them to her lips and extended her fangs, letting the poison drip upon the steel. The poison of a half-breed, a changeling, was not so lethal as the kiss of a full San-keth. But even so, one scratch of her poison daggers would kill in a matter of moments.

She poisoned the last blade and set it in place.

At last, she was ready.

Sykhana left her room, not bothering to close the door, and made for the anteroom.

And Aldane's crib.

~

RACHEL AWOKE IN THE DARKNESS.

She looked at the ceiling of the bedroom, working moisture into her mouth. Gerald lay against her, eyes closed, breathing slow and steady. Some moonlight leaked through the window, staining the room silver. Everything was still and silent.

So why did she feel so troubled?

Aldane, that was it. She didn't hear him crying. He usually woke up hungry this time of night.

She stared at the bedroom door.

This was absurd. So Aldane hadn't woken up hungry - that was surely no cause for concern. She ought to take the opportunity to get some sleep. The gods knew she hadn't slept the night through since Aldane had been born.

But he always woke up hungry this time of night.

Rachel slipped naked out of bed, shivering at the cool night air against her skin, and tugged on a robe. She would check on Aldane, she decided. Just to make sure that he was all right. Then she could go back to bed.

She opened the door, taking care to keep silent, lest she wake Gerald, and stepped into the anteroom.

And stopped in her tracks.

A dark shape stood over the crib, gazing down at Aldane. The figure looked up, and Rachel caught a glimpse of a pale face, of yellow eyes gleaming beneath a hood.

Of San-keth eyes.

Rachel opened her mouth to scream.

The dark figure moved in a blur, steel gleaming. Rachel threw herself to the side, but not before a throwing knife nicked her jaw. She gasped in pain, numbness spreading from the cut.

Her legs began to tremble.

Poison, she realized. The throwing knife had been poisoned.

The cloaked figure sprang forward, arm curling around Rachel's waist. Rachel tried to scream, tried to fight, but her limbs trembled, and she could not seem to form words. Her head rocked back, muscles twitching, and she stared into the dark hood.

Sarah's face gazed down at her. Only Sarah had ivory fangs curling over her lips, and her eyes had turned yellow, with vertical black pupils. Sarah was a calibah, a changeling, the product of a San-keth father and a human mother. Rachel would have given birth to calibah herself, had Mazael and Gerald not saved her from such a fate.

But that meant Sarah had been a changeling all along. A San-keth changeling had been in her rooms for months. A San-keth changeling had been watching her, spying on her.

A San-keth changeling had touched her son.

Rachel tried to scream, but Sarah's gloved hand clamped over her mouth.

"You stupid weakling," hissed Sarah. "You don't deserve him. I will make him immortal and strong, and he will reign in splendor over the earth forever." She leaned close, and Rachel smelled the harsh tang of calibah poison on Sarah's breath. "He won't even remember you."

She shoved, and Rachel fell to the floor, still twitching. Rachel clawed at her robe, pawing at her pocket. Sarah crossed the room, reached into the crib, and picked up Aldane. The baby lay silent and motionless in the calibah's arms, and Rachel realized that he had been drugged for silence.

Rage exploded through her, and she tried to sit up, tried to scream for help, but her muscles kept jerking.

Sarah looked at her once more, lip curled with contempt, and then vanished through the doorway.

Rachel slumped against the wall, her heart hammering, her head throbbing. She knew the changeling poison wasn't nearly as deadly as the venom of a full-blooded San-keth. Yet it was still lethal enough, and she had only moments to live.

She clawed at her robe's pockets, and pulled out a handful of dried yellow leaves. She lifted her trembling hand to her lips and forced the leaves into her mouth, making herself chew and swallow. She bit her tongue, blood filling her mouth, but still forced herself to chew. Once she had been betrothed to Skhath, a San-keth cleric of

Sepharivaim, and she had learned many of the secrets of the San-keth.

Including the antidotes for their poison. Ever since Mazael had killed Skhath, she had lived in terror of the retribution of the San-keth, and had carried dried succorleaf with her wherever she went.

Thank the gods for that.

But Aldane. Gods, oh, gods, she had taken Aldane...

Bit by bit the cold numbness of the succorleaf spread through her veins, easing the pain, her limbs stilling. Rachel worked moisture into her mouth, trying to ignore the taste of blood.

"Gerald," she whispered, when at last she could speak again. "Gerald. Gerald." She lashed out with her foot, kicking the door. Her bare sole did not make much noise against the heavy oak. "Gerald, gods, Gerald. Gerald. Gerald. Gerald!"

Her voice came out in a ragged, rusty shriek.

The door burst open, and Gerald sprang into the anteroom, naked but for the sword in his right hand. His eyes widened when he saw her, and he knelt by her side, sword still ready.

"Rachel!" he said. "Gods, what happened, are..."

"Aldane!" said Rachel. "Sarah's a changeling, she took Aldane. Stop her. Stop her!"

Gerald rose to his feet, hesitated, looked back at her.

"You're bleed..."

"I'm fine!" shouted Rachel, clawing at the wall as she tried to stand. "Get Aldane. Get Aldane!"

Gerald raced from the room, not even bothering to cover himself, and shouted for the guards.

Rachel levered herself to her knees, panic filling. Sarah had taken Aldane. Sarah had taken her son.

A San-keth changeling had taken her son!

A moment later she heard the horns ring over Knightcastle.

～

ON THE SECOND tier of Knightcastle, Sykhana froze in place, listening to the horns ring over the towers.

"Damn," she muttered.

She had erred. In her excitement, she had left at once, trusting in her poison to finish off Rachel Roland. Sykhana should have simply cut the woman's throat. No doubt Sir Gerald had awakened to find his son missing and his wife dying upon the floor.

He would be wroth. Again the horns rang out, summoning Knightcastle's guards and knights to arms. They would seal the castle, hunt her down, and kill her.

And Aldane would lose his chance for eternal power and bliss.

Sykhana cursed and broke into a run. Around her she heard the clatter of arms and armor rising from Knightcastle's courtyards, the shouts of sergeants and knights bellowing orders, the tramp of boots against flagstones. She had spent months observing Gerald Roland firsthand, and though he was trusting and naive, he was no fool in matters of arms. He would order Knightcastle sealed, send search parties to slay her and reclaim Aldane.

But there was more than one way out of Knightcastle.

Knightcastle was ancient, expanded and rebuilt and expanded again throughout its long history. One long-dead Roland king had wished to visit his mistresses in secret, so he had constructed the Trysting Ways, a network of secret passages connecting his chamber to his mistresses' rooms. Later Roland kings and lords had expanded the Trysting Ways, until a maze of hidden passages threaded through Knightcastle like veins in living flesh. Not even the Rolands themselves knew all the hidden twists and turns of the Trysting Ways.

But the San-keth knew of them. Last year, the archpriest Straganis had used the Trysting Ways to attack Lord Malden. Mazael Cravenlock and the Dragon's Shadow had baffled the attack, driving Straganis and the calibah back into the Trysting Ways. No doubt Lord Malden and Sir Tobias had since ordered the entrances guarded.

But there were many entrances into the Ways, and if Sykhana could reach them before the guards did...

She heard men running, heard someone shout. Had they spotted her? She slid through the door at the base of a tower, and into a dusty round chamber, once used as an armory, to judge from the racks on the walls. The fireplace had a secret entrance into the Trysting Ways. Three more steps, and...

The door on the far wall swung open, and four armsmen in Roland tabards stepped into the room.

"Aye, I don't see the point," said the first man, "but orders are..."

He fell silent.

Sykhana hissed, lips drawing back from her fangs.

"Gods, that's a changeling!" said one of the men.

"Kill it!" said another man.

All four armsmen drew their swords.

Sykhana stooped, set Aldane on the floor, and straightened up. The first of the armsmen, with the silver trim of a sergeant on his helm, lunged at her, his sword glittering in the dim moonlight. Sykhana spun past the thrust, grabbed his wrist, and pulled herself close.

Then she kissed him. The sergeant's eyes widened in astonishment, and screamed as her fangs plunged into his lip and chin. Rachel Roland had received only the smallest drop of Sykhana's poison. The sergeant received a full dose. His screams cut off as his face turned black and his windpipe closed up.

The remaining three men hesitated, and Sykhana yanked a throwing knife from her belt, drew back her arm, and flung it. The armsman on the left ducked, but the blade nicked his jaw.

He was dead. He just didn't know it yet.

Sykhana danced back and yanked a pair of daggers from her belt. The armsmen came at her, swords stabbing and slashing. She dodged their attacks and lashed out with her daggers. All three men were armored, and competent fighters, and there was no way she could land a killing blow with one of her daggers.

But it was easy enough to land scratches on their hands and faces. Sykhana dodged another swing, and a sword thrust scraped along her side, her leather armor just barely stopping the blow. Just another moment, just another moment longer...

The man she had struck with the throwing knife fell to his knees, eyes wide, breath wheezing. Then the second man toppled, and then the third, overcome by the potency of Sykhana's poison. A changeling's poison was not nearly as deadly as that of a San-keth.

But it was still deadly enough.

Sykhana stepped towards the men, daggers in hand.

She had left Rachel Roland alive...but she would not make the same mistake twice.

After it was done, she cleaned her blades on the dead men's tabards, picked up Aldane, and walked to the fireplace. A moment's search, and she found the trigger, hidden in a crack between two stones. She pressed it, and the back of the fireplace swung open, revealing a narrow, darkened passageway.

Sykhana vanished into the Trysting Ways.

~

AN HOUR later she hurried through the streets of Castle Town, wrapped in a cloak, Aldane hidden beneath its folds.

She paused to hide in an alley as a troop of the town's militia marched past, torches and spears in hand. The horns from Knight-castle had roused the militia, though the militia likely didn't know the reason for the alarms. No doubt Gerald Roland thought that Sykhana was still in the castle, and hadn't yet dispatched a messenger to warn the town.

By the time he did, Sykhana intended to be long gone.

She hurried through the alleys until she came to the prosperous streets of Castle Town's northeastern quarter. The house she chose was not a mansion, not quite, but nonetheless stood four stories tall, faced with cut white stone and polished wooden timbers. She slipped around to the side, to the servants' entrance. It was locked, of course, but Sykhana picked it with ease. Inside she crept down a corridor lined with wooden paneling, and stopped before an open door, candlelight spilling against the walls.

Paul Korren sat at his desk, writing. A thin man with a well-trimmed goatee, he was a powerful merchant and trader. His ware-houses in Knightport bulged with good from across the world, and he sold them at a tidy profit. He was friends with Lord Malden, and on good terms with a dozen other powerful lords in the kingdom.

He was also a proselyte, a human follower of Sepharivaim, and had a shrine dedicated to Sepharivaim hidden beneath his wine cellar. He had been clever enough to remain hidden during Stragan-is's attack last year, but Sykhana felt nothing but contempt for prose-lytes. The San-keth utterly loathed humans, considered them vermin, and the archpriests could not decide whether to kill them all or merely enslave them once Sepharivaim returned in power.

And yet some humans still chose to follow the San-keth way? Pathetic.

"Korren," said Sykhana, stepping into the merchant's study.

Korren looked up from his desk, scowling. "What is this? Who are the devil are you? I..."

He fell silent as he saw Sykhana's eyes.

"You are a messenger, yes?" he said. "From the archpriests? I have been faithful. I have remained hidden, even after many calibah were slain in Knightcastle last year. I retain the ear of Lord Malden, and neither he nor his sons suspect my true loyalties."

"I require a horse," said Sykhana. "At once."

Korren frowned. "A horse?"

"Aye," said Sykhana. "And, also, the entrance to your tunnel."

Korren's face grew hard. "I have no tunnel."

"Don't lie to me, fool," said Sykhana, lips peeling back from her fangs. "I know you have a secret tunnel out of the city walls, so you can smuggle goods in and out with out paying Lord Malden's taxes. I also know that the tunnel is large enough to handle horse-drawn carts. You will give me a horse at once, and tell me the way to your smugglers' tunnel."

"What is that you have there?" said Korren, rising and stepping around the desk. "An infant? Whose? What are kind of business is this?" He glared at her. "I received no word from the archpriests. Before I give you anything, you will tell..."

Sykhana snarled and leapt at him, her arm snaking around his shoulders. She yanked him close, her fangs stopping a half-inch from his throat.

Korren went very still, his face white.

"You will," hissed Sykhana, " stop wasting my time and do as I bid. Now."

Korren hastened to obey.

A FEW MOMENTS later Sykhana led one of Korren's best horses across Castle Town's square, across from the Inn of the Crowned Helm. She had changed her armor for the dress of a serving maid, the slumbering Aldane hidden in her cloak. Her transparent inner eyelids closed, giving her eyes a human appearance.

Four men stood on the front steps of the Crowned Helm. The innkeeper, she suspected, and his porters, come to watch the fuss.

"Aye, lass?" said the innkeeper. "Why are you wandering the streets at night? Isn't safe."

"My pardons, sir," said Sykhana. "But my brother is in the militia, and my mother bade me to bring him some bread." She lifted Aldane. The baby, wrapped as he was, did almost look like a loaf of bread.

The innkeeper nodded, and Sykhana had a sudden thought.

She hid a smile.

"I just saw the strangest thing," said Sykhana. "Do you know Paul Korren, the merchant?"

"Aye," said the innkeeper. "Pompous windbag. Never pays his bills on time."

"I saw a woman hurrying into his wine cellar," said Sykhana. "Dressed all in black, carrying a baby. The strangest thing. Perhaps she was frightened by the horns."

The innkeeper frowned. "That must be it."

Sykhana smiled and led the horse away, leaving the seed to take root in their minds.

~

AN HOUR later she galloped to the east, into the rising sun, along the road to the village of Tristgard.

The road to the Grim Marches.

Aldane started to wake, and Sykhana touched his face.

"Don't cry, my precious one," she murmured. "For soon you will be a god, and I will be your mother."

6

PURSUIT

Rachel awoke with a pounding headache and a vile taste in her mouth.

She sat up, blinking. Cheery dawn sunlight streamed through the windows. Blood stained her nightgown, and a tight bandage rested against the left side of her jaw.

A wave of dizziness washed over her, and she leaned back against the pillows, confused. How had she end up here? And why did her mouth taste like succorleaf? The last thing she remembered was getting up to check on Aldane, and then...and then...

"Oh, gods," said Rachel, sitting back up. "Aldane. Aldane!"

Dizziness spun through her, stronger than before, and Rachel clutched at the bed for balance.

"My lady!" said a girl's voice. "I think she's awake!"

Rachel tried to get to her feet. Aldane, she had to get to Aldane...

A strong hand took her elbow, steadying her.

"Careful," said Lady Rhea, Lord Malden's wife and Gerald's mother. She was a tall, lean woman in her middle fifties, with long gray-streaked brown hair and pale blue eyes. "Circan says you were poisoned, that you saved yourself with succorleaf. That was very clever."

Compliments from Lady Rhea were rarer than pearls, and another time Rachel would have been pleased. But she could not think of anything other than Aldane. "Where's Aldane? Where's Gerald? Did he find Aldane? And Sarah..." Her face twisted in rage as she remembered the treacherous maid.

"Knightcastle is sealed," said Lady Rhea. "The gates were barred and guarded moments after Gerald found you. My sons and their men are searching the castle from top to bottom. We will find this vile changeling and make her pay."

"I don't care about Sarah," said Rachel. "I want Aldane back."

"So do we all, dear," said Rhea, patting her hand. "But you need to rest..."

"No!" said Rachel, clawing to her feet. Once she would never have dared to defy Gerald's mother. But a San-keth changeling had taken her son. "I've got to find Aldane, I've got to get him back..."

"You must lie down," said Rhea, her voice firm.

"I cannot lie abed when my son is gone," said Rachel. "Please, my lady. You...have lost sons." The very thought of losing Aldane made her stomach twist. "Could you lie waiting, if you knew...if you knew..."

Lady Rhea said nothing for a moment, her face blank. For a moment Rachel feared that she had taken offense. Rhea had lost three sons. Belifane, slain by Lord Richard Mandragon. Mandor, killed by the Knights Dominiar. And Garain, cut down last year, murdered by a San-keth changeling...

"Your maid," said Rhea, voice distant. "She was a San-keth changeling? All this time?"

Rachel nodded.

"I lost a son to the changelings," said Rhea. "I hope you do not have to know that pain, too."

She looked towards the door, where her maids, a half-dozen nervous young women, awaited her command.

"Help her dress," said Rhea, the maids surged forward.

〜

A SHORT TIME later Rachel hurried through the courtyards and arcades of Knightcastle, making for the castle's lowest circle, Lady Rhea and her maids following.

"Slow down, girl," said Lady Rhea. "You are a noblewoman of Knightcastle, not a fishwife hurrying to the docks on market day."

Again Rachel ignored her.

Ringed by towers and battlements, Knightcastle's vast barbican was larger than many villages. Rachel remembered standing here a year past, watching Mazael and Gerald and Tobias ride out with Knightcastle's armies to face Amalric Galbraith and the Dominiar Order. Now armsmen and squires ran back and forth across the flagstones. Gerald paced before the gates, wearing his armor, a blue cloak with the Roland sigil flaring behind him.

He stopped when he saw her.

"Gerald," said Rachel. She yearned to run to him, throw herself into his arms. But she did not want to make him look weak in front of his men. "Gerald...did..."

"Rachel," he said, stepping forward and taking her hands. "You're well? Thank the gods."

"Aldane?" she said. "Have you found Aldane?"

He grimaced. "Not yet. We've sealed the castle, and have men searching every room. Sarah will not long elude us."

"If she's even still here," said Rhea.

Gerald and his mother shared a look.

"What?" said Rachel. "How could she have escaped? You found me only a few moments after Sarah attacked me. She couldn't have gotten to the gates before you sounded the alarm."

"The Trysting Ways," said Rhea.

Gerald scowled. "Those damned Trysting Ways. I told Father to have them sealed up, all of them. And after Straganis almost killed us last year, I think he would have listened."

"The Trysting Ways are part of Knightcastle's traditions," said Rhea, "and your father respects tradition."

Gerald shook his head. "You mean he wants to visit his mistresses unseen."

"That's no way to talk about your father in public," said Rhea, without rancor. How she accepted Lord Malden's philandering so calmly, Rachel would never know.

"So she could have escaped through the Trysting Ways?" said Rachel.

Gerald sighed. "Yes. Father did at least agree to seal any passages that led outside the castle. But only Trocend knew them all, and the San-keth killed him. We could have easily overlooked one or two. Or more."

"Oh, gods," said Rachel. "Then she got away, she has our son and she..."

"We don't know that yet," said Rhea, her voice like iron.

Rachel clutched at Gerald's arm. "We have to ride out, we have to catch her before she gets away..."

"That would do no good," said Gerald, "until we knew where she was going. And why."

"There is a sensible question," said Rhea. "Why? Why did this changeling take my grandson?"

"Because the San-keth hate us!" said Rachel. "Because Mazael defeated Skhath, and so they'll take vengeance on him. On him, or any of his kin that they can reach."

And the San-keth hated her, too. For she was an apostate, a traitor. She had been a proselyte, pledged to Skhath, promised to bear his changeling offspring for the greater glory of Sepharivaim and the San-keth. And she had turned her back on them. They wanted revenge, she knew.

They might have taken Aldane in vengeance. The very thought that she might have done this, that she might have brought this upon her son, made her want to weep.

"But why?" said Rhea. "Why not just kill him? Why not just kill you, for that matter?"

Gerald blinked. "That's...a good point, Mother. When the San-keth have come for us before, they've always tried to kill Rachel. They've never tried to kidnap anyone before." He looked at Rachel. "Sarah. Did she say anything?"

"She did," said Rachel, shivering. "She was so angry. I had no idea she hated me so much. She said that she was going to make Aldane powerful and strong forever. What does that mean?"

"I don't know," said Gerald. "Speculation is pointless until we know more. And Sarah might very well be trapped in the castle."

"If she escaped," said Rhea, "she almost certainly would have made for Castle Town. No doubt she had allies there, or at the very least a hidden store of supplies. You should send men there at once."

"It's already done, Mother," said Gerald, squinting through the portcullis. "Tobias went himself, along with two score of reliable men. If there's a nest of San-keth proselytes hiding in Castle Town, Tobias will deal with...wait." He turned and shouted. "Open the portcullis. Tobias has returned!"

A column of horsemen rode towards the gate, and Rachel heard the thunder of steel-shod hooves against the road. The massive portcullis groaned open, and a moment later twenty horsemen galloped into the barbican, armor flashing in the sunlight, the Roland banner flapping overhead. The lead rider dropped from his saddle, armor clanking, and pulled off his helmet.

Sir Tobias Roland looked like a shorter, more muscular version of Gerald. He had a broad, ruddy face, made for laughing. But he had not laughed much, not since Garain's murder and Lord Malden's increasing illness, and today he looked even grimmer than usual.

"Gerald," said Tobias.

"Where are the rest of your men?" said Gerald.

"Keeping the innkeeper of the Crowned Helm under guard," said Tobias.

"You've found something," said Gerald.

"Aye," said Tobias. "There's news in Castle Town. You'd best come at once."

Gerald nodded. "Rachel, stay with..."

"No!" said Rachel, her fingers tightening against his arm. His armor felt cold and hard beneath her hand. "She has our son. I...I cannot wait."

Gerald hesitated, then gave a short nod.

~

A SHORT TIME later they reined up before the Inn of the Crowned Helm.

"Aye, sir knight," said the innkeeper, a stout man in a pristine white apron. "We were all up, my lads and I, when we heard the horns. Feared it was bandits or raiders, but nothing happened. Then I saw a peasant lass taking bread to her brother. She said she saw a woman in black carrying a baby, and Sir Tobias said your son had been taken..."

Rachel's heart leapt against her ribs.

"Where did she see the woman and the baby?" said Gerald.

"At the house of Paul Korren," said the innkeeper. He scowled. "Man's a scoundrel. Never pays his bills on time. Wouldn't surprise me if he hoped to hold your son for ransom, sir knight."

"If you've led me true," said Gerald, turning his horse around, "then you will be rewarded. To the house of Paul Korren! Quickly!"

~

KORREN LIVED IN A FINE HOUSE, four stories tall, fronted with white stone and polished timbers. It even had a good-sized garden in back, ringed by a low stone wall, where Korren's servants could grow vegetables. The double doors to a wine cellar lay against the house, the handles chained and locked shut.

Tobias grunted. "You, you, and you. Circle to the sides. You and you. Watch the back door and the windows. If there are any snakes here, they might try to slither away before we can cut off their heads. Keep anyone from running until Sir Gerald and I say they can go. The rest of you, follow me. Turn the house inside out."

"This Korren fellow might be innocent," said Gerald.

"Innocent?" said Rachel. "You heard what the innkeeper said!"

"Aye," said Tobias. "It might have been Sarah. Or it might have been Korren's wife, or one of his servants. Have no fear, sister. If Korren aided Sarah, I'll run my longsword up his arse."

He slid from his horse, Gerald and Rachel following, the armsmen marching behind. Tobias strode up to the door and pounded on it with his sword hilt, his pommel leaving gouges in the polished wood. After a moment the door opened a crack, and a nervous-looking serving girl peered out.

"Aye, sirs?" she said. "What is your business here?"

"I am Sir Tobias Roland," announced Tobias, "Marshal of Knightcastle, and this is my brother, Sir Gerald Roland, armsmaster of Knightcastle. We will speak with Paul Korren, now."

The serving girl blinked. "But...but the master said he should not be disturbed..."

Tobias smiled, pushed open the door, picked up the serving girl, and set her to the side. She stared at him with shocked eyes. "Oh, your master will want to see us, my dear. Now be a good girl and stay out of the way." He turned, beckoned to the waiting armsmen. "Lads! If either the changeling or my nephew are in this house, find them."

The armsmen trooped into the house and fanned out, hands on their swords hilts. Rachel heard crashes and bangs as they began searching, overturning furniture and looking in cupboards. There was a commotion further down the hall, and a thin man with a well-trimmed goatee stormed into sight, clad in the fine velvets and rich furs of a prosperous merchant.

"What is the meaning of this?" raged the well-dressed man, glaring at them. "Do you not know who I am? I am Paul Korren, Master of the Merchants' Guild and a close friend of Lord Malden Roland, and he will hear of this outrage, I assure you!"

"Really?" said Tobias, still smiling, though it did not reach his eyes. "I happen to dine with Lord Malden several times a week, and he rarely mentions you. He did talk about you once, though. He said you were a toad who would sell his own mother for a copper coin. But perhaps my father's standards for his close friends have slipped."

"Your father?" said Korren, and then his eyes widened with recognition. "Sir Tobias! Forgive me. I...I did not recognize you."

He was sweating, Rachel saw. The man was terrified.

"Quite all right," said Gerald. Like Tobias, he was smiling, and it did not touch his blue eyes. "I'm sure a master merchant is far too busy to speak with the sons of his lawful lord. Perhaps I should mention that to my father, the next time I see him."

Korren looked back and forth, licking his lips. "But what is this about, my lords? I am a loyal subject of Lord Malden. I have done nothing wrong."

"Merely a precaution, you see," said Gerald. "If it turns out we have made a mistake, I will pay you recompense myself."

"A mistake?" said Korren. "About what?"

"My son was abducted from Knightcastle early this morning," said Gerald, "by a San-keth changeling. Some eyewitnesses saw a woman entering your wine cellar, carrying a baby. I will have my son back, master merchant, and if I have to search the house of every man in Knightcastle, I will do it."

Korren's expression did not change, did not even flicker, but his face went pale.

Rachel's hands curled into fists. He knew something about Sarah, he knew where the changeling had taken Aldane, and he had the temerity to lie about it...

"My wine cellar?" said Korren. "But, my lords, I fear you are mistaken. My wine cellar is tiny. Surely not large enough to hide a creature so vile as a San-keth changeling and a stolen child. Let me speak with Lord Malden, and surely I can convince him of my innocence..."

"Liar!" shrieked Rachel, stepping past Gerald. Korren looked at her, shocked. "Liar! You know who took him! You helped her! You helped her!"

Her hands hooked into claws, and she would have leapt upon him, but Gerald caught her shoulder.

"Who is this woman?" said Korren. "Bad enough that you have accused me unjustly of this crime! Must I endure the hysterics of some deranged wench?"

"Have a care, master merchant," said Gerald, his tone cool, "how you speak of my wife."

Korren flinched. "Your wife? You mean she's the apostate that..."

He fill silent.

"You called her an apostate," said Gerald, his voice even cooler. "The only ones to call her that are San-keth proselytes. Those who betray the gods of the Amathavian church, and turn to the worship of Sepharivaim, plotting murder and torture and bloodshed."

"You think too much for me, brother," said Tobias. "All I know is that San-keth proselytes are dangerous scoundrels, and our father's lands are better off without them."

Korren opened his mouth to answer, but a shout from the garden interrupted him.

"My lords! You need to see the wine cellar at once!"

Korren turned and ran for the door.

Or he tried to, rather. Tobias's meaty fist lashed out and smashed into Korren's jaw. The master merchant struck the paneled wall and bounced off, staggering. Tobias barked an order, and two armsmen hurried forward, pinning Korren's arms behind his back.

"Come, sir," said Tobias, still smiling that cold smile. "Let's see what sort of vintages you stock in your cellar, hmm?"

PAUL KORREN'S wine cellar was small and dusty. The armsmen shoved aside a pair of wine casks, revealing a wooden trapdoor set on the stone floor.

The trapdoor opened onto a scene Rachel remembered all too well from her nightmares.

A shrine to Sepharivaim, the serpent god of the San-keth, lay hidden below the cellar. A bronze image of a great coiled serpent lay upon a wooden altar. Bronze bowls and daggers rested below the serpent idol, and the altar's side bore dark, crusted stains.

Sepharivaim was a jealous and cruel god, and demanded tribute in human blood from his servants. Was that why Sarah had taken Aldane? To kill him upon Sepharivaim's bloodstained altars?

The thought made her want to throw up. Or to rip out Korren's eyes. Or both.

"Oh, yes," said Tobias, looking over the gloomy shrine. "A loyal subject of my father, indeed."

Korren looked back and forth between Tobias and Gerald. "I don't...my lords, I swear it, I didn't even know this was here. The servants must pray to the serpent god here. Or...or it must have been here when I bought the house, yes, that's..."

"Do you really think we are stupid enough to believe your lies?" said Gerald.

Korren sputtered some more, and then his expression hardened, contempt flashing in his eyes. "Fools. You don't know the might of Sepharivaim. He will crush you utterly."

"I have seen San-keth clerics slain," said Gerald, "along with countless changelings. Sepharivaim must be a feeble god, if he has the loyalty of such pathetic servants." He looked at the altar. "And such incompetent hirelings."

Korren spat. "Sepharivaim will make you pay for such insolence, you..."

Tobias sighed and backhanded Korren across the face. The merchant fell with a cry of pain, blood flying from his lips. He slumped against the rough stone wall, and Tobias kicked him in the gut with a heavy boot. Korren fell, and would have toppled to the floor, but Tobias grabbed his collar with one hand and lifted him, Korren's feet hanging over the floor.

"You should listen to me," said Tobias in a pleasant tone. "My brother enjoys talking, and discussing theology and morality. I am a much simpler man, and so I will state this plainly. You will tell me what I want to know, or I will hurt you until you do."

Korren spat in Tobias's face. "I will never betray Sepharivaim! Never!"

Tobias shrugged and threw Korren against the wall. "Fair enough." He glanced at Gerald. "You may want to withdraw, brother. You always found this...distasteful, I recall."

"No," said Gerald. "He knows what happened to my son. I will watch. Rachel, wait outside for us."

She hesitated. If Korren knew what had happened to Aldane, she wanted to watch him suffer. But she knew that look in Gerald's eyes, so she took the ladder to the wine cellar and climbed the stairs to Korren's garden.

As soon as she stepped outside, she heard the screaming, and waited.

And as it turned out, Tobias only had to break four of Korren's fingers before he started talking.

~

"KORREN DIDN'T KNOW her name, or her purpose," said Gerald, voice grim.

Rachel watched him, her hands opening and closing over and over again.

They stood in the solar of the Old Keep, Knightcastle's oldest tower. Here, Rachel knew, the ancient Roland kings of Knightcastle had built their fortress, raising a keep to defend their people against the Malrag hordes unleashed after the fall of Tristafel. Now four men stood before the solar's high windows. Gerald, pacing as he described what Korren had confessed. Tobias, scowling, his massive arms crossed over his chest.

The third man was tall and slender, with hair so blond it was almost white, a marked contrast from his long black coat, cloak, trousers, and boots. Circan of Stormriver was Lord Malden's new court wizard, sent after the San-keth had murdered Trocend Castleson last year. Rachel did her very best not to glare at him. She detested magic, and loathed wizards.

Skhath, after all, had been an accomplished necromancer.

The final man leaned heavily upon a silver-headed cane, the folds of his rich cloak and robe hanging loosely about his body. Malden Roland, Lord of Knightcastle and Gerald's father, had aged greatly in the year since Sir Garain's death. Rachel did not think it would be very long before Tobias took his father's place as Lord of Knightcastle.

"She arrived in the middle of the night," said Gerald, still pacing before the solar's high windows. "She ordered him to give her a horse, and when he questioned her, she threatened to kill him. So Korren gave her the horse, and led her to his smugglers' tunnel. She took the horse and fled. I saw the tracks in the tunnel myself."

Lord Malden grunted. "Were you able to track her?"

"She made for the main road leading north from Castle Town," said Gerald. He shook his head. "From there her tracks merged with a thousand others. She could have taken any five roads from there."

"Did you kill Korren?" said Lord Malden. "Vile little rodent. All these years he is evaded my taxes with that smugglers' tunnel, and he kidnaps my grandson to boot. He deserves the blade. Or a dance at the end of a noose."

"Not yet, Father," said Tobias. "He still might know something useful, so I've got him in a cell. If we get Aldane back, we'll execute him then."

If? Rachel's hands trembled, and she tried to force them to stillness.

"What are we going to do?" said Rachel. Her voice quavered, and she hated herself for it. She had to stay strong. Aldane needed her to be strong. "We're not...we're not just going to let Sarah go, are we?"

"Of course not," said Gerald. "We will send word to every castle, town, village, and monastery in Knightrealm, with a description of Sarah and Aldane, and a bounty for his safe return and her head. I will organize the armsmen, to ride in parties along each of the roads she might have taken. A woman traveling alone with a baby will be unusual. She will almost certainly draw notice. We will find her, sooner or later."

He was trying to sound confident, she knew, for her sake. But she knew him too well by now. He doubted they would ever find Aldane again.

"There must," Rachel closed her eyes, trying to keep from weeping, "there must...be something else we can do. Something. Anything."

"There is."

Circan's voice was so soft Rachel scarce heard it.

"What?" said Gerald.

Circan's eyes were as pale as his hair, and they showed not a hint of emotion as they settled upon Rachel. "But you will not like it, my lady."

"What is it, man?" said Gerald. "My son is missing. I will do whatever it takes to get him back."

Circan hesitated, glanced at Lord Malden. The old lord nodded.

"When Aldane was born," said Circan, "my lord Malden bade me to draw a vial of his blood."

"Blood? Blood!" said Rachel. For a moment rage overrode her fear. She knew what kind of vile magic a necromancer could work with a vial of a victim's blood. Skhath had explained the spells, threatening to inflict them upon her should she ever betray him. "You touched my son, wizard? You used my son's blood for a spell. You scoundrel, I'll..."

"Father," said Gerald, "why did you not tell me of this?"

"Enough, daughter!" said Lord Malden. "And you as well, my son. Our house has made powerful enemies in the San-keth. Mazael dealt them a harsh blow, but I knew they would return someday. So I bade Circan to draw a vial of Aldane's blood. And yours, my daughter, and yours as well, my sons."

"But why?" said Rachel. "Why would you do such a thing?"

"Because," said Circan. "A vial of blood can be used to work terrible magic upon its owner. But it can also be used in a tracking spell."

"A...tracking spell?" said Tobias, frowning. "You mean, you can use your magic to...find Aldane?"

"In a manner of speaking," said Circan. "I cannot pinpoint the young lord's location with any degree of accuracy. But the vial of blood can act as a...compass, let us say. I can use it to follow him." He bowed in Rachel's direction. "Forgive me, my lady, for not mentioning this earlier. But I had to take caution. A skilled wizard can sense the presence of the spell, and work a counterspell that will destroy the vial of blood. But this Sarah of yours has no arcane skill. I can track your son with impunity."

"Then what the devil are we waiting for?" said Gerald. "I will ride at once to find Aldane, and you will ride with me, wizard."

"I shall come as well," said Tobias, rubbing his sword hilt.

"No," said Lord Malden. "You will remain here, Tobias." Tobias started to protest, but Lord Malden kept talking. "I am an old man, and tired, and you are my heirs. You must bear the burden of ruling Knightcastle when I die. And if all my sons die before me...then Knightrealm will fall into chaos after my death. I will not have it."

Tobias scowled, but gave a sharp nod.

"Gerald," said Lord Malden, "you will take Circan, and as many men as you need."

"No more than a hundred mounted armsmen, I think," said Gerald. "We can move faster that way. One woman and a baby on a horse can move very quickly."

"She will have to stop sooner or later," said Lord Malden. His tone grew stern, formal. "Sir Gerald of house Roland! My grandson has been kidnapped. I charge you to find this changeling, slay her, and bring my grandson back to Knightcastle."

"It shall be done, my lord," said Gerald.

"And I will come as well," said Rachel.

"No," said Gerald and Tobias and their father in unison.

"But I must!" said Rachel. "I have to get Aldane back. I will have no peace in my heart until he is safe again."

There was a silence.

"She is your wife, Gerald," said Lord Malden. "I leave the decision to you."

"This will be a hard journey, Rachel," said Gerald. "We shall have to ride fast. And Sarah might have allies she can call upon, other changelings, or maybe San-keth clerics. When we find her, there will be violence." His face twisted. "You could be hurt, or even killed..."

"I don't care," said Rachel, and she clutched his hands. "Do you know what it would be like to stay here, waiting for news? Knowing that every rider might carry word of Aldane's death, or yours? I cannot wait. She took him from me! I have to get him back. I have to! If...if I wait here, I am sure that I will go mad."

Gerald stared at her in silence for a long moment, his fingers kneading the back of her hands, emotions warring over his face.

At last he nodded.

AN HOUR later a hundred mounted armsmen left Knightcastle's barbican. Sir Gerald Roland rode at their head, clad in his shining armor, a flowing blue cloak billowing from his shoulders. Circan was at his side, holding a crystal vial of blood in his right hand, muttering a spell under his breath.

Rachel rode in the midst of the column, heart hammering.

She would get Aldane back, or she would die.

There were no other options.

7

THE DRAGONS

Mazael Cravenlock lay asleep and dreamed:

He stood on a battlefield, Lion in his hand, dead Malrags strewn at his feet. But some of his own men lay among them, their armor dented and torn by Malrag spears and axes.

Lion burned in his fist, the blade shining with blue flames.

Mazael turned as the Malrags rushed him.

He leapt to meet them, Lion in both hands. A cut took the hand from a Malrag's arm, and Mazael spun, ripping open the throat of another. Yet the still they came at him, swinging black axes and stabbing black spears. Mazael killed Malrag after Malrag, but more took their places, gray lips pulled back from yellowed fangs, colorless eyes narrowed in fury.

Mazael killed and killed, Lion's blade smoking with Malrag blood, but still the creatures continued their assault.

A snarl split the air, and a black shape blurred past Mazael, crashing into the Malrags. Two of the Malrags fell to the earth with roars of pain, their hamstrings torn, and Mazael saw the great black wolf, ivory fangs flashing. The wolf's savage fury drove the Malrags back, and Mazael flung himself into the fray. Four Malrags fell to

Lion in as many heartbeats, and the black wolf leapt and pounced, fangs and claws dealing death.

Soon the remaining Malrags broke and ran, fleeing to the south. Not east towards the Great Mountains, not west towards Castle Cravenlock, and not towards Lord Richard's castle of Swordgrim in the north.

Always towards the south, towards the Great Southern Forest.

Why?

Mazael turned, saw the black wolf staring at him, blue eyes blazing like Lion's blade. He stepped towards the wolf, and it slunk back, fangs bared. For a moment he thought the wolf would flee, or attack him, but it did not.

It only stared at him, trembling as if enraged, or terrified.

But it did not run, and it did not attack. Still those blue eyes stared at him, full of rage and fear and...longing?

"Who are you?" said Mazael.

The wolf snarled.

"I know you mean me no threat, whoever you are," said Mazael. "But...you must have some reason for aiding me against the Malrags. Who are you? What do you wish of me?"

The wolf growled, snapping in his direction...

~

"MY LORD?"

Mazael blinked awake.

He lay on one of the benches in Castle Cravenlock's lofty great hall, gazing up at the vaulted ceiling. Light from the sunset streamed through the western windows, filling the hall with bloody light. His shoulders and back ached - he'd fallen asleep wearing his armor again.

Not that there had been much opportunity to remove it, lately.

Rufus Highgate stood over him, concern on his haughty face. Beneath his Cravenlock tabard, the boy wore a coat of black Malrag mail that hung to his knees. He had kept his head and killed two

Malrags during the skirmish north of White Rock, and claimed his dead foe's armor as spoils. Mazael let his men claim weapons and armor from the slain Malrags as trophies. It helped keep their spirits up, let them boast of their deeds to their fellows.

Besides, the Malrag armor was very often better than their own gear anyway.

"My lord, the sentinels have seen Lord Richard's banners approaching," said Rufus. "You wanted to be informed at once."

"I did," said Mazael, sitting up. Around him workmen and servants labored in the great hall, carrying benches and raising tables. Tonight he would feast Lord Richard and his vassals, and the Dragonslayer would share his plans.

Tomorrow, they would march to battle against the Malrags.

"Go find Sir Hagen," said Mazael. "Tell him to meet me at the barbican. I'll be along shortly."

Rufus bowed and ran off, his black Malrag mail rattling.

Mazael rubbed his face, his beard scratching beneath his palms, and let out a long breath.

That damnable dream.

What did it mean? At first Mazael thought it had been a sending from the Old Demon. But the Old Demon's dreams had always been visions blood and death and power, meant to tempt Mazael's Demon-souled nature. Later he wondered if a different wizard, perhaps one of the Malrag shamans, had sent the dreams to damage his mind. But Lucan had cast a spell over him, probing for the presence of magic, and found nothing.

Whatever the dreams were, they had not been sent by the Old Demon or another wizard.

But what, then? Was it his Demonsouled essence, trying to take control? Or did it mean nothing at all? Merely his mind forming symbols as he slept?

No. Mazael had seen the wolf with his own eyes when it saved him from the balekhan in Cravenlock Town's square. Whatever the black wolf was, it was no symbol.

He gave an angry shake of his head. The frustration must have shown on his face, because the servants scurried to get out of his way, and he forced himself to calm. Mazael did not like mysteries, did not like lies. The Old Demon had tried to turn him into a puppet. Skhath had masqueraded as a human knight. Morebeth Galbraith had seduced him, hiding her Demonsouled nature.

Gods, but he was tired of being manipulated.

But he could not solve the mystery of the black wolf now, and the Lord of Swordgrim had arrived. And if Mazael was going to defend his lands and his people, he needed Lord Richard's help.

He left the great hall to greet the liege lord of the Grim Marches.

LORD RICHARD'S VASSALS, the lords and knights of the Grim Marches, gathered to feast in the great hall of Castle Cravenlock.

Mazael knew them all. Many he had known as a squire, in the years before Lord Adalon banished him from the Grim Marches. The others he had met after he becoming Lord of Castle Cravenlock. Many feared him. Even those who did not believe he had killed Mitor to take the lordship of Castle Cravenlock.

But no matter what the lords and knights of the Grim Marches thought of Mazael, they had one thing in common.

They all feared Lord Richard Mandragon more than they feared Mazael.

Mazael walked among the lords, his fellow vassals, greeting them and exchanging polite words. Most of the lords, like Mazael, wore armor. Many of them, like Rufus, wore Malrag armor. The Malrags had attacked dozens of castles and towns. Many of the lords had been victorious.

Some had not.

"Lord Robert Highgate," said Mazael.

Robert, Lord of Castle Highgate and Rufus's father, gave him a thin smile. He had the same arrogant expression as his son, albeit on a face that was twenty-five years older and considerably fatter. Nevertheless, Robert knew how to lead men in battle.

The necklace of Malrag claws hanging from his belt proved that. Some of the men had taken to wearing them as trophies.

"Lord Mazael," said Robert. "My leg has been hurting me, lately."

Mazael snorted. "Then you should have guarded your left better, my lord." Years ago, he and Robert had been squires together, and Mazael had broken Robert's leg in a sparring match. "But we have grimmer things to discuss than the fights of our boyhood."

Robert's expression sobered. "Aye. Those damned Malrag devils hit us hard. If Castle Highgate was not so well fortified, they would have swept us away in hours. Aye, we're prepared well enough for war with men. But these unnatural devils? Bah! Give me a man to fight, not some spawn out of the pits of hell." He looked haunted. There was a hint of uncertainty, even fear, in his arrogant expression.

"Devils or not," said Mazael, "the Malrags are still flesh and blood. A sword can kill them. They can be fought, just as any other foe. And if they can be killed and fought, they can be defeated. Just like any other foe. Do you think Lord Richard will let the Malrags roll over the Grim Marches without offering a fight?"

Robert snorted. "Certainly not. Aye, we stood against them at Castle Highgate, even if we paid dear for it. And you, Lord Mazael. We have heard how you harried every Malrag foolish enough to set foot upon your lands. With Lord Richard to lead us, and you at his right hand, we will send these devils scurrying back to their holes!"

He clasped hands with Mazael, and moved on.

Mazael watched him go. Morale, he realized. That was the key. A lord had to keep his men's spirits up, to make them believe in victory. And apparently the lords themselves needed encouragement.

He turned, and saw a dark figure leaning against one of the great hall's pillars, watching him.

Mazael took a deep breath.

Best to get this over with at once.

He walked to the dark figure and gave a shallow bow, one suitable for greeting an equal. "Lord Toraine."

Toraine Mandragon returned an identical bow, smirking. "Lord Mazael."

Toraine, Lord Richard's eldest son and Lord of Hanging Tower, looked a great deal like his brother Lucan. Even the smirk was almost identical. But Toraine was tall where Lucan was short, and muscular where Lucan was slender. The Black Dragon, men called Toraine, from the interlocking black scales covering his armor, taken from a great dragon that Toraine had slain with his own hand.

That, and Toraine's utter lack of mercy. Before Toraine had become its lord, the Hanging Tower had been known as the Western Tower.

"You've done better than I expected against the Malrags," said Toraine. "I expected to find Cravenlock Town in ashes and Castle Cravenlock in ruins. Instead you have driven the Malrags back and kept your lands secure. Perhaps your reputation is not so overstated as I believed."

Mazael smiled. "And the tales of your exploits match perfectly with your reputation, my lord Toraine."

Toraine lifted an eyebrow. "Oh?"

"Because the tales say you've slaughtered every Malrag you've come across," said Mazael. "Perhaps you confused them with peasants?"

Toraine's black eyes narrowed. "Lord Mazael. You are too soft-hearted. War is about killing, in the end. You kill more of them than they kill of you." He shook his head. "Even my father does not fully understand that."

"Oh?" said Mazael.

Toraine grinned. "After you killed Mitor, there were only two members of House Cravenlock left. You and Rachel Cravenlock. And for some reason, my father chose to spare both of you. He should have killed you and your sister. Had he done so, a potential enemy would have been removed, and the lands of Castle Cravenlock would have passed into my family's hands."

"Into your hands, you mean?" said Mazael, forcing himself to smile. Toraine, he knew, would respond to weakness the way a wild dog would respond to the smell of blood. "Lord Toraine of Castle Cravenlock?"

"Why not?" said Toraine. "I see how you coddle the peasants and the townsfolk, letting them flee into your lands. They are unnecessary mouths. You should have let the Malrags slay them, to save yourself the effort of feeding them. You're weak, Lord Mazael. You aren't strong enough to do what needs to be done. When I am liege lord of the Grim Marches, I will not tolerate such weakness in my vassals."

"You aren't liege lord yet," said Mazael. "Your father is a healthy man, and hopefully the gods shall grant him many long years."

"We may certainly hope," said Toraine. "After all, my father has shown you a great deal of mercy. Though he might change his mind, once he learns how you have been plotting with Lord Malden against him."

"Have I?" said Mazael. "Do enlighten me. I haven't spoken to Lord Malden in over a year. How have I plotted with him?"

Again that thin smile flashed across Toraine's face. "By joining your blood to his."

"My sister married Gerald Roland over a year ago," said Mazael. "Lord Richard has yet to express his disapproval."

"Perhaps my father will change his mind," said Toraine, "once he learns that Lady Rachel has given birth to a son."

Mazael blinked in surprise. "She has? The last letter I had from Knightcastle was five months past. She said she was pregnant, but I've heard no word since."

"Not surprising," said Toraine. "The Malrags have been killing anyone they can find. No doubt the courier bearing the news rode right into a Malrag warband. The boy's name is Aldane Roland. Which means your nephew is a son of House Roland, the mortal enemies of the Mandragons. When war between Mandragon and Roland comes - which it will - with whom shall you side, Lord Mazael? Hmm? Will you keep your oaths, and ride with my father? Or will you side your blood, and ride with Lord Malden against my father?"

Mazael laughed.

Toraine blinked, a scowl spreading across his face.

"To side with my blood," said Mazael, "would cost me more than you could possibly imagine, my lord Toraine. And I needn't worry about the choice. Neither Lord Richard nor Lord Malden can go to war with the other without my help. And they shall not have it. Knightcastle and the Grim Marches shall remain at peace."

Toraine's eyes narrowed.

"A good evening to you, my lord," said Mazael. "It is always a pleasure speaking with you."

He moved on before Toraine could answer him. That had not been wise, he knew, provoking Toraine like that. Lord Richard was not immortal. Someday he would die, and Toraine would become liege lord of the Grim Marches. And Toraine wanted Mazael dead, would not hesitate to kill every last man, woman, and child in Mazael's lands.

Part of Mazael's mind murmured that it would be best if Toraine met an "accident" while at Castle Cravenlock...

No. That impulse came from the Demonsouled part of Mazael's heart, and he would not give in to it. Not after the price Romaria had paid to save him from his Demonsouled essence.

Though perhaps it would be better if Toraine did die in the upcoming battles...

Mazael shook aside the thought and stopped. A lean man with a thin face and a crooked nose stepped into his path, green eyes glinting with amusement. He wore a green surcoat, embroidered with a black crow perched upon a gray rock.

"Lord Mazael!" said the thin-faced man, grinning. "Good to see you again. Though I hope this time you won't punch me in the face. That gets rather unpleasant, you know."

"Sir Tanam," said Mazael.

Toraine might have been Lord Richard's mailed right fist, but Sir Tanam Crowley of Crow's Rock was Lord Richard's cunning left hand. If Lord Richard wanted to put fear into his enemies, he sent Toraine after them. But if he wanted something done quietly, competently...then he sent Sir Tanam.

"You've been in the field?" said Mazael.

"Aye," said Tanam, making a flourishing bow. "Someone's got to keep an eye on these Malrag devils for Lord Richard. And if I happen to kill a few of them in the process...well, a man's got to have his fun, does he not?" He shook his head, locks of gray hair sliding over his pale forehead. "For all their cunning, the Malrags are dumber than rocks."

"How?" said Mazael. "The ones I've fought have been clever."

"Aye," said Tanam, "but they love killing too much. And they love preying upon anyone weaker than themselves. Send in one man on a horse, have him feign wounds, and you can lure the Malrags into a lovely trap. Worked my way through three warbands, doing that, on my way to your castle."

"Good," said Mazael. "The more you kill, the better."

"I agree," said Tanam. "Though this won't be over until we find and kill the Malrags' leader." He lowered his voice. "I spoke to Lucan, once I arrived...and I think I might have found the Demonsouled leading the Malrag host."

Mazael frowned. "You have?"

"Aye. And I think the Demonsouled is a Dominiar knight."

"A Dominiar," said Mazael. "But there are no more Dominiars. Amalric Galbraith killed their leadership, and I killed Amalric. The Order collapsed after that. The church withdrew its support of the order, and the Justiciar Order and Lord Malden divided the Dominiars' lands between them."

"The Dominiar Order is no more," said Tanam, "but there are still Dominiar knights left. Some have renounced their vows. Others turned to brigandage, or became mercenaries. And a few, I am told, have sworn revenge upon you, personally, my lord." He grinned. "It seems they hold the Battle of Tumblestone against you."

"That's hardly surprising," said Mazael. "But how would a Dominiar knight end up commanding a host of Malrags..."

And even as he spoke, the answer came to him.

"I spoke to Lucan," said Tanam. "He told me that only a powerful Demonsouled can command the Malrags. And you claimed that Amalric Galbraith was Demonsouled."

"I didn't claim he was Demonsouled," said Mazael. "He was

Demonsouled." Mazael's half-brother, in fact, another child of the Old Demon. He remembered the way the sword of the Destroyer had blazed with blood-colored flames in Amalric's black-armored fist, the forest of corpses impaled upon the stakes raised around Tumblestone.

Tanam shrugged. "I believe you. I saw what Simonian of Briault did, after all. But if Amalric was Demonsouled...then some of his men might have been, as well." He lowered his voice. "My men have been scouting the Malrag warbands, and they've brought back reports. The Malrags do not ride horses, yet a group of horsemen ride with the warbands, all in black armor. The horsemen fly the Dominiar banner, an eight-pointed silver star upon a black background, and the Malrags take orders from the horsemen."

"It is a Demonsouled," said Mazael, voice thick. "Amalric was in his late twenties when I killed him. More than old enough to have fathered a son." So was Morebeth - she had claimed to have never borne a son, but every word she had told him had been a lie. "Or it could be another Demonsouled, one that served Amalric."

Or it could be another child of the Old Demon, like Mazael and Amalric. Or even the Old Demon himself. Mazael knew his father had not forgotten him, that the Old Demon would someday come to fight him once more. Had the Old Demon loosed the Malrag warbands upon the Grim Marches?

"My lord?" said Tanam.

Mazael blinked, shook his mind free from its dark speculations. "Then that is good news, Sir Tanam. To defeat the Malrags, we need only find this Demonsouled and kill him." Or her, thought Mazael, remembering Morebeth. "Once we do, the Malrags will turn upon each other, and we can destroy their warbands one by one."

Tanam grinned and clapped Mazael on the shoulder. "I look forward to it."

"As do I," said Mazael.

But he spoke with a confidence he did not feel. Three times now, he had faced another Demonsouled. The Old Demon had almost corrupted and killed him. Amalric had come within a hair's breadth of killing him, and Morebeth had almost seduced him. Only chance, or fate, or the intervention of the gods, had saved Mazael.

He had no wish to face another Demonsouled.

But he would not abandon his people to the Malrags' cruelty and butchery. If he had to fight another Demonsouled, he would. Whatever the cost to himself.

Tanam looked across the hall. "My lord Richard would speak with you, I think."

Mazael nodded and crossed his great hall, exchanging words with the lords and knights he as passed. Lucan Mandragon stood at the foot of the dais, draped in his black cloak, face shadowed beneath his hood. The black metal staff rested in his right hand. Mazael rarely saw Lucan without that staff, now.

Lord Richard Mandragon waited besides his younger son.

He was a vigorous man in his late forties, and the streaks of white threading the Dragonslayer's red hair and beard made it took as if a mane of fire wreathed his lean face. He wore gleaming red armor, its overlapping scales taken from the great red dragon he had slain in his youth. His black eyes were like discs of coal , and they displayed neither anger nor fear. Mazael could not recall ever hearing Lord Richard raise his voice in anger, not once.

Yet no one in Castle Cravenlock's great hall would dare to betray him. Not even Toraine and Lucan.

"Lord Mazael," said Lord Richard, his voice deep and resonant. "Thank you for hosting this gathering."

Mazael bowed with more respect than he had shown Toraine. "It must be done, my lord. The Malrags threaten us all."

"Indeed," said Lord Richard. "This is the gravest threat the Grim Marches have faced since the San-keth took control of Lord Adalon and Lord Mitor. But we destroyed that threat, and we shall destroy the Malrags. Utterly."

Beneath his hood, Lucan's lip curled in contempt, but he said nothing.

"Might I ask how?" said Mazael. "I assume you have a plan?"

"I do," said Lord Richard. "Too long we have been on the defensive against the Malrags. It is time to bring the fight to them. My knights and vassals have gathered their men. Tomorrow we shall ride out and show the Malrags what it means to wage war in the Grim Marches."

Lord Richard stepped atop the dais and lifted his hand, and silence fell over the great hall.

"My lords of the Grim Marches," said Lord Richard, his voice falling over the crowd. "You have come at my call, bound by your oaths, but many of you have already faced the Malrags in battle. And for those of you who remain untouched by war, it is only a matter of time. The Malrags threaten us all, and we must combine our strength to overcome the Malrags and wipe them from the face of the earth." He beckoned. "Sir Tanam?"

Tanam Crowley cleared his throat and crossed to the dais. "My men have been scouting the Malrags. Warbands range back and forth across the eastern Grim Marches, but the bulk of the Malrags are gathered in the foothills of the Great Mountains. There are at least fifty thousand of them. Maybe even as many as sixty thousand."

Silence answered his pronouncement. If every lord and every knight called every man able to bear arms, the Grim Marches could muster twenty-five thousand fighting men, maybe thirty thousand.

"Then our path is clear," said Lord Jonaril Mandrake, a stout man with arms like oak trees. "We must withdraw behind our castle walls and prepare for a siege, and wait for aid from the king and the other lords."

"Wars are not won by hiding behind stone walls," said Lord Richard, "and the king cares nothing for us, and the other lords of the realm would be more than glad to take our lands after the Malrags have slain us. No, if we are to save ourselves, we must do so with our own hands."

"How, then?" said Lord Astor Hawking, a thin man with an ascetic face.

Lord Richard gestured to the side. Each of the lords had brought their court wizards, and they stood in silence a corner of the hall, clad in their long black coats and cloaks. Timothy stood with them, looking solemn.

"The wizards," said Lord Richard, "have told me of the nature of the Malrags, how they are soulless things, animated by evil spirits, controlled by cruelty and base impulse. Without a powerful leader to hold them together, they will turn upon each other, even in the face of their enemies. And almost certainly this leader is a powerful Demonsouled. Sir Tanam's men have seen a horseman in black armor leading the Malrags – and we all know that the Malrags do not ride horses. Our task, then, is a simple one. We shall find this Demonsouled and kill him. Once the Malrag warbands turn upon each other, we will destroy them one by one."

"And how shall we do that?" said Lord Jonaril. "Surely this Demonsouled creature is no fool."

"Neither are we," said Lord Richard. "Our great advantage is cavalry. The Malrags do not use beasts in warfare, it seems, and the plains of the Grim Marches favor horsemen. We shall use this to our advantage. The greater part of the footmen shall remain in the towns and castles, garrisoning them from Malrag attack. Our horsemen will gather in force, and attack Malrag warbands one by one, overwhelming them. Sooner or later the Demonsouled leader will throw the bulk of his forces at us, or come in person to deal with our threat." Lord Richard closed his fist. "And then we shall have him. If he has arcane abilities, our wizards will overwhelm him. Once he is slain, the Malrags will turn on each other, and we can destroy the warbands at our leisure."

It was a good plan.

But Mazael doubted that it would be so simple.

8

THE GRAND MASTER

Word came from Mazael's scouts the morning after the feast. Eight hundred Malrags had been spotted a few hours east of Castle Cravenlock, moving to the southeast, away from both the town and the castle. Yet a half-dozen small villages lay in their path.

If the Malrags wanted to cross Mazael's lands, they would pay a toll in blood.

He paused only long enough to send a message to Sir Tanam Crowley.

Mazael rode out at the head of three hundred horsemen, knights, armsmen, and archers, with Sir Hagen, Sir Aulus, Timothy, and Lucan at his side. Lion rested against Mazael's hip, a heavy lance ready in his right hand. The knights and the mounted armsmen followed him in a column, the horse archers covering the flanks.

It did not take long to find the Malrag warband. Mazael saw the column of dust first, the Malrags' armored boots churning at the dry earth. Then he saw the Malrags themselves, the warband hastening across the plains like some great black predator.

A predator that turned to face Mazael's men.

"They've seen us," said Hagen. He rubbed his close-cropped black beard and pulled on his helm.

"Good," said Mazael. "If they wish to visit my lands, it's only proper that we should greet them. Sir Aulus! Sound the halt, and release the archers!"

Sir Aulus lifted his horn to his lips. The thin knight blew a long blast on the horn, and Mazael's horsemen came to a halt. Another three short blasts in quick succession, and the mounted archers galloped forward. They rode small, quick horses, and bore light leather armor, a powerful short bow, and three quivers of arrows. The archers were neither knights nor armsmen, but militiamen, common peasants pressed into service against the Malrags. Most of the Grim Marches' commoners labored as farmers, but quite a few tended flocks of sheep and cattle.

Which meant that many of them had been born in the saddle, and learned how to shoot from horseback at an early age.

The archers galloped back and forth before the Malrag line, loosing arrow after arrow. The arrows plunged into black armor, and Mazael heard roars and bellows of pain, a few of the Malrags even toppling to the earth.

The warband wheeled, chasing after their tormentors. But the archers raced away, twisting in the saddle to release another barrage of arrows. More Malrags fell, trampled beneath their enraged comrades.

"Aulus," said Mazael. "Have them break!"

Aulus blew another series of blasts. The horse archers broke into three groups and fled in different directions. The maneuver went off smoothly; Sir Hagen's endless drilling of the militia had paid off. The Malrags scattered, attempting to chase down the archers.

"Aulus!" said Mazael, raising his lance and slinging his shield over his left arm. "The charge! Now!"

Aulus sounded a long blast, and Mazael kicked Challenger to a gallop, the big destrier surging forward with a snort of excitement. Behind him the knights and armsmen gave a shout and galloped after Mazael. Lucan and Timothy remained behind, ready to deal with any Malrag shamans.

The Malrags could not miss the thunderous charge of two hundred heavy horse, and tried to scramble into a spear wall. But they had scattered too far in pursuit, and the knights charged too fast. Mazael braced himself, his armored boots digging into his stirrups, and aimed his lance. A heartbeat latter Challenger crashed into the Malrag line, the lance plunging through a Malrag's chest, another dying beneath Challenger's steel-shod hooves. Some of his knights were thrown to the ground, cut down by Malrag axes, and others fell, their horses slain, but a score of Malrags perished for every one one of Mazael's men. Mazael caught a glimpse of the balekhan in its black plate armor, but a moment later the balekhan disappeared in a storm of flashing hooves.

The Malrags broke and ran.

Mazael reined up, his lance's head dark with Malrag blood. "Sir Aulus!" He looked around for his herald. "Sir Aulus!" Aulus trotted his horse over, one hand gripping the lance with the black Cravenlock standard, the other holding a bloody sword. "Sound the recall! We'll ride the rest of them down, kill them one by..."

"Lord Mazael!" Sir Hagen galloped to Mazael's side, pointing with his war axe. "Lord Mazael, look!"

Mazael turned, frowning.

He saw dark shapes perhaps two miles to the north, marching in precise order, black spears and axes glinting in the morning sunlight. Malrags. Another warband, at least five or six hundred strong. A warband with its own balekhan, and perhaps a shaman or two. Once the fleeing Malrags reached the balekhan, it would take command, and Mazael would face nearly a thousand Malrags with only three hundred horsemen.

He did not like those odds.

"Sir Aulus!" he bellowed. "Sound the recall. The men are to reform. We'll take action once we see what that second warband does." In war, it was better to force an enemy to respond, rather than to respond to the foe's actions. But until Mazael saw what the second warband intended, he dared not risk his men's lives in a futile charge.

Aulus stood up in his saddle, sounding the recall. One by one, Mazael's men broke off their pursuit and galloped back to Aulus's standard, moving into their place in the formation. Mazael's hand tightened around his lance, his gauntlet creaking, and he watched the fleeing Malrags join the new warband. He expected them to charge, to march forward, even to howl their bloodcurdling war cries.

But instead the Malrags stood motionless and silent. Waiting. But for what?

He looked around, saw Timothy and Lucan nearby.

"Timothy," said Mazael. "Those Malrags. Any shamans among them?"

Timothy's eyelids fluttered, his bearded lips moving, his right hand clenched tight about his wire-wrapped quartz crystal. "I don't think...wait. There's one. Just one. But, gods...strong." His eyes snapped open. "My lord, there's a human wizard among them, a powerful one."

"A human wizard?" said Mazael. Was the wizard the Demonsouled in command of the Malrags? Mazael possessed no magical ability, and neither had Amalric or Morebeth. But the Old Demon was a wizard of crushing power. "Demonsouled?"

"Perhaps. I...can't tell."

"There's another source of power among them," murmured Lucan, pointing with his staff. "Not a wizard, I think. Not even human. But strong nonetheless."

"Demonsouled?" said Mazael. Timothy, he knew, could not sense the presence of a Demonsouled. Otherwise he would have realized Mazael's secret long ago. But Lucan had some means of doing so.

"Perhaps," muttered Lucan. "I can't tell. It seems like...Demonsouled power, yes. But as if it's contained, somehow...like in an object."

He frowned, and glanced at his metal staff, for some reason.

Hagen cursed and pointed with his axe again. "Horsemen. Flying the Dominiar banner."

A group of Malrags emerged from the warband, one of them carrying a black banner with the silver Dominiar star. In their midst rode two horsemen. One wore a heavy black cloak, not very different from Lucan's. The other rider was much larger, and wore ornate black plate armor, the same sort of armor once worn by Dominiar commanders.

A Demonsouled Dominiar knight? Mazael remembered Amalric Galbraith, the sword of the Destroyer a crimson inferno in his fist.

The rider in the black cloak stood up the stirrups, hand gesturing in a spell.

"Parley!" His voice boomed over the distance separating Mazael's men and the Malrags. "Parley! The Grand Master wishes to speak with Lord Mazael! Come with one companion, and the Grand Master will parley with Lord Mazael!"

"My lord, do not," said Hagen. "It is a trap, plainly."

"Plainly," said Mazael.

"Undoubtedly they will kill you if you walk into their hands," said Timothy.

"They can try," said Mazael. "But if that big fellow on the horse is the Demonsouled in command of the Malrags, and I can get him within reach of Lion...that would be well worth the risk. And if he is indeed the Demonsouled and we can kill him, our lives will be well spent. Lucan! Come with me. Hagen! You have command until I return." He handed over his lance to Hagen. "If the Malrags show any sign of treachery, attack."

"But..." said Timothy, Aulus, and Hagen in unison.

"Do as I say," said Mazael. He turned Challenger around, and rode from his men, Lucan riding alongside him. After a moment the black-armored man and the rider in the black cloak rode out from the Malrags.

They met in the middle, halfway between the Malrag warband and Mazael's horsemen, and stared at each other in silence. The black-armored rider had the hilt of a two-handed greatsword rising over his shoulder. Besides him the second horseman sat in his saddle, wrapped in his black cloak. The wind tugged at the cloak, and Mazael saw a long black coat beneath the cloak.

A black wizard's coat.

The cloaked man drew back his hood. He was in his late fifties or early sixties, with a lean, lined face, pale blue eyes, and a wild shock of white hair. A small smile danced over his thin lips, as if secret jest amused him. He looked at Mazael, at Lucan, and then back at Mazael.

"You realize," he said, his voice sonorous, "that if we sit here in silence, this meeting is going to be dreadfully tedious."

"Then perhaps you ought to say something worth listening to," said Mazael. "Such as why you are riding with the Malrags. Or why one of you, or perhaps both of you, are commanding the Malrags. Or why the Malrags have attacked my lands and killed my people without justification. Or why I simply shouldn't kill the both of you."

The armored man shifted, and the cloaked man chuckled. "Really, my lord Mazael. Such bluster. We shall never accomplish anything, if you are so quick to violence."

"You have me at a disadvantage," said Mazael. "You know my name and title, but I do not know yours."

The cloaked man's smile widened. "Fair enough. I am called Malavost, once of Alborg, and I have no title." Lucan stirred. "Ah. The Dragon's Shadow recognizes the name, I see. Very good. That will save much tedious explanation."

The armored man pulled off his black helm. Beneath it he had a broad face, with iron-colored hair, a close-cropped iron-colored beard, and iron-colored eyes. Unlike Malavost, he did not smile. In fact, his gray eyes blazed with hate as they stared at Mazael.

"And I," said the Dominiar knight, "am Ultorin, Grand Master of the Dominiar Order."

"Grand Master? Of what? There is no more Dominiar Order," said Mazael.

Ultorin bared his teeth in a snarl. "Because you murdered the last Grand Master, Amalric Galbraith, and you butchered our brother knights below the walls of Tumblestone."

"Amalric was Demonsouled," said Mazael, "and he led your brother knights on a trail of rape and butchery through the Old Kingdoms and Knightrealm. He deserved his fate, and you were a fool to follow him."

"He would have conquered the world," said Ultorin, the hatred in his eyes shining brighter. "And we would have built a new world, a world of order, of peace, a world purged of weakness and corruption. All that we could have had...had you not murdered Grand Master Amalric."

"So that's what this is about?" said Mazael, waving his hand at the Malrags. Was Ultorin the Demonsouled? Or Malavost? Or both of them? "Vengeance for that butcher Amalric?"

"Not at all," said Malavost with his thin smile. "I'm afraid, Lord Mazael, that our true purpose is quite beyond your comprehension. Vengeance is merely a bonus for Ultorin here. Which he shall take presently."

Ultorin drew his greatsword from over his shoulder, holding it in one hand. The black blade was massive, as wide as Mazael's hand, the razor edges glimmering. Sigils had been carved down the length of the blade, jagged, irregular symbols that seemed to speak of death and madness.

Lucan flinched.

The sigils in Ultorin's sword brightened with blood-colored light, a haze of darkness shimmering around the blade. It looked as if Ultorin held a thunderhead in his fist, a storm illuminated from within by crimson lightning. Mazael felt power washing off from the blade in waves, and he yanked Lion from its scabbard. At once the sword jolted in his hand, azure flames running up the blade.

Lion only reacted that way to things of dark magic. Whatever power filled Ultorin's sword, it was not benevolent.

"You're going to die, Lord Mazael," said Malavost. "Here and now. Along with the Dragon's Shadow. You will not impede our plans."

He lifted his hands and began a spell, green light flickering around his fingertips.

Ultorin roared and spurred his horse towards Mazael, greatsword lifted for a two-handed blow.

LUCAN SAW Malavost lift his hands in the beginnings of a spell.

He gestured and muttered a spell of his own, unleashing a blast of psychokinetic force. Malavost flinched as the spell struck him, his cloak billowing about him, but his wards absorbed the worst of the spell.

Malavost turned his horse in a circle, eyes falling on Lucan.

"Ah," he said, as Ultorin charged at Mazael. "The Dragon's Shadow. Marstan's little apprentice. Let us see if you are everything your reputation claims."

He lifted his left hand, wisps of darkness churning around his hooked fingers. Lucan felt the power of the spell, its raw potency, and began a defensive spell, strengthening his own protective wards.

He finished an instant before Malavost did.

A black shadow leapt from Malavost's hands to strike Lucan, tentacles of darkness wrapping around him and stretching into his horse. The horse reared up, screaming in agony, and collapsed dead to the ground. Lucan's wards absorbed the spell, protecting him from harm, but the backlash of struggling energies flung him from the saddle.

He struck the ground and heard Malavost begin another spell.

ULTORIN GALLOPED AT MAZAEL, snarling in fury. Mazael booted Challenger to a run, gripping Lion for a thrust, intending to stab below Ultorin's raised arms. No – Ultorin was moving too fast. Mazael shifted, bringing his shield around to block Ultorin's attack.

It just barely saved his life.

The black greatsword hammered down in a blaze of red light, and Mazael's shield exploded in a spray of oaken shards. Pain burned up his arm, and the force of the blow almost knocked him from the saddle. Only by plunging his boots into the stirrups did he keep his seat. Challenger and Ultorin's black horse galloped past each other, and Mazael seized the reins with his aching left hand, spinning his destrier around.

Ultorin reined up, stood in his stirrups, waving his greatsword overhead.

The Malrags loosed their war cry and leapt forward, their line dissolving as they charged. A horn blast rang over the plains, and Mazael's horsemen charged forward with a shout. A thunderclap and a flash of green light, and Mazael saw Lucan go sprawling, Malavost wreathed in ghostly green flames. Ultorin urged his horse to a gallop, the massive greatsword spinning in his right hand as if it weighed nothing at all.

Mazael gritted his teeth and put his spurs to Challenger's flanks, moving to meet Ultorin's charge.

~

LUCAN SCRAMBLED BACK to his feet, leaning upon his staff, free hand gesturing as he muttered another spell. Power surged through him, his will plunging into the spirit world and opening a passageway.

Two creatures answered his call. They looked like great lions, albeit lions with scorpions' wings and tails, and a mass of barbed tentacles for manes. The spirit beasts screamed with piercing, unearthly wails and raced forward, mouths yawning wide as they closed on Malavost.

But Malavost was already casting another spell. He flung out his hands, and a shimmering corona of blue light enveloped both him and his horse. The lions flinched away from the light, snarling. Malavost gestured again, and the blue light pulsed. Then the glow vanished, and the lions with it, banished back to the spirit world.

"Competent enough, I suppose," said Malavost, smirking. "But still elementary. Were you really Marstan's student? Marstan would never have attempted anything so utterly pedestrian against..."

"Stop talking," said Lucan, and lifted his staff.

The staff answered his need. Demonsouled power flooded into Lucan, easing his weariness, filling him with fresh strength. The sigils carved into the staff flared and pulsed with blood-colored light.

With light, he realized, exactly the same color as the sigils upon Ultorin's sword.

Malavost's pale eyes narrowed in alarm, his smile vanishing for the first time, and he began a defensive spell.

But this time Lucan had the initiative. He poured his will into the staff and unleashed a blast of invisible force. It caught Malavost in the chest and flung him to the ground. Malavost scrambled to his feet, scowling, and Lucan struck again. This time Malavost crossed his arms before him and snarled out a short spell. A fresh ward crackled into existence around him, and Lucan's spell crashed into it. For a moment snarling force surrounded Malavost, his cloak snapping in the sudden gale, and then Lucan's spell faded away.

Malavost's ward had held.

Lucan began another spell, but Malavost's words cut him short.

"You little fool," he said, amused. "A bloodstaff? Infused with the blood of some hapless Demonsouled you slew, no doubt. I'm sure it provides you with quite a power surge...but is it really worth the cost?"

Lucan hesitated. The staff's power screamed through him, urging him to destroy Malavost, to crush him utterly, and then to start butchering the Malrags.

"Ah," said Malavost. "You don't know. Do you have any idea what that staff is doing to you? I thought not." He laughed. "Ultorin doesn't know what his bloodsword is doing to him, either. And if he did...he would not have dared to come within a mile of it."

Lucan risked a glance to the side, where Ultorin and Lord Mazael dueled each either, Lion sheathed in azure flame, Ultorin's greatsword cloaked in darkness and crimson fire. The Malrags ran at them, screaming, while the horsemen of Castle Cravenlock thundered towards the duel...

And in that moment of distraction, Malavost unleashed his full power at Lucan.

~

ULTORIN AND MAZAEL DUELED, their horses circling around each other.

Mazael swung and stabbed, shifting his grip on Lion's hilt from one-handed to two-handed as his blows demanded. Ultorin was strong, as strong as Mazael, and his massive greatsword gave him a longer reach. Yet the magic of Lion's blade proved capable of blocking the dark power in Ultorin's sword, and Mazael's lighter longsword was quicker than Ultorin's heavy weapon. Again and again Lion slipped past Ultorin's guard, leaving scratches in the Dominiar's massive black armor. If only Mazael could get Lion's point into the armor's weak points, he could end this fight.

And he could break the Malrags. Ultorin was their Demonsouled leader, he was sure of it.

An explosion rang out, a column of dirt shooting into the air. Mazael risked a glance to the side, saw Malavost wreathed in swirling darkness, saw Lucan gesturing with his black staff, its sigils ablaze with fiery light. Lucan looked exhausted, his face pale, his hands trembling, while Malavost...

Malavost only looked amused.

Ultorin took advantage of Mazael's distraction. His black horse spun around, his blade looping for Mazael's head. Mazael ducked, the edge of the greatsword scraping along the top of his helm. A deathly chill radiated from the weapon, and the force of the blow nearly snapped Mazael's neck. But he kept his seat, and lunged forward, all his strength behind Lion.

His sword's point crunched into Ultorin's right shoulder, the azure flames blazing hotter. If Ultorin was Demonsouled, no doubt he could heal wounds in a matter of moments. But those moments counted, and if Mazael could drive home his advantage and land a killing blow...

At that moment his horsemen and Ultorin's Malrags crashed together around them.

A pair of Malrags attacked Mazael, cutting him off from Ultorin. He spun Challenger, trying to avoid their blows, wishing he still had a shield. A black axe missed his leg, while a spearhead dug through his armor, digging into his calf. Mazael snarled in pain and lashed out with Lion, ripping open a Malrag's neck. The second Malrag sprang forward, raising its axe for a blow, only to lose its head to the sword of a passing knight. Mazael pressed his knees to Challenger's flanks and the horse started forward, moving in pursuit of Ultorin.

His leg hurt, badly, but he already felt the pain subsiding as his Demonsouled essence healed the wound.

A pair of armsmen in Cravenlock tabards attacked Ultorin, each man wielding a shield and a heavy mace. Ultorin bellowed, his black sword whipping about in a sideways cut. The blade smashed through a heavy shield and ripped into the unfortunate armsman's chest, the bloody light from the sigils shining ever brighter. Ultorin wheeled his horse around, turning to face the remaining armsman, lifting his greatsword for a deadly blow.

It was the perfect opportunity. As Challenger galloped past, Mazael struck out, all his strength and his horse's speed behind the blow. Lion's point struck below Ultorin's upraised left arm, sinking deep into his armpit. Ultorin howled in rage and pain, sagging in the saddle, his horse carrying him towards the Malrags. Blood streamed down his armor, dark against his darker cuirass. The wound was mortal - Mazael had seen enough mortal wounds, and dealt enough of them, to know one when he saw it. Ultorin would bleed out in a matter of moments.

Strange that it had been so easy. Malavost must have been the Demonsouled, not Ultorin. Mazael struck down a passing Malrag, and then another, looking for the wizard...

Ultorin screamed.

Mazael turned and saw Ultorin plunge his greatsword into a Malrag's back. The carved sigils blazed, the darkness surrounding the blade thickening. The Malrag thrashed and heaved, colorless eyes bulging, its fanged mouth open in a silent scream.

And then the Malrag...withered. There was no other word to describe it. The Malrag shrank into a desiccated skeleton, draped in leathery skin. Then it crumbled into smoking black ash, chunks of disintegrating bone raining to the earth. Ultorin whipped his sword free from the ruin, lifted his face to the sky, and howled like a maddened beast. His face was flushed with fresh vitality, and he even looked slightly younger.

The black sword, Mazael realized. It had drained the Malrag's life, pouring the energy into Ultorin...and healing his wound in the process.

And then there was no more time for thought.

Ultorin galloped towards him, still roaring in fury, and Mazael rode to meet his attack.

MALAVOST'S full power drove at Lucan, a psychokinetic hammer that tore at the earth. Yet Lucan gripped both hands around his staff, the burning Demonsouled power filling him with might, and his ward turned the worst of the attack. With a howl of rage, he flung out his hands and shouted a spell. Malavost's attack dissipated, and Lucan's own will lashed out. A jet of blood-colored flame burst from his staff, drilling towards Malavost.

Malavost snarled, both his hands held out before him, shouting a spell of his own. A ward shimmered into existence before him, and Lucan's fire parted a few inches before Malavost, flowing around him like a river around a stone. The blast of magical flame killed two Malrags and sent a third fleeing, its armor melted to its skin, but left Malavost untouched.

Still Malavost laughed.

"Fool," he said. "All that power, and you still can barely touch me? Shameful! If Marstan had wielded that kind of power, he would have ripped me to shreds."

Lucan spat in fury, his mind pulsing with rage, every instinct screaming for him to rip Malavost to shreds, to dance laughing in his blood. But a small part of his mind, the part still sane, knew that Malavost was right. Malavost could not match his power with the staff, but Lucan could not match Malavost's skill. No matter how much raw magical force Lucan flung at Malavost, the older wizard managed to deflect it, or turn it back upon Lucan.

He needed a distraction.

And even as the thought crossed Lucan's mind, the air behind Malavost blurred, and Timothy stepped out of nothingness. In the raging madness of the Demonsouled power burning through him, Lucan had forgotten all about Timothy.

And so, it seemed, had Malavost.

Timothy lifted his arm, a copper tube clutched in his fist, his mouth flying through an incantation. Malavost whirled and began a spell, but it was too late. A roaring gout of orange-yellow flame exploded from the copper tube, engulfing Malavost and a half-dozen nearby Malrags in a howling firestorm. Timothy lacked Lucan's power and skill, and came nowhere near to Malavost's level. Yet he could still unleash a powerful blast of flame, and Lucan sensed Malavost's wards shuddering beneath the strain.

It was the opportunity he needed to attack.

Lucan struck out with all his will, his spell augmented by the staff's power. Malavost staggered in the midst of Timothy's firestorm, his wards trembling around him. Lucan only need to collapse Malavost's failing wards, and then Timothy's flames would reduce Malavost to smoking char...

Malavost flung out his arms and shouted.

And psychokinetic force exploded in all directions. The sudden gale blew out the flames, flinging Malrags and Cravenlock armsmen alike to the ground. Timothy fell backwards, bounced, and did not move. Malavost's will struck Lucan like a falling boulder, and he fell, hitting the ground hard.

And as he did, his concentration broke, and his connection to the staff vanished.

Lucan got to his knees, only to empty his stomach. His arms and legs felt like wet paper, and wave after wave of pain pulsed through his head. His vision swam, and for a moment he saw two of everything. Only by leaning upon the staff did he keep from falling upon his face.

He saw Malavost walking towards him, smiling once more.

Lucan struggled to rise, to cast a spell, but could do nothing through the pain filling his head.

He cursed himself for a fool. He'd known that the Demonsouled power would probably kill him, sooner or later...but hadn't even given him the strength to defeat Malavost.

A horn rang out.

Malavost stopped, his smile vanishing, and looked to the west.

With some effort, Lucan turned his head, and saw horsemen riding from the west, horsemen flying a banner of a black crow upon a field of green.

~

Mazael and Ultorin danced through the battle, Lion's blue flame struggling against the greatsword's burning darkness.

Again and again they fought, and again and again the press of Malrags and Cravenlock armsmen drove them apart. Mazael cut his way free from the Malrags, his armor splattered with black Malrag blood, and came at Ultorin. Ultorin's dark armor bore dozens of shiny marks from Mazael's blows, and Ultorin himself had been forced to kill three more Malrags to heal the wounds Mazael had dealt him.

Challenger crashed into Ultorin's horse, and Mazael brought Lion down in an overhead cut. Ultorin parried the blow a few inches from his head, and reversed his grip, driving his blade towards Mazael's heart. Mazael whipped Lion in a circle and beat aside the massive thrust, his sword's point digging another groove in Ultorin's cuirass.

Mazael's pulse thundered in his ears, the battle rage filling him with speed and power. It was his Demonsouled nature, he knew, but he remained in control, focusing his rage upon Ultorin. Ultorin, who led the Malrags. Ultorin, who had brought sword and fire to Mazael's lands.

Ultorin, who Mazael could defeat.

He knew it. He felt it in his bones. Ultorin was just as strong as Mazael, and his blazing greatsword made for a terrifying weapon, but Mazael was the better swordsman. Four times he had landed serious wounds upon Ultorin, while the Dominiar had left only minor scratches across Mazael's armor. If he could just land a solid blow upon Ultorin, the fight would be over.

And with it, perhaps, the Malrag invasion. He doubted that Ultorin was Demonsouled. Yet the Malrags seemed to obey Ultorin, and again and again he had flung them into Mazael's path.

But Demonsouled or not, Mazael would strike him down.

His next thrust came within a hair's breadth of splitting Ultorin's throat, leaving a bloody line down his bearded jaw. Ultorin snarled and spurred his horse to a gallop, waving his greatsword and bellowing a command. Five Malrags raced at Mazael, howling their inhuman war cries. Challenger crashed into them, trampling one beneath steel-shod hooves, and Mazael swung and thrust, Lion plunging through the Malrags' gray skins and into their innards.

Ultorin galloped away, trampling down Malrags that got in his path.

A horn rang out.

Mazael ripped Lion free from a Malrag skull and looked west. Horsemen raced across the plain, swords and spears in hand, their banners showing a black crow upon a green field. Sir Tanam Crowley's men. Mazael had sent word to him, before leaving Castle Cravenlock, to ride to battle. Now Crowley's men had arrived, and the Malrags were trapped.

The battle was soon over.

But both Ultorin and Malavost got away.

"I was wrong. Neither one of them," said Lucan, sagging in his saddle, "are actually Demonsouled."

They rode back to Castle Cravenlock, Mazael riding besides Sir Hagen, Lucan, Timothy, and Sir Tanam. The knights and armsmen rode behind Mazael, and many of the horses had empty saddles, or bore wounded men. He had lost far more men than he liked - but less than he had feared.

Going after Ultorin like that had been a hideous gamble, but Mazael had not lost it. Nor had he won the throw.

Yet.

"If neither Ultorin nor Malavost are Demonsouled," said Mazael, "then how are they commanding the Malrags? Do they both serve another Demonsouled?" Yet he had seen Ultorin give commands to the Malrags, seen them obey.

"His greatsword," said Lucan. He looked terrible, his skin sallow, his eyes sunken and feverish. He held his black staff like a dying man clutching his cane. Surviving the fight with Malavost must have been a terrible strain. "It's called a bloodsword. And...I think I know what it is."

Tanam Crowley frowned. "Other than magical, you mean? I saw the thing, if only from afar. Blood and darkness." He shook his head. "Maybe the sword itself is Demonsouled."

"Yes," said Lucan, looking up. "Yes, that's exactly it."

Tanam blinked. "It was only a jest."

"But a jest that struck the mark," said Lucan. "It...is possible to take the blood of a powerful Demonsouled, to use it in the forging of a weapon. Such a weapon is called a bloodsword, and it bestows the power of a Demonsouled on whosoever wields it. Along with other abilities, as well...you saw how Ultorin could heal his wounds by killing Malrags. I suspect the sword drains the life of its victims and transfers that energy to its wielders." His lip twitched. "Though drinking the life of a Malrag, I suspect, is rather like drinking poisoned wine."

"Where would Ultorin have gotten a bloodsword?" said Mazael.

Had the Old Demon given it to him, unleashed him and the Malrags upon the Grim Marches?

"From a Demonsouled, presumably," said Lucan. "And with the Demonsouled's cooperation." His hand tightened about the black staff. "It would undoubtedly be impossible to take a living Demonsouled's blood without his cooperation."

"Undoubtedly," said Mazael, thinking of how he would react to such an attempt.

"I suspect Ultorin obtained the bloodsword from Amalric Galbraith," said Lucan. "Ultorin declared his loyalty to Amalric during our...parley. No doubt Amalric created the sword as a reward for Ultorin's fealty, and to make him a more effective servant. But regardless of where he obtained it, the sword gives Ultorin the powers of a Demonsouled. And it lets him control the Malrags."

"This is grim news," said Tanam.

"No," said Mazael. "No, it's not."

The others gave him a puzzled look.

"I almost had him," said Mazael, voice quiet. "I fought Amalric Galbraith, and he would have killed me, had Sir Adalar not intervened. That bloodsword makes Ultorin fast and strong, but he's not Amalric Galbraith. I can kill him. Or we don't even need to kill him. We need only destroy the bloodsword. If we can, the Malrags will no longer obey Ultorin. They may even kill him for us, before they turn on each other."

Lucan grimaced. "Assuming we can defeat Malavost, first. I suspect he is more dangerous than Ultorin by far."

"You seemed to know who he was," said Mazael.

Lucan looked at Timothy.

Timothy cleared his throat. There was soot on his forehead and hands from the fire spell. "He is renegade, a necromancer and a warlock. Once he was a master wizard of the Order of Alborg, until his crimes were discovered." He sighed. "They say, my lord...they say that he studied under the necromancer Simonian of Briault."

Mazael's frown deepened. Few men knew that Simonian of

Briault was actually the Old Demon, eldest of the Demonsouled and Mazael's father.

"Whether that story is true, I know not, and Malavost is unlikely to confirm it for us," said Lucan. "But I do know that he was one of Marstan's teachers. And he always excelled Marstan in both skill and power. He has friends among the San-keth, both the serpent people themselves and their human proselytes."

Mazael pulled off his helmet and ran a hand through his sweat-soaked hair. Lucan had inherited all of Marstan's skill and power, and Lucan was one of the most powerful wizards Mazael had ever seen. If he could not defeat Malavost in a straight fight...

"Grim news, indeed," said Tanam, shaking his head.

"Grim or not," said Mazael, "Malavost is still a mortal man, and he can still die upon a sword blade like any other."

"I hope, my lord," said Lucan, "that you are correct."

9

THE CLERIC OF SEPHARIVAIM

Sykhana fled east, towards the Grim Marches and the village of Gray Pillar.

She rode her horse to death, and stole another one. She dared not linger. With Rachel Roland's death and her subterfuge with Paul Korren, she had left a tangled trail for any pursuers. Yet she had not lived this long by taking foolish chances, and when Gerald Roland tracked down Korren, she had no doubt the wretched merchant will tell everything to save his own hide.

Not that Lord Malden would show any mercy to a San-keth proselyte, not after a calibah had murdered his eldest son.

So Sykhana rode hard, stopping only to tend to Aldane.

Her Aldane.

The baby rode in a basket on her saddle, padded to protect him from the bouncing ride. She fed him fruit and meat ground into a paste, and milk she stole from passing farms. Her training at Karag Tormeth had been brutal, but it gave her the ability to move unseen and unnoticed with ease. At the time she had hated the training, but now she blessed it.

Sometimes Aldane cried, screaming at the top of his lungs, and Sykhana cradled him against her chest.

"Don't cry," she murmured. "Don't cry. Forget your mother. She was weak and stupid, unworthy of you. I will love and cherish you, always."

She kissed him on the forehead.

"And you will be a god," she said, "and live in power and splendor forever."

~

SOON SHE CAME to the town of Tristgard.

Most travelers going to the Grim Marches from Knightcastle took the road that looped north through the High Plain. But Sykhana hoped to avoid as many witnesses as possible - a lone woman traveling with a baby would draw notice. And some travelers would not hesitate to take advantage of one woman, apparently unarmed.

Sykhana grinned and licked her lips, her hidden fangs rasping against her tongue.

If anyone tried to stop her, they would regret it sorely.

But she did not expect any trouble at Tristgard, a pretty little town, with houses and walls of stone, it was a place for merchants to stop and rest as they made the journey from Knightcastle to the Grim Marches, or from Cadlyn in the High Plain to Knightport. Though the townspeople might be more vigilant - last year the archpriest Straganis and a band of calibah tried to kill Rachel and Mazael Cravenlock here as they journeyed to Knightcastle. But the attack had been a year past, and she suspected the townspeople would have fallen back into complacency by now.

So Sykhana was surprised to see militia patrolling both the road and the ford below the town. She reined up, frowning. Townsmen in leather armor, spears in hand, stood guard at the Black River's ford. Others waited on the walls, crossbows in hand. Below the walls of Tristgard, she saw a ragged camp of dozens tents and wagons. Frightened, tired-looking people moved among the tents - hollow-eyed men with dirty faces, weeping children clutching at the skirts of tired women.

Refugees. But why had they fled here?

A pair of militiamen approached her, and Sykhana made sure to look properly frightened, her eyes downcast.

"Here now, lass," said the older of the two men, "what's your business here? Did you come from the Grim Marches?"

The Grim Marches?

"Nay, sir," she said. "My father's farm is in the hills. My sister came down with the flux, so she bade me to take her baby into town until she recovers, lest he catch the sickness."

"What's your father's name?" said the younger man, scowling.

"Brand," said Sykhana, picking the first name that came to mind.

"I don't know any Brand," said the younger man.

The older man snorted. "Don't be a fool, boy. One woman with a baby's no danger. And she doesn't have the flux - babies with the flux last only six hours, if they're lucky. You can enter the town, lass, but stay away from the common rooms - some of the lads will take liberties with a lone woman."

"Thank you, sir," Sykhana said, giving him a shy smile. "But...why are all these folk here, in the tents?"

"War's coming," said the younger man.

"Perhaps," said the older one. "There are rumors of trouble in the Grim Marches. The refugees say that Malrags have come down out of the mountains to burn and kill. Some Marcher folk have fled here, to get away from the troubles."

"Malrags?" said Sykhana. She had heard of Malrags - the clerics said they were real, though she had doubted to ever see one. Malrags had invaded the Grim Marches? She did not believe for a moment that it was a coincidence.

Just what had Malavost wrought?

"Aye," said the younger man. "Devils, without conscience or mercy. They'll burn the Grim Marches and come for us, you mark my words."

"Bah," said the older man. "It's Lord Mazael's lands they're attacking, I hear. And I saw Lord Mazael when the snake folk tried to kill him. He cut through them like wheat, and he'll do the same to the Malrags. You should go, lass - the road is no place for a lone woman."

Sykhana gave him the shy smile again and kept riding.

She slipped past the guards at the ford, stole one of their horses, and rode for the east.

~

SOON SHE CAME to the endless rolling plains of the Grim Marches, with the distant shape of the Great Mountains rising to the east.

And she realized that the rumors were true.

Everywhere she saw the signs of war. The Malrags had not yet come this far west. But she saw men drilling in the squares of villages and towns, saw knights galloping from castles, saw armsmen marching in formation, armor and weapons flashing in the sunlight. Wagons and horses choked the roads, as men and supplies moved east to the fighting, and peasants fled west to avoid it.

It was marvelous. In all this chaos, no one paid any attention to one woman with a baby.

She rode over the Northwater bridge and deeper into the Grim Marches.

~

THREE DAYS later she came to Castle Cravenlock itself.

The castle squatted atop its crag, dark and ominous, fortified with a strong wall and tall towers. It looked like a dark wizard's stronghold from a child's tale. Which was not surprising - the founder of the House of Cravenlock, a thousand years past, had been a San-keth proselyte, and built a hidden temple to Sepharivaim beneath his castle. The temple remained hidden and secret until Mazael Cravenlock killed Skhath, expelled the proselytes, and sealed the temple's entrances.

Not that Sykhana cared. She had served Sepharivaim and the

San-keth loyally, but they had never given her a child to carry in her arms.

A short distance from the castle stood Cravenlock Town, an overgrown village of four thousand people. Or it had been, at any rate. Sykhana saw new construction in the town, and the stone walls had been fortified with additional towers and platforms for archers and siege engines. No doubt the refugees had swollen the town's population. And Mazael Cravenlock was no fool, which explained the additional fortifications.

But better to avoid both the town and the castle. Aldane was only two and a half months old, and Lord Mazael had never seen his nephew. But if Sykhana chanced to cross Mazael's path, if he recognized something of his sister or Gerald in Aldane's face...no. Better to avoid him entirely.

Even as the thought crossed her mind, she saw the horsemen riding towards her.

Sykhana reined up, her stolen horse breathing hard. A score of armored men in Cravenlock tabards rode up, led by a villainous-looking knight with a close-cropped black beard and a chest like a barrel. A patrol, and unlike the men at Tristgard, they would be on their guard.

She made herself look frightened as they approached.

The men reined up around her.

"Hold," said the knight, not unkindly. "From where do you hail?"

Sykhana blinked, as if fighting back tears. "My name's Jenna, and I come from my father's farm, near the Northwater Inn. But...but three days ago those devils came, and my," she started to cry, "my father and my husband went out to fight them, and told me to take the baby and a horse and run, so I did, and the devils cut them down, and I ran, and ran..."

She dissolved into tears, weeping, huddling Aldane close to her chest.

Sympathy flashed over the knight's hard-bitten face, and Sykhana managed not to smirk.

"You're safe now," said the knight. "I am Sir Hagen Bridgebane, armsmaster to Lord Mazael of Castle Cravenlock. Lord Mazael has decreed that any driven from their homes by the Malrags may find refugee at Cravenlock Town. You'll have to work for your bread, aye, but the Malrags are pressing us hard, and every hand is needed."

"Truly, sir knight?" said Sykhana, her voice trembling. "Oh, thank you. Thank you!"

"Go to the town," said Sir Hagen, pointing. "Speak to Neville, the mayor. Tell him I sent you, and he'll find a place for you and your child. You might have to share a room with three or four other women, but it's still better than another night out in the open."

"Thank you, sir," she said again.

She rode past the gates of the town and made for the east, towards the looming shapes of the Great Mountains.

~

EAST OF CASTLE CRAVENLOCK, things were not so orderly.

Sykhana passed a half-dozen ruined villages, their houses and barns reduced to piles of blackened bricks. The corpses of butchered peasants lay bloated and decaying in the spring sunlight. She saw the corpses of Malrags as well, hundreds upon hundreds of them. They were hideous things, with gray skin, fanged mouths, six-fingered hands, and colorless eyes. And to judge from the number of dead Malrags, Lord Mazael and the other nobles of the Grim Marches were putting up a terrific fight.

She wondered why Malavost had brought the Malrags to the Grim Marches. Lord Mazael and Lord Richard were mortal foes of the San-keth, but Sykhana did not care about their emnity, and Malavost certainly did not. Ultorin hated Mazael, but Ultorin was nothing more than a rabid dog.

It puzzled her as she rode through more ruined villages and sacked towns.

~

TWO DAYS AFTER CASTLE CRAVENLOCK, she saw a Malrag warband.

Sykhana rode through the main street of a burned village. Wisps of smoke still rose from the wrecked houses, and fires crackled here and there. The villagers lay where they had been slain, their bodies hacked and torn by Malrag axes. Sykhana ignored them. Their deaths at the hands of the Malrags meant nothing to her.

Then she saw the dead woman.

Sykhana reined up, transfixed. A peasant woman of perhaps twenty years lay on her belly in the dirt, the back of her dress stiff with dried blood. Her eyes bulged with pain and horror.

A tiny white hand lay beneath her shoulder, the fingers loose.

The woman had tried to flee the Malrags, clutching her baby to her chest, and a Malrag plunged its spear into her back as she tried to save her child. Only the baby had been killed in her fall, crushed by the mother's weight. Or the Malrag's spear had plunged through the woman's chest to transfix the child.

For a moment Sykhana wondered what it would be like to lose Aldane, to see him die, and the pain that burned through her was so fierce that she gasped aloud. She touched his sleeping face with trembling fingers. He was so tiny, so perfect. She would not lose him. He would be a god and live forever, Malavost had promised. She would not lose him!

When she looked up, the Malrags were watching her.

A dozen of the creatures stood at the end of the street. They wore black armor, and carried black axes and spears. Black veins threaded beneath their leathery gray hides, and their colorless eyes showed no hint of mercy.

Sykhana hissed, her fangs extending over her lips, and snatched her hidden daggers from their hiding places.

One of the Malrags stepped forward. It was smaller than the others, almost spindly, and wore a robe of ragged black leather. Unlike its companions, it had a third eye in the center of its forehead, an eye that glowed with a ghostly green light. The three-eyed Malrag stared at her for a moment, and began to speak. Sykhana did not recognize the hissing, growling language...but somehow the meaning of the words echoed in her mind.

-You are not human-

"No," said Sykhana. "I am calibah, of both human and San-keth blood."

The three-eyed Malrag stepped closer to her, titling its head to the side. Suddenly Sykhana felt the cold prickle of magical power. The Malrag had arcane abilities, and she remembered some of her lessons in Karag Tormeth. The creature was a shaman, she realized, a Malrag spell caster.

The shaman began speaking again.

-But the young one is fully human. And the young ones are weak, helpless. They make the sweetest screams when they die-

Sykhana snarled, pointing her daggers at the shaman's face. "Dare to lift a finger against him, wretch, and I will spill your black blood upon the earth."

The shaman and the other Malrags hissed, their cold laughter echoing inside Sykhana's skull.

-Do you think death frightens me, little changeling? I have been slain many times, and I shall be slain many more ere the Great Demon is enfleshed once more. I have killed humans, and I have killed San-keth...and I have killed your kind, little changeling. A calibah woman screams much the same as any other as you strip the flesh from her arms one inch at a time-

"Try it," spat Sykhana, trying to hide her fear, "and I'll send you to meet your precious Great Demon."

Again the Malrags laughed at her.

-Fear not, little calibah. The Master bade us to watch for a calibah woman and a human infant. We are to take you to him at once-

"Yes," said Sykhana, trying to retake control of the conversation. She was used to inspiring fear, not feeling it. And the Malrag shaman's three-eyed gaze unsettled her. "The village of Gray Pillar. Your Master awaits me there."

-Come-

The Malrags left the village, and Sykhana followed them.

~

GRAY PILLAR LAY to the east, at the very edge of the foothills, a village that earned its bread mining the gold veins of the Great Mountains. Or at least it had, until the Malrags had arrived.

And as the shaman led Sykhana east, she saw more and more Malrags.

At first it was only scouting parties of three or four. Then she saw an entire warband, led by a towering balekhan in black plate, two shamans at the creature's side. And then more warbands, and still more, until the Malrags covered the Grim Marches like a black tide, like steel-armored locusts.

Sykhana tried to count the numbers, and finally gave up. There had to be at least seventy thousand of the creatures. Maybe even as many as a hundred thousand, and still more were gathering. Lord Richard Mandragon and all his vassals together could not muster more than twenty-five thousand fighting men. The Malrags, if they wanted, could slaughter every living human in the Grim Marches.

But why did Malavost care?

Later that day they came to Gray Pillar.

The village took its name from the tall column of gray stone rising from its square, some monument left over from a long-forgotten kingdom. Houses built of rough-mortared fieldstone ringed the square, their roofs burned, dead peasants rotting in the sun. Hundreds of Malrags thronged the village, watching as the shaman led her past.

Malavost and Ultorin waited for her at the base of the pillar. Ultorin was massive in his black plate armor, one armored hand resting loosely around the hilt of his bloodsword. Besides him, Malavost almost looked like a scarecrow in black, albeit a scarecrow with white hair and pale blue eyes.

Yet Sykhana knew that Malavost was the more dangerous by far.

Ultorin sneered as she approached, and then he laughed. "So. The snake's little pet has returned."

"I have," said Sykhana, hiding a frown.

Ultorin looked a bit paler than she remembered, with dark circles under his iron-colored eyes. He seemed ill at ease, as if the sun's light pained him. Malavost had mentioned that the bloodsword might have...deleterious effects upon Ultorin, but she hadn't expected to see them so soon.

"There's no need for hostility, Grand Master," said Malavost in his resonant voice. "We could not begin until Sykhana brought the child. And she has." His ever-present smile widened. "Now we can act in force. Our goals shall be accomplished...and you will have your vengeance when Lord Mazael moves to stop us."

Ultorin spat upon the ground. "Let him try."

"You've done well, Sykhana," said Malavost. "Are you ready to present the child to the cleric?"

Sykhana stiffened in the saddle. Aldane was hers. Hers! Every instinct screamed against showing Aldane to the miserable old priest.

She calmed down. Malavost had promised that Aldane would be hers forever. And Skaloban would never have him.

"Yes," said Sykhana, swinging down from the saddle. She lifted Aldane from his padded basket. "You may take me to Skaloban now."

Malavost gave a bow that had just a hint of mockery to it, and beckoned. Ultorin snorted, shook his head, and stalked away, hand still caressing the hilt of his bloodsword. He cared nothing for the San-keth, viewing them only as a means to the end, even before Malavost had given him that sword.

Sykhana wondered how badly it had chewed into his sanity.

"This way," said Malavost, and he led her to Gray Pillar's church.

Or what was left of it. It had once been a fine domed church, in the style of old Dracaryl, similar to the church in Cravenlock Town. Now the windows had been smashed, the doors lying splintered and ruined. From within the chapel came the stench of clotted blood and rotting flesh.

Again Sykhana felt that strange, unfamiliar fear. She did not want to take Aldane into that place. But Malavost walked through the ruined doors, and she would not show fear before him. So she took a deep breath and followed him.

Inside the church's altar had been desecrated, profaned by the blood of murdered victims. Crude scenes had been painted upon the walls, showing the San-keth, murdering and torturing humans. The corpses of sacrificial victims to Sepharivaim lay piled against the wall, filling the church with their stench.

Skaloban, a San-keth priest of Sepharivaim, stood before the altar.

He rode a rotting human skeleton, the bones animated by the power of his necromancy, as did all San-keth clerics. According to the ancient lore, the serpent people had once possessed arms and legs, as did the humans and the Elderborn and the Malrags. But the gods of the humans and the Elderborn betrayed Sepharivaim, banishing him in the outer darkness beyond the circles of the world and stripping the San-keth of their limbs, forcing them to crawl in the dust. In vengeance, the San-keth clerics used necromancy to animate the bones of slain humans, using them as undead carriers.

"Honored Skaloban," said Malavost, bowing. "Sykhana has returned."

"Yes," said Skaloban, his voice a faint hiss, his forked tongue lashing at the air. "I can taste her scent." Skaloban was twenty feet long, his coils wrapped tight around the skeleton's spine, his enormous wedge-shaped head rearing up where the skeleton's skull had once been. "So you have returned, child, have you?" The skeleton walked towards her, green fire flickering around its joints, Skaloban's head swaying. "Were you successful?"

"I was," said Sykhana. It was no effort to keep her voice firm. Once the clerics of great Sepharivaim had filled her with fear and awe. Now she felt only contempt. They had not been able to give her what she wanted. "Behold, chosen of Sepharivaim. The unmarked child of a human apostate, just as you bid."

Skaloban's tongue flicked the air over Aldane.

"Good," murmured Skaloban. "Very good. He is worthy of our great purpose. The child shall be the Vessel. Your task, calibah, will be to make sure the Vessel lives to reach the Door of Souls. You must guard him every moment, waking and sleeping. Fail, and your life shall be forfeit. Do you understand?"

Sykhana bowed low to hide her smile. "Yes, honored one. I shall do as you bid."

"Good," said Skaloban, his head rotating to face Malavost. "Wizard. Instruct your pet to rouse the Malrags. We march at once."

Malavost smiled. "As you command, honored Skaloban."

LATER SYKHANA STOOD with Malavost outside the ruined church, Aldane in her arms, watching the Malrag host rumble into motion.

"Do I have your promise, wizard?" she said.

Malavost nodded. "You shall be Aldane's mother for all your days. And Skaloban shall never touch him."

"I have your word?" Sykhana said.

Malavost nodded, his pale eyes glittering.

"You do," he said.

10

REUNION

Rachel wanted to scream at her husband.

"We have to conserve the horses," said Gerald. "If the San-keth wanted Aldane dead, that changeling would have killed him on the spot. No, they want him alive for some vile purpose."

"Then we should ride with all speed," said Rachel, her voice tight, "to stop Sykhana before she achieves that vile purpose."

Sykhana. That name filled Rachel with a rage beyond anything she had ever known. The changeling would pay for having dared to lift a finger against Aldane, for betraying Rachel.

"Circan thinks she is alone, but she won't remain alone for long," said Gerald. "Undoubtedly she has allies. We'll need to fight them, and we'll need fresh horses and men to win that fight." He reached over his saddle and took her hand. "If we're going to get our son back, we'll need to keep our wits about us."

Rachel shivered with fury. Their son had been taken, and Gerald wanted her to remain calm? Rachel wanted to ride the horses to death, to gallop to the horizon until she saw Sykhana, until she could hold Aldane in her arms once more...

She sighed.

"You're right," she whispered. She knew well the deep cunning of the San-keth and their calibah servants. If she did not keep her head, if she urged Gerald into doing something rash...then her folly might well get Aldane killed. "I just...I have to get him back, Gerald. I have to."

"We shall," said Gerald. He looked to the side, where Circan rode at the head of the column. "It's not as if Sykhana can elude us, after all."

"Yes," whispered Rachel, her gloved hand tightening against her horse's reins until the leather squealed.

So long as Circan had the vial of Aldane's blood, they could follow her son anywhere. Let Sykhana run all she wanted! Rachel would hound her to the ends of the earth.

~

THEY STOPPED AT TRISTGARD.

Sykhana had gone east since fleeing Knightcastle, and Tristgard defended the ford over the Black River. Someone certainly would have seen Sykhana, Gerald said, and he wanted to question the town's militia.

He was right. Much as Rachel wanted to ride on, Gerald was right. So she stood beside her horse outside the town's gates and waited. Tristgard held no good memories for her. Here the San-keth had attacked her as she had ridden to her wedding at Knightcastle. Here she had seen Mazael take a half-dozen crossbow bolts to the chest, surviving only by a miracle.

But Tristgard had changed in the last year.

A small city of tents and wagons surrounded the town, filled with terrified people. Refugees, she realized. Some of the armsmen spoke to them, and brought back disturbing stories. All the refugees had come from the Grim Marches, and spoke harrowing tales of war. Of Malrags descending like locusts from the Great Mountains, killing everything in their path.

Mazael's lands. Many of the refugees had come from her brother's lands.

And if Circan was correct, Sykhana was making for Castle Cravenlock.

Gerald returned after an hour, his expression grim.

"What is it?" said Rachel. "Did someone see Sykhana here?"

He led her away from the other knights and the armsmen, far enough that they could not be overheard.

"I think so," said Gerald. "One of the militiamen saw a lone woman, on a horse, carrying a baby. She was here two days ago."

"Two days!" said Rachel. Her heart soared. They could close the gap easily. Especially once they got to the open plains of the Grim Marches.

"She slipped past the guards at the ford and rode east. They haven't seen her since." He sighed. "She's almost certainly going to the Grim Marches."

"But that's good news!" said Rachel. "We can catch her there, we can get help from Mazael..."

"The Grim Marches are at war," said Gerald, waving his hand at the ragged tents. "Look at those refugees."

"We already knew about the Malrags," said Rachel. "Mazael mentioned them in his last letter."

"He mentioned warbands," said Gerald. "The situation has clearly gotten much worse. If we go into the Grim Marches, we'll be riding into a war."

"Surely you aren't thinking of turning back!" said Rachel.

"Of course not," said Gerald. "But...if the reports of the Malrag numbers are true, we very well might not come back, if we find ourselves in the wrong place at the wrong time. I should send you back to Knightcastle, to keep you safe until I can return with Aldane."

"No!" said Rachel. "I told you, I will not be left behind. Bad enough to wait not knowing what that vile changeling is doing to Aldane. But to wait knowing that you might be slain...no, no I couldn't bear it."

"And what of me?" said Gerald, anger flashing over his face. "Suppose we are attacked and I cannot defend you? Do you think I want to watch you die in front of me? Or suppose you get to watch me die? We'll be riding into a war, Rachel. You will be safer at Knightcastle."

"I am not turning back," said Rachel, "without our son."

They stared at each other for a moment.

Finally Gerald sighed and gave a nod.

"All right," he said. "I've heard it said that the gods love fools and madmen. Well, I hope it is true, for I am certainly a fool and a madman to allow my wife to ride with me into a war."

"To get Aldane back," said Rachel, "I would ride to hell and back."

"Let's hope it doesn't come to that," said Gerald. "Sir Cavilion!" The lean knight in command of the armsmen rode over. "We ride for the Grim Marches."

They left an hour later, riding over the Black River and towards the Grim Marches.

A FEW DAYS later they rode over the Northwater bridge.

Everywhere Rachel saw the signs of war. The men marching east, clad in leather armor and bearing spears and bows. The terrified men, women, and children fleeing west, their worldly goods piled in wagons and carried on their backs. Upon every tongue were stories of the Malrags, of their cruelty, of their atrocities.

"Your son is now east of Castle Cravenlock, my lord," said Circan, riding besides Gerald. The wizard's face was grim, his brow furrowed beneath his pale hair. "Or the changeling may be at Castle Cravenlock now. The distance is difficult to judge."

"If only we had a way to send a message to Mazael," said Rachel. "He could stop Sykhana." And Castle Cravenlock was three days ride from the bridge. Sykhana was adding to her lead.

Gerald shook his head. "I suspect Mazael is busy with the Malrags. If Castle Cravenlock hasn't already fallen."

"None of the refugees spoke of it," said Sir Cavilion.

"Surely would have seen more peasants on the road, had the castle fallen," said Circan, his fingers still closed about the vial of Aldane's blood.

"We should stop at Castle Cravenlock," said Rachel. "Mazael will aid us."

"I am sure of it," said Gerald. "If he has any aid left to spare."

⁓

TWO AND A HALF DAYS LATER, they saw the signs of battle in the hilly country west of Castle Cravenlock.

Rachel shivered and pulled her cloak tighter. A dozen dead Malrags lay across the road. To judge from their wounds and the decay of the corpses, they had been dead no more than two or three days. Rachel had never seen anything quite so hideous as the dead Malrags. The creatures seemed like something out of a nightmare, or a demented artist's fevered imaginings.

"What are they?" said Sir Cavilion, hand on his sword hilt.

"Malrags," said Gerald. "And it seems they are certainly not a myth." He grimaced and took a look around the hills, as if expecting a Malrag ambush to fall upon them. "Cavilion. Put out scouts. Have them ride at least a mile in every direction around us. If we're going to run into a Malrag warband, I want to know in advance."

"My lord," said Cavilion, and gave the orders.

They rode on.

⁓

A FEW HOURS later they left the hill country, riding hard for Castle Cravenlock.

Rachel gripped her reins, her heart churning within her. Since leaving Knightcastle, she had thought of little but Aldane. But now her impending return to Castle Cravenlock filled her with trepidation. She had endured terrible things there.

She had made terrible mistakes there.

But Mazael was at Castle Cravenlock, and she smiled at the thought of seeing her elder brother once more. She loved Gerald, of course, but Mazael was a warrior without peer. He had defeated Skhath, he had defeated Simonian of Briault, he had destroyed the Dominiars, and he would help her get Aldane back...

"My lord!"

Rachel looked up. One of the scouts galloped towards them, horse sweating, cloak billowing behind him.

"What is it, man?" said Gerald.

"Devils, my lord," said the scout, trembling. "Devils! I've never seen..."

A bloodcurdling scream split the air.

And Malrags, hundreds of Malrags, boiled over the crest of a nearby hill.

Rachel gaped at them. The dead Malrags strewn across the road had been horrible. Living ones, their fangs bared, their colorless eyes wide as they charged, were infinitely worse. Gerald shouted orders, and the knights and armsmen turned, preparing their mounts for a charge.

But they were too late, and the Malrags were too fast.

They crashed howling into the line, and men and horses died. Rachel saw a dozen Malrags go down, their black blood spilling into the dirt, but more pressed into the melee, stabbing and hacking.

And then a Malrag leapt at Rachel, grinning a fanged grin.

She jerked at the reins of her horse, but too late. The Malrag's black axe plunged into her horse's neck, and the poor beast screamed, rearing up. Rachel lost her seat and fell to the ground, the jolt shooting up her back and making her teeth clack. She scrambled backwards, legs tangled in her long skirt. The Malrag leapt over the dying horse, bloody axe in hand.

The creature's mouth moved, speaking in a strange language, but she heard its voice inside her head.

-Scream, mortal child. Scream for me-

Rachel screamed.

And then Gerald was there, his sword and surcoat splattered with blood both Malrag and human. His shield caught the Malrag across the face, and the creature stumbled, giving Gerald the opening he needed to cut its throat. The Malrag fell, and Gerald killed another, and still another, standing over Rachel.

"Rachel!" he bellowed, catching a spear thrust on his shield. "Run! Now! Run to Castle Cravenlock. Damn it, run! Run!"

Rachel scrambled to her knees, breathing hard. She saw the Roland knights and armsmen falling, succumbing to the Malrag attack. Gerald killed another Malrag with a vicious slash, hot black blood splattering across Rachel's face.

"Run!" he shouted, raising his shield.

She stared at him, frozen with horror. All the men were going to die, she realized. Gerald was going to die. He was sacrificing himself to save her, to gain even a chance of her survival, and it was her fault. If only she had not insisted upon coming. If only she had seen Sykhana for what she was. And now she would perish, and Gerald would die for her mistakes, and their son would remain in Sykhana's vile hands.

But she could find neither words to say nor the will to act as the Malrags closed around them. There was a thunderclap, and a dozen Malrags went sprawling, thrown to the earth by Circan's war spells. For a moment the Malrags wavered, and Rachel felt a surge of hope.

Then the Malrags bellowed and charged to the attack, leaping over the bodies of dead men and Malrags alike. Gerald grimaced and set himself, battered shield raised, and Rachel waited for the end.

She hoped it would be quick.

A horn rang out, long and loud.

Rachel saw the first wave of horsemen thunder down the hillside, lances leveled. They flew the Cravenlock banner, three silver swords upon a field of black. At their head rode a tall man in steel armor, clad in a Cravenlock surcoat.

A sword of blue flame blazed in his fist.

∾

AFTER THE BATTLE, Rachel tended to Gerald's wounds. Her husband had not been hurt badly, thank the gods - a minor cut, some scrapes and bruises. The rest of the men were not so lucky. Fifteen dead, and another twenty wounded, six seriously. Circan moved among the men, treating their wounds, while Mazael's court wizard Timothy did the same.

Mazael himself stood nearby, leaning upon Lion. Her brother looked little different than she remembered. Tall and strong, with the same brown hair and beard, the sharp gray eyes. He looked grim and sad, as he always had since Romaria Greenshield had been killed, but now he seemed grimmer and harder than ever.

Fighting Malrags, she supposed, could do that to a man.

"Gods, Mazael," said Gerald. "You arrival was most timely. The Malrags had us. Another few moments and it would have been over."

"We were fortunate," said Mazael. "All my scouts have been riding to the east, looking for Malrag warbands. We spotted this group hastening to the west and followed them, lest they raid the untouched villages near the Northwater. It is well that we did."

"I was a fool," said Gerald. He had the strained look he got when men died under his command. Rachel would do her best to comfort him later. "I should have put out more scouts, have been better prepared."

"You couldn't have been," said Mazael. "Until three months ago, no living man had ever fought a Malrag. We took horrible losses, until we learned to fight them properly. Though our situation is still dire. We are in sore need of any aid you can provide." He paused, looked at Rachel for a moment. "But you have Rachel with you."

Gerald nodded.

"Whatever madness possessed you to bring her here," said Mazael, "your need must have been great indeed. So I assume you did not come to our aid."

Gerald took a deep breath. "No. Mazael, I..."

"The San-keth took our son!" said Rachel.

He stared at her, and for a moment Rachel remembered Mazael

in his younger days, filled with wrath, ready to destroy anyone in his path.

It heartened her. The San-keth would regret ever touching Aldane.

"Tell me everything," said Mazael. He looked over the battlefield and scowled. "But as we ride. There are more warbands about, and I would rather not encounter them, not until we have Rachel safe in Castle Cravenlock."

LATER SHE SAT in the great hall of Castle Cravenlock, surrounded by the lords and knights of the Grim Marches, as Gerald told Mazael what had happened.

And told Lord Richard Mandragon, as well.

Rachel tried not to stare at the Dragonslayer. She had lived in terror of Richard Mandragon for years. He had defeated her father Lord Adalon, and she had believed that one day he would defeat Mitor and kill her. Mitor had believed that as well, and in desperation, had turned to the San-keth for aid.

To Skhath, to whom he had promised Rachel.

"Those damned San-keth," said Mazael when Gerald had finished. "It would not surprise me if they took Aldane out of spite."

"No doubt spite played a role," said Lucan Mandragon. Rachel feared and loathed Lord Richard, but she feared his wizard son even more. Mazael should never have trusted him. "But if they acted from mere spite, they would have simply killed the child then and there. They have some other motive."

"Also," added Sir Tanam Crowley. Rachel remembered him very well - he had kidnapped her from Castle Cravenlock on Lord Richard's orders. "This Sykhana is working with Malavost and Ultorin, I doubt not."

"That seems correct, Sir Tanam," said Circan, bowing. "If my spell is accurate, Aldane is three or four days' ride to the east of here. And he has not moved since we arrived at Castle Cravenlock."

"So almost certainly my son is with Ultorin and Malavost," said Gerald.

"Most probably," said Tanam. "My scouts think the main Malrag host is three days' ride east of here."

"So," said Rachel, "we ride out and get Aldane back."

The men looked at each other, and then back at her.

"Sir Gerald, Lady Rachel," said Lord Richard in his calm voice, "I am sorry to hear of your son's abduction. But it changes little. Our task is still the same. We must find Ultorin and kill him. Or destroy his bloodsword, at the very least. Once he is dead, the Malrag host will fall apart, and we can destroy them easily. That will give us the best chance to recover your son."

"But we know where Aldane is!" said Rachel. "We can get him back, we..."

"Through tens of thousands of Malrags, my lady?" said Lucan. "No scout, no matter how skillful, can slip through such numbers. Nor could I or the other wizards use a spell to elude the Malrags. The shamans would sense such a spell, not to mention what Malavost might..."

"Shut up!" said Rachel. "I don't care what you think, wizard, or what you can do with your filthy spells! What do you know about losing a son? Or someone you love? I doubt someone like you has ever loved anyone!"

Lucan said nothing, but his expression shifted, and Rachel knew she had stung him.

"Lord Richard is right, I fear," said Gerald. "If Aldane is surrounded by thousands of Malrags, our best chance of getting him back is to kill Ultorin. If I could, I would take our remaining men and get Aldane back. But we have only eighty men left, and there are fifty thousand Malrags around our son. If we try to get him back, we will die, and accomplish nothing."

"But the others have more men," said Rachel, looking around at the lords and knights of the Grim Marches. "Mazael has men. We could take them, could strike at the Malrags, could..."

"No," said Lord Richard.

She blinked at him.

"I will forbid my vassals to send any men on a fruitless attempt to retrieve the child," said Lord Richard. "I will do what is necessary to defeat the Malrags and save the Grim Marches. If I must spend the lives of my men to achieve that, so be it. I have done it before and I shall do it again. But I will not throw away their lives on a fruitless attempt to retrieve one child."

"But he is my son!" said Rachel.

Lord Richard's eyes, cold and black, met hers. "Thousands of sons have died already, Lady Rachel, and thousands more may well die before we defeat Ultorin. And I will not waste their lives to merely save one child."

Rachel could not bear another word.

"Rachel," said Gerald, reaching for her hand.

She rose and stalked from the hall.

LATER RACHEL STOOD IN A GARDEN, crying.

Her father had constructed this garden, built onto a massive balcony on the side of the castle's main keep, as a gift for her mother. But Lady Arissa had hated Lord Adalon, and never used the balcony. No one ever came here. So Rachel had often hidden here as a child, crying. Later, as she had grown, and Mitor had made his alliance with the San-keth, she had still come here to cry. When she had left Castle Cravenlock a year past, she had rejoiced, knowing she would never need to come to this garden to cry again.

And here she was, again.

She bowed her head, hands spread on the railing, her tears falling against the stone.

Boots rustled against the grass.

Rachel turned, saw Mazael walking towards her.

They stood in silence for a moment.

"Lord Richard is right, you know," said Mazael.

"I know," whispered Rachel. "I know." She closed her eyes. He put his arm around her, and she leaned against him, his armor hard against her side. "I don't have the right to ask anyone to die for Aldane. But, gods forgive me, Mazael. If I could spend the lives of a hundred men, or even a thousand men, to get Aldane back, I would do it. I would do it without hesitating." She sniffled. "I would spend my life, if it only meant he would be safe."

Mazael nodded.

"You've changed," said Rachel. "Five years ago you would have ridden after Aldane, and damned anyone who tried to stop you."

He laughed quietly. "You're right. I would have, five years ago. And gotten myself killed in the process. Or worse." Rachel wondered what he meant by that.

"It is my fault, Mazael," she said. "I was the one who prayed to Sepharivaim, not Aldane. Sykhana took Aldane because of me." Her lip trembled. "My son will suffer for my mistakes."

"Perhaps," said Mazael. "I've had men suffer for my mistakes. I've had men die for my mistakes. You can either learn from them, or give up and die."

"I will not give up," said Rachel. "Not until I have Aldane back." She hesitated. "Do...you really think Lord Richard's plan will work."

"It will. If we kill Ultorin, or destroy his bloodsword, he loses his command over the Malrags," said Mazael, and there was heat in his voice. "I can take him. I had him, Rachel. If I can get close enough, I can kill Ultorin. Then we'll drive the Malrags from the Grim Marches, get your son back, and have peace once more."

"Yes," said Rachel. She hesitated. "When you kill Ultorin, the Malrags will turn on each other, won't they?"

Mazael nodded.

"And that means they'll kill anything in sight," said Rachel. "Including Aldane and Sykhana."

There was a long pause.

"I don't know," said Mazael. "But...you're probably right. Ultorin and Malavost must want Aldane alive for some reason. Once Ultorin is dead...then there will be nothing to stop the Malrags from killing Aldane."

"Save him," said Rachel. "If anyone can save Aldane, you can. Promise me, Mazael. Promise me that you will save my son."

For a long time Mazael said nothing.

"I will," he said at last. "If I can."

MALAVOST OPENED HIS EYES.

He rode at the head of the Malrag host, near Ultorin atop his great armored steed. Nearby rode Sykhana, Aldane in her arms, and Skaloban, the San-keth cleric's horse enspelled to keep it from bolting in terror. The Malrags stretched behind them, a vast host, covering the plains of the Grim Marches like a black ocean. They would kill him if they had a chance, he knew, but he did not care. The Malrags would kill everything in their path if they had a chance.

But they were expendable tools, and nothing more.

Just as Sykhana and Skaloban were expendable tools. Even Ultorin, with his bloodsword, was nothing a tool. Malavost needed the Malrags, if only for a little while longer, and he was certainly not foolish enough to wield a weapon forged with Demonsouled blood himself.

Unlike, say, the Dragon's Shadow.

Malavost smiled at the thought. Lord Richard's little whelp had no idea what the bloodstaff would do to him. What it already had done to him.

But that was a pleasure for another time.

He rode to Ultorin's side.

"We have a problem," said Malavost.

Ultorin glared at him. Flecks of venomous yellow showed in his gray eyes, and there were hints of black veins forming beneath his skin.

A weapon forged in Demonsouled blood was not a...healthy thing to wield.

"What kind of problem?" said Ultorin.

"Someone knows exactly where Aldane Roland is," said Malavost.

Sykhana looked up in alarm, her eyes turning yellow as her inner eyelids opened, fangs curling over her teeth.

"How?" she said.

"A spell," said Malavost. "I've sensed it twice, now. I suspect one of Lord Malden's court wizards drew a sample of the child's blood. With that blood, the wizard could follow Aldane anywhere."

Skaloban hissed. "Then block the spell."

"Sadly, honored Skaloban, I fear I cannot," said Malavost, hiding his contempt. The San-keth clerics claimed to be masters of necromancy, but he had found their skills lacking. "A blood link is the most powerful connection possible. Short of killing Aldane, there is nothing I can do to obscure the child's location."

Sykhana fanged glare turned in his direction.

"The Vessel must be protected," said Skaloban.

Ultorin threw back his head and roared with laughter, the cords in his neck standing out. His mood swings had gotten worse, lately. "Let them come. Let them come! I will leave them screaming in pools of their own blood!"

"Undoubtedly," said Malavost. "However, if I agree with honored Skaloban. The Vessel's security is paramount. Even you must agree, Ultorin - without the Vessel, you shall not have your vengeance."

Ultorin's gray-bearded lips twisted into a scowl, but he nodded.

"Sykhana was pursued from Knightcastle," said Malavost, "and most likely her pursuers have joined forces with Lord Mazael. Who, as I need not remind you, is a most dangerous foe." Ultorin's snarl intensified - Mazael's escape from their trap had left him in a rage for days. "Therefore, I suggest we take action."

"What is your plan, wizard?" said Skaloban.

Malavost told them.

Ultorin laughed again, mad and wild, Skaloban hissed in approval, and even Sykhana gave a cautious nod.

Of course, Malavost's plan might get Ultorin killed. But that was acceptable. He was an expendable tool. The only one Malavost really needed alive was Aldane Roland.

The Vessel.

~

MAZAEL SLEPT, and dreamed:

He galloped across the plains, Lion blazing in his fist, Challenger breathing hard beneath him. A calibah, a changeling, raced before him, Aldane Roland trapped in her arms. He heard the baby wailing, heard Rachel sobbing in fear.

Mazael gritted his teeth and urged Challenger faster.

The changeling would not escape him.

Suddenly the changeling veered to the right, moving away from the dark mass of the Great Mountains.

Veering towards the south.

Always towards the south.

And then Ultorin appeared, his bloodsword a swirl of darkness and flame in his armored fist. His eyes had turned a sulfurous yellow, and veins of darkness pulsed and throbbed beneath his skin. He looked demonic, deformed, a man taken by dark powers and twisted into a monster.

Mazael leapt from Challenger's back and raced to meet him. Lion met bloodsword in a dozen blows, blue flame struggling against shadow and blood-colored light. But Ultorin had grown stronger, and faster, and he drove Mazael back. Mazael jerked Lion back and forth to meet Ultorin's blows, looking for an opening.

And then a blur of black fur shot past Mazael.

Ultorin bellowed, and the great black wolf ripped at his hamstrings. The Dominiar knight fell to his knees, screaming, and Mazael whipped Lion around in a two-handed cut.

Ultorin's head jumped off his shoulders and rolled across the ground. Black slime oozed and trickled from his neck, and his headless corpse slumped to the earth with a rattle of armor. Mazael stared at the black wolf, Ultorin forgotten, looking into the wolf's blazing blue eyes.

They looked so familiar, so very familiar...

Then he realized that the wolf was female.

"Who are you?" whispered Mazael.

The wolf trembled, and for a moment Mazael thought she would flee from him. But she took a step forward, fangs bared, and Mazael followed her gaze.

To the west, towards Cravenlock Town.

MAZAEL AWOKE, dawn sunlight streaming through the balcony door.

War horns echoed in his ears.

Cravenlock Town was under attack again.

11

THE BLACK WOLF

"Aye, my lord," said Sir Tanam Crowley, "it's bad."

Mazael hurried across the courtyard towards the stables. Rufus handed him his gauntlets, and then sprinted off to prepare Challenger.

"How many?" said Mazael.

"At least five thousand strong," said Tanam. "Almost certainly more. They're heading straight for Cravenlock Town."

Mazael cursed. "There are only three hundred militiamen at the town. Five thousand Malrags will crush them. That's enough to take the castle itself, if the balekhan keeps its wits."

Or if Ultorin led them. Or Malavost. Especially Malavost. Ultorin might command the Malrags, but Mazael suspected that Malavost did a great deal of Ultorin's thinking.

"We've not enough men here, my lord," said Tanam. "I am loath to say this, but the wisest course is to fall back to the castle and wait for Lord Richard to relieve you. Castle Cravenlock is strong. You can hold out until my lord Richard arrives."

"No," said Mazael. "I will not abandon my people to death at the hands of the Malrags. Toraine is camped to the south of the castle, with seven hundred horsemen. Send your fastest scouts to him, Sir

Tanam, and ask him to ride north with all speed. We can destroy the Malrags, if we catch them between the town's walls, my men, and Toraine's men."

Assuming, of course, that Toraine simply did not sit back and let Mazael get slaughtered. He hoped Toraine's lust for battle would overcome his desire to see Mazael dead.

Tanam frowned, but nodded. "Aye, my lord, as you say. The gods go with you."

"And you," said Mazael. "Sir Hagen! We ride at once!"

Hagen bellowed orders to the knights and armsmen, who hastened to their horses.

"Mazael!"

Gerald ran towards him, clad in armor and surcoat. Behind him hurried the sixty Roland armsmen and knights still fit to fight, the grooms leading their horses.

"We are with you," said Gerald.

Mazael shook his head. "This isn't your fight. And if you die in the Grim Marches, Lord Malden will have war with Lord Richard."

Gerald shook his head. "The San-keth have my son, and my only path to getting him back lies through the Malrags. Besides, you need every man who can ride and fight."

He was right about that.

"Then I am glad to have you with me," said Mazael, as Rufus led Challenger over. Mazael swung up into the saddle, looking around as Rufus passed up his shield and lance. Timothy, Gerald's wizard Circan, and Lucan sat atop their horses, ready to fight, though Lucan looked ill, as usually did of late. Sir Aulus was ready with the banner and the war horn, while Sir Tanam and his raiders moved into position behind Mazael's men. Mazael was glad the Old Crow remained at Castle Cravenlock – few had Tanam's skill at hit-and-run tactics.

Tactics Mazael would need to come through this battle victorious.

"Sir Hagen!" said Mazael. "We ride for the town!"

Mazael kicked Challenger to a trot and rode for the castle's gate. Hagen bellowed orders, and the horsemen fell in behind Mazael, alongside Gerald's and Tanam's men. Mazael looked up, his eyes sweeping the wall.

He saw Rachel upon the battlements, her hands at her throat. She would be able to see the entire battle from the castle's wall.

Mazael hoped he did not get her husband killed in front of her.

They rode for Cravenlock Town.

~

A BLACK STORM of Malrags swept towards Cravenlock Town. Crossbowmen on the walls fired into the Malrags, as did militiamen with short horse bows. Every arrow and every quarrel found a mark, throwing dead Malrags onto earth that had already been soaked in black blood.

But for every Malrag slain, a dozen more surged forward.

They had ropes with grappling hooks, using them to scale the walls like misshapen, black-armored spiders. Militiamen on the ramparts attacked with long spears or thrown rocks, and Malrags fell from the ropes to crush others beneath them. But more and more Malrags gained the battlements, struggling against the militiamen.

"We should charge them, at once," said Gerald. "If we get them away from the gate..."

"No," said Mazael. "Too many of them. We need to distract them until Toraine gets here. Sir Aulus! The archers!"

Aulus blew three quick blasts on his horn, and the mounted archers surged into the gap between Mazael's horsemen and the Malrags. A storm of arrows fell into the Malrag lines, and the archers veered into two groups, still releasing arrow after arrow. The Malrags howled in rage, and the outer ranks broke away, chasing after the mounted archers.

Lucan had been right. The Malrags were cunning and clever, but lacked the ability to override their bloody lusts. Without a strong mind to direct them, their desire to kill and torture often overrode their thinking.

Such as the Malrags now chasing mounted archers they had no chance of catching.

"Now?" said Gerald.

"Not yet," said Mazael, looking to the south. He saw a plume of dust around the castle's hill. "Sir Aulus! Tell Sir Tanam to make the Malrags bleed!"

Aulus blew the signal on his horn.

And the Old Crow's light horsemen leapt into the fray. Unlike Mazael's heavy knights, Tanam Crowley's men wore leather armor, and bore curved sabers, light spears, and bundled javelins. As the scattered groups of Malrags pursued the mounted archers, Tanam's men crashed into them. They stabbed with spears and slashed with sabers as they galloped past, leaving Malrags bleeding in the dirt.

In a matter of moments Tanam's men killed every Malrag that had broken ranks, and still crossbow bolts and arrows fell from the battlements. The Malrag attack stalled, and the creatures began to break in confusion. The mounted archers and Tanam's raiders returned to their places alongside Mazael's knights and armsmen, ready for another attack.

A distant trumpet blast rang over the battle.

Mazael turned again, saw horsemen racing from the direction of Castle Cravenlock, hundreds of them. At their head they flew a banner with a black dragon on a red field, and below that, the sigil of a gray tower with a dead man hanging from its balcony.

The banner of Toraine Mandragon, Lord of Hanging Tower.

Mazael grinned. It seemed that Toraine's desire for glory had won over his wish to become Lord of Castle Cravenlock.

"Now," he said to Gerald, "we charge. Aulus! Send the archers and the raiders to attack the flanks. Hagen! Take command of the knights and armsmen, and ride for the center. We'll throw them into disarray, and when Toraine arrives, he'll smash them like a melon beneath a hammer."

Aulus blew a string of blasts on his horn, the mounted archers and the raiders galloping forward at the signal. Mazael wheeled Challenger around, shield on his left arm, the lance ready in his right hand, Lion waiting in its scabbard at his hip. Behind him he heard the clank of armor as the knights settled into position.

Aulus sounded the charge.

Challenger leapt forward with an excited whiny, the earth rumbling as Mazael's heavy horsemen galloped forward. The Malrags tried to scramble into a defensive position. But as before, Mazael's tactics had worked, and the Malrags efforts were too little, too late. Mazael's lance plunged through a Malrag's throat, even as another perished under Challenger's heavy hooves, and all around him knights and armsmen smashed into the Malrags.

The Malrag lines collapsed like rotten ice.

Lucan kept well to the rear of the battle, Circan and Timothy on either side of him.

His hand tightened around his staff's cold black metal. He had expected Circan to react badly to him, to the Dragon's Shadow, the final student of the renegade Marstan. But the pale-haired wizard had followed Lucan into battle without question.

Lucan felt the staff against his palm, the edges of the sigils digging into his fingers.

He wanted to draw the staff's power into him, wanted to fill his veins with its fiery strength and strike down the Malrags. But he dared not, not unless the need was dire. The staff's power was too much, its strength overthrowing his reason and turning him into a murderous madman.

And the power left something behind. Some darkness, some illness. Like silt left behind when floodwaters retreated. A taint, building up within him, leaving a little more every time he used the staff's Demonsouled power. Lucan didn't know what the accumulation of darkness would do to him.

He suspected it would not be good.

He watched as Mazael's knights crashed into the Malrags, ripping through their lines like a thunderbolt.

"We should aid Lord Mazael," said Timothy, flexing his hands.

"No," said Lucan. "Not yet. Lord Mazael can take care of himself." He looked to the south, scowling. "And my brother shall be here soon. If the Black Dragon is good at anything, it's killing things. But neither of them can deal with the Malrag shamans on their own."

Or with Malavost. And Lucan doubted that he could handle Malavost on his own. Even with Circan's and Timothy's aid.

Another war horn rang out, and Toraine Mandragon's knights plunged into the collapsing Malrag lines. Lucan saw his brother, clad in his armor of black dragon scales, his sword carving through the Malrags' gray hides.

"Such a large warband," said Timothy, shaking his head. "We've never yet seen so many Malrags grouped for a single attack. To what purpose?"

"I know not," said Lucan. "Whatever the reason, we shall kill..."

He felt the surge of power in the air, his skin crawling with the presence of potent magical force.

Malavost.

THE MALRAGS BROKE AND RAN, Mazael's men driving them towards the open plains. He saw Toraine's men slam into the Malrags, heard the ring of steel on steel, men and Malrags screaming in rage and pain. Mazael drove his lance through a Malrag's chest, pinning the creature to the earth, and lost his grip on the weapon as Challenger galloped past.

He ripped Lion free from its scabbard, the blade an inferno of azure light, and the Malrags shied away from him.

Oh, yes. They had learned to fear Lion's flames.

Then he saw the banner flying over the nearby Malrags. A black banner, adorned with a silver eight-pointed star, once the sigil of the Knights Dominiar, now the banner of Ultorin.

Mazael spun Challenger around and raced for the banner, striking left and right, Lion trailing blue flame. Ultorin was here. If

Mazael could get close enough, if he could engage the renegade Dominiar, he could end this war here and now.

He ripped through the last rank of Malrags before the banner.

Ultorin sat atop his black-armored warhorse, gray-bearded face snarling. The expression made him look bestial, and for a moment Mazael thought that Ultorin's eyes flashed yellow. The bloodsword rested in his right hand, wreathed in darkness and crimson flame. A dozen Malrags stood around Ultorin, crossbows ready in their hands.

Mazael blinked in surprise. Crossbows? He had not yet seen the Malrags use any bows, and...

As one the Malrags lifted their crossbows and squeezed the trigger.

Mazael brought his shield up, two bolts thudding into the heavy wood. But another bolt plunged into his shoulder, and another into his leg, and three slammed into Chariot's flank. The big horse screamed and reared even as another bolt slammed into Mazael's hip, knocking him from the saddle to the ground.

He heard the clatter of armor as Ultorin's horse raced forward.

LUCAN SPOTTED MALAVOST.

The renegade wizard sat atop his horse, green flame sparking and flashing around his hands. Lucan started a spell of his own, and just in time. A blast of green lightning sizzled out of the sky and exploded against Lucan's wards, the air spitting and snarling with the strain of competing magical energies.

Apparently Malavost had learned a trick or two from the Malrag shamans.

"Timothy!" shouted Lucan. "Now!"

Malavost was not the only one with tricks. Timothy deBlanc was a good and brave man, but only a mediocre wizard. No matter how hard he tried, he would never match Lucan's level of power and skill, and certainly never approach the power of someone like Malavost.

But he was rather good with spells of illusion.

Timothy muttered the incantation, silver light dancing around his fingers, and gestured. The air shimmered, and a duplicate of Lucan upon his horse appeared, an image wrought of light and magic. And then another duplicate, and another, and images of Circan and Timothy as well.

Only a minor magic, a simple trick...but an effective one.

Malavost's pale blue eyes darted back and forth as the images raced in circles around him. He flung out his hands, green sparks flying from his fingers, and every spark caused an image to shatter into shards of silver light. But there were too many of them, far too many, and he came nowhere near striking Lucan and the others.

And as Timothy maintained the illusion spell, Lucan cast a spell of his own, as did Circan. Circan conjured spirit beasts, a half-dozen translucent lions with manes of hissing snakes and barbed tails, beasts that leapt past the Malrags to spring upon Malavost. Lucan unleashed his will and power in a strike, hammering at Malavost's wards. The blast knocked Malavost off his horse, sending the wizard sprawling to the ground.

Two of Circan's spirit beasts leapt upon Malavost's horse, ripping it to shreds, while the remaining four attacked Malavost himself. For a burning moment Lucan thought they had succeeded, that Malavost was finished. But instead Malavost rolled to one knee and thrust out a hand. Silver mist swirled around him, and he conjured spirit beasts of his own, creatures that looked like the monstrous offspring of squids and rabid dogs. His beasts tore into Circan's, driving them away.

Lucan loosed another psychokinetic blast, but Malavost deflected it, redirecting the spell into one of Mazael's armsmen, knocking the unfortunate man from his horse. Malavost launched into another spell at once, silver light flashing around him, and clapped his hands with a shout.

The air rippled, and all of the illusionary images vanished without a trace. Timothy groaned and fell to his knees, hands flying to his temples. Circan grimaced, his face a mask of concentration as he drove his spirit beasts against Malavost's creatures.

Malavost's pale blue gaze fell upon Lucan, a smile spreading over his face.

~

MAZAEL STRUGGLED to his feet as Ultorin's massive horse thundered towards him. Agony shot up his wounded arm and leg, but he threw himself to the side, throwing up his shield to protect himself.

Just in time, too.

Ultorin's bloodsword plunged down, the edge clipping the top of Mazael's shield, and even the glancing hit was enough to shatter the heavy wood. Mazael staggered back, his arm numb from the blow, his head swimming, his heart pounding, his vision blurring.

Behind him, Challenger groaned and collapsed, flanks motionless.

His horse was dead. But how? None of the crossbow bolts had dealt him a fatal wound. Had they struck an artery?

A wave of dizziness washed over Mazael, his blurred vision worsening, and he realized the answer with a chill.

Poison. Specifically, the poison produced by the fangs of a calibah - Sykhana herself, no doubt. One bite from a calibah's fangs had enough poison to kill a man, and Mazael had taken three crossbow bolts topped with the stuff. No doubt his Demonsouled essence had kept him alive, and would soon heal the damage from the poison.

But not soon enough to keep Ultorin from taking his head.

This hadn't been an attack. It was a trap.

Ultorin brought his horse around for another pass, and Mazael braced himself, trying to keep his balance.

~

THERE WAS no other choice left.

Lucan drew the staff's power into himself. The carvings along the staff's black length burned with blood-colored light - the same light, he realized, that surrounded Malavost's bloodsword. The power surged up, reaching for Lucan...but he only drew upon a portion of it, a pittance.

A trickle. He yearned to take more, to fill himself with the burning might, but he dared not.

Besides, the bloodstaff's raw power had failed against Malavost's skill. Lucan would need something else to defeat him.

Malavost laughed and again brought emerald lightning thundering down out of the sky. Lucan thrust out his staff, casting a ward, and sent the blast into the earth.

"Fool," said Malavost. "Even with that bloodstaff you cannot hope to overcome me. Why not simply lie down and wait for the end? I promise you that it will be quick and..."

Lucan ignored his taunts and cast another spell, reaching out with his will. With the staff's power churning through him, he felt the darkness of the Malrags all around him, the joy their malignant spirits took in slaying and killing.

He also felt a veneer of power over their darkness, something like chains of fire.

Ultorin's control.

Lucan severed those chains, and forced his own will over the nearby Malrags.

A dozen Malrags froze, their colorless eyes going wide, their gray lips peeling back from yellow fangs in a furious snarl. Lucan felt their hatred, their endless rage. He was not Demonsouled...but the staff had been infused with the might of Mazael Cravenlock's blood, and that gave Lucan the power to command them.

"Kill him!" he bellowed, pointing his burning staff at Malavost. "Kill him now!"

The Malrags under his control sprang at Malavost, black spears and axes drawn back for the kill.

Malavost's eyes widened in shock for just a moment, and then narrowed as he struck out. A psychokinetic blast flung four Malrags to the ground. His spirit beasts turned from Circan's and leapt upon the Malrags. Lucan let more of the staff's power pour into him and extended his spell, forcing his will and control over more of Ultorin's

Malrags. Dozens of the creatures threw themselves at Malavost, obeying Lucan's command. Circan staggered forward, panting, and cast another spell, conjuring more spirit creatures to unleash against Malavost.

Malavost snarled and threw his hands at the sky.

And a torrent of emerald lightning bolts screamed down around him, four, five, a dozen, ripping at the earth, dissipating Circan's spirit creatures, and tearing Lucan's enslaved Malrags to smoking chunks of charred flesh. The shock wave of hot air knocked Lucan to the ground, breaking his concentration.

His link to the bloodstaff broke, and again nausea and dizziness flooded through him.

But not as much as before.

When the air cleared he staggered to his feet, looking for Malavost.

But Malavost had vanished.

~

AGAIN ULTORIN'S bloodsword came down, and Mazael only just avoided having his head split in half. Instead the sword clanged off his left shoulder, destroying the armor plates and aggravating the crossbow wound. He had ripped the quarrels from his arm and leg, blood gushing over his armor, and the wounds began to knit themselves closed.

But not nearly fast enough.

Ultorin wheeled around for another pass, his horse's iron-shod hooves tearing at the earth. Then a blast of green lighting flashed out of the sky to the west, and then another, the thunderclaps rolling over the clamor of the battle. Ultorin stopped, his iron-colored eyes narrowed, and he lifted his bloodsword.

A shiver went through the battling Malrags.

"What?" roared Ultorin, looking around. "Someone dares? The Malrags are mine! Mine!"

For a moment he forgot Mazael.

Mazael surged forward, staggering like a drunk, and swung with both hands on Lion's hilt. He doubted he could penetrate Ultorin's black armor, or even the horse's coat of mail.

A coat that did not reach to the great black horse's fetlocks. Lion sank deep into the horse's right front leg, and the great beast screamed in agony, rearing up. But it could not support the weight of its armor on two legs, and collapsed with another scream, Ultorin falling from the saddle.

Mazael sprang at Ultorin, hoping to end their fight and the war with one solid blow. But his aim was off, and Lion's point tore a groove in Ultorin's cuirass Ultorin kicked out, his armored boot crashing against Mazael's wounded hip. Mazael staggered back, his leg pulsing with agony, and only just managed to keep from falling.

Ultorin sprang to his feet, his bloodsword a blur of darkness and flame. Mazael parried and blocked, staggering, barely keeping ahead of Ultorin's furious attacks. His head swam, and he cursed his folly. He could have taken Ultorin, could have defeated the rogue Dominiar.

But not with calibah poison pumping through his veins.

Ultorin drew back his bloodsword, his eyes filled with enraged glee, and Mazael knew that he could not block the attack in time.

And then a black blur shot past him and sprang upon Ultorin.

Mazael caught a glimpse of the great black wolf from his dreams, her blue eyes alight with wrath, her fangs flashing like daggers of white ice. Ultorin screamed, lashing at the wolf's side with his bloodsword, but he could not get enough momentum behind his blow to pierce the thick black fur.

Mazael staggered forward, all his weight and faltering strength behind Lion's point. The blade crunched through black armor and plunged into Ultorin's side, azure flame pouring into the wound. Ultorin roared in agony, his free hand raking at the wolf.

"Aid me!" bellowed Ultorin. "Aid me, now!"

As one, a dozen nearby Malrags turned, ignoring their foes, and sprinted at Mazael. He ripped Lion free from Ultorin's side and parried a swing, sidestepped, and killed a Malrag with a slash across the throat. Two Malrags leapt at the wolf, and she sprang off Ultorin with a snarl.

Mazael wheeled, killed another Malrag, and tried to force his way towards Ultorin. Even wounded, even with calibah poison in his blood, he could still match the Malrags. And Ultorin did not look well. Blood poured from the wound Mazael had carved in his side, and the black wolf's claws had torn away the right half of his face, rending skin and muscle to reveal the bone underneath. If Mazael could just get close enough to deal a mortal wound...

Ultorin plunged his bloodsword into the chest of a passing Malrag. The sigils carved into the blade blazed, the darkness surrounding the sword deepening. The Malrag withered, crumbling into ashes, and as it did, Ultorin's wounds vanished, the bloody gashes in his face and side disappearing. He growled and stalked through the Malrags, his yellow-flecked gray eyes locked on Mazael's face. Mazael tried to cut his way through the Malrags, but to no avail. There were simply too many of them, and more and more flung themselves at him. For a moment he wondered if Ultorin had called every Malrag on the battlefield to attack him.

The Malrags drove Mazael back, and Ultorin circled around to the side. Mazael gritted his teeth, trying to break free from the press, but to no avail. With his attention fixed on the Malrags, it would be the easier thing in the world for Ultorin to plunge his bloodsword into Mazael's back.

The darkness-wreathed blade came up...

The black wolf crashed into Ultorin once more, snarling, fangs and claws raking at armor. Ultorin spat out a curse and swung, the edge of his sword digging into the wolf's side. She reared back with a snarl of pain, blood flowing over the cut, and stumbled back.

And for a moment, Mazael felt a ghostly pain along his ribs, as if he had been struck there. As if Ultorin's bloodsword had wounded him, instead of the wolf. Ultorin stalked towards the wolf, murder in his eyes, and sudden fury erupted in Mazael.

The wolf staggered back, her hind right leg twitching as it tried to support her weight.

"No!" roared Mazael, sprinting towards Ultorin, his pain and weakness forgotten. Ultorin would not harm her. He would not! Ultorin whirled and snarled a command, and Malrags, dozens of Malrags, turned towards Mazael.

Mazael raised Lion's burning blade before his face, the azure light brighter than the bloody glow around Ultorin's sword...

Then Mazael's knights crashed into the gathered Malrags, swinging swords and heavy maces. Gerald rode at their head, shouting commands, his silver longsword flashing. The Malrags fell, overwhelmed by the charge of heavy horse. Ultorin's eyes narrowed, and he seized the reins of a passing horse and swung up into the empty saddle. Mazael started after him, but it was too late. Ultorin galloped from the field, trampling down any Malrags that got in his way. The knights continued their charge, the Malrags fleeing before them, and soon Mazael was alone on the battlefield, save for the dead.

And the black wolf.

She stood a short distance away, glaring at him, sides heaving with her breath.

"You save my life," said Mazael, taking a hesitant step towards the wolf. Now that the fury of battle had passed, his head ached and swam, and his half-healed crossbow wounds throbbed with pain.

The wolf backed away, snarling.

"Who are you?" said Mazael. "I mean you no harm. You've saved my life, twice now, whoever or whatever you are." He took another step forward, and this time the wolf did not move. "You're wounded. Come back with me, to Castle Cravenlock, and I'll see that you..."

The wolf backed away, eyes fixed on him.

No. Not at him. The wolf was staring at his belt.

At his belt?

Mazael looked down. Lion's empty scabbard hung from his right hip, and his sheathed dagger waited on his right. Besides his dagger dangled a slender chain, threaded through a large silver coin.

The silver coin that Romaria had once carried.

"This?" said Mazael, lifting the chain. The silver coin swung and flashed. "Is this what you want? It belonged to the only woman I ever loved, and..."

The wolf trembled...and changed. Her form melted and blurred, flowing like water, and then shrank. One moment a black wolf the size of a horse crouched a dozen steps from Mazael. The next a naked woman stood in the wolf's place, her black hair wild and tangled, her blue eyes ablaze with madness, her pale skin streaked with Malrag blood.

And for a moment Mazael could do nothing but stare, his mind frozen.

Romaria.

It was Romaria Greenshield. The only woman he had ever loved, dead now for two years. Dead at the hands of the Old Demon, his father, her chest reduced to a blackened ruin as she lay motionless upon the floor of Castle Cravenlock's chapel.

Impossible. It was impossible. Mazael had seen her die.

"Romaria?" he whispered.

She stared at him, face half-hidden behind a curtain of tangled black hair, and a strange mixture of longing and fear and rage crossed over her features, all mingled together.

She looked utterly insane.

"This can't be," whispered Mazael. "I saw you die. I saw you die. How..."

It couldn't be her. He had watched as her body had been laid in a crypt below Castle Cravenlock. He had sent a letter to her father, the Lord of Deepforest Keep, informing him of her death, though he had never heard an answer. This had to be a trick, some phantom conjured out of Malavost's magic.

Yet this was Romaria Greenshield. He knew it, knew it in his very bones.

He reached for her, and she backed away, lips pulled back from her teeth in a snarl, fingers hooked into claws.

"I'm sorry," said Mazael, the words pouring out of him. "I'm sorry, it was my fault you died, I brought you to your death, I..."

She trembled, anguish filling her face, and lifted a shaking hand towards him.

Metal rasped against the earth.

"My lord? I..."

Lucan Mandragon limped towards him, leaning upon his black staff. His cowl was thrown back, and he looked weary, bone-weary. Then he saw Romaria, and his black eyes grew wide with alarm.

Romaria growled, and her form blurred. In an instant she became the great black wolf once more, her blue eyes blazing like frozen stars. Then she turned and ran, moving with superhuman speed.

"Romaria!" said Mazael. "Romaria!"

But she did not turn back.

12

CENOTAPH

For a moment Lucan seemed at a loss for words.

"That," he said at last. "That was Lady Romaria, wasn't it?"

Mazael nodded, too shocked to answer.

"You said she had been killed," said Lucan.

"She was killed!" said Mazael in sudden anger. "Do you think me a liar? I saw the Old Demon strike her down with a spell. I saw her die. I saw them put her body in the tomb. She...she cannot possibly be alive."

Lucan scowled. "A trick, then. Some spell of Malavost's. Or perhaps a phantasm conjured by a Malrag shaman. It sounds like the sort of petty cruelty they would enjoy."

"But...it was her," said Mazael. "I was sure of it. And she was the black wolf, too. She tried to kill Ultorin, and helped me against the balekhan in Cravenlock Town. If Malavost or the shamans conjured the illusion, why would it attack Ultorin?" He pulled off his helmet, raked a hand through his sweating hair. "For that matter, the black wolf was no illusion. It left wounds on both Ultorin and the balekhan. But how could it be Romaria?"

"She wasn't human," said Lucan, voice quiet. "At least not entirely.

One half of her soul was human, while the other half was Elderborn."

"I know that," said Mazael, and his frown deepened. "You know something, don't you? Something from Marstan's knowledge."

"It is only a suspicion," said Lucan. "Nothing more. And what you saw could very well have been an illusion. You loved Romaria...much as I once loved Tymaen. If Tymaen appeared before me again, beckoning to me...I don't know if I could disbelieve it. Could you?"

Mazael said nothing.

"But there is a way," said Lucan, "to determine whether what you saw was the real Romaria Greenshield or not."

"How?" said Mazael.

"The tomb," said Lucan. "Go to the crypt below the chapel. If her body remains there, then you will know that you saw only an illusion of some kind."

Mazael nodded. That made sense. But first, he had responsibilities. He walked along the town's wall, to the Cravenlock banner flying over a mass of horsemen. Dead Malrags carpeted the ground, interspersed here and there with the body of a slain knight or armsman.

Mazael saw no sign of Ultorin. The renegade Dominiar had escaped, again.

Lucan paused for a moment, frowning at the ground. Then he knelt, scooped up some dirt, and followed Mazael.

"This was a trap for us," said Mazael, "wasn't it?"

"Aye," said Lucan. "We survived it, though."

If just barely.

A short walk brought Mazael to his gathered men.

"My lord!" said Sir Aulus, straightening in the saddle. "We thought you slain!"

Mazael made himself smile. "It will take more than Ultorin and his Malrags to finish me. What news?"

"The Malrags are broken," said Sir Hagen, maneuvering his horse alongside Aulus's. "Most of them are slain, taken in the charge or shot down by the militiamen on the walls, and the rest have fled. Sir Tanam's men are pursuing them."

"Where's Sir Gerald?" said Mazael. Gods, if he had gotten Rachel's husband and Lord Malden's youngest son killed...

"I'm here," said Gerald, striding past the horses. His armor was battered, and stained with Malrag blood, but he looked otherwise unharmed. "I lost my horse to a Malrag spear. Gods, those devils are fierce fighters."

"Aye," said Hagen, "but we sent them running! Didn't we, lads?"

A cheer went up from the men.

"Hagen," said Mazael. "Take command here. Have Timothy and Circan see to the wounded."

"Where will you be?" said Gerald. "Surely you don't mean to ride out in pursuit of Ultorin by yourself?"

"No," said Mazael. "I...have an urgent errand at the castle that cannot wait. See to things here, Hagen. I will return shortly."

He took the horse of a slain armsman and left, Lucan following him.

A SHORT TIME later Mazael reined up before the doors of Castle Cravenlock's chapel. It looked like a smaller version of the town's church, with the same domed roof, high windows, and solid walls of dark stone. Rufus raced from the stables to take his reins.

"My lord," said Rufus. "What has happened? Are..."

"We are victorious," said Mazael. "The Malrags have been driven back. Wait here." He saw Rachel hurrying down from the ramparts, skirts gathered in her hands as she ran. "Tell Lady Rachel that the Malrags were defeated and Gerald is safe. Don't let her follow me."

"But my lord," said Rufus. "I..."

"Do as I say!" said Mazael, pushing open the chapel's doors, Lucan following.

The chapel was almost full, mostly with women and the priests. The wives and mothers and sisters and daughters of his knights and armsmen, come to pray for their sons and brothers and husbands and fathers. They turned hopeful, terrified eyes towards him.

Some of those women had become widows and orphans today.

One of the priests hurried over, his brown robe rustling against the floor. "My lord? Are...are we victorious?"

"We are," said Mazael, and a relieved sigh went through the women. He wondered how many of them would weep before the day was done. "I need to get into the crypt. Now."

The priest blinked. "The crypt? But..."

"Now," said Mazael.

The priest took one look at his expression and hastened to obey. He led Mazael around the dais and altar, past the spot where the Old Demon had slain Romaria, to the back of the chapel. A massive iron door stood in the wall, and the priest unlocked it, revealing a set of stone stairs descending into darkness.

"I will fetch candles, my lord," said the priest.

Lucan smiled and lifted his hand, a ball of blue light hovering over his palm. "No need. I brought my own."

The priest made the sign to ward off evil, and Mazael descended into the crypt. Lucan followed, his ball of light throwing back the darkness, bathing everything in a pale blue glow. The stairs ended in Castle Cravenlock's crypt, a massive series of vaults supported by pillars of glistening brick. The air was damp and cold and chill. The dead of the House of Cravenlock lined the walls, lying in stone niches sealed by leaden plates. Each plate held the name of the deceased, along with an epitaph.

"Here," said Mazael. "We laid her here."

He walked along the wall, past the tomb of Lord Adalon, whom he had believed to be his father, and Lady Arissa, his mother, who had hated him. Next to them lay his two older brothers, both slain in Lord Adalon's war with Lord Richard. Besides them rested a niche for Mitor Cravenlock. An empty niche - Skhath's necromancy had destroyed Mitor's body utterly, leaving not even ashes to bury.

Romaria Greenshield's tomb lay besides them.

Mazael took a deep breath...and stopped.

The niche was open. The leaden plate lay forgotten upon the floor. Mazael stepped forward, reaching into the niche.

"Light, damn it," he said. "Get the light here."

Lucan lifted his hand, the blue light shining brighter. Inside the niche Mazael saw an open wooden coffin, its lids and sides scored with deep grooves, as if from razor-edged claws. Within the coffin lay the shattered remains of a bastard sword, its blade broken by the Old Demon's powerful magic.

But there was no trace of Romaria. No corpse, no bones. Nothing. She was gone.

"Oh, gods," said Mazael. "I buried her alive."

Lucan blinked. "My lord?"

"I buried her alive," said Mazael. He barely recognized the sound of his own voice. "I loved her, and she was wounded, and I buried her alive! I am fool!" He had Lion in his hand now, his shouts echoing off the vaulted ceiling. "Those damned priests! Why didn't they tell me? It is their responsibility to tend the crypt, why didn't they tell me?"

"Lord Mazael..."

"I did this to her!" said Mazael. He started towards the crypt stairs, Lion still in his hand. "The priests will answer to me! They'll tell me why they didn't hear her screaming, asking for help..."

Something slapped him hard across the shoulders, sent him to the crypt floor with a clatter of armor. Mazael rolled to one knee, stunned. Lucan stood over him, hand raised, eyes narrowed and pale face tense.

He had just cast a spell at Mazael. That alone shocked Mazael back to lucidity. Lucan had never before lifted his hand against him.

"Forgive me," said Lucan, "but in your...state of mind, it seemed unwise to let you confront the priests."

"Yes," said Mazael. The chapel was still no doubt full of frightened women. How would they have reacted to their lord stalking out the crypt, waving his sword and screaming threats at the priests? "Yes, yes, you're right." He got to his feet, rammed Lion back into its scabbard. "But...Romaria. How is this even possible? I know what death looks like, and I saw her die."

"Perhaps," said Lucan.

"You said you had a suspicion?" said Mazael.

Lucan nodded. "Lady Romaria was half-human, half-Elderborn. Such hybrids are incredibly rare, for a very good reason. The souls of humans and Elderborn do not easily mingle, and the soul of a child born to an Elderborn parent and a human parent is often...unstable. Sometimes spectacularly so."

"Unstable?" said Mazael. "What do you mean?"

Lucan's voice took on the cold, distant tone it often did when he spoke with Marstan's knowledge. "The Elderborn are not like us, Lord Mazael. Their souls are infused with earth magic, ancient and fell. Much in the same way that the Demonsouled half of your soul is infused with power, though the Elderborn are not tainted in the same way as the Demonsouled. The Elderborn can become far more powerful wizards than any human. They command the earth and elements, make the very rocks attack their foes. And they often have the power to change their shapes, to take on the forms of birds and beasts."

"Beasts?" said Mazael. "Like the a black wolf?"

"Yes. And that explains how she...survived the Old Demon's attack. The Old Demon struck her down with magic. And when he did, I believe, he fractured her soul. The spell expelled the human half of her soul from her body, and it latched onto the nearest available home."

"Where?" said Mazael.

Lucan smirked. No doubt Marstan had once smirked in the same way. "Why, you, my lord."

"Me?"

"You are only half-human yourself. Or a quarter-human, technically, since I suppose the Old Demon is only half-human. Which means you do not possess a complete human soul." His dark eyes bored into Mazael. "The human half of Romaria's soul fused with yours. And you made her effectively immortal, my lord. Death is the permanent sundering of soul and flesh, with the soul moving to the world beyond ours. But the human half of her soul was anchored to yours. It could not move on. Which means, I believe, the Elderborn half of her soul remained trapped in her damaged body. And the Elderborn half healed the wound the Old Demon dealt her."

"So she lay in agony for the last two years?" said Mazael, horrified.

"Probably not," said Lucan. "From what you described, the Old Demon's spell likely destroyed her heart and lungs. It would take years to repair the damage. Look – see the edges on the coffin, on the lead plate? Those cuts are fresh. No dust. Odds are she only clawed her way out of the tomb recently. Perhaps only a few hours before the first Malrag raid on Cravenlock Town."

"And that's why I dreamed of a black wolf," said Mazael. In some ways it was a relief – he had feared the Old Demon had sent the dreams. "Because half her soul was fused to mine. Ultorin wounded her, during our fight, and I...felt it. Only faintly. But I still felt it."

Lucan nodded.

"We have to find a way to help her," said Mazael. "If there is a way to help her?"

"Perhaps," said Lucan. "I...know a spell. A bit of Marstan's lore. It will expel the human half of Romaria's soul from you. It will return to her body, if you're close enough."

"How close?" said Mazael.

Lucan shrugged. "Close. At least five yards. You might have to be touching her for it to work."

"And how am I to manage that?" said Mazael. "She's terrified of me. And why not? I brought about her death, even if I did not will it. Whenever I've tried to approach her, she fled."

"Yet she aided you in battle," said Lucan. "Against the balekhan, against Ultorin himself. Clearly, she still has some feeling for you." He sighed. "Though, I must warn you. Obviously she has undergone a great deal of torment. Even if we restore her soul, her mind might well be destroyed."

"She might go mad, you mean," said Mazael.

Lucan nodded.

"We must still try," said Mazael. "I cannot...leave her like this. I owe her too much. I love her too much."

"So be it," said Lucan. "You will have my aid."

"How will we even find her?" said Mazael.

Lucan grinned, just for a moment. It made him look young. "With this." He reached into his cloak, withdrew a pouch filled with earth. "Romaria's blood spilled upon the earth when Ultorin wounded her. Not much, true...but enough that I can track her. To the ends of the earth, if need be."

"Much as Circan can do with my nephew," said Mazael.

"Yes," said Lucan.

"Then we shall go at once," said Mazael, gripping the younger man's shoulder. "Lucan, thank you. You are a true and loyal friend. Without your aid, I would have been slain a dozen times over the last year. And probably a dozen more times since the Malrags came."

Guilt flickered over Lucan's expression. "I am not a good man, my lord. I am not. I have only done the best I can."

Mazael nodded. "Let us go."

~

MAZAEL WALKED into the courtyard to find his men and Sir Tanam's waiting for him. Rachel clung to Gerald, cleaning the blood and sweat from his face and armor. Squires hurried back and forth, tending to the horses and armor.

"We're here, my lord," said Sir Hagen, his black-bearded face grim.

"Good," said Mazael. "Gerald!" Gerald walked over, Rachel still at his side. "Sir Hagen, Gerald. Both of you take command here. I...have a task, and I will return by nightfall."

"A task?" said Gerald. "What manner of task? Do you require my aid?"

"No," said Mazael. "Lucan and I will go alone. Any extra men will only slow us."

Sir Hagen scowled. "That is not wise, my lord. The countryside is crawling with Malrag scouting parties."

"Aye," said Sir Tanam. "My men think the Malrags' main host is on the move. So they'll have scouting parties out. As formidable as you are with that burning sword, and as powerful as my lord Lucan's arts are, I doubt the two of you can overcome a hundred Malrags."

"This is something I must do alone," said Mazael. "I owe a debt, and must discharge it. Trust me on this."

Rachel stared at him, a strange expression on her face. Ever since they had been children, she had been able to judge his mood simply by looking at him.

"This is," said Rachel, voice soft, "something Lord Mazael has to do, I think."

At last the men nodded. They did not look happy, but they nodded.

"Keep Toraine from making trouble while I'm gone," said Mazael, and he called for Rufus to bring him a horse.

∾

AN HOUR later Mazael rode south, atop an ill-tempered destrier named Hauberk, Lucan riding at his side. Lucan held a vial of blood-stained earth in his left hand, staff in his right, and every so often muttered a spell.

"Perhaps four miles to the south," said Lucan, blinking. "Maybe five. She's moving...but not quickly. We can overtake her, I think, and..."

He frowned, twisting in his saddle.

Mazael followed his gaze, saw a group of horsemen riding across the plains.

Towards them, actually. They flew no banners, and from a distance, their armor and clothing looked...strange. As they drew closer, Mazael saw that they wore leather and furs, cloaks of gray wolfskin hanging heavy from their shoulders.

A breath hissed through Lucan's teeth.

"What is it?" said Mazael.

"Those riders," said Lucan. "They're Elderborn."

13

THE LORD OF DEEPFOREST KEEP

"The Elderborn?" said Mazael, astonished. "Here?"

"Perhaps they've come to aid us against the Malrags," said Lucan, but there was doubt in his voice. "Sil Tarithyn came to White Rock, to fight against the Old Demon's undead."

"Only because they strayed into the Great Southern Forest," said Mazael. "And I have never heard of the Elderborn coming this far north."

"Perhaps they came in pursuit of a Malrag warband," said Lucan.

Mazael squinted. One of the Elderborn riders carried a banner, a black field with a green shield upon it.

"That banner," he said.

"I don't recognize it," said Lucan.

Mazael took a deep breath. "Romaria described it to me. It's the banner of Deepforest Keep. Of her father, Lord Athaelin."

"Did you not write him, telling him of her death?" said Lucan.

"I did," said Mazael, watching the riders draw closer. "I sent the letter with a messenger. A messenger that never returned." All the Elderborn were armed with the great bows they fired to deadly effect, quivers of obsidian-tipped arrows at their belts. At their head rode a human man, tall and strong, with thick black hair and a graying beard. A bronze shield hung from his back, and the hilt of a bastard sword jutted over his right shoulder.

Similar to the sword that lay broken in Romaria's empty tomb.

"Ah," said Lucan, raising his staff. "They want to kill you, don't they?"

"Possibly," said Mazael. "Don't attack unless I give the word."

He remained motionless atop Hauberk as the approaching riders reined up. There were a dozen Elderborn in all, their pale features angular and inhuman, their eyes like polished disks of silver and gold. Their leader, the human man, rode a few steps forward. Unlike the Elderborn, he wore a leather cuirass with steel studs, his cloak held in place by an elaborate bronze brooch. A bronze torque encircled his right arm, and a slender bronze diadem rested upon his brow. Age and weather had turned his face to seamed brown leather, but his blue eyes remained sharp and intense beneath his black hair.

Blue eyes, Mazael realized, exactly the same shape and color as Romaria's.

"So," said the blue-eyed man, his voice thick and rough. "You are Mazael Cravenlock?"

"I am," said Mazael.

"And do you know who I am?"

"No," said Mazael. "But if were to guess, I would say you were Athaelin Greenshield, Lord of Deepforest Keep."

The blue-eyed man gave a sharp nod. "Aye. That I am." He thumped his chest. "I am Athaelin, the Greenshield, Champion of Deepforest Keep and Defender of the Mountain."

"What brings you to the Grim Marches, my lord?" said Mazael. "Have you ridden to aid us against the Malrags? For we have sore need of help."

"A year ago," said Athaelin, as if Mazael had not spoken, "a messenger staggered beneath the Champion's Tower, wounded unto death. He bore a letter from you, telling of my daughter's death at the hands of the Old Demon. I would have ridden north, to take my vengeance at once, but the Seer bade caution. That, and I had no idea where to find you. At last the druids fashioned this for me with their spells," he held up a stone compass, its obsidian needle pointing straight at Mazael, "and I rode to the Grim Marches. And when I came to the Grim Marches, I found the land overrun with Malrags."

The Seer. Mazael remembered Romaria telling him of the ancient Elderborn druid, mighty in the magical arts of his people. He had prophesied that Mazael and Romaria would save each other, and that Romaria would save Deepforest Keep itself. His prophecy had proven half-correct; Romaria had indeed saved Mazael from himself. But after Romaria's death, he had thought the rest of the Seer's prophecy to be rubbish.

Now he was not so sure.

"Are you Demonsouled?" said Athaelin, his rough voice snapping Mazael out of his recollections.

"What?" said Mazael.

"The Seer and the druids will not give me a straight answer," said Athaelin, moving his horse closer. "They do not see such things as humans do. But if you are Demonsouled, I will kill you for what you did to my daughter."

"I did not kill Romaria!" said Mazael, voice hot with sudden anger.

"Oh?" said Athaelin. "The Seer told me her destiny was bound with yours. And she came north, and rode with you against your brother and the Old Demon. And now she is slain." There was a hint of pain in the rough voice, the blue eyes tight. "A curious coincidence, no?"

"I did not kill her!" said Mazael. He would not tell Athaelin the truth about his nature, not unless necessary. If the Elderborn knew that he was a child of the Old Demon, they would shoot him on the spot. "I tried to save her. I loved her."

A stir went through the Elderborn, and Athaelin's eyes seemed to throw sparks.

"You loved her?" he spat. "A curious way to show it, since she lies cold and dead!"

"It was the Old Demon," said Mazael. "He slew her, before I could stop him."

"A fine tale," said Athaelin. "I think it more likely that you are Demonsouled, that you slew Romaria with your own hands. That you now summoned the Malrags to the Grim Marches, and make war upon your neighbors..."

Mazael hands curled into fists, Hauberk's reins squealing against his gauntlets. He did not want to waste time while Romaria needed his aid. "Listen to me! Romaria is still alive."

"What?" said Athaelin, his voice cracking like a whip.

"She was half-human, half-Elderborn," said Mazael. "When the Old Demon struck her down, the spell sundered her soul. The human half broke loose, while the Elderborn half remained in her flesh. The power of her Elderborn soul changed her, forced her into the form of a beast. But Lucan," he gestured at the black-cloaked wizard, "has a spell that can repair the damage. I have to find her. She was wounded in a fight against the Malrags, and I fear it is only a matter of time before they catch up to her."

Athaelin glared, his expression becoming cold and deadly.

"Do you seriously," he said, "expect me to believe such tripe? You slew my daughter, Demonsouled, and I will have vengeance for it." His glare shifted to Lucan. "And I know of you, Dragon's Shadow. Richard Mandragon's pet necromancer, isn't it? Try to use your filthy arts, and I'll see you dead."

Lucan sneered. "Raise your hand against me, fool, and I will show you what my filthy arts can do."

The Elderborn lifted their bows, and Lucan gestured, green light crackling around his fingertips. Mazael yanked Lion from its scabbard, sure that things had come to a fight, but Athaelin spurred his horse between Lucan and the Elderborn.

"No!" said Athaelin. "This is between Mazael and me. I will not have anyone's blood shed to avenge my daughter but my own. Will you face me fairly, Mazael Cravenlock? Or will you hide behind your wizard?"

"Are you mad?" said Mazael. "Romaria is out there, we are surrounded by Malrag warbands, and you want to fight?"

"Among the men of Deepforest Keep," said Athaelin, "we settle our disputes with our own hands, and do not hide behind others. And you murdered my daughter. Will you then face me and answer my challenge?" His lip curled in contempt. "Or will you run and hide like a beaten dog?"

"I did not kill Romaria," said Mazael. "And if fighting you is the only way to prove it, then so be it."

"This is folly," hissed Lucan, voice low. "You have nothing to gain and everything to lose by killing Athaelin. Assuming you do even can kill him. I wager he is a capable swordsman, and you haven't recovered fully from those poisoned crossbow bolts."

Lucan was right. Athaelin had the hard hands and easy balance of a master swordsman. Mazael's wounds had closed, but his shoulder and leg still ached, and from time to time a wave of dizziness from the calibah poison swept through him.

"Nevertheless," said Mazael, "I must do this."

He slid from Hauberk's saddle, gripping the reins until the dizziness passed. Athaelin dismounted and dropped to the ground, moving with fluid grace. The Elderborn backed off, leaving Mazael and Athaelin in a ring about twenty paces across.

"If he gains the upper hand," murmured Lucan, "I will strike him down."

"Don't," said Mazael, though he doubted Lucan would listen.

Athaelin drew his bastard sword over his shoulder, the steel glimmering, its edges razor-sharp. "Are you ready?"

Mazael drew Lion. No azure flames appeared around its blade. Neither the Elderborn nor Athaelin were creatures of dark magic, after all. "I am."

"The defend yourself!"

Athaelin came at him in a run, his sword blurring over his hand in a two-handed grip. Mazael parried, dodged the next blow, launched a thrust of his own. Athaelin beat aside the thrust and side-stepped, his sword swinging for Mazael's neck. Mazael blocked the swing, Lion ringing against the bastard sword's blade.

For a moment they regarded each other in silence.

"I did not kill Romaria," said Mazael.

"I doubt that very much," said Athaelin. He circled to the left, and Mazael moved right. "First your letter arrives, claiming that Romaria died at the Old Demon's hands. The Seer confirms that a Demonsouled slew her. Then I arrive to find the Grim Marches overrun by Malrags, and you claim that she lives again? Yes, I doubt that very much."

He attacked, his sword like a bar of steel lightning. Mazael parried once, twice, thrice. Athaelin's fourth blow slipped past his guard and skidded across his chest, his armor just turning it. Had Mazael not been wearing his cuirass, the blow would have plunged into his heart.

He backed away, breathing hard, his chest aching from the thrust.

"Do you think I summoned the Malrags to make war upon my own lands?" said Mazael.

Athaelin's teeth flashed in his weathered face. "The Demonsouled are filled with bloodlust. And a Demonsouled of sufficient power can command the Malrags." He shifted his sword to his right hand, the blade spinning in a slow circle at his side, like a serpent preparing to strike. "Perhaps you take joy in watching bloodshed and suffering. As you took joy in watching my daughter die."

"I did not!" said Mazael, anger starting to fill him. "The Old Demon slew her in front of me! I would have stopped him, had I the power."

"Ah!" said Athaelin, pointing his sword at Mazael. "A moment ago you said she still lives. Now you say that the Old Demon slew her in front of you..."

"I thought the Old Demon slew her in front of me," said Mazael. "I didn't know his spell would cleave her soul."

"Your story changes from minute to minute," said Athaelin. "Are you really such a miserable liar? Or perhaps you believe your tales yourself. The Demonsouled often go mad, their minds destroyed by the taint of their souls."

Mazael hesitated, for an instant wondering if perhaps Athaelin spoke the truth.

And in that moment, Athaelin struck.

He leapt forward, all his strength and speed behind a two-handed slash. Mazael parried, but only just, and the force of the blow sent him staggering. He backed away as Athaelin came at him, the bastard sword rising and falling, his grip shifting from two-handed to one-handed and back again.

And in a flash, Mazael recognized the movements.

Romaria had used them against him, when they fought with practice swords in the courtyard of Castle Cravenlock. Athaelin's routines, his swings and slashes, were the same as the ones Romaria had used that spring morning. No doubt Romaria had learned them from him.

And Mazael knew what he would do next.

As Athaelin sidestepped and brought his sword around in a backhanded slash, Mazael dodged, the blade plunging past his face. Athaelin pivoted to recover his balance, but for a moment, he was open. Mazael could have plunged Lion into Athaelin's stomach, ripping through the leather cuirass and into muscle and flesh.

Instead he slammed Lion's pommel into Athaelin's stomach, knocking the older man back. Athaelin recovered quickly, his bastard sword coming up in guard, his eyes narrowed with fresh wariness.

"Do you know how I did that?" said Mazael, circling to his right. "Romaria showed me those attacks. Because she trusted me. Because I loved her."

"Your mouth pollutes her name," said Athaelin.

"She told me about you," said Mazael. "How you taught her to fight. How she loved Deepforest Keep, but she couldn't stay there."

For a moment anguish flickered over Athaelin's face, but he kept circling Mazael.

"And she could fight," said Mazael. "I would never have believed a woman could handle a sword so well. And she was the best archer I ever met. The best scout, the best tracker. Brave and bold, even though she was terrified of her fate. She told me about that, too, how half-breeds always succumb to the Elderborn half of their souls. And yet she carried on in the face of that. How could I not love her?"

"You know nothing," said Athaelin.

He attacked again, feinting in a low thrust, then bringing his blade up for a high cut. But Mazael had seen Romaria use this attack, and blocked it with ease.

"She saved my life," Mazael said, Lion straining against Athaelin's sword. "I have many regrets, but my greatest is that I failed to save her." They broke apart, still circling. "I did not kill her...but if she had never met me, she would still live. I curse myself for it."

"Do you think to inspire sympathy with this?" spat Athaelin.

"And when I learned that she still lived," said Mazael, shaking his head, "that she still lived, and I could help her...I set out at once. I will help her, my lord Athaelin. Whatever the cost to myself, I will help her. Even if I have to go through you to do it."

"Silence!" roared Athaelin, and sprinted at Mazael.

His attack came with such fury and power that Mazael, in his weakened state, barely deflected it. He parried, and tried to dodge, but Athaelin bulled forward, one hand seizing Mazael's shoulder. The other drew back his bastard sword for a lethal thrust. Mazael twisted, caught the wrist of Athaelin's sword hand, and yanked. Athaelin stumbled, his sword point skidding off Mazael's cuirass. Mazael ripped free and brought his sword up, laying the edge against Athaelin's throat.

In the same instant Athaelin's blade came to rest against Mazael's throat.

For a moment they stood like that, staring at each other.

He heard the creak as the Elderborn raised their bows, saw the flash of green light as Lucan began muttering a spell.

"Lucan," said Mazael, Lion resting against the side of Athaelin's neck.

"Hold," said Athaelin, his blade motionless against Mazael's throat.

"Perhaps we should kill each other and have done with it," said Mazael.

Athaelin said nothing, his fingers tight against his sword's hilt.

"But if I'm right," said Mazael. "I'm the only one who can help Romaria. Her only chance for aid. And if you kill me, she'll lose that chance."

"You could be lying," hissed Athaelin, "preying upon an old man's grief."

"Perhaps," said Mazael. "Or I'm telling the truth. I make this oath to you, Lord Athaelin. Go to Castle Cravenlock, seek out my arms-master Sir Hagen Bridgebane, and tell him that I sent you. He will give you lodgings. I will return within two days, and I will have Romaria with me."

"Or?" said Athaelin.

"Or I will be dead," said Mazael. "And if I am not, if I do return without Romaria...you can cut me down yourself. I won't stop you."

Lucan muttered something. It did not sound complimentary.

"Your oath?" said Athaelin.

"You have it," said Mazael.

For a long moment Athaelin did not move. Then he lowered his sword, his eyes and face tight with anger and...hope, perhaps?

"If you've led me false," said Athaelin. "I will kill you."

"If I've led you false," said Mazael, lowering his own sword, "then I've also led myself false, and I won't be alive for you to kill, my lord."

A wintry smile flickered across Athaelin's face. "I hope you are right. I hope I will see my daughter again, alive and well. But I fear you have only played upon an old man's foolish hope."

He walked back to his horse, swung into his saddle, and gestured to the Elderborn.

As one they rode to the north, towards Castle Cravenlock, leaving Mazael and Lucan behind.

14

THE DUEL

"You should have killed him," said Lucan at last.

"No," said Mazael.

Lucan snorted. "Then you should have let me kill him."

"No!" said Mazael. "I will not kill Romaria's father."

"Then he will kill you," said Lucan, "if we fail to return with Romaria. Or if she has gone mad, or..."

"Enough," said Mazael. "If you are so displeased, I can do this without you."

Lucan sighed. "No, you can't. You cannot cast the necessary spell without my aid."

Mazael swung back up into Hauberk's saddle. "Can you still sense her?"

"Aye." Lucan's eyes fluttered. "Three and a half miles to the south, I think. She's moving closer to us."

"Then let's find her," said Mazael, and put his boots to Hauberk's flanks.

~

THE SKY GREW darker as they rode south, heavy gray clouds rolling overhead. The corpses of dead Malrags lay scattered here and there. To judge from their wounds and the black blood drying upon their gray flesh, they had not been dead for very long. No more than a few hours. No doubt they had fled from the battle outside Cravenlock Town, only to perish from their wounds here.

Until their dark spirits were reborn once more.

"That one is missing its throat," said Lucan, pointing. "And that one was hamstrung."

"Romaria," said Mazael.

Lucan nodded.

"Where is she?" said Mazael.

"Nearby," said Lucan. He frowned, and pointed. "There. There!"

Mazael twisted in his saddle, and saw the great black wolf.

Romaria.

She half ran, half limped, across the plain, making for a low hill. A ring of weathered stones, the foundation of some long-forgotten tower, topped the hill. The wolf had been wounded, her dark fur wet in places with blood.

Mazael saw the reason why a moment later.

A score of Malrags raced after her, axes and spears in hand, their colorless eyes wide and eager for the kill.

"No," said Mazael, drawing Lion and kicking Hauberk to a gallop.

The Malrags turned to look as Lion erupted into blazing azure flame. And as they did, the black wolf lunged forward, fangs ripping, and two of the Malrags fell, hamstrung. The rest hesitated, caught between fear of the wolf and fear of Lion's flame, and Hauberk crashed into them, knocking one Malrag to the earth. Mazael struck, driving Lion into a Malrag's skull, even as Hauberk kicked another Malrag.

But there were too many of them. Mazael urged Hauberk forward, but the Malrags followed, stabbing and slashing. He parried one blow, then another, but a spear bit into his hip, and the edge of an axe grazed his calf. He snarled in pain and killed another Malrag, even as a spear dug through his armor and into his shoulder.

Then a thunderclap rang out, and invisible force seized the nearest Malrags. Lucan stood in his saddle, hand raised, gray light flickering around his fingertips. Mist swirled below his horse, and a pair of shadowy beasts leapt from the mist, each looking like a cross between a hyena and a scorpion. The spirit beasts tore into the Malrags, rending them to pieces. Hauberk screamed in pain and fury and ripped free of the Malrags. Mazael leaned forward, putting the horse's momentum behind his swing, and Lion took another Malrag's head.

Even wounded, the wolf moved with grace and power, dealing death at every turn.

It was over soon, most of the Malrags slain, the rest fleeing. Mazael brought his panting horse to a stop, Lion dangling from his fist.

The wolf stared at him. Her flanks heaved with exhaustion, her legs trembling, her blue eyes glittering.

Mazael slid Lion back into its scabbard and dropped from the saddle.

The wolf backed away, fangs bared in a noiseless snarl.

"Romaria," said Mazael.

The wolf went rigid.

"Careful," murmured Lucan. "She might rip your throat out."

Mazael risked a glance at Lucan. The younger man's hood was thrown back, his dark eyes fixed on the wolf.

"Closer," said Lucan.

Mazael took a step towards the wolf, and she crept back.

"Do you remember me?" said Mazael. "I remember you. I remember kissing you for the first time, on the steps of the King's Tower. I remember watching you use a bow, or give coins to the hungry children in Cravenlock Town."

He took another step, and this time the she did not back away.

LUCAN WATCHED as Mazael drew closer to the great black wolf.

Every line of the wolf's form shivered with tension. Lucan could not tell if she was about to flee in terror, or spring upon Mazael in rage.

And if she did, Mazael was in a great deal of danger. His Demonsouled nature allowed him to recover from all but the most grievous wounds. But if his heart was pierced or his head smashed, he almost certainly would die. There had never been a chance to test it, of course, but Lucan knew that Mazael's regenerative power would only go so far.

And he needed Mazael alive.

He sat atop his horse, ready to cast the spell.

And if that failed, if she attacked Mazael, Lucan would kill her. He would regret doing it, of course. He, too, knew what it was like to lose a woman one loved.

But Mazael had lost Romaria once before...and Lucan was reasonably certain that he could endure losing her again.

~

"AND YOU STOOD with me against the Old Demon, at the end," said Mazael.

He was only a few paces from the wolf, now, and still she gazed at him with that mixture of fear and terror. How close did he have to be for Lucan to cast the spell? Did he have to touch the wolf? The gods only knew how she might respond to that – she might flee, or she might rip his hand off.

"You saved me," said Mazael, "you kept me from murdering Rachel, from murdering Mitor. You kept the Demonsouled part of my nature from overwhelming me, from turning me into a monster."

The wolf did not move.

"Do you remember this?" said Mazael, lifting the silver coin on its chain. The wolf trembled, blue eyes fixed upon the coin. "You used to carry this. I kept it, to remember you. To remind myself of all you did for me." He took a deep breath. "To remind myself of how much I love you."

Another spasm went through the wolf, worse than before.

And then she changed, the lines of her form blurring and melting, her body shrinking and reshaping itself. One moment a great black wolf stood before Mazael. The next Romaria Greenshield crouched naked before him, her black hair wild and tangled, her pale skin marked with both Malrag blood and her own.

Bit by bit she straightened up, heedless of her nudity, blue eyes fixed upon his face. Her expression flickered from rage to fear and back again.

"Romaria," he said.

Something like recognition came into her expression. "Mazael?" Her voice was thick, rusty, as if she had not used it for a long time. "You...are Mazael?"

He nodded. They stood face to face now, perhaps a foot or so apart.

"Yes," he said. "You remember me?"

"Remember?" said Romaria, as if the word confused her. "It...I... you. I...remember you. We kissed." A smile flickered over her lips. "There was...we fought together. I remember a chapel. A demon. Red light." Her hands twitched towards her chest, where the Old Demon's spell had burned away her heart and lungs. "Pain. I...remember pain."

"The Old Demon," said Mazael. "He killed you. Or, I thought he killed you. Instead, his spell did...this to you."

"I can't remember," said Romaria. "Anything. I want to remember."

"I can help," said Mazael, holding out his hand. "The Old Demon's spell tore your soul in half. It can be healed. Just take my hand, and you'll remember."

She hesitated, staring at him for. Then she reached out, and put her hand, thin and strong, against his.

~

LUCAN WATCHED as Mazael and Romaria stood staring at each other. His magic waited for his command. Ready to restore Romaria's torn soul...or to strike her dead.

She took Mazael's hand.

Touching. They were close enough for the spell to work.

Lucan began casting the spell, green light flickering around his fingertips, and Romaria's face twisted with fury.

~

ROMARIA SNARLED, every muscle in her body going rigid.

"What is it?" said Mazael. He half-expected to see another band of Malrags charging at them. But the only Malrags he saw were dead. Lucan sat atop his horse, muttering, green light flashing around his hands.

The spell.

"Magic!" screamed Romaria, her eyes wild. "Magic killed me. The Old Demon's magic!"

"This spell will help you..."

"You lie!" said Romaria. "You lured me to my death. You let the Old Demon kill me! And now you're trying to kill me again!"

"No!" said Mazael. "I'm not, I swear it, I..."

She changed.

The woman vanished, and in her place stood the great black wolf, pressed up against Mazael, eyes ablaze with fury, claws sliding against his armor. And before Mazael could react she drove him to the ground, paws straining against his shoulders.

Her jaws closed around his throat, fangs stabbing through his skin. Mazael heard the sound of ripping meat, felt the hot blood splatter across his face and neck, and everything went black.

~

LUCAN CURSED as the black wolf's jaws closed around Mazael's throat.

There was no more time.

He finished his spell, flung out his hands, and the wolf disappeared in flash of swirling green flame.

15

REBIRTH

For a long time, Romaria Greenshield had been lost to herself. She had lain in darkness, full of pain, her mind drifting in oblivion. Bit by bit she forgot herself, forgot the pain, forgot everything. Sometimes images flickered through her mind. Fire and magic. A man, tall and strong, with a brown beard and gray eyes.

Then she awoke, clawed her way free from the crypt, and fled across the wild plains.

Yet dark things stalked the plains, filled with corruption and malevolence. And still the gray-eyed man with the sword of azure fire haunted her dreams. Seeing him filled her with fear, as if something horrible had happened to her the last time she had met him. Yet seeing him in danger from the dark things filled her with even greater fear, so she went to battle besides him, rending the dark creatures with fang and claw.

And her fear for him warred with her fear of him.

And then green fire devoured her world.

∾

ROMARIA AWOKE on the hard ground, naked and cold, her body aching and her skin smeared with dried blood.

She got to her knees, blinking with confusion. How had she come to be here? This was the Grim Marches, wasn't it? Her father had sent her north, to investigate the undead things. Her memory churned. She remembered Castle Cravenlock. A stone chapel. A Demonsouled wizard, standing upon an altar.

His magic plunging into her chest, burning her, killing her...

She looked down at herself, at the unmarked skin of her breasts, at Mazael Cravenlock lying before her, bleeding to death from a torn throat.

The memories came back in a rush.

"Oh, gods!" said Romaria, trying to staunch the blood flowing from his throat. "Mazael. Mazael!"

"He'll be fine."

Romaria looked up.

Lucan Mandragon stood a short distance away, leaning on a black metal staff.

There was something...wrong about him.

In her wolf form, Romaria's sense of smell had been enhanced, and she smelled something vile inside Lucan. Some poison working its way through his veins, killing him, corrupting him, changing him into something monstrous.

But even that was nothing compared to the vile stench of his staff.

"Lucan," said Romaria. She remembered him, from Lord Richard's war against Mazael's brother Mitor. "What have you done to yourself?"

Lucan slumped against the staff, and for a moment he looked so young, so tired. "What was necessary. I...needed greater power, to meet the threats that faced me. And so I found it..."

Mazael shuddered, drawing a gagging breath, and Romaria forgot about Lucan and his corrupted staff.

"Oh, gods," she whispered. "I killed him."

"No," said Lucan. "He is Demonsouled, remember? Even now his wound closes."

He was right. Romaria saw the edges of the terrible gash in his throat closing, the blood flow slackening. She had seen his Demonsouled power close his wounds before. Soon he would recover.

But Mazael looked different than she remembered. Older. A little leaner. Fresh lines on his face. As if he bore new cares and worries since she had last seen him...

How long ago had that been?

"Lucan," said Romaria, "how long...how long...was I like that?"

"A little over two years," said Lucan.

"Gods of the earth and forest," said Romaria, repeating the old Elderborn oath she had often heard her father use. "Two years? How is that even possible?"

Lucan hesitated. "The Old Demon's spell was meant to kill you, but it instead split your soul asunder. The human half merged with Mazael's. The Elderborn half remained in your body, and its latent magic had...unusual effects. Hence your transformation into a wolf."

"Two years," repeated Romaria. "Did I kill anyone?"

"Only Malrags," said Lucan. "And you saved Lord Mazael's life several times. Do you remember anything?"

"Some," said Romaria. "It was like a dream. Or a nightmare. And only now have I awakened. I think..."

Mazael trembled, his mouth yawning wide as he gasped for breath.

∾

RED PAIN FLOODED MAZAEL, and darkness drowned him.

Then consciousness filled him once more, and he wheezed for breath, coughing up a great deal of blood. He tried to sit up, and warm, strong hands took his shoulders, helping him up.

"Breathe," said a woman's voice. A woman's familiar voice. "You took quite a wound. Even you will need a moment to heal it."

Mazael opened his eyes, the world swimming into focus around him. He sat at the base of the hill and its ruined tower, dead Malrags scattered over the grasses. Lucan stood a short distance away, leaning on his staff.

Romaria knelt besides him, hands on his shoulders, steadying him. She looked utterly exhausted. Yet the madness had vanished from her face. And those blue eyes looked so familiar.

"Romaria?" said Mazael, his voice no more than a cracked whisper.

She nodded, blinking.

Mazael grabbed her hands. "I'm sorry. I'm so sorry. I led you to your death. It was my fault, my mistake..."

"Enough," said Romaria, squeezing his hands. "Enough! You didn't kill me. The Old Demon did." Her familiar crooked grin spread over her lips. "Though it seems the old devil didn't even do a very good job, did he? Not if I'm sitting here." She took a shuddering breath. "And you saved me."

"No," said Mazael, turning his head. "Lucan did that. Thank you."

Lucan inclined his head, but Romaria frowned, her muscles tensing beneath Mazael's hands.

"I suggest," said Lucan, "that we return to Castle Cravenlock at once. There are still Malrag warbands roaming nearby, and we are exhausted."

"The Malrags," said Romaria. "What are Malrags doing in the Grim Marches, anyway? I've fought Malrags before, but I never through to see any out of the mountains."

Mazael blinked. "You've fought Malrags?" Until a few months ago, no living man had seen a Malrag for over a century. Or so Mazael had thought.

"Aye," said Romaria. "When I traveled in the Great Mountains, before I went west to the Old Kingdoms. Vile things, full of cunning, and the only thing they enjoy is cruelty and butchery. Have they been raiding the Grim Marches?"

"With a host tens of thousands strong, commanded by a man wielding a Demonsouled bloodsword."

"For the gods' sake!" said Lucan. "We can discuss this at Castle

Cravenlock. Might I remind you that I am exhausted, you are weakened, and Romaria is both unarmed and naked? If we encounter any Malrags now, we are probably finished."

Mazael looked at Romaria. In the chaos of the moment, he had almost forgotten that she was naked. He had thought her beautiful, two years ago, and he thought her beautiful now. Even beneath the dried blood and the scratches and cuts, even through his exhaustion, she was still beautiful.

Gods, how he had missed looking at her. How he had wanted her.

She stared at him, and he wanted to kiss her. But not here. Lucan was right about the Malrags.

Mazael climbed to his feet, his damaged armor clanking, Romaria putting a steadying hand on his arm. "Here." He tugged off his cloak and put it around her shoulders. "I doubt I should ride into the courtyard with you naked upon my horse."

That crooked grin flashed across her face once more. "Well. It would make quite a stir, wouldn't it?"

ROMARIA SAT BEHIND MAZAEL, wrapped in his black cloak, as they rode north.

And as they rode, he told her what had happened over the last two years. Some of it she had expected. Gerald Roland married to Rachel. Mazael keeping peace between Lord Malden and Lord Richard. Some of it she had not expected. The Dominiar Order destroyed at the Battle of Tumblestone?

"You killed Amalric Galbraith?" said Romaria.

"Aye," said Mazael. His voice was distant, as if recalling a memory that pained him. "He was Demonsouled. A child of the Old Demon. As am I."

"No," said Romaria. "No. You're nothing like Amalric Galbraith. He was a monster. The crimes he committed in the Old Kingdoms... he would put entire villages to the sword. Men, women, children."

"He did the same, near Tumblestone," said Mazael.

She squeezed his shoulder, beneath the damaged armor. "You did well to stop him."

And what Mazael had to tell her about the last few months was bad, very bad. A host of Malrags. A renegade wizard. Gerald's and Rachel's son kidnapped by a calibah. And the Malrag horde led by a madman with a sword forged from Demonsouled blood.

"Ultorin," she said, spitting the name like a curse.

Mazael looked surprised. "You know him?"

"I do," said Romaria. "He was Amalric Galbraith's right hand. He did much of Amalric's killing, and was just as cruel and brutal as his master. I told you I traveled in the Old Kingdoms, fought against the Dominiars." She remembered those days, hiding the forests, ambushing the haughty Dominiar knights as they rode to collect taxes. "I foiled Ultorin, once, in a battle. I wonder if he remembers me. I hope he remembers me. Even if he hadn't brought the Malrags to the Grim Marches, I would still put an arrow through his chest."

Castle Cravenlock came into sight, grim and dark atop its crag, with Cravenlock Town resting at its base. The town had grown in the last two years. Mostly from refugees fleeing the Malrags, no doubt. The walls had been strengthened, and she saw crossbow-armed militia patrolling the ramparts. Despite the Malrags, men and women alike moved about their tasks with purpose, and while Romaria saw fear, she saw no sign of despair.

Mazael had rallied his people well.

They rode to the castle and clattered through the barbican. Armed men milled about the courtyard, while squires ran to and fro, tending to their knights. Romaria saw Sir Gerald Roland waiting near the gate, Rachel at his side. She looked up as Mazael approached, a relieved smile spreading over her face.

Then she saw Romaria, and her green eyes got very wide.

"Mazael, you're back, thank the gods," said Gerald. "Were you successful..."

He saw Romaria, and his voice trailed off.

"Evidently you were," said Gerald after a moment. "This must be quite a tale."

"It is," said Mazael, smiling. "We..."

"Romaria!"

She turned her head. A group of Elderborn stood near the curtain wall, aloof and alien in their furs and leathers, bows resting in their hands. A man ran across the courtyard, a man with graying black hair and blue eyes, a bronze diadem on his brow and a bronze shield slung across his back...

"Father!" said Romaria.

She slid from the saddle and ran to him.

~

MAZAEL WATCHED Romaria run to Athaelin.

"You're smiling."

Rachel looked at him, eyes wide with wonder.

"You never smile," said Rachel. "At least, not as you once did, when we were young."

He dropped from Hauberk's back. Rufus Highgate came to take the reins, frowning at Romaria.

"My lord," he said. "If I might ask. Who is that...lady?"

"Lady Romaria Greenshield," said Mazael. "Daughter of Athaelin Greenshield, Lord of Deepforest Keep. And yes, she was slain, I know." Now it was Rufus's turn to wear an astonished expression. "Take care of Hauberk. And send word to the seneschal. Lady Romaria will need rooms at once."

"And clothes," added Rachel.

"You heard the lady," said Mazael. "Go."

Rufus bowed and led Hauberk away.

"Lord Mazael."

Athaelin approached, Romaria at his side. Some of the anger had fallen from his expression, and he no longer looked quite so grim.

"I have kept my oath to you," said Mazael. "Here is your daughter, safe and sound once more. You, your daughter, and your companions are my guests, and may remain at Castle Cravenlock as long as you like. Though we would welcome any aid you could give against the Malrags. We are sore pressed, as I'm sure you can see."

"I was wrong about you," said Athaelin.

You aren't, thought Mazael.

He was truly Demonsouled, a child of the Old Demon. And even if he had not killed Romaria with his own hands, even if she forgave him, he still blamed himself for what had happened. If Athaelin had cut him down during their fight, it would not have been murder.

It would have been justice.

"I see Romaria before me, alive and well," said Athaelin. "And I see what you have done here. How you have rallied your people, and fought to defend your lands. I had heard rumors of Malrags in the Grim Marches, but I never dreamed they would come in such numbers." He shook his head. "You have my aid, and the aid of my companions. And I shall send word to Deepforest Keep, to summon additional help. The Malrags must be defeated. Otherwise they will threaten the Elderborn of the Great Southern Forest, and even Deepforest Keep itself."

"Thank you," said Mazael. "We shall be glad to have your aid."

THAT NIGHT MAZAEL HELD A FEAST, to celebrate the victory over the Malrag warband outside of the Cravenlock Town, and Lord Athaelin's arrival.

And Romaria's safe return.

She dressed as she always had, in boots and trousers and leather armor, and drew a few disapproving looks from the ladies of the castle. But she did not care, and neither did Mazael.

The lords and knights assembled from their various camps around Cravenlock Town. Lord Richard greeted Athaelin with his usual calm courtesy.

"Our host marches east tomorrow," said Lord Richard. "We will draw out the Malrags, find Ultorin, and kill him. Your presence would be welcome, my lord Athaelin. The Elderborn are known to be archers without peer. Perhaps you would accept command of the archers and the skirmishers? Most of my lords and knights are accustomed to commanding heavy horse, and I have few men experienced as archers."

"It would please me," said Athaelin. He laughed. "You men of the plains know how to fight from the back of a horse, but on your feet? We men of Deepforest Keep could teach you a thing or two."

"Indeed," said Lord Richard.

Romaria sat at Mazael's side throughout the feast, and sometimes her hand strayed to touch his beneath the table.

From time to time Mazael saw Lucan standing on the balcony, wrapped in his cloak, eyes glittering beneath his hood as he leaned upon that black staff.

AFTER THE FEAST, Romaria joined Mazael in his rooms atop the King's Tower.

"There's something wrong with Lucan," said Romaria.

Mazael snorted. "There's quite a bit wrong with Lucan."

"No," said Romaria. "He...smells wrong."

"Smells?"

Romaria paced to the balcony doors, arms wrapped around herself. "My senses are...different, after what happened to me. Sharper, somehow. I can see more clearly. And I can smell things...wolves have a sharper sense of smell, after all. And Lucan smells rotten. Corrupted. Like meat that's gone bad."

Mazael crossed to her, took her hands. She did not pull away. "He's sick, you mean?" He had wondered at that himself. Lately Lucan had looked tired, and had been prone to collapses. It had begun when the Malrags invaded, almost after Mazael had first seen Lucan with that black staff.

"No. At least, I don't think so. He almost smells...he smells Demonsouled."

Mazael closed his eyes. "Like me, you mean."

Romaria turned to face him. "No. No. You smell," the crooked grin appeared, briefly, "you smell dangerous. Like a wolf. There's power in you, but you've learned to control it. Lucan smells...worse." She sighed in frustration. "I cannot explain it any better."

"He has been of great help to me," said Mazael. "Without his aid, I would have been killed, several times. And his spell restored you. But if you are wary, I will watch him."

"Thank you," said Romaria.

They stood in silence for a moment.

"I've missed you," said Mazael. "More than I can say."

She smiled. "I told you the Seer prophesied that we would save each other. Well, we have, haven't we?" She took a deep breath. "You know this doesn't change anything."

"What do you mean?"

"You have control of yourself," said Romaria. She closed her eyes, moved closer to him. He felt the heat of her body against his, the warmth of her hands, her breath against his neck. "But I am still half-human, half-Elderborn. The power in the Elderborn half of my soul...I cannot control it. Sooner or later, it will consume me. As happens to all half-breeds. I don't know how much time I have."

"No one knows how much time they have left," said Mazael. "We could all die tomorrow. You...just know more clearly how you will die."

"I know," said Romaria, voice quiet. "So I will spend what time I have left doing something worthwhile. Fighting the Malrags. And spending time with those I love. Like my father." She hesitated. "And with you."

"I love you," said Mazael.

He drew her face closer, and she kissed him. Slowly, gently, at first.

Then with greater urgency.

∾

THEY WOUND up together in Mazael's bed, their clothes gone, joined together in body as they were in spirit and fate.

Mazael knew he might die tomorrow, that she might die tomorrow. But he did not care, did not care about anything but Romaria's eyes and lips and body.

HE AWOKE the next morning with Romaria's legs tangled in his, her arm thrown across him, her head resting against his chest, the feel of her breath against his skin.

The sound of horns in his ears.

Mazael sat up, alarmed, and Romaria's eyes shot open.

War horns.

The Malrag host had come.

16

THE MARCH

The door to Mazael's bedchamber burst open, and Rufus Highgate ran in.

Mazael remembered that night when Rufus had run into his room, bearing news that Cravenlock Town was under attack. It had been the first time he had seen the Malrags.

The first time he had seen the great black wolf.

Rufus skidded to a stop, gaping at Romaria.

"Damn it, boy," said Mazael. "Stop gawking." Again he heard the sound of horns, and the rattle of armor and the clamor of raised voices from the courtyard. "What is it?"

"The Malrags, my lord," said Rufus. "Sir Tanam's men say that are marching for the castle, in greater numbers than we have ever seen before. The...the entire Malrag host might be on the move, my lord.

"Help me dress," said Mazael, climbing to his feet, while Romaria pulled on her clothes and armor. Had Ultorin decided to avenge his defeat outside the walls of Cravenlock Town, his two failed traps to kill Mazael? Or had he simply decided to break the resistance of the Grim Marches once and for all? The entire might of the Grim Marches had gathered in camps around Castle Cravenlock – nearly twenty-five thousand men – but Ultorin had at least seventy-five thousand Malrags. Maybe even more. Knights and mounted armsmen could tear their way through the Malrag lines with ease, but Lord Richard's combined armies had only seven thousand heavy horse.

How many Malrags could they overcome?

Or perhaps Malavost, or the San-keth, had some other goal in mind.

"It doesn't matter why," said Romaria, slinging her sword over her shoulder. Mazael had found a bastard sword for her, and she carried one of the short horse bows favored by the militia, a quiver of arrows at her belt. "We'll stop him first. Then we'll figure out why he did it."

"Aye," said Mazael, and then realized that she knew what he had been thinking. Either they still shared some strange link due to Lucan's spell, or she just knew him very well. He adjusted his armor as Rufus buckled his sword belt. His armor felt strange – many of the damaged steel plates had been replaced.

"If we can find Ultorin," said Romaria as Mazael tugged on his black surcoat, "it doesn't matter what he plans. We can end this, today. Malavost can't control the Malrags without him, and they'll turn on each other." Her voice darkened. "And Ultorin deserves death, anyway, for the things he did in the Old Kingdoms."

"Then let's see if we can give it to him," said Mazael.

He hurried down the stairs, Romaria and Rufus following, and entered the courtyard. Knights ran back and forth, climbing into their saddles, their squires adjusting their arms and armor. Gerald sat atop his horse near the steps to the keep, talking with Sir Hagen. Rachel stood in the doorway, watching him, her face a calm mask.

She was terrified, Mazael knew. Her husband, her brother, and her son might all die before the sun set.

"What news?" said Mazael.

"The Malrags are on the move, my lord," said Hagen, face grim beneath his black beard. He alone, of Mazael's friends and vassals, seemed unmoved by Romaria's return. Of course, he had only entered Mazael's service a year after the Old Demon had killed her.

"Sir Tanam's scouts spotted them. A great host, marching directly for Castle Cravenlock."

Rufus sprinted in the direction of the stables. "How many?" said Mazael.

Hagen hesitated. "At least a hundred thousand strong, at a minimum. Most likely one hundred and fifty thousand, and perhaps as many as a quarter of a million. The Malrag host...it simply covered too much ground for Sir Tanam's scouts to get an accurate count."

"So many of them," murmured Rachel, her face white.

"A quarter of a million," said Mazael. Perhaps a hundred and twenty thousand men, women, and children lived upon the lands of Lord Richard and his vassals.

And now twice as many Malrags prepared to fling themselves at Castle Cravenlock.

"Lord Richard sends word," said Hagen. "The host is to assemble four miles east of Castle Cravenlock." He grimaced. "There we will take our stand against the Malrags, or so he says."

"Lord Richard has a plan, I hope?" said Mazael. Hagen did not answer. But there was only one hope of victory, wasn't there? They had to find Ultorin and kill him. Anything else was useless.

"So many of them," repeated Rachel. "And my son is in the middle of them."

"Fear not, Lady Rachel," said Romaria. "With so many of them, it will make it all the harder to miss."

Rufus returned, leading Hauberk, and Mazael pulled himself into the saddle. Romaria took one of the lighter, swifter beasts favored by the mounted archers in the militia. She turned the horse in a quick circle, nodded in satisfaction.

"Then we had best make haste," said Mazael. "We wouldn't Lord Richard to keep all the Malrags for himself, would we?"

"The gods go with you," said Rachel.

Gerald stooped, kissed her, and rode with Mazael to the barbican. Lucan and Timothy were there, grim in their black coats, while Lord Athaelin waited with his Elderborn companion. The Elderborn carried their massive bows, while Athaelin bore his bastard sword in his right hand and his bronze shield upon his left arm. The shield looked ancient, a ring of runes carved around its edge, and the bronze had acquired the green patina of age.

Ah. Greenshield. Of course.

"You're looking well, daughter," said Athaelin.

Romaria grinned. "And you as well, father."

"Lord Mazael!" Athaelin clashed the flat of his blade against his ancient shield. "We are ready to ride with you."

"Good," said Mazael.

He took one look around the courtyard, at the men ready on their horses, at the women watching from the walls. At Rachel, standing alone and forlorn upon the steps to the keep. Mazael knew he might well die today. Everyone in this courtyard might fall in battle against the Malrags.

Yet he would not surrender his lands and the lives of his people without a fight. And if he could fight his way to Ultorin, if he could cut down the renegade Dominiar...Mazael could end war. He could save his people and his lands. The Grim Marches could have peace.

Mazael could have more nights with Romaria.

But even if he fell in battle today, he was glad, so glad, that they had shared at least one night together.

He felt Romaria's eyes on him, saw her nod.

"Come," said Mazael. "Let's not keep Lord Richard waiting."

SYKHANA RODE in the heart of the vast host, Aldane cradled in her arms.

All around her marched Malrags, Malrags beyond count, armed with spears and axes, their black armor seeming to drink the sunlight itself. The balekhans marched with their warbands, the hilts of their massive swords rising over their shoulders. She also saw the Malrag shamans striding along, ragged black robes fluttering around their gaunt bodies, their third eyes flickering with ghostly light.

So many of them. Malavost had told her that Ultorin had gathered one hundred and sixty thousand Malrags under his command. Sykhana looked over them and felt a shiver of fear. Ultorin's will - and the power of his bloodsword - kept the Malrags in check. If not for that bloodsword, that Malrags would turn on each other in a heartbeat, enslaved to their endless lust for pain and death. They would rip apart Aldane, if not for Ultorin.

And Ultorin was going insane.

Sykhana glanced at Ultorin, a tower of black armor atop his horse, the bloodsword strapped to his back. For the moment, at least, he was not raving. His skin had gone deathly pale, and the veins in his neck and hands looked more black than blue. Flecks of venomous yellow dotted his gray eyes, and he flinched away from the sunlight as if it caused him physical pain.

The bloodsword was killing him. Sykhana only hoped he lasted long enough to reach their goal, for Aldane to become immortal and powerful. Because if he did not, if he died before they did...

"No," she hissed. Malavost would keep his promise. Aldane would live forever.

She cradled the child, her child, close against her chest, and watched as Malavost and Skaloban approached Ultorin.

"The scouts report," said Malavost in his calm voice. "The knights and lords of the Grim Marches have gathered east of Cravenlock Town. Twenty-five thousand of them in all, with perhaps seven or eight thousand heavy horse."

Skaloban's tongue flicked at the air. "A powerful force."

"Bah!" said Ultorin. Dark circles ringed his eyes. "Nothing. They are nothing! I have a hundred and sixty thousand Malrags at my command." His hand touched the hilt of his bloodsword. "My command! I will sweep away our enemies and dance through their corpses!"

He laughed then, long and loud and full of madness.

Skaloban's head reared back in alarm, the skeletal hands of his carrier coming up in the beginnings of a spell.

"Most certainly, Grand Master," said Malavost, unmoved by Ultorin's display. "You could indeed smash the army of the Grim

Marches. But that would not bring you your vengeance against Mazael Cravenlock, would it? Not in the way that you desire."

"Vengeance?" said Ultorin, his voice dropping to a growl. "I will have my vengeance upon him. I will see blood and death and misery wreaked across the Grim Marches." He smiled, yellow-flecked eyes growing wide. "I will see fire and death wreaked upon the entire world!" He ripped his bloodsword free and lifted it over his head. "I will watch the world burn!"

"And so you shall," said Malavost. "If you proceed as we have discussed." Sykhana marveled at his ability to remain so calm. "For once we reach our goal, you can rain death upon the entire world, and no one will be able to stop you."

Ultorin snarled, and then all at once lucidity seemed to fill his eyes once more. "Yes. Yes, you are right, wizard. We must hew to the original goal." He looked at his bloodsword, as if confused to how it had gotten there, and returned the weapon to its scabbard. "I can smash the army of the Grim Marches, yes. But there are twenty-five thousand of them, and Lord Richard's seven thousand heavy horse could make us pay heavily. If they damage us enough, they could keep us from reaching our goal."

"The solution is simple, Grand Master," said Malavost, and laid out a plan.

Ultorin nodded. "That will work. I will command the balekhans to make it so. Again you have proven your worth to me, wizard." His face screwed up with rage once more. "I will make Mazael pay for what he has done! I will avenge Grand Master Amalric's death!" He ripped the bloodsword free and pointed it to the west, towards Castle Cravenlock. "Do you hear me, Mazael? I will make you scream!"

"I suggest we move at once, Grand Master," said Malavost.

Ultorin rode into the ranks of Malrags, shouting for the balekhans to attend him.

For a moment Skaloban and Malavost stood in silence. Aldane squirmed in Sykhana's arms, frightened by Ultorin's outburst, and she soothed him.

"That human is insane," said Skaloban.

"Oh, unquestionably," said Malavost, unperturbed. "And it's only going to get worse, I'm afraid. Amalric Galbraith was a potent Demonsouled, and any weapon forged with his blood will be too powerful for a mortal to handle. The bloodsword will induce a slow but steady deterioration of Ultorin's sanity. And he's used it to heal his wounds, as well, by draining the life force of Malrags. This will increase his strength and stamina, true, but greatly increases the risk of certain...physical abnormalities developing."

"The man is unreliable!" said Skaloban. "His madness places our plan, indeed, the Vessel himself, in dire jeopardy! You should have wielded the bloodsword yourself."

Malavost lifted his eyebrows. "Pardon, honored Skaloban, but do I look like a fool? I have survived this long by knowing my limitations. And no mortal can safely wield the power of the Demonsouled - most Demonsouled themselves eventually descend into homicidal madness." He smiled, briefly. "As the Dragon's Shadow will soon discover. No, honored Skaloban, Ultorin is...disposable. A necessary sacrifice to reach our goal. His sanity will continue to deteriorate, true, but he will last long enough for us to fulfill the Vessel's purpose."

"See that he does," said Skaloban, his black-slit eyes turning to Sykhana. "And you see that the Vessel reaches the Door of Souls safely. Fail, and it will not go well with you."

He turned and stalked away, green sparks flashing from the joints of his skeletal carrier.

"It is," murmured Malavost, so softly Sykhana almost didn't hear, "always such a pleasure conversing with you."

"How soon," said Sykhana, "until Ultorin decides to kill us?"

"He won't," said Malavost, glancing at her. "And even if he does, I will dispose of him, and find another fool to wield the bloodsword. We need the bloodsword's control over the Malrags. We do not particularly need Ultorin to be the one to wield it." He smiled. "Now, come. We have a battle to watch. And is it not fitting that the Vessel should witness the destruction of his enemies?"

~

WAR DRUMS BOOMED over the plain.

Mazael rode past rank after rank of pikemen, their chain mail covered by black tabards marked with the red dragon of the House of Mandragon. Rows of horse archers, sitting ready with their short bows and javelins. Footmen equipped with shields and heavy maces. And the heavy horse, knights and mounted armsmen, armored in plate and chain, lances and swords ready in their hands.

Twenty-five thousand men, led by one of the most cunning and battle-hardened lords in the kingdom.

Mazael hoped that would be enough.

He found Lord Richard beneath the black Mandragon standard, clad in his armor of red dragon scales. With him waited Lord Robert, Lord Astor, Lord Jonaril, Sir Tanam, and his other chief vassals. Toraine waited atop his horse, a black shadow in his dark armor.

"Lord Mazael," said Richard Mandragon, utterly calm. "Welcome."

"My men are at your disposal, my lord," said Mazael.

"Good," said Richard. "Lord Athaelin, Lady Romaria, Sir Hagen, welcome. Today we shall end this fight."

"What is the plan, then?" said Lord Robert Highgate. In his mail and surcoat, Lord Robert looked rather like a shiny metal pear.

"Our task is simple," said Lord Richard. "We find Ultorin and kill him. Once he is dead, the Malrags will turn upon each other, and we can destroy them at our leisure."

"How shall we draw him out?" said Lord Astor. "He must know we will try to kill him. Surely we would not be foolish enough to expose himself to unnecessary risk."

"We have an unfair advantage, my lord Astor," said Lucan, face shrouded in his cowl. "Ultorin hates Mazael, hates him beyond all reason. And the bloodsword is eating at his mind." His hand tightened on his black staff. "He will take foolish risks, if he thinks he can cut down Lord Mazael. And twice now Ultorin has set traps for Mazael."

"I shall command the reserve," said Lord Richard. "Lord Astor, you will command the footmen in the center. Lord Robert, you will command the horsemen of the left wing. Toraine, you shall command the horsemen of the right. Sir Tanam, you have charge of the mounted archers. My lord Athaelin, I would be honored if you would take command of the foot archers."

"The honor shall be mine," said Athaelin.

"You, my lord Mazael, shall command the vanguard," said Lord Richard.

Romaria frowned.

"Of course," said Mazael. "But why?"

"Because Ultorin hates you," said Lord Richard. "You presence at the forefront of the battle line will draw him out. And once he is drawn out, we can strike him down and end this war."

Mazael nodded. It made perfect sense. And if both Mazael and Gerald were killed in the battle, and Aldane was not recovered from the San-keth...then Rachel would be the heir to Castle Cravenlock. And Lord Richard could force her to marry Toraine, and forever end any threat from the Cravenlocks.

Lord Richard would do anything to ensure the peace of the Grim Marches.

"If I find Ultorin," said Mazael, "I will kill him."

"Good," said Lord Richard, turning. "Lucan. Join the other wizards with the reserve. We will need your skills to counter any attacks from the Malrag shamans." Lucan nodded. "Sir Gerald, you may do as you wish, of course. But I would be grateful if you would remain with me in the reserve. Your father, as you know, does not think highly of me, and I would not give him further cause for grievance."

"Of course," said Gerald with a bow. "But if I see my son, I will take whatever action I think best."

"As you will," said Lord Richard. "To your commands, my lord."

Mazael turned Hauberk, towards the banners of the vanguard. Romaria steered her horse besides his.

"He's hoping you will fall in the battle," said Romaria, her voice low.

"I know," said Mazael. "I'll just have to disappoint him, won't I?" He paused. "Where will you go?"

"With the mounted archers," said Romaria. "I'd ride into battle with you, but I'm not a knight." She gave him a sad smile. "Good luck to you, my love."

He reached over and took her hand. "And to you, my love."

Mazael turned and rode for the vanguard, while Romaria left for the mounted archers.

~

ALDANE CRIED in Sykhana's arms.

The constant booming of Richard Mandragon's war drums had frightened him. Sykhana rocked the baby in her arms, trying to soothe him. None of the Malrags cared about his cries, of course. Except from time to time a pair of white eyes turned towards him, and Sykhana knew the creatures were thinking about killing him, torturing him.

As they had killed and tortured that woman and her baby in the burned village...

Sykhana shook aside the image and made herself listen.

-We are ready-

The voice echoed in Sykhana's mind. A balekhan stood next to Ultorin's horse, its massive black sword in hand.

-Release us to battle. We shall slaughter your enemies, great Master. Their blood shall fill the earth, and their screams shall be music to your ears-

"Richard Mandragon's host has drawn itself into battle formation!" said Skaloban, his voice croaking with alarm. "They are ready for us!"

"Of course they are, honored Skaloban," said Malavost. Sykhana wondered if the San-keth cleric noticed the faint note of scorn in

Malavost's voice. "That is the entire point of the plan, is it not? That we draw the full attention of Lord Richard's host?"

"Yes," said Ultorin, drawing his bloodsword. "We will draw his attention...and then the whole world shall feel my vengeance!"

He lifted the bloodsword into the air and roared, and a hundred thousand Malrag throats answered him, the creatures howling their terrible battle cries to the sky. It was louder than thunder, louder than an earthquake, the most terrible noise Sykhana had ever heard.

"Kill them!" bellowed Ultorin. "Kill them all! Kill them all!"

The Malrag attack surged forward.

THE MALRAG WAR cry died away, its echoes lingering over the plain.

A half mile away Mazael saw the vast dark mass of the Malrag host, thousands upon thousands of them.

And then as one, the Malrags began running forward, still howling, the earth thundering beneath their armored boots.

17

THE BATTLE OF CASTLE CRAVENLOCK

"My lord," said Sir Hagen, voice low and urgent. "My lord, your orders?" For the first time that Mazael could remember, Hagen Bridgebane sounded anxious.

Looking at the charging Malrag horde, Mazael could hardly blame him.

"Hold," said Mazael. Sir Hagen waited at his right, and Sir Aulus at his left, the black Cravenlock standard flying from his lance. Hopefully Ultorin would see it.

The Malrags thundered closer.

"My lord," said Hagen. "Your commands?"

"Hold," said Mazael, risking a look over his shoulder, at the Mandragon banner flying over the reserves. Far in the distance he saw the walls and towers of Castle Cravenlock atop the crag. Rachel could see the battle from the walls, along with the wives and mothers and daughters of his vassals and knights.

He hoped he could bring them victory. That he could return their husbands and sons and brothers.

"My lord!" said Hagen.

Lord Richard's war drums boomed out, sounding the charge.

"Now!" said Mazael. "Charge!" He lifted his lance. "Charge!"

Sir Aulus blew a long blast on his horn, and the vanguard, two thousand heavy horse, roared in answer. Hauberk leapt forward in excitement, and around Mazael the knights of the Grim Marches rolled forward, lances lowered.

SYKHANA WATCHED the wall of horsemen gallop at the charging Malrags, and felt a shiver of fear. They couldn't possibly reach her and Aldane. They couldn't cut their way through tens of thousands of Malrags.

But she wondered if Gerald Roland rode among them, eager to retrieve his son and avenge the death of his wife, and Sykhana felt something cold touch her spine.

No! Aldane was hers!

"Shamans!" bellowed Ultorin, gesturing with his bloodsword. "Give them a welcome!"

BLASTS of green lightning screamed down from the sky, plunging into the vanguard like knives. One struck a dozen feet from Mazael, sending two knights screaming to the earth.

They died, trampled beneath the hooves of their comrades.

"Charge!" said Mazael, gritting his teeth. They had to reach the Malrags. They had to reach Ultorin.

LUCAN FELT the magical energy swirl overhead, saw green lightning rip out of the sky.

"Wards!" he said to fifty men in long black coats and cloaks near him, the court wizards of the lords of the Grim Marches. "To counter the lightning. Follow my lead."

He lifted his hand and began casting a spell. The wizards of the Grim Marches, save for Timothy, feared him, or hated him. They knew Marstan's reputation.

But they would obey him.

Lucan lifted his hand, and the wizards released their spells.

The next bolt of lightning struck an invisible barrier and vanished. Lucan gestured, throwing his full power into the spell. Two more lightning bolts screamed down, only to strike his barrier and rebound into the Malrag ranks, ripping them apart.

MORE LIGHTNING CAME THUNDERING out of the sky, only to bend at the last minute, twisting to strike down the Malrags.

Lucan and Timothy and the other wizards had come through.

Then there was no more time. Mazael lowered his lance and set himself, boots digging into Hauberk's stirrups. The vanguard crashed into the charging Malrags, the air filling with the clang of armor and the sound of tearing flesh and cracking bone. A Malrag fell beneath Hauberk's hooves, the big horse barely slowing, and Mazael rammed his lance through a Malrag's jaw with such force that the steel point exploded out of the back of the creature's head. Some horsemen fell, dying beneath Malrag spears and axes, but more, far more, Malrags perished.

Mazael killed another Malrag, and another, his mind racing. Again and again the Malrags had proven that they could not stand up to a charge of heavy horsemen on level ground. Yet Ultorin had thrown the Malrags in a huge attack against the knights. Why? Did he hope simply to bury the army of the Grim Marches in sheer numbers?

The lance ripped from Mazael's hand, buried in a Malrag's chest, and he swept Lion free from its scabbard, the blade ablaze with azure fire.

He cut down more Malrags, and more, always more.

And looking at the sea of Malrags that stretched before him, he realized that Ultorin might indeed be able to bury them under sheer numbers.

⚬

THE WAR DRUMS BOOMED OUT, and Romaria's light horse sprang forward.

Around her galloped Mazael's militia horse archers and Sir Tanam's raiders. Before them the vanguard plunged into the Malrag horse, driving through them like a scythe through wheat, and Romaria saw a flash of blue flame.

Mazael's sword.

The horse archers veered past the vanguard, moving along the Malrag lines, and Romaria drew an arrow from her quiver. The horse bow was smaller than she preferred, and the arrows not quite so well made. But she had learned to shoot a bow from the Elder-born of the Great Southern Forest, and there were no finer archers in the world.

Ahead of her, Sir Tanam's standard-bearer, the banner of Crow's Rock fluttering from his lance, blew out three blasts upon his war horn.

Romaria raised the bow, drew, and released. Then again, and again, and again. Every arrow found a mark, and Malrags bellowed in pain, wounded, or fell dead upon the earth. Around her hundreds of archers loosed their arrows, sending volley after volley into the Malrag lines. The Malrag ranks disintegrated as some fell back, trying to take cover from the arrows, while others broke free and moved in pursuit of the horse archers.

Which made it all the easier for Mazael's horsemen to ride them down.

Romaria leaned to the left as she loosed another arrow into the pursuing Malrags. Her sturdy little horse had been well trained, and it mirrored her movement, veering to the left to follow the other horse archers. She twisted in the saddle, loosing arrow after arrow into the Malrags. Sir Tanam's standard-bearer blew a long blast, the call to reform the line, and Romaria stopped shooting to join the other archers.

They had killed hundreds of Malrags, and Mazael's charge had killed thousands more. Yet Ultorin's host held tens of thousands more. Could they possibly kill all of them?

Even as the thought passed through her mind, green lightning crackled across the sky, followed by a sheet of sizzling flame.

~

"Again!" bellowed Lucan, lifting his hands to the sky.

Timothy and the other wizards obeyed, combining their powers to cast warding spells. Emerald lightning streaked towards Richard Mandragon's host, only to crash against the combined warding spells of the wizards. Some of the lightning blasts fizzled into nothingness, or veered into the ground, digging glassy furrows into the earth. And still others rebounded into the Malrag ranks, burning the creatures to ashes and charred bone.

Yet the shamans' attack continued. Lucan rather doubted that the shamans, or Ultorin himself, cared how many casualties the Malrags took.

So long as the humans died.

Then the lightning barrage doubled, and doubled again, hammering at the wards, all the blasts focused over the wizards. The black-cloaked men gritted their teeth, sweat pouring down their faces, hands thrust at the sky. The wards shimmered and crackled beneath the strain.

"Counterattack!" shouted Timothy. "Lucan, we must strike back!"

Lucan nodded. "Do it!" Timothy began casting a spell, yellow-orange flames dancing around his fingertips. "The rest of you, lend him your power. Do it now!"

The wizards complied, channeling their power into Timothy's casting. Lucan focused upon the wards, pouring his full skill and power into them. At once he felt the strain against his will...and the black staff waiting ready in his hands. He yearned to send his will into it, to summon the blazing power and to lay waste to the Malrag shamans.

No. He didn't dare. Not until the need was dire...

Timothy raised his hand, shouting the final words of his spell. A fireball blazed around his fist, and then erupted into a sheet of flame that burst across the sky. An instant later the green lightning sputtered, and then stopped entirely. Either the flame spell had killed the Malrag shamans, or distracted them enough to stop the attack.

Lucan frowned, gripping his staff.

Where was Malavost? The magical attacks had been powerful, but lacked skill and precision. Otherwise Lucan and the other wizards would never have been able to deflect them so easily. He expected Malavost to launch an attack at any moment.

Yet he still saw no sign of Malavost.

"THEY ARE ADVANCING TOO QUICKLY!" said Skaloban, his voice full of alarm. And, perhaps, a hint of fear. Sykhana's contempt redoubled. The cleric of Sepharivaim was a coward. She had come to hold the San-keth priests in contempt years ago, and Skaloban in particular seemed weak and pathetic.

Malavost would give her more than the San-keth ever would.

She kissed Aldane on his forehead and watched the confrontation.

"Do not fear, honored Skaloban," said Malavost, calm as ever. "If Lord Richard's men advance too far, we shall simply unleash the Ogrags."

Sykhana flinched. The normal Malrags were bad enough.

The Ogrags were worse.

"You said we would need the Ogrags later," said Skaloban.

"This is true," said Malavost. "However, a few Ogrags lost now would not make much of a difference later. And the men of the Grim Marches have not yet seen an Ograg, have they? They would not know how to fight them. They would slaughter the men of the Grim

Marches most effectively." He glanced at Ultorin. "Of course, it is the Grand Master's decision."

Though when he phrased it that way, Ultorin's decision was certain.

"A dozen Ogrags," said Ultorin, grinning. "That will give us enough time." He laughed, eyes wide, the cords in his neck bulging. "And I'll enjoy watching the Ogrags tear Mazael's knights to pulp."

~

LION BLAZED in Mazael's fist.

He struck down a Malrag, and then another, and then another, Lion cleaving through Malrag flesh with ease. Steel weapons wounded and slew the Malrags, but Lion had been forged to slay things of dark magic, and the Malrags feared the sword's fire. They shied away from Mazael, flinching from the sword's fire...and his knights and armsmen crashed into the distracted Malrags, cutting them down.

The Malrag charge had stopped, and now the momentum lay with Mazael and the rest of the vanguard.

He heard the distant boom of the war drums, followed by the roar of men and the thunder of hooves. Lord Richard had released the right and left wings under Lord Robert and Toraine. Once they arrived, they would crush the Malrag attack, and send any survivors fleeing.

Back to Ultorin's host.

Where, no doubt, tens of thousands more Malrags waited to attack. And still Ultorin had shown no sign of himself. If he stayed to the rear, if he simply sent wave after wave of Malrags at the host of the Grim Marches without exposing himself to danger...then he would win.

And then a different kind of roar cut into Mazael's thoughts.

He turned, smoke rising from Lion's blade as the magical flames burned away black Malrag blood. A huge gray shape lumbered through the Malrag lines, clad in clanking black armor. It looked like a Malrag, but most Malrags stood no more than five or six feet tall. This creature, this giant, stood at least fifteen feet tall, sheathed in armor plates like black dragon's scales. It looked even more deformed and gruesome than the smaller Malrags, its gray skin gnarled with growths and cysts.

The giant bellowed and ran forward, a spiked mace ready in its right hand.

~

ROMARIA HEARD THE ROAR, and it sent a cold shiver through her.

She knew the Malrags well. She had fought them in the craggy valleys and narrow passes of the Great Mountains, guiding travelers and merchant caravans through the high roads.

And only an Ograg made a roar like that. She had seen such a nightmare, the larger cousin of a Malrag, only twice. The second time, it had killed half the caravan before she had managed to bring the creature down with an arrow through its eye.

Turning, she spotted an Ograg, and then another, shoving their way through the ranks of Malrags, spiked maces in their hands. From what Mazael had said, his men had not yet seen an Ograg. They wouldn't know how to fight the creatures.

They would be slaughtered.

She galloped to Sir Tanam Crowley's side. The Old Crow sat staring at the Ogrags, his mouth drawn into a hard line.

"Lady Romaria," he said. Most men would have dismissed her without a second thought, but whatever else he was, the Old Crow was no fool. "You know what these things are?"

"Aye," said Romaria. "They're called Ogrags. Like Malrags, but bigger."

Tanam snorted. "I can see that."

"They grow in the same sort of dark hives as Malrags," said Romaria. "But the Ogrags keep growing and growing...almost like a tumor. They have incredible strength, but their growth deranges their minds. They're absolutely insane, and almost always stupider than the normal Malrags."

Tanam nodded. "So how do you fight the big devils?"

"From a distance," said Romaria, fitting an arrow to her bow. "Shoot them full of arrows until they bleed to death. Their eyes and throats are vulnerable - an arrow there can finish them off, if you're lucky."

Tanam grunted. "It's as good as plan as any. We'll shoot down the Ograge, and leave the Malrags to the heavy horse." He nodded to his standard-bearer, who lifted his horn and blew a short string of blasts. The horse archers surged forward, raising their bows. A storm of arrows fell upon the nearest Ograg. Most bounced from the giant's armor plates, but several struck home.

The Ograg roared in fury and came at them, mace raised high.

~

"SCATTER!" shouted Mazael, standing in his stirrups and waving Lion over his head. "Don't let it get close..."

Too late.

The misshapen giant crashed into the nearest group of knights, laying about with its spiked mace. Its first blow sent both a knight and his horse flying into the air, man and beast screaming. The giant kicked, and sent a mounted armsman sprawling to the earth. The man tried to scramble to his feet, only to have his head crushed like an egg beneath the giant's stump-like foot.

Mazael leaned from the saddle, snatched a fallen Malrag spear, and urged Hauberk forward. Yet the big horse hesitated, no doubt frightened by the giant's hideous appearance, or perhaps its vile stench. Mazael shouted and dug his spurs into the horse's side, and Hauberk whinnied and broke into a gallop.

The giant turned as Mazael thundered towards it. The spiked mace came up, ready to deliver a killing blow.

Exposing the creature's unarmored armpit.

Hauberk galloped under the upraised arm, and Mazael thrust

with all his strength. The spearhead, a foot of black steel, sank into the giant's exposed gray flesh. The creature howled and lashed out with its mace, the spikes passing so close to Mazael's face that he felt the wind of their passage. The giant flailed, mad with pain, slimy black blood dripping down its black-armored chest.

Mazael wheeled Hauberk around and drew Lion. The giant flinched away from the sword's flames, and Mazael set Hauberk forward in a charge. The creature lifted its mace for another blow, and Mazael stood up in his stirrups as he passed, whipping Lion through a high overhand swing.

The sword's tip ripped through the giant's throat, black blood spraying.

It let out of a gurgling bellow and fell to its knees, clutching at its torn throat.

Mazael wheeled, snatched another spear from a slain Malrag, and went looking for another giant.

ROMARIA BALANCED IN HER SADDLE, loosing arrow after arrow.

Almost every arrow found a mark in Ograg flesh. Most of the other horse archers and skirmishers lacked her skill. But when a hundred men shot at the Ograg, some of the arrows found a mark. The Ograg bellowed, lumbering after them, but the swift horses with their light-armored riders moved far faster than the massive creature.

Romaria drew and released once more. Her arrow streaked across the empty space and buried itself in the Ograg's throat. The creature roared, shaking in rage and pain, and Sir Tanam's raiders veered close and loosed a volley of steel-tipped javelins. Most of the weapons bounced away from the heavy armor, but a half-dozen buried themselves in the Ograg's face and throat.

The Ograg collapsed with a groan, the earth shuddering with the impact.

Romaria spun her horse, galloping for the next Ograg. All around her the heavy horsemen crashed through the Malrags, while the mounted archers and the skirmishers harried the Ogrags, luring them away from the knights. Her heart thundered beneath her ribs, her black hair streaming behind her head, and a wild grin spread over her face. They would win! They would smash the Malrags, drive them across the plains. And then Romaria would find Ultorin and put an arrow through his rotten heart, and they would have victory and peace.

She wanted to lift her face to the sky and howl.

Howl...

Her bow creaked, and Romaria looked at her hand in horror, the Ogrags and the Malrags momentarily forgotten.

Slender claws sprouted from her fingertips, digging into the wood and horn of her bow. Her hand looked more sinewy and muscular than usual, and a fuzz of fine black fur covered her fingers.

It was the beast within. The Elderborn half of her soul, charged with earth magic. Lucan's spell had restored her, but her nature had not changed. The human half of her soul was not strong enough to contain the raw power of the Elderborn half. And sooner or later, that power would overwhelm her, and she would become the great black wolf once more.

And then no spell could change her back.

Shuddering, she forced herself to calm, forced back the eagerness for the hunt, and her hand returned to normal, the claws and fur vanishing.

But she still felt the beast stirring within her, just below the surface.

Romaria was the child of a human father and an Elderborn mother...and half-blooded children all met the same fate. Sooner or later, their Elderborn souls overwhelmed them. Sooner or later, they became the beast, and nothing could stop it.

Her heart cold, Romaria lifted her bow and joined the battle, losing herself in the killing.

~

"Spears!" said Mazael, brandishing Lion.

His men obeyed, lances and spears in hand, and galloped past the Ograg. The long spears let them stay out of reach of the Ograg's massive fists and enormous spiked mace. The creature bellowed in frustration, lashing out with the mace, but the horsemen evaded its blow. Then Sir Hagen galloped past, and flung an axe in a smooth overhand throw. The heavy axe buried itself in the Ograg's brow, and the creature fell to its knees with a snarl. Another knight thundered forward, lance extended, and plunged the steel point into the Ograg's featureless white eye.

The Ograg collapsed with a thunderous clang of black armor.

Mazael turned Hauberk, spear in his left hand, sword in his right, and looked for new foes.

And found none.

Lion's flame dimmed in his hand.

Mazael looked around, frowning.

He saw no remaining Ogrags. Dead Malrags, dead Malrags beyond count, carpeted the plains, along with many slain knights, militia, and armsmen. He saw a few bands of Malrags left, fleeing in all directions, pursued by groups of horsemen.

But no other Malrags.

There had been no more than fifteen or twenty thousand Malrags in the attack, Mazael guessed.

What had happened to the rest of them?

Sykhana swayed in the saddle, Aldane cradled in her arms.

To the north, far to the north, she saw the dust raised by the battle. Or, rather, raised by the distraction. Twenty thousand Malrags, flung at Lord Richard's army, while the rest of the Malrag host slipped away to the south. Perhaps the twenty thousand would prevail over the men of the Grim Marches, or perhaps they would be slaughtered. Either way, it would not matter.

Aldane was safe. That was what mattered.

"Do you see?" murmured Malavost, riding besides her. "I told you I would keep my word."

Sykhana nodded, her heart racing. Soon Aldane would reign in splendor forevermore.

And she would be his mother.

Forever,

In the distance, she saw the green mass of the Great Southern Forest.

~

"To the south?" said Mazael, astonished. "Why would they go to the south?"

Sir Tanam shrugged. "My scouts didn't get close enough to ask. The Malrags are not the conversational sort. But the rest of the host is marching to the south."

Lord Richard's principal vassals gathered below his standard, overlooking the carnage of the battlefield. Vast tents had been raised to house the wounded, and Mazael heard the groans and cries of the injured men. Twenty thousand Malrags had been wiped out, slaughtered to the last creature. Yet two thousand men of the Grim Marches lay dead upon the field, with at least twice as many wounded, if not more.

Some of them might even live out the night.

"And they've all gone," said Tanam. "My lads saw other Malrag warbands scattered across the plains. Yet they're all marching south."

"Why go south?" said Toraine. Unlike the rest of the lords, Lord Richard's oldest son looked relaxed. Almost exhilarated. No doubt he had enjoyed the battle. "There's nothing to the south. Nothing but the Great Southern Forest, and no one lives there."

"No," said Mazael, looking at Romaria. She looked haggard and tired. Lord Athaelin stood besides her, ragged and spattered with Malrag blood. "The Elderborn live in the Great Southern Forest."

He looked at Lord Richard.

"Ultorin is going to Deepforest Keep."

18

THE PURSUIT

The morning after the battle, the lords and knights of the Grim Marches met in council atop the King's Tower of Castle Cravenlock.

They would have met in the great hall, but the wizards and the priests had filled it with cots for the wounded. The same had happened with the chapel, the courtyards, and the church in Cravenlock Town. The turret atop the King's Tower was the only flat space not filled with the wounded and the dying.

And the men of the Grim Marches had won the battle.

Mazael leaned against the battlements, still tired from the fighting, and listened to the other lords.

"It's confirmed, my lord," said Sir Tanam Crowley. "All my scouts say the same thing. The Malrags are marching into the Great Southern Forest. Every last warband. Most of them have already entered the Forest, and in another two days, there won't be a single Malrag left in the Grim Marches." He looked towards the town, and the battlefield beyond it. "A single living Malrag, anyway."

"Why?" said Lord Richard, still clad in his armor of crimson dragon scales. "Had Ultorin acted more boldly, he could have destroyed our host and taken Castle Cravenlock. Does he bear you some enmity, my lord Athaelin?"

"I cannot see how," said Athaelin. The sunlight caught on the bronze diadem encircling his gray hair. "I have never met a Dominiar knight. Neither the Elderborn nor the men of Deepforest Keep leave the Forest often."

"I fought against Ultorin," said Romaria. She looked better than yesterday, but dark circles ringed her blue eyes. "When the Dominiars waged war against the Old Kingdoms. But that was years ago. No doubt he remembers me...but he has far more cause to hate Mazael. And I doubt he even knew I was from Deepforest Keep."

"Will the Elderborn tribes fight against the Malrags?" said Lord Richard.

"Aye," said Athaelin. "Every step of the way. The Malrags hate the Elderborn even more than they hate humans. The Elderborn are archers without peer, and the Forest offers a thousand places to launch an ambush. But there are no more than two thousand Elderborn living in the Forest."

"They will not be able to stop the Malrags from reaching Deepforest Keep?" said Lord Richard.

"No," said Athaelin, voice grim. "They will not. My people will need aid."

"Then our course is clear," said Gerald. Somehow, he had managed to find a clean surcoat, his armor polished back to its usual mirror shine. "We must ride to the aid of Deepforest Keep and defeat Ultorin once and for all."

Lord Richard and Toraine shared a look. Lucan shook his head, a faint smirk on his lips.

"I see no reason for us to do so," said Toraine, and many of the lords nodded in agreement.

"What?" said Gerald, baffled. "But...you're simply going to let them go?"

"We have driven the Malrags out of the Grim Marches," said Toraine. "And now they have gone in search of easier prey. Our lands have been defended – that is all that matters."

"You would stand by and do nothing?" said Gerald.

"Lord Athaelin is not my father's vassal," said Toraine. "He need not obey my father. But neither is he entitled to the protection of the Mandragons."

"I agree with Lord Toraine," said Lord Robert. "My lands have suffered grievously from the Malrags. The Grim Marches have suffered grievously. Women have been made into orphans and widows, and we shall be lucky if we do not have a famine. If we have driven off the Malrag devils, I say let them go."

"So my father and the Elderborn fought with you against the Malrags," said Romaria, voice cold as she glared at Toraine, "and you..." She stopped, closed her eyes, flexed her right hand for a moment. "And you will simply abandon them?"

"Lord Athaelin," said Toraine, "despite his prowess, brought a dozen Elderborn to our fight. That hardly merits sending the host of the Grim Marches through the Great Southern Forest." He smiled, black eyes glittering. "And we lords of the Grim Marches must look after ourselves first. Perhaps the Elderborn and the Malrags will slaughter each other, and we need not deal with them ever again."

Romaria's expression turned thunderous, and Athaelin's eyes narrowed, but Lord Richard raised his hand.

"Enough, Toraine," he said. Again Mazael saw Lucan roll his eyes. "Lord Athaelin, we are grateful for your aid. But Lord Robert and Lord Toraine are correct. The Grim Marches have lost thousands of fighting men in the last four months, losses we can ill-afford. And the survivors must return home soon to plant crops, or we shall indeed suffer famine. And I dare not send men south to fight the Malrags. The neighboring lords will look upon our injured state and watch for any sign of weakness. The Castagenets of the High Plain, or perhaps Lord Malden of Knightcastle."

Gerald scowled. "My lord father would do no such thing."

Lord Richard raised a single flame-colored eyebrow. "Would he not, Sir Gerald?"

Gerald's frown deepened, but he said nothing.

"Lord Richard," said Athaelin, "this argument is pointless. There is no bond between our peoples. You have your duties, and I have mine. I must leave at once and return to Deepforest Keep. War is coming, and my people shall need me."

Lord Richard nodded. "It grieves me that I cannot send more aid, my lord Athaelin. Ultorin and his Malrags have done great injury to my lands, injury that I would see repaid tenfold." He paused, and looked at Mazael for a moment. "If any of my vassals wish to accompany you south, to win glory fighting the Malrags, I will not oppose them."

"I will ride with you, Lord Athaelin, along with my remaining men," said Gerald. "The San-keth have my son. The only way I will get Aldane back is over Ultorin's corpse."

Athaelin nodded. "You would be welcome, sir knight, along with all your men."

"And I shall come, as well," said Lucan, voice quiet.

Toraine snorted. "You, brother? What will you do? Strike the Malrags with that metal stick of yours?"

Lucan's fingers slid over the black staff. "Perhaps, brother, one day I shall show you just what this staff can do."

Toraine's sneer intensified. "And perhaps I shall show you just what my sword can do."

"Enough," said Lord Richard.

"I will come," said Lucan to his father, ignoring Toraine. "I suspect that Malavost is pulling Ultorin's strings. And I very much wish to know what Malavost wants, why he desires to attack Deepforest Keep, why he kidnapped Sir Gerald's son. Malavost is a skilled wizard and a necromancer of considerable power. Whatever he wants, whatever goal he pursues, it will be something baleful. And I will see him stopped."

"Very well," said Lord Richard. "I give you leave."

"I...would be glad of your assistance," said Athaelin, but Mazael heard the hesitation in his voice. No doubt Romaria had shared her fears about Lucan with him.

"And you, Lord Mazael?" said Lord Richard.

Mazael hesitated. There was a great deal of truth in what Lord

Richard had said. Mazael needed to defend his lands. Hundreds of his fighting men had been slain, and the gods alone knew how many peasants. He needed to stay, to rebuild, to prepare if the Malrags returned.

But Ultorin had brought fire and sword to Mazael's lands, crimes that cried out for vengeance. And Ultorin had to be stopped, lest he bring war to Deepforest Keep and even lands beyond.

And the San-keth had taken Mazael's nephew.

Rachel's son

He remembered the pain on her face.

And Lucan was right. Ultorin was the master of the Malrag host, but Mazael suspected Malavost was the master of Ultorin. Whatever the wizard wanted, it could not bode well for the people of the Grim Marches.

Mazael felt Romaria's eyes on him.

For her, he would ride to the ends of the earth.

"Yes," said Mazael. "I will go."

"A word, Lord Mazael," said Lord Richard, beckoning.

They walked to the corner of the tower's roof, away from the other lords.

"Are you sure this is wise?" said Lord Richard. "I will not command you to stay. But there are only two thousand Elderborn in the Great Southern Forest, and no more than seven or eight thousand humans living in Deepforest Keep. No matter how puissant their skill in battle, Ultorin and the Malrags will destroy them utterly."

"Not unless Ultorin is slain first," said Mazael.

"Perhaps," said Lord Richard.

"I will only take a few hundred men with me," said Mazael. "A small force, so I can get ahead of the Malrags and reach Deepforest Keep before Ultorin. In my absence, I will name Sir Nathan Great-heart as castellan, to hold my castle and lands in my name until I return."

"Very well," said Lord Richard. "What of Lady Rachel?" He paused for a moment. "Will she remain in Sir Nathan's care, as well?"

"She will want to come," said Mazael. "She pursued Sykhana this far, after all."

Lord Richard said nothing.

"But you knew that," said Mazael, "and that does not trouble you. And I know why."

"Do you?" said Lord Richard.

"Because if I am killed, and Rachel is killed, and Aldane is slain or never reclaimed from the San-keth," said Mazael, voice quiet, "then there are no Cravenlocks left. As liege lord, you can then claim Castle Cravenlock and its lands and bestow them upon whoever you wish. Perhaps Toraine, or one of your more loyal vassals."

"You see very deeply, my lord Mazael," said Lord Richard. "Your father and your brother both worshiped Sepharivaim, and ripped apart the Grim Marches in futile war. You have been a loyal vassal and worthy ally, which is why I have not lifted my hand against you." He paused. "Yet I do what is necessary for the security and safety of my lands. Whatever that might be."

"I understand," said Mazael.

"Then I wish you well, Lord Mazael," said Richard Mandragon. "I hope you return victorious, with Ultorin slain, Deepforest Keep saved, and your nephew rescued. And if you do not...then I will do what must be done."

RACHEL PACED her rooms in the King's Tower, back and forth, back and forth. At last she flung herself into a chair, forced herself to sit, to remain motionless.

Her hands shook.

It had been so very long since she had seen her son.

Her hands balled into fists, and she stood again. Even now, she knew, the Malrag host marched south, to Deepforest Keep. And Sykhana was with them, and Sykhana had her son. Circan had confirmed it, when she asked him. He still had the crystal vial of Aldane's blood, and Sykhana was moving south with the Malrags.

With her son.

She felt her lips tremble.

Oh, gods, when would she ever see Aldane again?

Rachel heard footsteps outside the door and wiped her eyes. She recognized Gerald's tread, and would not fall apart in front of him. His men relied on him, needed him to stay strong. And she would help him to stay strong.

No matter how much Rachel wanted to scream and weep.

The door opened, and Gerald stepped inside. His armor gleamed, his blue surcoat crisp and clean. She badgered his squire and pages into making sure his armor looked its best. Gerald was the youngest son of Lord Malden Roland – he might even be Lord of Knightcastle one day, if Tobias died childless. He had to look the part.

"What did they say?" said Rachel. She had wanted to attend the council, but she could not bear to face Lord Richard and his vassals again, not after her outburst the last time.

"Mazael and Lord Athaelin are certain that Ultorin means to attack Deepforest Keep," said Gerald. He sighed. "Lord Richard will not send any aid."

"Why not?" said Rachel, aghast.

"He will not risk his army against the Malrags," said Gerald. "Apparently, he is afraid that my father will take advantage of any weakness."

Rachel opened her mouth to protest, but fell silent. She knew her father-in-law, and Lord Richard was not wrong.

"But Mazael will go," said Gerald. "He plans to take two hundred men and ride south at once. I will go with him."

"Only two hundred?" said Rachel.

"Mazael thinks that Ultorin will besiege Deepforest Keep," said Gerald. "And a siege is quite different than an open battle – one man upon a wall can hold off ten men below it. Or ten Malrags, one hopes. With only two hundred men – and my men – we can get to Deepforest Keep before the Malrags. It's our best chance to kill Ultorin and get Aldane back."

Rachel nodded. She yearned to ride into the Malrag horde,

snatch her son back, and take him to safety at Knightcastle. But if she tried that, she would die. She wouldn't even get within sight of her son. They had to use their wits to get Aldane back.

"I'm coming with you," said Rachel.

Gerald closed his eyes. "No, Rachel."

"I've come this far," said Rachel.

He took her hands, his fingers hard with calluses from the hilt of his sword. "That was different. I thought we were only pursuing Sykhana. Dangerous enough, aye, but I didn't know we would ride into a war. If you come with me to Deepforest Keep...I know the Malrags will attack it. They might kill every man, woman, and child at Deepforest Keep. They might kill us before we even reach it. And if you are with us..."

"If I stay here and you are slain," said Rachel, "Lord Richard will force me to wed Toraine."

"Then you should go back to Knightcastle," said Gerald. "Some men are taking the wounded back to Knightcastle. Sir Cavilion could escort you..."

"No!" said Rachel. "If you die, if Aldane dies, then I will die with you. You are my husband and he is my son. I will not be parted from you."

"But you could live," said Gerald, his fingers rubbing hers. "You needn't perish. You could remarry, you could..."

"Remarry?" said Rachel. "To Toraine Mandragon? To one of your father's knights? No. No!" She shook her head. "The San-keth promised Mitor power and wealth and immortality, and look how that ended. The priests of the Amathavian church say that we all must die sooner or later. Well, they are right. But I would rather die as your wife and Aldane's mother than as an elderly widow or some other man's wife."

For a long time Gerald stared at her, the skin tight around his eyes.

Then at last he nodded.

"The gods forgive me," he said.

Rachel blinked back tears, and hugged him.

~

"WHAT IS IT?" said Mazael, his fingers tracing the smooth skin of Romaria's back.

They lay together in his bed, the moonlight leaking through the balcony doors. Romaria lay against him, her cheek resting on his chest, her long legs tangled with his. Her breathing came slow and steady, yet he felt the tension beneath her skin

"The beast almost took me," she said.

"The beast?" said Mazael.

She smiled, faintly. "It's what I call the Elderborn part of my soul. The part infused with earth magic, the way part of yours is infused with the power of the Demonsouled."

"But the Elderborn aren't evil, the way the Demonsouled power is," said Mazael.

"No," said Romaria. "But it's still terribly strong." She closed her eyes. "I cannot control it. Sooner or later it will overwhelm me. And then I will become that black wolf again, forever."

"I know," said Mazael. "But we all die of something, do we not?" His hand moved up her back, caressing her neck. "And...I am glad you chose to spend your remaining time here, with me."

She smiled, her eyes still closed. "How could I not?" For a moment they lay in silence. And then she said, "I don't want to go back to Deepforest Keep."

Mazael frowned. "You told me that it was your home. That it was the most beautiful place you had ever seen."

"It is," said Romaria. "But half-breeds like myself are...not favored among the Elderborn. Most Elderborn find a half-human, half-Elderborn child disgraceful. And some think we are outright abominations." He hesitated. "My mother...she is the High Druid of the Elderborn, the chief of their priestesses. Traditionally the Greenshield, the Lord of Deepforest Keep, lies with her upon taking up the diadem. Only rarely does the High Druid become pregnant. But she did. She wanted to purge her womb of me, but my father insisted that she carry me to term." Her voice grew soft. "She hates me."

"You never told me this," said Mazael.

Romaria shrugged. "I never thought I would go back to Deepforest Keep."

"You must have known you would," said Mazael. "The Seer prophesied it. He said we would meet, that we would save each other. You kept me from giving in to my Demonsouled side..."

"And you brought me back from the beast," said Romaria.

"And the Seer said you would save Deepforest Keep," said Mazael.

"I was hoping he was wrong," said Romaria.

"But he was right about us," said Mazael.

There was a long pause.

"Yes," said Romaria at last. "There are...caves beneath Deepforest Keep. Inside Mount Tynagis, leading to the ruins atop the mountain. Every man of woman of Deepforest Keep enters those caves on their sixteenth birthday, to come of age. And inside the caves, the Seer shows us visions of our future. I hoped the visions would not come true." She shook her head, black hair sliding over Mazael's chest. "I don't know how I can save Deepforest Keep."

"Shoot Ultorin," said Mazael. "That will solve everything."

She laughed. "Simple. Yet effective." She slid a hand over his shoulder and onto his chest. "But why are you going to Deepforest Keep? I have to go – it is my home, even if the Elderborn hate me. But Lord Richard was right. You have no obligation to defend it."

Mazael took a deep breath. "Ultorin brought the Malrags to the Grim Marches, brought them to attack my lands and my people. I will be damned before I let him escape retribution for that. And the San-keth have my nephew. I will get him back. If I can." His arm tightened against her back. "And because Deepforest Keep is your home. If you fight to defend it, I will go with you."

Romaria hesitated. "Is this guilt, Mazael? Because you blame yourself for what happened to me? I told you, it was the Old Demon's fault, not yours."

"That's not it," said Mazael. "I do blame myself, but that's not the reason I'm going to Deepforest Keep. It's your home. And I will help you defend it. I love you." His fingers stroked her cheek, her neck. "And if I kill Ultorin and rescue Aldane while defending your home... I suppose I can live with that."

Romaria grinned. "I suppose you can. I love you."

"I love you," said Mazael.

He kissed her once more, and they drifted off to sleep.

MAZAEL LEFT Castle Cravenlock before dawn, riding at the head of two hundred and fifty men. Two hundred of his own men – one hundred heavy horse and one hundred armsmen trained in the bow and crossbow. The survivors from Gerald's party. Lord Athaelin and his Elderborn, screening out around them to act as scouts.

Romaria rode alongside Mazael, bow balanced atop her saddle, the hilt of her new bastard sword rising over her shoulder. Gerald and Rachel followed, and then Circan and Lucan. Mazael had left Timothy and Sir Hagen behind to aid Sir Nathan. Mazael's lands would rest in capable hands until he returned.

One of the Elderborn rode up to Athaelin.

"There's not a sign of Malrags for five miles in any direction," said Athaelin.

Mazael nodded, and lifted Hauberk's reins. "Then let's reach Deepforest Keep before they do," he said, "and make Ultorin regret ever setting foot into the Grim Marches."

They rode to the south.

19

THE GREAT SOUTHERN FOREST

A day later they reached the Great Southern Forest.

The Grim Marches' rolling plains ended at a wall of trees. Massive, ancient trees, their trunks heavy with moss, their roots a tangled web covering the earth. The sun shone over the plains, but inside the Forest, Mazael saw only cool shadows, the ground shaded by the overlapping branches.

A thousand places for a Malrag ambush to hide.

"One man on foot can reach Deepforest Keep in two weeks, if he takes the most direct path," said Athaelin, reining up alongside Mazael. "Ultorin will take the most direct route, I think. Though he will not be able to move quickly, not with a hundred and fifty thousand Malrags. It will take him at least three weeks to reach Deepforest Keep. Maybe four."

Mazael shared a look with Gerald.

"The enemy always moves quicker than you expect, my lord Athaelin," said Gerald. "Far quicker."

"I assume you will not take us on the direct path to Deepforest Keep?" said Mazael. "Not with a hundred and fifty thousand Malrags blocking the way."

Athaelin shook his head.

"There are dozens of paths throughout the Forest," said Romaria, scanning the trees, one had resting on her bow. "The Elderborn tribes use them to hunt game. One path will take us around the main route, get us to Deepforest Keep in two and a half weeks. If we hasten. The ground is uneven, and we will need to walk the horses."

"It should keep us clear of the Malrags, though," said Athaelin.

"I doubt it," said Mazael.

Athaelin looked puzzled, which surprised Mazael. Romaria's father was a capable fighter, but Mazael wondered how much experience Athaelin had leading men in battle.

"I suspect these paths are narrow," said Mazael, "and a hundred thousand Malrags would clog them quickly. So Ultorin will move his host in groups. I also suspect the Elderborn tribes will attack the Malrags," Romaria nodded, "and so Ultorin will send out scouting parties and warbands to deal with the Elderborn. We may stumble across them. For that matter, the Forest is vast, and Ultorin will not have the benefit of you and Romaria to guide him. Some of the Malrags will get lost, or separated from the main host. We might cross their paths, as well."

"Then we will fight them," said Athaelin, "and be victorious, and arrive at Deepforest Keep."

"It will take hard fighting," said Mazael. "Our great advantage over the Malrags has always been cavalry. On the plains, our horsemen broke the Malrags over and over again. In the Forest, the advantage will belong to the Malrags. Fortunately, we have rarely seen them use bows or missile weapons."

"Your men should use javelins," said Romaria.

Mazael shook his head. "Hard to use in the forest. Bows are better."

Athaelin nodded. "That's why half your men are archers."

"Aye," said Mazael. "I hope to avoid the Malrags, with the aid of your scouts. But if it comes to a fight, then knights and armsmen will make a shield wall to protect the archers." He glanced up at the sky. "We had best get moving."

Gerald nodded. "I'll get the men ready." He rode off.

"Romaria," said Athaelin, "tell the Elderborn to start scouting. Teams of two. If there are any Malrags within five miles, I want to know about it."

"As you say, Father," said Romaria, and rode towards the Elderborn, leaving Mazael alone with Athaelin.

"I am glad you are here," said Athaelin. "I have little experience in this kind of war."

Mazael snorted. "I doubt that. You almost took my head off, as I recall."

"Aye," said Athaelin, "but fighting man-to-man, or in a small band, is different from this. I've led men in raids, in small battles...but never against such numbers."

Mazael shrugged. "It's little different. Fighting man-to-man, you slay your foe. In this kind of war, there are simply more to slay. And the only one we really need to kill is Ultorin."

Athaelin laughed. "Spoken truly. Then let us return to Deepforest Keep, and show Ultorin how to wage a war."

Mazael nodded, and led his men into the trees.

THEY SAW the signs of the first skirmish before noon.

A dozen Malrags lay at the base of an ancient oak, their black blood soaking into the mossy earth. Arrows jutted from their bodies, fired with inhuman precision into the gaps in their armor. Romaria swung from her saddle, knelt by a dead Malrag, and wrenched an arrow from its wounds.

"An obsidian head," she announced. "The Elderborn did this."

One of the Elderborn reined up by Athaelin, speaking in their strange tongue.

"The scouts say there are more dead Malrags, dozens of them, scattered over the next five miles or so," said Athaelin. "No sign of any living ones. Or of any Elderborn, for that matter."

"They must have been pressed hard," said Mazael.

"Why?" said Athaelin. "Obviously, they won."

"But they did not stop to collect their arrows," said Mazael. "I imagine those obsidian arrowheads break easily and take some time to replace."

The Elderborn shared a look amongst themselves, speaking in their own language.

"You're right," said Romaria. "The Elderborn always collect their arrows after a battle."

Athaelin listened to the Elderborn for a moment, nodded. "They say there are signs of flight on the ground. A hunting party of maybe twenty Elderborn. But they cover their tracks too well. We cannot trace them."

"Then that hunting party is on their own," said Mazael. "If we come across the Elderborn, we will aid them, but chasing them is a fool's errand. I suggest we keep moving, Lord Athaelin."

Athaelin nodded, and they traveled deeper into the Forest.

THEY MADE camp among the great trees, tents going up, banked firepits dug to mask the smoke from the cooking fires. At least they had no shortage of wood, and the Forest's small streams provided ample drinking water. Mazael stood at the edge of the camp with Gerald and Romaria, staring into the gathering darkness.

"It's so quiet," said Gerald.

"Too quiet," said Romaria. "We should be able to hear the birds singing, the animals moving through the brush."

"Perhaps we've scared them all off," said Mazael.

"Aye," said Romaria, "or something else has."

But no Malrags came during the night.

THEY SAW the first traig the next morning.

Athaelin and the Elderborn led them along a trail that broadened until it became something resembling a road. The roots of the massive trees had dug into the path, and moss and brush grew thick upon the earth, but here and there Mazael saw ancient, lichen-spotted white paving stones. From time to time half-crumbled columns rose out of the underbrush, some toppled by the roots of the trees.

Then the road narrowed, and Mazael saw the traig.

Rachel gasped. "What is that thing?"

A statue of white stone, nearly fifteen feet tall, stood in a ring of trees. At first Mazael mistook it for a massive boulder, but despite the weathering and the lichen, the stone had been worked by skilled hands. It had been carved in the shape of a great armored warrior, leaning upon a greatsword, covered head to toe in ornate plate armor. As they drew closer, Mazael saw that the armor had once been covered in intricate reliefs. Time and weather had eroded the scenes, but they still showed some long-forgotten battle.

"The Elderborn call them traigs," said Romaria, voice soft. Most of the Elderborn were out scouting, but three rode near Athaelin. They looked at the traig with reverence in their alien faces.

"What are they?" said Mazael. "Tombs, perhaps?"

Athaelin shook his head. "No one really knows, not even the Elderborn, or even the druids themselves. The traigs are relics left by the High Elderborn, the ancestors of the Elderborn tribes who now hunt the Great Southern Forest." His voice grew formal, as if reciting a long-remembered story. "In ancient times, the High Elderborn built mighty cities of marble and glass, reared with skill and magic spells, and their kingdoms sprawled across the face of the earth. Then the children of the Old Demon came, bringing with the San-keth and Malrags beyond count. The Elderborn kingdoms fell in ruin and fire, their knowledge lost. Now only a few Elderborn tribes still roam the world, and revere the ancient ruins of their ancestors."

"That's so sad," said Rachel, blinking.

"The traigs represent, I think, the defenders of the ancient Elderborn kingdoms," said Athaelin. "Warriors clad in spell-wrought armor, with magical blades in their hands. Their like cannot be found today...except, perhaps, for the sword at your hip." He nodded at Mazael, at where Lion hung in its scabbard.

"Elderborn knights of old," said Rachel. She always did like old stories.

"Perhaps," said Athaelin. "Though if they were the warriors of old, I would like to have a legion of them at my command. Then I would sweep the Forest clean of the Malrags, and return your son to your arms, Lady Rachel."

For a moment Rachel gave the traig a longing look, and then they left it behind.

～

LATER THAT NIGHT they saw a living Malrag for the first time.

The creature staggered along the ancient road, wounded, black blood leaking from its armor. The Elderborn shot the Malrag before it even came within sight of the horsemen.

"More arrow wounds," said Romaria, examining the dead creature. "At least a day old, I think."

"The only survivor from a battle, no doubt," said Gerald.

"Then the Elderborn are having the better of it," said Athaelin. "We have not yet seen a single slain Elderborn."

"Good," said Mazael.

But he did not allow the Elderborn, or his own scouts, to relax their vigilance, and he made sure to pick a defensible location for their camp.

～

THAT NIGHT MAZAEL saw flashes of green lightning far to the south.

He walked to the edge of the camp. Lucan stood there, black staff clenched in his pale hands. For an instant Mazael thought the sigils upon the staff's length blazed with hellish light, and he reached for his sword, but the light vanished.

He blinked, shaking his head.

Lucan saw him, nodded.

"How far away are they?" said Mazael.

Lucan shrugged. "Twenty miles. Perhaps thirty. Far enough away that I cannot sense them with any accuracy. I feel the disturbances, though. Someone is using a great deal of magic."

"Are the Elderborn druids are fighting the Malrag shamans?" said Mazael. Another flash lit the southern sky.

"Perhaps," said Lucan. "If they are, I wish them a great deal of luck. The shamans lack fine skill, but they make up for it in raw power." He snorted. "Maybe we'll get fortunate and the Elderborn will kill Ultorin and Malavost for us."

"We," said Mazael, "are not that fortunate."

"No. No, we are not."

They stood in silence for a moment.

"Are you ill?" said Mazael at last.

He saw a dark eyebrow lift in Lucan's cowl. "Why do you say that?"

"Because you look ill, frankly," said Mazael. "You've collapsed during battle, repeatedly." He hesitated, unsure of what to say. "And Romaria...thinks you smell ill."

Lucan laughed. "None of us have bathed since leaving Castle Cravenlock. A few more days and we all shall smell ill."

"It is more than that," said Mazael. "Her senses have...changed, since you merged the pieces of her soul. She thinks something is very wrong with you." He reached out, gripped the younger man's shoulder. "You have been a loyal friend and ally against some terrible foes, Lucan. If I can aid you, I will."

Lucan's expression did not change, but for a moment he no longer seemed the sneering, cynical necromancer, but a young man of twenty-two, exhausted and confused by a terrible burden.

"Thank you, my lord," said Lucan, voice soft. "And...you are a lord worthy to follow. I am pleased to serve you, as I was never pleased to serve my lord father." He bowed his head. "And...yes, I am ill. It is...the strain of drawing too much magical power for too long. Not all of us have your...vigorous nature, my lord. I have to turn to other sources of power to sustain myself. And some of those sources have unpleasant side effects."

"Are you in danger?" said Mazael. "Timothy never suffers these side effects."

"Timothy is a good man, my lord, but he is only a mediocre wizard," said Lucan. "And so I can access...sources of power that he cannot." He took a deep breath, leaning on the black staff. "I know the risks. I know what I am doing. It is necessary, if I am to stand against the likes of Malavost." His voice dropped. "And you understand, my lord. You have fought long and hard against your...nature, but without its power, you would have been slain a dozen times in the last few years. In the last few months."

Mazael looked into the camp, where Romaria sat with Athaelin by a fire. "You may be right. But...the price for that power was still more than I wanted to pay."

Lucan's smile was brittle. "What we want, my lord, has little bearing upon what we actually receive."

⁓

THE NEXT DAY Romaria and her father went scouting together.

It had been too long, she realized. Too long since she had glided through the trees of the Great Southern Forest, moving from shadow to shadow without making a sound. Too long since she had felt her boots grip the mossy soil, since she had heard the wind rustle through the leaves of the great oak trees.

Deepforest Keep was her home, but she had not missed it very much. But, gods, she had missed the Great Southern Forest.

She and Athaelin moved silently through the trees. They had both learned from the hunters of the Elderborn, and years of practice proved just as effective a teacher. Now Romaria could move through the Forest without a whisper of sound.

Athaelin held up a hand. "Let's rest for a moment. I doubt there are any Malrags in the area."

Romaria nodded and leaned against a tree. Her father reached into his pack, handed her some hard bread and jerky. She took a bite, washed it down with a swig from her waterskin. The salty food was less than pleasant, but certainly better than nothing.

"I wonder where all the Malrags went," said Athaelin around a mouthful of bread.

"Deepforest Keep," said Romaria. "Ultorin wants to attack it, and the Malrags follow him. Or at least his bloodsword."

Athaelin nodded. "Your mother asked about you."

Romaria froze. After a moment she forced herself to relax. "Did she?"

"Ardanna wanted to know what had become of you," said Athaelin. "At the time I thought Mazael had killed you."

Romaria scowled. "And I suppose the High Druid was delighted to hear the news."

Athaelin hesitated, which was all the answer Romaria needed.

"Did she want to send Mazael congratulations?" said Romaria, voice tighter than she would have liked.

Athaelin sighed, pulled his shield over his shoulders, rested it against his knees. The ancient bronze shield with its patina of age, the symbol of the Greenshield, the Champion of Deepforest Keep and Defender of the Mountain.

"No," he said at last.

"But I doubt she was grief-stricken to hear of my death," said Romaria.

"She thought it should be avenged," said Athaelin. "That the Elderborn blood within you should not have been spilled with impunity."

"Even if the blood was in a filthy abomination of a half-breed," said Romaria.

"Do not speak of yourself like that," said Athaelin, scowling. "You are brave, and skilled, and have survived trials that few could endure. Ardanna will accept that you have returned to Deepforest Keep. I will make her."

Despite herself, Romaria almost smiled. "And when have you ever been able to make her do anything?"

"There is a first time for everything under the sun," said Athaelin. "Besides. You know what the Seer said about you."

Romaria sighed. "That I would save Deepforest Keep."

"You doubt him?"

"No," said Romaria. "I've seen his visions come true enough times. He said that Mazael and I would save each other, and so we have. But they never come true in the way you might expect. And I wonder what his vision means."

"Mazael," said Athaelin.

Romaria snorted. "Is this the part, Father, where you express disapproval? You already tried to kill him once."

"He's Demonsouled," said Athaelin, "is he not?"

Romaria said nothing.

"I've seen him in battle," said Athaelin. "I've seen how he mows down the Malrags like so much wheat, how his minor wounds seem to heal up very quickly. I've seen how his men follow him without question." He shook his head. "Gods, I've even started following his commands without thinking. But he has control of himself, does he not?"

Romaria closed her eyes. "Aye. The Old Demon himself is Mazael's father. Do you remember those undead things that appeared in the Forest? The Old Demon raised them, disguised as the necromancer Simonian of Briault. And he was the one who killed me." She shook her head. "Or...struck me down, I should say."

"But Mazael does have control of himself?" said Athaelin.

"Yes," said Romaria. "The Old Demon tried to corrupt him. Rachel betrayed him, left him to die in the San-keth temple below Castle Cravenlock. Mazael would have killed her, but I stopped him. Or I helped him stop himself. But he does have control of himself. The Demonsouled power has not warped him into a monster."

"Good," said Athaelin. "I've killed minor Demonsouled before, but never have I seen one who mastered the darkness within. I always heard that such a man would be a warrior without peer." He shook his head, and raked a hand through his gray hair. "Watching Mazael fight, I can believe it."

"So...you will not act against him?" said Romaria. "Even knowing what he is?"

Athaelin snorted. "You're in love with him, daughter, and you're no fool. I doubt you would take a monster to your bed. If you trust him, then so do I."

Romaria smiled. "Thank you."

He reached over and touched her cheek. "And he seems to make you happy. You haven't had much joy in your life, Romaria, I know. And much of that is my fault. But..."

Something moved in the trees behind Athaelin.

Romaria exploded to her feet, snatched her bow from her shoulder, drew an arrow, and released, all in one smooth motion. Athaelin scrambled to his feet, reaching for his sword, and Romaria shot another arrow.

She laughed at his expression.

"What?" said Athaelin, scowling, looking back and forth. "What is it? Malrags?"

She laughed again, pointing with the bow. "Look!"

Two deer lay upon the ground, her arrows jutting from their throats.

Athaelin grinned. "Good shooting."

"At least we'll have fresh meat tonight," said Romaria.

RACHEL RODE in the center of the column, surrounded by knights. Mazael had insisted - she wore no armor, and one arrow fired from the trees could kill her. Rachel agreed without any protest. She needed to stay alive to get her son back.

"Thirty-seven," she said.

Gerald looked at her, his armor flashing in the rays of sunlight leaking through the leafy canopy overhead. "Thirty-seven what?"

"Days," said Rachel. "Thirty-seven days since I last held Aldane."

Gerald closed his eyes, nodded. "I know."

They rode without speaking for a while, the only sound the crack of branches beneath the horses' hooves. Mazael rode with Athaelin and Sir Cavilion at the head of the column, speaking in low voices. Romaria and most of the Elderborn were gone, scouting for Malrags and hunting for provisions. Romaria said that the Malrag invasion had sent the deer herds fleeing in all directions. They might have fresh venison and pheasant every night until they reached Deepforest Keep.

"Do you think we'll ever see Aldane again?" said Rachel.

Gerald nodded. "We'll get him back."

"Do you really believe that?" said Rachel. "Tell me the truth."

Again they rode in silence.

"I don't know," said Gerald at last. "This...has turned out to be more than I ever expected. At first I thought the San-keth only wanted revenge on you. But then we rode into a war. And the San-keth are working with Ultorin and his Malrags..." He sighed, pulled off his gauntlets, and rubbed his face. "We are caught up in great events, my wife. Our son is caught up in great events."

"I just wish I knew why," said Rachel. "If the San-keth...if the San-keth wanted to hurt Aldane, I could understand that. But why kidnap him? Why take him with the Malrags to Deepforest Keep?" She gazed at the endless tangled branches of massive trees. "I wish I knew why."

"We will know why," said Gerald. "We'll find Ultorin and kill him. And when the Malrag host turns on itself, we'll get Aldane back."

He spoke so confidently. Rachel wondered if he believed it himself. But she understood. He could not show weakness in front of his men.

"It's almost midday," said Gerald. Both Mazael and Athaelin insisted that they travel all day, and take their meals in the saddle. Or on foot, when the ground became too uneven, and they had to lead their horses. "There's still some fresh pheasant left. I think..."

The distant sound of a war horn rang out, echoing through the trees.

Gerald frowned, hand flying to his sword hilt.

An instant later a blast of green lightning blazed down from the sky, the thunderclap following.

20

FALLING LEAVES

"**F**orm up!" roared Mazael, jumping from his saddle. "Knights to the front! Archers, ready your bows!"

Fighting from horseback in the dense forest would be useless at best and suicidal at worst. The knights and armsmen scrambled from their saddles, shields on their arms, swords in their hands. Behind them the archers stood ready, arrows resting against their bows.

"The reserve!" said Mazael. "Stay with the animals!" Twenty-five armsmen and twenty-five archers, along with Circan, fell in guard formation around the pack horses and the destriers. Rachel waited by the pack horses, her face tight with anxiety. Gods, how many times had she watched Mazael and Gerald go into battle, wondering if today they would not return?

He swallowed. Romaria was out there, with the Elderborn scouts. Another blast of emerald lightning flashed to the west, the roll of thunder coming a few heartbeats later. Had the Malrags caught Romaria and the Elderborn? Were they fighting for their lives even now? Mazael wondered if he should lead the men in the direction of the lightning, if...

A moment later Romaria crashed through the trees, breathing hard, four Elderborn scouts at her heels.

"Mazael!" she said. "Two miles south of here, in a circle of traigs. Forty Elderborn are trying to hold off a hundred and fifty Malrags. The Elderborn are holding their own..."

"But the Malrags have one of those damned shamans," said Mazael, glancing at Lucan.

"Two, actually," said Romaria. "The Elderborn have a druid, but she's overmatched. I don't know how much longer they can hold."

Mazael glanced at Lucan, who stood a short distance away, wrapped in his black cloak. He nodded, his eyes glinting beneath his hood. He was ready.

"Should we aid them?" said Sir Cavilion, frowning. "I mean no disrespect to your people, my lord Athaelin, my lord Romaria. But our best chance at reaching Deepforest Keep lies in speed and stealth. If the Malrags notice us, or if they call up reinforcements..."

"No," said Mazael. "We aid them. If we come across more bands of Elderborn, we'll assist them as well. The more we can gather and take with us to Deepforest Keep, the better chance we'll have against the Malrags when Ultorin launches his assault."

Cavilion nodded and drew his sword.

"Let's go," said Mazael. "Romaria, lead the way."

Romaria nodded and moved into the trees, the Elderborn fanning around her. Athaelin drew his bastard sword in his right hand, the ancient bronze shield upon his left arm. Mazael kept Lion in its scabbard. The sword would burn with azure flames as they drew closer to the Malrags, and he did not know how far the light would carry in the trees.

His men marched south, keeping as close together as the massive trees and the tangled underbrush allowed. Mazael scanned the trees, hand resting on Lion's hilt. Had the Malrags used archers or javelin-equipped skirmishers, the close-packed formation of his men would have made them easy targets. Fortunately, the Malrags preferred hand-to-hand combat. Perhaps their love of cruelty and torture demanded it.

Again a green lightning flashed down, followed by a thunderclap, much louder this time. Then the earth trembled for a moment beneath Mazael's feet, and he heard a distant rushing noise. He looked at Lucan.

"Earth magic," muttered Lucan, staff held at the ready. "The druid is fighting back, I think."

Mazael nodded, and they kept marching.

Soon he heard the familiar bellow of Malrag war cries, and something else - voices shouting in the lyrical tongue of the Elderborn. He smelled smoke, the harsh scent of burning wood.

Then, all at once, he saw the battle.

A low hill rose in the forest, crowned by a ring of a dozen traigs, like white teeth jutting from a bone. About fifty Elderborn stood in the ring, clad in gray furs, firing their bows. Over two hundred Malrags milled at the base of the hill, armed with shields and axes. They crept slowly up the slope, the Elderborn sending volleys of obsidian-tipped arrows at every opening in the line. For every volley, some of the Malrags fell dying to the earth. Yet there were too many Malrags, and they were too well-armored. Mazael saw a balekhan at the rear of the Malrags, bellowing commands. The Malrags had formed a shield wall, and the Elderborn arrows could not penetrate. When the Malrags reached the crest of the hill, they would slaughter the Elderborn.

A green lightning bolt streaked towards the Elderborn, only to veer aside and rip apart a tree in a spray of burning splinters. Mazael saw an Elderborn woman, clad in a cloak of brown fur, thrust her arms at the sky, an oaken staff in her hands. A druid then - and one on the brink of exhaustion, to judge from the trembling of her arms.

Then the balekhan saw Mazael. It roared a command, and the Malrags turned, howling.

Mazael ripped Lion free from its scabbard, the blade shining with azure fire.

"Stand fast!" yelled Mazael as the Malrags charged.

His men raised their shields, forming a wall, and behind him he heard the creak of the militiamen's bows.

LUCAN MUTTERED A SPELL, wrapping himself in a veil of concealment. The spell Timothy had used against Malavost, it wrapped the light and shadow of the forest around him. It was not powerful enough to draw the notice of the Malrag shamans, and it would hide him from their eyes.

He smiled. He might possess the greater power, but it seemed Timothy still had a thing or two to teach him.

The Malrags charged at Mazael's men, heedless of the Elderborn arrows that ripped into their flanks. The creatures struck into the shield wall with a great crash, swinging their axes with abandon. Yet the shield wall held, the knights stabbing over the top of the shields, arrows from the militia hissing over their shoulders to plunge into gray Malrag flesh. Mazael fought at the front, Lion a storm of blue flame in his fist, and every blow flung a Malrag upon the earth. Lord Athaelin and Sir Gerald fought at his side, protecting each others' flanks. Arrows hissed out of the trees, and Lucan saw Romaria and the Elderborn scouts, picking off the Malrags one by one.

They were winning.

At least until the shamans took a hand. Two or three well-placed lightning bolts would kill half the knights.

Unless Lucan took action.

He strode through the trees, bloodstaff ready in his hands. He felt its Demonsouled power beneath his fingers, half-asleep, waited for him to call upon it, to fill him with strength and blazing might. But he dared not use it. Mazael was right - the staff's power let him perform feats of magic far beyond even his considerable skills, but it was killing him. He dared not draw upon that power.

Not unless, of course, the situation was hopeless...

He shook aside the thought. This situation, at least, was not hopeless. Two Malrag shamans were not beyond his powers, especially with surprise on his side.

The first Malrag shaman stood in the shadows of a nearby tree, no doubt to provide cover from the Elderborn arrows. The shaman's third eye blazed with emerald light, and the creature turned towards the battle, hands lifted in the beginnings of a spell. Lucan felt the tremendous surge of power as the shaman summoned a lightning bolt.

But this time, Lucan had the advantage.

He drew in power and thrust out his hand. A psychokinetic burst erupted from his fingers, ripping into the Malrag with the force of a sledgehammer. The blast picked the creature up and smashed it against the oak tree with such force that its head shattered, black blood spraying across the trunk.

Lucan whirled, preparing another spell, ready to strike before the other shaman could attack.

His heart sank.

Another shaman stood perhaps twenty yards away, all three eyes focused upon Lucan.

A third shaman stood besides the second.

They cast their spells as one, and green fire thundered upon Lucan.

~

MAZAEL CUT THROUGH THE MALRAGS, Lion blazing in his fist.

He struck down a Malrag, and another, and then another, black blood sizzling against Lion's blade. Besides him Athaelin fought with the same dancelike movements he had seen Romaria use in battle, while Gerald remained immovable, Malrag axe and spear alike rebounding from his shield.

A Malrag bellowed, and Mazael heard the words echo inside his skull.

-Fight! Fight and die! We shall be reborn, but they shall not-

Mazael saw the balekhan striding through the mass of Malrags, a black greatsword ready in a mailed fist. It stood almost eight feet tall, covered head to toe in black plate mail.

The creature came to a sudden halt when it saw Mazael.

-You! I have heard of you. The one who could have the Master, yet turned his back upon his heritage. I will slay you, and enjoy your screams of torment, pitiful one-

The balekhan lifted its black sword, and Mazael sprang to meet it.

Lucan had no other choice.

The bloodstaff's power flooded him, filling him with strength, with vitality, with manic and wild glee. Twin lightning bolts screamed down to slay him, and Lucan lifted his staff, casting a warding spell. A sphere of blood-colored light shimmered around him, and the lightning blasts smashed against it. One rebounded to rip apart a tree, sending burning splinters flying in all directions.

The other lashed across the clearing to slam into a Malrag shaman. The creature's head and torso simply disappeared, the charred remains of its body toppling to the forest floor. Lucan attacked at once, channeling another psychokinetic burst through his staff and flinging it at the remaining Malrag. But the shaman cast a ward, and the blast redirected into the ground at its feet, throwing up clods of torn earth.

The shaman began casting again, and Lucan slammed his staff against the ground, calling into the spirit world. Gray mist swirled at his feet, and a score of spirit beasts, more than he had ever summoned before, leapt forth. This time they looked like great black cats with the heads of vultures, the wings of bats, and the tails of scorpions. With a horrid skittering sound, they raced forward, the ground visible through their translucent forms.

The Malrag shaman put up a good fight. A blast of emerald lightning sent two of the beasts back to the spirit world, while a psychokinetic burst sent three more tumbling through the air. But the rest sprang upon the shaman, claws and breaks ripping at its flesh. The shaman staggered, black blood spraying, and collapsed, the spirit beasts feasting.

Lucan laughed with delight and forgot the shaman and spirit beasts both.

So many things to kill, so little time. Where to begin? The Elderborn first - their supernatural accuracy with their bows might inconvenience him. Then Lucan would mow down the Malrags and Mazael's men both. Or perhaps he would only kill Mazael's men, and keep the Malrags for himself. He would kill Ultorin, take command of the Malrag host, and march north to make his father and brother pay for all the pain they had inflicted upon him.

He lifted his hand. The bloodstaff's sigils blazed brighter, and darkness swirled around the staff. Power flooded into Lucan like molten iron, and he focused his will, preparing to unleash death upon the Elderborn...

The ground heaved beneath his feet. Roots erupted from the ground, twining around his legs.

Lucan staggered, leaning upon the bloodstaff for balance. The Elderborn druid raced towards him, disgust and horror upon her angular face, and began to cast another spell.

MAZAEL DUELED THE BALEKHAN, black sword straining against Lion's azure flame.

The balekhan was stronger, but Mazael was faster. As the mass of Malrags crashed against the shield wall, as Elderborn arrows whistled through the air, Mazael danced around the balekhan's strokes, whipping Lion at the weak points in the towering creature's armor. His blade crunched through the elbow joint on the balekhan's left arm, and it bellowed in rage and pain.

Then a steel-tipped arrow thudded into the back of the balekhan's leg, and then another. The creature stumbled to one knee, roaring, and Mazael glimpsed Romaria in the shadows of the trees, her bow in hand.

He surged forward, and plunged Lion into the eye slit of the balekhan's helm. A storm of azure fire erupted down Lion's blade, and the balekhan toppled backwards with a clatter of black armor. A ripple went through the Malrags, and they fell back, white eyes fixed upon Mazael.

"Take them!" shouted Mazael. "Strike hard!"

His men surged forward, and the storm of arrows from the Elderborn redoubled.

"VILE CREATURE," said the Elderborn druid. "You defile the Forest with your dark magic. No more! You will pay for your..."

Lucan snarled and struck his staff against the earth. Ribbons of blood-colored flame erupted from the sigils, cutting the roots to pieces. The druid's silver eyes widened, and she pointed at Lucan, pale blue light flashing around her fingers.

He struck first.

His psychokinetic burst picked her up, flung her a dozen yards, and smashed her against a traig. Her blood splattered against the statue, shockingly red against the white stone, and the dead druid crumpled to the ground, eyes staring at him.

Lucan strode forward, the bloodstaff burning in his hand. The fool woman had dared to use her spells against him? Then so be it! First he would slay every last Elderborn in the clearing, and then he would...

The staff's light winked out.

The strength drained out of Lucan. He collapsed to his knees, his limbs like wet string, and vomited . Then his vision blacked out, and for a terrible moment he thought he had gone blind. He blinked, and his sight returned, but everything looked distorted, rotting, as if the world had died.

Bit by bit, his vision returned to normal, though his stomach churned and his head felt as if iron spikes had been hammered into his temples. Gods, gods, why did he use that damned staff? He should throw it away, destroy it before it destroyed him.

But the stolen Demonsouled power was so very sweet...

He saw the dead druid slumped against the traig, eyes staring at him as if in accusation.

Lucan's nausea redoubled, but there was nothing left to come up.

He had murdered her. Caught in the frenzy of the bloodstaff's power, he had butchered her without a second thought. His hands shook against the staff. He had only acted in self-defense. If she had not attacked him first...

But that was a feeble justification. She had only attacked him because she thought him a threat. Because she had seen the Demon-souled power of its bloodstaff for what it really was. And he had killed her without mercy.

Lucan closed his eyes and waited for the Elderborn arrows to sink into his flesh.

Nothing happened.

He opened his eyes, and saw that the battle was over. Most of the Malrags lay slaughtered upon the earth. The rest had fled in all directions, the Elderborn moving to speak join Mazael's men. Most likely, no one had seen Lucan kill the druid. When they found her corpse, they would blame the shamans, or one of the common Malrags.

For a wild moment he wanted to confess, to tell them everything...

No. A foolish thought. He had to see this through. He had to stop Malavost. Whatever the cost to himself. He would not permit others to suffer from dark magic as he had...

But the Elderborn druid had suffered from dark magic, hadn't she?

His dark magic.

Lucan pushed the thought aside and got to his feet.

～

THE BATTLE WAS OVER.

And to Mazael's astonishment, he had not lost a single man. Some had suffered wounds, but none fatal. Between the valor of his men and the uncanny skill of the Elderborn, the Malrags had been slaughtered.

The Elderborn descended from the hill and its ring of traigs. They wore clothes of leather, and mantles made from gray wolf fur. Their leader walked in front, carrying a great bow and a spear with an onyx head. His eyes were a strange shade of purple, and fixed upon Mazael with electric intensity.

Mazael bowed. "Ardmorgan Sil Tarithyn."

He knew this Elderborn. Sil Tarithyn was the ardmorgan, or high chief, of the Tribe of the Wolf. They had come north two years ago, to fight the undead abominations raised by the Old Demon, and had helped Mazael in the final fight against Skhath and the San-keth.

"Mazael Cravenlock," said Sil Tarithyn. He stopped, gazed at Mazael for a moment, and then his angular face split in a smile. "So. You have faced yourself, and conquered yourself."

"You could say that," said Mazael.

Romaria strode from the trees, Athaelin's Elderborn following, and Sil Tarithyn looked at her. "And the Greenshield's daughter. For a dead woman, you look most hale."

Romaria grinned. "Clean living."

"Do not speak to her, ardmorgan!" said another of the Elderborn, scowling. "She is an abomination!"

Romaria's grin faded, and Athaelin scowled.

"Abomination?" said Sil Tarithyn. "You should hold your tongue, Gardan. Her skill helped save our lives." Lucan limped over, looking exhausted, leaning upon his staff. The battle with the shamans must have drained him. "If she is an abomination, I would have a dozen more. The Malrags have us sore pressed."

Gardan's scowl deepened, but the Elderborn looked away.

"Lucan," said Mazael. "You did well. I fear those shamans would strike us all down, but here we are. Thank you."

Lucan nodded, not meeting his gaze.

"A dozen of my tribe were slain this day," said Sil Tarithyn, "along with one of our druids. Your arrival was most timely, Mazael Craven-lock and Romaria daughter of the Greenshield. Without your intervention, we would all have been slain. And the Elderborn are a dwindling people. "

"You have our aid," said Mazael.

"And mine," said Gerald. "The Malrags' leaders took my son, and I will not rest until he is returned to me."

Sil Tarithyn blinked in surprise. "They took your firstborn, Gerald Roland? That is strange. The Malrags slay. They do not take captives."

"It is a long story," said Mazael. "Suffice it to say, the Malrags are led by a Dominiar knight named Ultorin. He has a sword forged in Demonsouled blood, which gives him the power to command the Malrags."

"Ah," said Sil Tarithyn. "That explains much."

"The San-keth kidnapped Sir Gerald's son," said Mazael, "and took him to Ultorin. A renegade necromancer named Malavost is also traveling with Ultorin, aiding the Malrags in their battles. Why Ultorin, Malavost, and the San-keth have allied to attack Deepforest Keep, I don't know. Whatever their goal, I hope to kill them before they reach it."

"Nor do we know," said Gerald, "why they have taken my son, instead of simply killing him."

Sil Tarithyn bowed his head, deep in thought. When he looked up, his purple eyes were hard with anger.

"The temple," said Sil Tarithyn. "They come to defile the temple."

"Temple?" said Mazael. "What temple?"

"The temple atop Mount Tynagis," said Sil Tarithyn. "Long ages ago, our forebears, the High Elderborn, ruled this land, and they built a great temple to our gods atop the crown of Mount Tynagis. The Malrags and the Demonsouled destroyed the High Elderborn. But we guard the ruins of the temple to this day, for it remains sacred."

"Wait," said Mazael. "Mount Tynagis. Deepforest Keep is built upon its slopes, is it not?"

"Aye," said Athaelin, "upon a spur of the mountain, overlooking the Forest itself."

"And the only way to this ruined temple is through Deepforest Keep?" said Mazael.

Romaria nodded. "Mount Tynagis is too rocky to be climbed. The only path to the peak is through the caverns. The Ritual of Rulership takes place in those caves." Athaelin's face tightened, as if at a painful memory. "And when we of Deepforest Keep come of age, we go into the caves, and the Seer shows us our vision of the future."

"Defender of the Mountain," said Mazael to Athaelin. "That's one of your titles, isn't it? I assume you're defending Mount Tynagis and its ruins."

Athaelin drew himself up. "I am the Greenshield, the Champion of Deepforest Keep and the Defender of the Mountain. You northerners might call me 'Lord' Athaelin, but that is only your word. I am the protector of Deepforest Keep, and the defender of the road to the mountain's top. The only way to the temple is through the mountain's caverns, and the only way to the caverns is through Deepforest Keep."

"Which is why Ultorin is attacking Deepforest Keep," said Mazael. "He wants to get to this ruined temple."

"Why go to such effort and trouble for some ancient ruin?" said Gerald.

"He wishes to defile it," said Sil Tarithyn.

"But why?" said Gerald, smacking a fist into his palm with frustration. "Ultorin cannot have even seen an Elderborn until a week ago. Most men outside the Grim Marches believe the Elderborn to be nothing more than a legend. Why would he bear your people such enmity?"

"I fear you misunderstand, Sir Gerald," said Lucan, his voice bone-weary. He looked terrible. "The ancient High Elderborn were wizards of tremendous strength. Any temple they built would be a place of great power. Or it would contain magical relics of vast potency." He looked at Sil Tarithyn. "Am I not correct?"

"You speak truly," said Sil Tarithyn. "The High Elderborn wielded great magic. We believe there is a mighty power in the temple atop the mountain, though none of my people have trodden there for many centuries."

"I think this is Malavost's doing," said Lucan. "Ultorin cares only about carnage. Malavost must know about the temple, and he's using Ultorin and the Malrags as a club to clear the path. Once Deepforest Keep is destroyed, Malavost can claim the temple, and whatever it contains, without interference."

"Then what do the San-keth want with my son?" said Gerald.

Lucan shook his head, sweaty black hair sliding across his pallid forehead. "I don't know. Perhaps they are Malavost's partners. Or perhaps Malavost promised them some share of the power from the temple."

"We cannot allow Ultorin and the San-keth to defile the temple," said Sil Tarithyn. "We must return to Deepforest Keep at once with his news. Ardanna, the High Druid, will know more."

Romaria flinched at the name. It was only for a moment, but her eyes remained steely afterward.

"I ride for Deepforest Keep, to take command of our defense against the Malrags," said Athaelin. "Lord Mazael and Sir Gerald and their men have agreed to aid us, in vengeance for what Ultorin did to the Grim Marches, and to reclaim Sir Gerald's son from the San-keth."

"Noble goals," said Sil Tarithyn.

"I suggest we travel together," said Mazael. "The closer we come to Deepforest Keep, the more likely we are to encounter Malrags."

"And we should gather up any other of my people we encounter," said Sil Tarithyn. "The Malrag onslaught came without warning, and we are scattered before it like leaves upon a storm. We shall need to shelter within the walls of Deepforest Keep, if we are to have any chance of victory."

"Then let's get moving," said Mazael.

~

SYKHANA SAT UPON HER HORSE, feeding Aldane milk and ground-up beets, when she heard Ultorin's enraged bellow. Aldane jerked against her chest, his blue eyes wide in surprise, and started to cough. She pounded him on the back, and Aldane paused, took a deep breath, and started to scream at the top of his lungs.

Sykhana hushed Aldane, rocking him back and forth, and looked around for danger.

She rode in the heart of the Malrag host, tens of thousands of Malrags surrounding her in every direction. The tangled roots and towering trees of the Forest often blocked the Malrag host, and the Malrags responded by attacking the Forest, ripping down the trees and tearing up the ground. Sometimes the shamans called lightning to scorch the earth, so that nothing would ever grow there again.

That made Sykhana uneasy.

It was the sure and certain knowledge that the Malrags would do the same thing to Aldane, if they could.

Ultorin sat on his black horse, towering over a Malrag, blood-sword in his hand. Ultorin looked...Ultorin did not look at all well. His gray eyes had taken a distinct yellowish cast, as if lit from by sulfurous flames. His skin had turned pale and waxy, his veins black, like corruption spreading through dead meat. His teeth had become jagged and uneven.

Almost like fangs.

Sometimes the mere sight of him was enough to make Aldane cry.

"What is this?" said Ultorin, gesturing with the bloodsword. "What do you mean to say?"

The Malrag growled in response, and if Sykhana concentrated, she heard the creature's loathsome voice echoing inside her head.

-It is as you say, great master. Mazael Cravenlock has come south-

Ultorin shivered like an enraged animal.

-I escaped from the fight. Mazael Cravenlock has two hundred men with him. And more of the cursed Elderborn. Mazael gathers them to his side, and makes his way south, faster than we can pursue. He will reach Deepforest Keep before we do, will defend it from our host-

"I will crush him!" said Ultorin. "I will break him utterly, I will hear him scream and beg for mercy, and then, only then, will I kill him!"

-You will not-

Ultorin frowned at the Malrag, shocked. "What did you say?"

-You will not. Mazael Cravenlock could have been greater than you. Yet he has denied his power. Even so, he is still stronger than you, far stronger than a fool wielding stolen power even as it kills him-

Ultorin roared and brought the bloodsword crashing down. The Malrag collapsed to the earth, its skull a ruin of shattered bone and black blood. The bloodsword's sigils flared, and Ultorin shivered as the blade drained the Malrag's life energy. Again Ultorin bellowed, and he leapt from the saddle, landing with light grace, despite his bulk.

The bloodsword and the stolen Malrag life forces were making him stronger and faster. It was, however, turning him into a ravening nightmare.

"Hold still!" said Ultorin, and the nearest Malrags went motionless. Ultorin stalked over and began butchering them one by one, his black armor splattered with blacker Malrag blood. A strange combination of ecstasy and agony filled his features.

Aldane wailed in Sykhana's arms.

Ultorin turned, glaring at Sykhana. His yellow-shot eyes fell upon Aldane, and a wide smile lit up his face.

He stepped forward, lifting the bloodsword.

"No," said Sykhana, snatching the poisoned dagger from her belt. "No. Stay back! Stay back!"

Ultorin grinned, eyes wide with madness, and stalked forward.

"Grand Master!"

Malavost's calm voice cracked like a whip. The wizard hurried past the ranks of Malrags, the hem of his long black coat whispering against the forest floor. Skaloban followed upon his skeletal carrier, ghostly green flames flickering around the joints. Ultorin blinked, confusion on his face.

"Grand Master," said Malavost, his tone soothing. "I congratulate you on your victory."

"Victory?" said Ultorin. "What victory? Do not speak in riddles!"

"Over the Elderborn, of course," said Malavost. "You must have slain them all, surely. Else why would you be slaying your own Malrags?"

For a moment Ultorin blinked in chagrin. Then the rage returned. "Mazael Cravenlock has come south! He has followed us, wizard!"

"And this is bad news?" said Malavost, raising his white eyebrows.

Again Ultorin seemed confused.

"You wished vengeance on him, did you not?" said Malavost. "And now he is close at hand. When our goals are achieved, when we have power beyond the wildest dreams of mortal man...you shall take your vengeance upon him. It will last for ten thousand years. And then the world shall be yours, Grand Master."

Ultorin nodded. "Yes. Yes. You are right. See to it."

He climbed back into his saddle and rode into the ranks of Malrags, the horse's black armor clanking.

For a moment Skaloban and Malavost stood in silence, the ranks of Malrags marching past them, Sykhana motionless upon her horse.

"He threatened the Vessel!" hissed Skaloban, pointing at Malavost. "He has gone utterly insane!"

"Quite right," said Malavost, unruffled. "I fear poor Ultorin's sanity has passed a tipping point. He has a month, perhaps, before he descends into raving madness. Or he transforms into something utterly inhuman and begins slaying everything in sight."

"What are you going to do about it?" said Sykhana. "He would have killed Aldane!" The thought of Aldane dying upon the blood-sword, his life force sucked into Ultorin's body, was hideous.

"Nothing at all," said Malavost, smiling. "In another month, Deep-forest Keep will be destroyed, and the Vessel shall be immortal and invincible. Just as I promised you."

21

DEEPFOREST KEEP

Mazael and his men rode southeast.

After another week, the terrain grew hillier, the ground rockier. Great hills rose out of the earth, their crowns and sides dotted with weathered granite boulders. Yet the trees remained enormous, some of them standing higher than the hills themselves. The rocky ground forced Mazael and the others to dismount, to lead their horses along by foot. He cursed the delay. Every day Ultorin and his hordes drew closer to Deepforest Keep, to whatever powers and treasures lay hidden in the ruined temple atop Mount Tynagis.

To whatever fate they intended for Aldane.

Mazael pushed on as fast as he dared.

OF COURSE, wooded hills made perfect terrain for an ambush.

Twice Athaelin's and Sil Tarithyn's Elderborn scouts found roving Malrag warbands making their way through the hills, converging in the direction of Deepforest Keep. The first time Mazael's men plowed into the Malrags from behind, while the Elderborn sent volley after volley of arrows into the creatures.

He lost three men in that fight, with two more wounded.

The second time was easier. Romaria and Athaelin lured a band of three hundred Malrags into a narrow, dead-end gully. Mazael's men prepared the gully beforehand, chopping down trees and piling rocks, and when the Malrags charged, the men unleashed avalanches, sealing the Malrags in the gully while Romaria and her father scrambled up ropes to safety.

After that, the Elderborn archers made short work of the trapped Malrags.

~

THE NEXT DAY, they found a band of Elderborn, from the Tribe of the Bear, fighting a losing battle against a Malrag warband. Mazael's men attacked them from the flank, while the Elderborn loosed a storm of arrows, and Lucan and Circan unleashed conjured spirit beasts. The Malrags, taken by surprise, fell without inflicting a single loss upon Mazael's men.

The Tribe of the Bear joined the Tribe of the Wolf, and Mazael found himself leading a hundred and fifty Elderborn south to Deepforest Keep.

He did not mind. The extra archers, no doubt, would come in handy.

They hastened south, and the ground grew ever hillier.

~

TWO DAYS after they rescued the Tribe of the Bear, Mazael saw Mount Tynagis for the first time.

"Mazael!" called Romaria, running down one of the slopes. Mazael turned, dropping Hauberk's reins, and drawing Lion. But no flames erupted from the sword's blue-tinted steel blade. There were no Malrags nearby.

And Romaria had a smile on her face.

"What is it?" said Mazael.

"Come look at this," said Romaria. "It will take just a moment."

Mazael shrugged, left Gerald in command of the column, and followed Romaria up the side of the stony hill. He was stronger than her, but she was more agile, and from time to time she had to stop and wait as he hauled himself over a boulder or around a jutting tree trunk.

"I hope," said Mazael, "this is worth the climb."

She grinned. "Trust me."

He kept following. The hill was large enough to rise above even the Great Southern Forest's massive oaks, and only a few scraggly trees marked its crown. Romaria led him to the top of the hill and pointed to the south.

"Look," she said. "Mount Tynagis."

And it was, Mazael admitted, an impressive sight.

The mountain rose out of the trees like an island jutting above a sea of green leaves. It was not a large mountain, no more than five thousand feet high, not tall enough for a crown of ice and snow. Yet he did see something white gleaming atop the mountain's crest, something white and jagged...

He squinted. "Is that..."

"Aye," said Romaria. "Those are the ruins of the High Elderborn, atop the mountain."

Mazael stared for a long moment. The mountain was still three or four days' travel distant. He could just make out the faint white shape of walls and soaring arches atop the mountain, of towering buttresses and broad courtyards. To be visible at this distance, the temple had to be truly enormous.

"The High Elderborn," said Mazael, "must have been mighty builders."

"They were," said Romaria. "No one has set foot in that place for years beyond count. Yet still it stands."

"And whatever Ultorin and Malavost want," said Mazael, "it's in there."

Romaria's face hardened. "What they want, and what they shall not have."

Mazael gave her a tight smile. "Yes. We will stop them."

Her answering smile was just as hard. "You almost make me believe it."

"We have a fair chance," said Mazael, gazing at the distant mountain. "We cannot defeat one hundred and fifty thousand Malrags, true. But Ultorin is the key to everything. If we can slay him, or if we can destroy his bloodsword, then victory will be ours. And I can take him, Romaria. I've almost defeated him before. If I can get close enough, if I can get him away from any aid, I can slay him."

"Or I can just put an arrow through his eye," said Romaria.

Mazael snorted. "That will work too, I suppose."

She leaned forward and kissed him. "Whatever happens, Mazael...I am glad you are here with me. That I had a chance to show you my home."

Mazael nodded, took her hand.

"I love you," said Romaria.

"I love you, too," said Mazael.

They kissed once more and descended the hill to join the others.

THE NEXT DAY they encountered a band of a dozen Malrags.

The creatures tried to flee, but the Elderborn hunted them down and shot them without mercy.

"Scouts, most likely," said Athaelin, examining the bodies.

"That's good news, then," said Gerald.

"Why?" said Athaelin.

"Because," said Mazael, "these Malrags were likely scouting ahead of the larger warbands, or the main part of Ultorin's host. Which means that we're ahead of him, and we will reach Deepforest Keep before the Malrags."

But not, Mazael suspected, by very much.

They would reach Deepforest Keep no more than a day or two ahead of the Malrags.

~

"ALMOST HOME," said Athaelin, leading his horse over a root.

They traveled through the foothills around Mount Tynagis. The forests here were even thicker, the trees tall and massive, their gnarled trunks heavy with layers of moss. Only dim sunlight leaked through the overlapping canopies of leaves, and the Forest here seemed dim and cool and silent.

At least, Mazael thought, until the Malrags arrived.

"So desolate," said Rachel, steering her mount around a massive traig.

Athaelin looked back. "Desolate? A desert is desolate, my dear lady." He swept out a hand. "The Great Southern Forest is filled with life."

"Forgive me, my lord Athaelin," said Rachel. "It's just...we have traveled so very far, and seen no one else but Elderborn and Malrags. No other humans. And yet you said nine thousand people live at Deepforest Keep? How did so many people come to live in such a remote place?"

Romaria laughed.

"What?" said Rachel, annoyed. "I was only asking."

"Aye," said Romaria, "but Father loves to speak of Deepforest Keep's history. If you let him, he will talk until we cross Deepforest Keep's gates, and then perhaps some more."

"Pay no heed to these doubters," said Athaelin. "For you, my lady...I think you like stories, you like tales."

"I do," said Rachel, and Mazael smiled. When they had traveled to her wedding, she had listened raptly to Gerald's and Tobias's stories of Knightcastle's long history. "Though...I prefer the stories that have happy endings, my lord. My life has had too many sad tales, of late."

"Ah!" said Athaelin. "Then I'm pleased to oblige. For Deepforest Keep's tale is a glorious one, and it will have a happy ending, once we slay Ultorin, retrieve your son, and drive the Malrags back to their mountain holes. You know that the dragon kings of Old Dracaryl once ruled the Grim Marches?"

Rachel nodded.

"Then you know that Dracaryl fell in fire and blood," said Athaelin. "Many were slain. A few survived to found new towns and castles. Young Lucan's family, I believe, descended from old Dracaryl nobles." Lucan gave a slow nod. "But many others fled the horrors that plagued the Grim Marches. They escaped into the Great Southern Forest, hoping to find refuge on the other side of the mountains."

"How did they end up at Mount Tygnais?" said Rachel.

Athaelin laughed. "They got lost. They were starving and freezing, and hoped to take shelter in the ruins atop the mountain. At the very least, they thought, the ruins might keep them safe from the dark magic that had destroyed Dracaryl."

"But my people stopped them," said Sil Tarithyn, who had come over to listen. "The temple of Mount Tynagis is sacred to our gods, and we will not let it be defiled by the foot of man or Elderborn or San-keth or Malrag."

"It almost came to a fight," said Athaelin. "But the leader of the refugees was a wise man. He bore a shield of bronze and a diadem, both ancient, both magical, and his people called him the Green-shield. And the Greenshield in his wisdom made a pact with the High Druid of the Elderborn. The Elderborn would let the refugees settle upon the slopes of Mount Tynagis. And in exchange, the refugees would remain the friends and allies of the Elderborn, and forever guard the path to the sacred temple atop the mountain. And Deepforest Keep was born. To bind their pact, the Greenshield and the High Druid lay together as man and wife, to symbolize the union of their two peoples, and my ancestors raised the first stones of Deep-forest Keeper. And the Greenshield became the Champion of the Deepforest Keep and Defender of the Mountain, a title that has been passed down from generation to generation to me."

"It is a good tale," said Sil Tarithyn. "Only rarely have Elderborn and human been able to dwell together in peace. But here, in the shadows of Mount Tynagis, we have done so, and together we have defended the temple against all who would defile it. The Elderborn dwell in the forests, and the humans in Deepforest Keep and their farms."

"Why did they lie together?" said Rachel. "The first Greenshield and the High Druid, I mean. Did they wed, to join their peoples together?"

"A ritual," said Athaelin. "To symbolize the joining of human and Elderborn. It is now a tradition. Every new Champion of Deepforest Keep, upon taking up the Greenshield and his diadem, will lie once with the High Druid."

Rachel frowned. "It seems a strange way to make an alliance."

Athaelin shrugged. "Perhaps. But you wed Sir Gerald, did you not? And there is now peace between Lord Mazael and Lord Malden."

"I hadn't looked at it that way," said Rachel. "When the Greenshield and the High Druid lie together, do children ever..." She looked at Romaria, and Mazael saw the understanding fill her eyes. "Oh."

"Aye," said Romaria. "Humans and Elderborn rarely lie together. It is...frowned upon. And when they do, only rarely are half-breed children born. The Elderborn do not approve of such children, of the mingling of the blood." Her eyes grew distant. "Some of the Elderborn call such children abominations, and believe they should be left in the woods to die of exposure."

"A folly," said Mazael. "Your skill and cunning has saved my life, several times."

"When I was young," said Sil Tarithyn, "I thought much the same way. But now I am older, and have seen more of the world. A half-breed may be just as valorous as an Elderborn or a human." His purple eyes shifted to Romaria. "Though her path may be harder."

Romaria looked away.

～

THEY SAW farms as they drew closer to Deepforest Keep, scattered here and there among the trees. Carved terraces climbed up the hillside, and Mazael saw that the men of Deepforest Keep grew wheat and olives and grapes there, or fruit in small orchards. A traig stood by a wine press, its martial appearance strange against the peaceful look of the farm.

Yet every last farm was deserted. Some had been burned to the ground.

"Malrags' work," said Athaelin, looking at a burned farm, voice hard with anger. "They'll pay for driving my people from their homes."

They saw more and more farms, Mount Tynagis looming ever larger over them.

The next day, three weeks after leaving Castle Cravenlock, Mazael saw Deepforest Keep for the first time.

The city sat upon an outthrust spur of Mount Tynagis, perhaps three hundred feet above the foothills, with its walls rising another forty feet. Inside he saw houses and towers built in the same graceful style as the ruins atop the mountain, though constructed of the mountain's gray stone rather than white marble. Massive oak trees also grew within the walls, rising over the houses and some of the towers as well. Behind the city, Mazael saw terraces climbing up the mountain's sides, lush and green with crops. Hundreds of traigs dotted the hills below the city, all of them facing outward, as if to watch for enemies.

"Earth magic," murmured Lucan.

Mazael glanced at him. Lucan looked worse than ever, his face almost white, his eyes glittering and feverish.

"That's how those trees are growing inside Deepforest Keep," said Lucan. "The soil should be too rocky to support them. Earth magic. The walls are enhanced with it, as well, warded against magical attack." He almost smiled. "Which means Malavost and the shamans won't be able to simply blast the walls down."

"And the city is strongly situated," said Mazael, looking it over. "East, west...and south, I think, we have nothing to fear. The mountain is too steeply pitched for anyone to assault the walls from those directions. The city is only vulnerable from the north, where the spur joins the rest of the mountain. Ultorin will have to order the Malrags to climb that road, there," he pointed, "and then circle to the south."

"And that road goes directly under the western wall," said Lucan. "Where the Elderborn will be able to pour down arrows."

"Aye," said Mazael. "An attacker would need an ocean of blood to take Deepforest Keep."

"And Ultorin has oceans of Malrag blood to spend," said Lucan. "He will not care how many Malrags are slain, so as Malavost and the San-keth can reach the temple atop the mountain."

"Ultorin may have Malrags beyond count to spend," said Mazael, "but we need only spill his blood."

"To deal with the Malrags, yes," said Lucan. "I suspect Malavost will prove more troublesome."

"Perhaps," said Mazael, "but Malavost is still only a mortal man. A blade through the throat will slay him, just like any other man."

Lucan lifted an eyebrow. "Bloodthirsty today, my lord."

Mazael pushed back his anger. "You are right. But, gods, it makes me angry. The men of Deepforest Keep live in peace. Save to trade, I doubt any of them have left the Great Southern Forest for years. And yet Ultorin and Malavost and the San-keth have made war upon them, and for what? Some magical bauble from the temple." He made a fist, forced himself to relax. "It reminds me of Amalric Galbraith. Or of Morebeth. Both of them were willing to trade away anything for power. And Ultorin and Malavost are willing to slaughter everyone in Deepforest Keep for power. No. I will stop them, Lucan."

"Be careful of that," said Lucan, his voice soft. "The temptation to wield the necessary power...the consequences can be unpleasant."

"I know," said Mazael. "And I know of what you speak. But I will not use that...part of myself. I will defeat Ultorin as a man, not as a monster. Or I will die trying."

Lucan stared at him a long moment, then bowed his head and looked away. No doubt he thought Mazael a fool. But Mazael did not care. He knew that if he gave in to his Demonsouled nature, he would have vast powers at his disposal. And he knew the price those powers would carry, how they would twist him into a ravening monster like Amalric Galbraith or Ultorin. And he would not do that.

Romaria had paid too steep a price for it.

"Perhaps you are right," said Lucan, his voice faint. He rubbed the black metal staff he always carried. "Perhaps...I always thought that power was worth any price, because once I had power, I could do good with it. I could keep innocents safe from dark magic, keep them from suffering as I had suffered. But perhaps I was wrong. Perhaps the price is too steep," he looked in the direction of Sil Tarithyn's Elderborn, "if innocents pay the price for my power."

"He who fights monsters must take care," said Mazael, "lest he become one."

Lucan blinked at him.

Mazael shrugged. "Sir Nathan and Master Othar used to tell me that when I was a boy. Some ancient priest said it – I don't remember his name." He snorted. "Though, considering who and what I am...it turned out to be good advice."

"Excellent advice," murmured Lucan, and a shout caught Mazael's attention.

"Mazael!" Gerald strode to his side, armor clanking. "Someone's coming."

A group of armed men hurried down the road from the city, thirty or so of them, clad in mail with long spears in their right hands. At their head walked a tall man, perhaps ten years Mazael's junior, with the hilt of a bastard sword jutting over his shoulder.

"We've been seen," said Mazael. "Tell everyone to stop." Athaelin and Romaria came to the head of the column, staring at the approaching men. "And stay calm. I'm sure the men of Deepforest Keep are eager for aid, but it's best to remain polite."

The column stopped, and the men from Deepforest Keep approached them.

The leader frowned at Mazael. He looked a great deal like both Romaria and Athaelin, with the same strong features, the same blue eyes, and the same thick black hair. Unlike Romaria, the man bore no trace of Elderborn ancestry upon his face or ears. A half-brother, Mazael thought, a son Athaelin had gotten on a human woman.

Then the leader saw Athaelin, and his eyes widened.

"Well, Rhodemar?" said Athaelin. "No greeting your father? Or for your sister?"

"Father!" said Rhodemar, grinning, and walked over and caught the older man in a vigorous hug. Still grinning, he reached over and pulled Romaria close, and she laughed in surprise. "It is good to see you. Especially in this dark hour." He stepped away, looking at Romaria. "And you, sister. I had thought you dead, slain at the hands of some lord in the north."

"Not quite," said Romaria, stepping between Mazael and Rhodemar. "This is Mazael, Lord of Castle Cravenlock." Mazael offered a grave bow, and Rhodemar answered in kind. "And he saved my life."

Rhodemar looked at Athaelin, and then back at Romaria. "And he is the one in the Seer's prophecy..."

"Aye," said Romaria.

"So the Seer's prophecy did indeed come true," said Rhodemar. "And I hope he spoke truly, as well, when he said you would save Deepforest Keep." He looked at Mazael. "I am glad Father brought you here, Lord Mazael, along with your men. We are sore pressed, and every man or Elderborn able to swing a sword or draw a bow is welcome."

"What news?" said Athaelin. "Have any Malrags attacked the city itself yet?"

"No," said Rhodemar. "The outlying farms have been raided, with grievous loss of life. I have ordered all the farmers and herders within the walls – their farms and flocks can be rebuilt, but their lives cannot. Every man able to fight has been impressed into our militia, and the Elderborn tribes have sheltered within our walls as well. When the Malrags come, we shall have three thousand fighting men, and fifteen hundred Elderborn with their bows."

Three thousand spearmen and fifteen hundred Elderborn archers. Even with the strong walls of Deepforest Keep, that would not be nearly enough against one hundred and fifty thousand Malrags.

"How far are the Malrags from the city?" said Athaelin. "We have gathered every Elderborn we can, and led them here, but our scouting ability is limited."

"We didn't dare send out too many scouts," said Gerald, "lest the Malrags follow them back, and send numbers enough to overwhelm us."

"There are Malrag warbands prowling all over the foothills," said Rhodemar. "None of them have yet come within a day's travel of the city, though that will change, I deem, once more arrive. The Elder-born say that the main host of the Malrags is no more than two days' march from Deepforest Keep."

Two days.

Mazael looked at the towering height of Mount Tynagis.

Within a week, this would be settled. Either he would slay Ultorin and break up the Malrag host, or the Malrags would raze Deepforest Keep and Ultorin would seize the ruins atop the mountain.

"What of provisions?" said Athaelin.

"As many foodstuffs and flocks as we could manage have been gathered within the walls," said Rhodemar. "We food enough to last for a year."

"Good," said Athaelin. "Very good."

"That won't be necessary," said Mazael.

Father, son, and daughter looked at him.

"Ultorin has one hundred and fifty thousand Malrags," said Mazael. "Even with my men, Deepforest Keep has four thousand defenders. Ultorin has strength enough to simply storm the city."

"This Ultorin - I assume he is the leader of the Malrags - will pay a grievous price for doing so," said Rhodemar, "and we have the magic of the druids to aid us."

"But Ultorin doesn't care about the price," said Mazael, and he explained to Rhodemar about the bloodsword and Malavost's desire to seize the temple atop the mountain. "The Malrags are nothing more than his tools, his weapons. He cares nothing for them. If he has to butcher every last one of them to destroy Deepforest Keep and take the ruined temple, he will do it. No, this will not be a long siege. Ultorin will try to take Deepforest Keep by storm. In a week's time, either we all shall be dead - or we will kill him first."

"Gods of wood and stone," said Rhodemar, shaking his head. "What sort of fool would wield a blade forged in the blood of a Demonsouled?"

Lucan stepped to Mazael's side, gazing at Rhodemar, face expressionless.

"Come," said Athaelin. "Join me in the Champion's Tower. We must discuss our defense."

"That is why I am here," said Rhodemar. He took a deep breath. "The High Druid requests the presence of the Champion and his guests, in the courtyard below the Great Traig."

Romaria's face grew hard.

Athaelin sighed. "Ardanna wants to speak with us, does she? I suspect she did not quite say it that way, Rhodemar."

Rhodemar nodded. "She demanded your presence, Father. As if you were a servant."

"No matter. Come, then," said Athaelin. "Let us see what Ardanna has to say about the defense of Deepforest Keep."

22

THE HIGH DRUID

Rhodemar led them through the gates and into the main plaza of Deepforest Keep. Houses and towers of gray stone lined the plaza, their walls faced with lichen and long green vines. A massive oak tree rose overhead, looming higher than both the towers and the houses. A group of spearmen in mail drilled in the square, following the directions of a grim-faced sergeant.

"Find quarters for Mazael and his men," said Athaelin.

Rhodemar nodded. "We can quarter them in the Northern Tower, along with the horses. Lord Mazael, Sir Gerald, and Lucan Mandragon will be our guests in the Champion's Tower."

Mazael left his men and Gerald's at the foot of the Northern Tower, a tall fortress of gray stone, telling them to follow the instructions of Rhodemar's men. Then he followed Athaelin and Rhodemar into Deepforest Keep, Romaria, Gerald, Rachel, and Lucan following after him. Romaria walked at his side, her face grim, her right hand clenching and unclenching.

"Is she that bad?" said Mazael.

Romaria gave a sharp nod. "You'll see for yourself, soon enough."

He looked at Deepforest Keep as they walked. Mazael had visited numerous cities in his younger wanderings, but he had never seen one quite like Deepforest Keep. Gardens and groves lay among the stone houses and towers, tended with skill and care. Some of the gardens had white traigs, their sides spotted with lichen. The great oak trees were enormous, often bigger than the towers. Most cities smelled of smoke and waste, but the air of Deepforest Keep was clean and clear, the sun shaded by the trees.

The Champion's Tower, a round tower of gray granite, stood at the southern corner of Deepforest Keep's walls, overlooking the foothills below. A ring of smaller oak trees encircled a courtyard at the base of the Tower, surrounding an enormous traig, twice as large as any of the others Mazael had seen. This traig bore a stone sword in either hand, its head concealed with a crowned helm.

The Great Traig itself, no doubt.

A dozen Elderborn women waited below the Great Traig, each clad in a ragged robe made from animal furs. Every woman bore an oak staff in her right hand, and wore strange amulets of polished bone and stone. Piercing eyes of gold and silver and purple fixed upon Mazael.

"The druids," murmured Lucan. "Each one is powerful. Tread carefully."

Mazael nodded.

One of the Elderborn women stepped forward, her oaken staff tapping against the weathered flagstones of the courtyard. Her amulets were more intricate than the others, and she wore a diadem of woven cord and uncut sapphires. Her golden eyes gleamed like coins, cold and hard, and swept over Mazael and his companions.

Then the golden eyes narrowed as they fixed upon Romaria, and Romaria glared back.

Ardanna, Mazael realized. The High Druid of the Elderborn.

"Athaelin," said Ardanna, her voice clear and cold as a crystal. "So good of you to come, and deign to fill your responsibilities as Champion of Deepforest Keep and the Defender of the Mountain."

Athaelin made a grand bow that had more than a hint of mockery to it. "And it is good to see you again, most noble High Druid."

"Do not make a joke, Champion," said Ardanna. "I weary of your japery. And this latest joke is the worst of all." She looked back at Romaria. "I see you have brought your pet abomination to Deepforest Keep."

"Mother," said Romaria, her voice ice.

Ardanna ignored her. "I told you not to bring it back to Deepforest Keep, after you sent it north to investigate the undead. And I was relieved when I heard word that it was dead. And yet you have returned it to Deepforest Keep. In this hour of trail, when both the Elderborn and your people face grave threat, you choose to run north and chase after your pet abomination."

"I chose to go north and avenge my daughter's death," said Athaelin, all trace of good humor gone from his tone. "I returned with my daughter, our daughter, still alive, and allies willing to fight on our side against the Malrags. And instead you choose to mock our daughter and scorn me, instead of discussing the danger."

Ardanna's nostrils flared in rage. "You insult me by bringing this abomination into my presence, and..."

Rhodemar frowned. "Should we not discuss our defense? The Malrag host is almost upon us. This is not the time to bring up old quarrels."

Neither Athaelin nor Ardanna heeded him, and both began to shout.

"Enough!" said Romaria, glaring at the High Druid. "You will not discuss me like I am a piece of furniture, Mother. Not when I am right in front of you."

Ardanna's voice dripped with contempt. "I have nothing to say to you, abomination."

"It seems like you have plenty to say," said Romaria. "You have always had plenty to say, even if you are too cowardly to say it to my face. Plenty to say, while Father does the hard work of defending Deepforest Keep."

The golden eyes flashed. "Cowardly, you call me, you miserable vermin?" She stepped closer to Romaria, every inch of her body taut with rage. "Then let me tell you the truth. To your face, if you prefer. You were a mistake. No child is supposed to be born of the ritual coupling between the High Druid and the Champion. When I learned of you, I would have purged my womb of your tainted presence, but the Champion and the druids forbade it. When at last you were born and I was free of you, I would have left you to die of exposure in the woods, but again your foolish father forbade it."

Ardanna continued to rant, and Romaria said nothing, but Mazael saw the muscles twitching in her face, and he had heard enough.

"Stop," he said. "Not another word."

"Do not interfere, human lord," said Ardanna. "You think her worthy? I will prove you wrong."

Ardanna pointed her staff, and Romaria went rigid.

"She is half-human, half-Elderborn," said Ardanna, the tip of her staff glowing with blue light. "The Elderborn live in harmony with themselves. But a half-breed, an abomination, cannot. Sooner or later the Elderborn half of her soul will overwhelm her, and she will become a ravening beast, out of harmony with herself and the world. Sooner or later...or sooner, if I hasten the process. As I should have done long ago."

The blue light around the staff brightened, and Romaria began to shudder. Mazael saw claws appear on her fingers, fangs upon her lips, and black fur sprout from her hands. Rhodemar reached for her, and she growled, face looking more wolfish by the second.

"Stop!" said Athaelin. "Stop this now, Ardanna! Damn you, stop this now!"

But Ardanna ignored him. The Greenshield, Mazael realized, had no power over the High Druid.

"Stop," said Mazael, "now."

Ardanna ignored him, and Romaria screamed.

And fury blossomed in his mind.

One moment he stood between Romaria and Athaelin. The next he stood over the High Druid, his boot upon her chest, Lion's tip resting at her throat. Ardanna's haughty arrogance disappeared in shock, and for the first time a hint of fear appeared in her golden eyes.

"I told you," said Mazael, voice quiet, "to stop."

Every Elderborn man in the courtyard had his bow drawn, the arrows pointed at Mazael.

Romaria collapsed to the ground, shivering, and Athaelin bent over her.

"You must leave at once!" said one of the Elderborn druids, her face livid with fury. "You have dared to draw a blade against the High Druid! Leave, or we shall shoot you and all your men where you stand."

Gerald drew his sword, and Lucan lifted his hand, green flames writhing around his fingertips. Rachel backed away from him, eyes wide.

"Stop this folly!" bellowed Athaelin, still on one knee besides Romaria. "Have you gone mad, Ardanna? You attacked your daughter!"

"She is a vile abomination," spat Ardanna, "and not my daughter." Her golden eyes remained fixed on Mazael. "You must go, human lord. You must go now. Take your precious abomination and do not return to Deepforest Keep."

"As you wish," said Mazael, taking his boot from the High Druid's chest "I will take her, and my men, and go."

Athaelin surged to his feet. "You are indeed mad, Ardanna! One hundred thousand Malrags descend upon Deepforest Keep, and you turn away aid? Because you cannot get over your useless hatred of Romaria?"

"As you wish," said Ardanna. "The human lord and his men may stay. But the abomination must be expelled from Deepforest Keep."

"No," said Mazael. He slid Lion back into its scabbard. Whatever else happened, he would not start a bloodbath here that would deprive Deepforest Keep of its ablest defenders. "No, you've shown me your true colors, my lady Ardanna. If you will expel Romaria, then I will go with her, and you may face the Malrags on your own." He would find a way to get to Ultorin, to get Aldane back from the San-keth. "Romaria has saved my life, and shown her valor to me many times over. If you expel a woman of her courage...then you do not deserve my aid."

"As you will!" spat Ardanna, climbing to her feet, but the fear returned as she looked at Mazael. "Go! Take your filthy abomination, and go..."

"No."

The deep voice was soft, yet it carried over the shouting.

An Elderborn man stood at the base of the Champion's Tower, leaning hard upon an oak staff. He was the first Elderborn Mazael had seen to show signs of age, his hair long and gray, his face weathered and marked with deep lines. The Elderborn, Romaria had told him, could live for a thousand years, which meant that this man had to be truly ancient. His eyes were silver, clear and bright, like polished coins.

"Seer," said Ardanna, dipping her head in a quick bow.

The Seer. The Elderborn druid who had foreseen that Mazael and Romaria would meet, that she would save him, and he would save her.

Who had predicted that she would save Deepforest Keep.

The Seer's silver eyes settled upon Mazael, and he stared back without flinching.

"So," said the Seer. "It has come at last."

"The abomination must be expelled, Seer," said Ardanna, and Mazael realized that the Seer's words carried greater weight than the High Druid's. "It will bring disaster upon us, and..."

"No," said the Seer. He walked into the circle of trees, limping, leaning on his staff. "No future is certain. And doom lies heavy upon Deepforest Keep, upon the world. For if Deepforest Keep falls, then all the world shall fall with it. If Romaria, the daughter of the Greenshield, remains here, then Deepforest Keep might fall." He gazed at Ardanna. "But if she departs, then Deepforest Keep shall certainly be destroyed. This I have foreseen."

"But..."

"This," repeated the Seer, with perfect, calm, "I have foreseen."

Ardanna stared at him, hands tight around her staff, but at last gave a short, sharp nod.

Romaria climbed to her feet, dark circles under her eyes, gazing at her mother with loathing.

"Mazael, son of House Cravenlock," said the Seer. "Will you stay, and fight alongside us?"

"I see no reason why I should," said Mazael. "My men and I hardly seem welcome here."

"This is so," said the Seer. "But I know what you seek. You seek your nephew's safe return, and the destruction of your foes, the necromancer and the corrupted knight."

"So?" said Mazael. "I suppose you'll tell me that if I leave Deepforest Keep, I will surely die?"

"All men die," said the Seer. "Whether human or Elderborn. And no one can see the future. Not even I. But if you leave Deepforest Keep, your nephew will surely die. And your foes will gain power beyond your ability to oppose, and will come north to seek your ruin. This I have foreseen."

"Mazael," said Rachel, voice tight. "Aldane. If you go, Aldane will die."

And Ultorin and Malavost had to be stopped. Whatever they wanted from the ruined temple atop Mount Tynagis, Mazael had to keep them from it.

"Very well," said Mazael, looking to the Seer. "I will fight alongside you against the Malrags. But let me make myself clear. If anyone tries to harm Romaria again, I will leave. Is this understood?"

"Ardanna," said Athaelin.

The High Druid's voice could have cut stone. "Your terms are acceptable."

"Now," said Rhodemar with some asperity, "perhaps we can discuss our defense? Or shall we stand here and bicker until the Malrags cut us all to pieces?"

Both Athaelin and Ardanna looked ashamed, if only slightly, but Romaria's venomous glare at her mother did not waver.

"The Malrags come in great numbers," said Rhodemar. "Our

scouts counted at least one hundred and twenty thousand of them. Undoubtedly there are more, but Lord Mazael says one hundred and fifty thousand of them left the Grim Marches."

"Our tribes will have put up a fierce fight," said Ardanna, lifting her chin, "and our arrows shall have thinned the ranks of the foe."

"But not by very much," said Rhodemar. "As to what they want, or who leads them, we do not yet know."

"But I do," said Mazael. "The Malrags are led by Ultorin, a Dominiar knight, Malavost, a necromancer of power, and an unknown number of San-keth clerics. Ultorin has a sword forged in Demonsouled blood, which gives him the power to command the Malrags."

"A bloodsword?" said Ardanna. "My people have encountered such weapons before. They bestow terrible power, but inevitably drive their wielders into madness."

Lucan looked away, rolling the black staff between his palms.

"Malavost is probably controlling Ultorin somehow," said Mazael. "The San-keth also kidnapped my nephew, Sir Gerald's son. Ardmorgan Sil Tarithyn of the Tribe of the Wolf believes that Malavost and the San-keth want to seize the ruined temple atop Mount Tynagis and claim it for themselves."

Ardanna's golden eyes narrowed. "They would dare," she hissed, "to defile the sacred temple. We shall not allow it. We..."

"The Door of Souls," said the Seer.

Again everyone looked at the ancient Elderborn.

Lucan frowned. "The...Door of Souls? What is that?"

"I know what your foes seek," said the Seer. He looked at Gerald. "And I know why your son has been kidnapped."

"Why?" said Rachel, stepping to Mazael's side. "Why? For the love of all the gods, please tell me why."

"In ancient times," said the Seer, "the High Elderborn communed with the spirit world and spoke with its princes and lords. Their mightiest wizards could even enter the spirit world, through an artifact called the Door of Souls."

"An artifact," said Mazael, understanding, "within the temple atop Mount Tynagis."

"You speak true," said the Seer. "The Door of Souls is perilous, which is why my people have guarded Mount Tynagis for long centuries, why we made the pact with the men of Deepforest Keep. If Malavost acted alone, I would say he simply wished to seize the Door's power for himself. But with the San-keth, and the child...no, he wishes something different."

"What?" said Rachel. Gerald grabbed at her arm to support her. "What is he going to do?"

The Seer looked at her, his weathered face grave. "Your son shall become Sepharivaim reborn."

"I don't understand," said Rachel.

"Do you know the story of the San-keth?" said the Seer. "How once they walked as you and I do, with arms and legs, until they followed their god Sepharivaim into wickedness, and the rest of the gods stripped the San-keth of their limbs and forced them to crawl in the dust to humble their pride. And Sepharivaim himself was cast down and defeated. But a god cannot be slain, even by other gods. Sepharivaim's body was destroyed, and his spirit cast into the dark void between the worlds. A mortal wizard of sufficient skill could use the Door of Souls to draw Sepharivaim's spirit back into the world and infuse it into a mortal body."

"A mortal body," said Mazael, understanding like at last, "like Rachel's son."

Rachel's hands were at her mouth, her face white.

"If it were as simple as that," said Lucan, "why have the San-keth not done this long ago?"

"Because it is not simple," said the Seer. "They would need a wizard of great skill and power to even attempt the summoning spell."

"Malavost," said Mazael.

"And they would need a way to force their way past Deepforest Keep and reach the temple," said the Seer.

"Ultorin and the Malrags," said Mazael.

"And they would need a special child," said the Seer. "Not just any mortal body could receive the soul of a god. The child would need to be young, in his first year. And he would need to be born of a woman who had been marked by Sepharivaim, yet had rejected him. For an apostate's child would be vulnerable to such possession..."

Rachel started to weep. "I did this. I did this. Oh, Aldane. Oh, I'm sorry. Gerald, I'm sorry. This is my fault, my fault, all my fault..."

Gerald led her to a stone bench and sat her down, and Rachel buried her face in her hands, still weeping.

"Then we know the purposes of our enemy," said Ardanna, but even she looked shaken, "and we must find a way to defeat him."

"The way is simple," said Mazael.

"Oh?" said the High Druid. "So confident?"

"No," said Mazael. "But the path to victory is clear. We must kill Ultorin and destroy his bloodsword. Then the Malrags will turn up each other, and we can destroy them in the aftermath. It is the only way. I have seen your defenses, my lord Athaelin, my lady Ardanna, and I have seen your men and Elderborn. Your walls are high, and your men skilled. But Ultorin will smash your walls and slay your men. The sorcery of Malavost and the Malrag shamans will overpower your druids. They will leave Deepforest Keep a desolate ruin."

"And open the Door of Souls to unleash a horror upon the world," said the Seer.

"We must slay Ultorin," said Mazael. "It is our only hope of victory or survival. Whatever else happens, we must find a way to kill him."

"Perhaps we should consider killing the child, as well," said Ardanna, "should the opportunity present itself."

Rachel surged to her feet, her hands curled into fists, and for a moment Mazael thought she would throw herself upon the High Druid, but Gerald's hands closed about her shoulders.

And even Gerald looked angry.

"It is only sensible," said Ardanna. "Even if we fail, even if Deepforest Keep falls, perhaps we can spare the rest of the world..."

"You would like that, I'm sure," said Athaelin. "The men of Deepforest Keep slain. But the Elderborn can wait in the forests until the Malrags depart, and..."

"Damn it, enough!" said Mazael. "Your are on the verge of destruction, and yet both of you squabble like children! You will cooperate, or by the gods, I will leave you to your fate."

Athaelin gave a nod, and Ardanna looked away, saying nothing.

"What do you suggest we do, then?" said Rhodemar.

"Prepare for a siege," said Mazael, "as you have been doing. Ultorin will send the Malrags against the walls. We must hold him off as long as we can, to exploit our advantage."

"What advantage?" said Ardanna.

"Ultorin is insane," said Lucan, voice quiet. "The bloodsword is destroying his mind, piece by piece. He will take risks, expose himself to dangers that a sensible man would otherwise avoid."

"Malavost and the San-keth will try to restrain him," said Mazael, "but sooner or later he will make a mistake, and that will be our chance to strike."

"So be it," said Athaelin.

"The scouts say the main bulk of the Malrag host will be here in two days," said Rhodemar.

"Then I suggest we get to work," said Athaelin.

23

THE SEER

"I am sorry about Ardanna," said Athaelin.

Mazael, Romaria, and Athaelin stood on one of the balconies of the Champion's Tower, the foothills sloping away into the Great Southern Forest below them. Mazael saw men marching on the walls, spears in hand, while the Elderborn followed, carrying their great bows. Women and children hurried back and forth, stacking quivers of arrows and bales of spears.

"Why does she hate you so much?" said Mazael. "Because of Romaria?

Romaria had not spoken since their confrontation with the High Druid and gazed grim-faced at the activity below.

"Her hatred is nothing personal, either for me," said Athaelin, "or Romaria. Ardanna...simply detests humans. She believes the Elderborn to be the superior race, because of their longer lives and greater magical prowess. It galls her that humans now possess most of the world, while only a few remnants of the Elderborn linger on in remote places. And it infuriates her that a child of mixed human and Elderborn blood walks Deepforest Keep."

"Infuriated or not," said Mazael, "she will help defend Deepforest Keep, whether she likes it or no."

"Aye," said Athaelin. "Ardanna is proud and cruel, but she will fight to save the city. And we have something more important to discuss than Ardanna's temper."

"What is it?" said Mazael.

Athaelin took a deep breath. "I need you to take command of our defense."

"Father?" said Romaria.

"You are the Greenshield, the Champion of Deepforest Keep," said Mazael. "The command should be yours."

"The Champion's task is to defend Deepforest Keep and Mount Tynagis," said Athaelin. "And I cannot do that, not as well as you can. I am skilled with sword and bow, true. But I have never led more than five hundred men in battle. Certainly I have never commanded the entire host of Deepforest Keep. But my daughter told me how you have commanded mighty armies in great battles, and Romaria is not one to exaggerate. In this, Mazael, your hands are more capable than mine. Take command of our defense."

"But your men respect you," said Mazael. "I've seen the way they heed you. I am a stranger to them. They will not follow my lead."

"The men of Deepforest Keep respect me," said Athaelin, "but..."

"They love you, Father," said Romaria.

"Perhaps," said Athaelin. "They may respect me, but I cannot save them. Even you might not be able to save them. But you have a better chance of keeping them alive than I do."

For a long moment they stood in silence, staring at each other.

"Very well," said Mazael. "I will take command of the defense."

Athaelin closed his eyes and let out a long sigh. "Thank you."

"But you will remain in command," said Mazael. "This is your city and your people. They will follow you, not me. So I will advise you. Whether you follow my suggestions or not is up to you. But you will retain command of Deepforest Keep."

Athaelin smiled at Romaria. "He is a clever one, isn't he?"

For the first time since arriving in Deepforest Keep, Romaria smiled. "I've always thought so, Father."

Mazael squinted at the sky. "We've still three or four hours of daylight left, and we should put it to use. Here are my first suggestions..."

They got to work.

~

THAT NIGHT MAZAEL and Romaria returned to their rooms atop the Champion's Tower, gazing into the darkened forest.

"It's so quiet," said Romaria. "It's never this quiet in the Forest at night."

"The Malrags," said Mazael. "Everything flees before them. This is the last quiet night Deepforest Keep will know for a while, I think."

She nodded, and they stood in silence for a moment.

"Your mother," said Mazael.

"I hate her," said Romaria, and he saw the unshed tears shining in her eyes. "I thought...I thought I was past this. I left Deepforest Keep for years, to travel in the Great Mountains and the Old Kingdoms. I forgot about her. Even when I returned to Deepforest Keep to visit Father, I stayed away from her. Not hard, since the great High Druid would have nothing to do with a wretched abomination." She sniffled. "It is so foolish to say...but I hoped, perhaps, that she would think differently of me, after all that I have done. That perhaps she would see that I had some value."

"It is not so foolish," said Mazael, putting his arm around her. "I thought the same way once, about my father."

She gave him a puzzled look. "The Old Demon?"

"No. Lord Adalon," said Mazael, naming the man he had thought was his father. "He banished me from the Grim Marches when I was eighteen. He gave me a horse and a sword and a chain mail shirt, and told me never to return. For a while, I thought that if I did great deeds, he would take me back."

"What changed?" said Romaria. "By the time I met you, you didn't give a damn what anyone in your family thought. Except for Rachel."

Mazael shrugged. "I moved on. I joined Lord Malden's court as a sworn knight, and by the time I heard that Lord Adalon had died and Mitor had become the new lord of Castle Cravenlock, I no longer cared. I would never have returned to the Grim Marches, had Lord Malden not sent me to investigate."

She leaned against him. "I am glad that you did."

Mazael pulled her closer against him. "So am I."

They went to bed together.

MAZAEL WOKE before dawn the next morning, blinking.

Romaria lay against his side, her black hair pooling across his chest. Dim gray light came through the balcony doors, along with the sounds of men moving along the city's walls. For a moment Mazael thought that the Ultorin had come, that the Malrags had launched an assault against the walls.

Romaria sat up, sensing his alarm. "What is it?"

But no sounds of combat filtered through the window.

"Nothing," said Mazael, climbing out of bed. He began to get dressed, and Romaria did the same. "It's going to be a long day. Best to..."

"Mazael," said Romaria.

Mazael turned.

A huge black raven settled upon the balcony's stone railing, watching them with gleaming black eyes. It was the biggest raven Mazael had ever seen. Even as he stared at it, the raven hopped to the floor of the balcony.

And as it did, it changed, its form blurring. The raven became an Elderborn man, gray-haired and weary-faced, leaning upon an oak staff.

Romaria bowed. "Seer."

"Just how long," said Mazael, "have you been there watching us? All night, I suppose?"

To his surprise, the Seer smiled. "Fear not. I do not spy upon things which are rightly private." His smile faded. "And I have learned this well. Once something has been seen, it cannot be unseen. And I have seen much that I would otherwise forget."

"But...you were a raven," said Romaria, confused. "How is that possible? I've never seen any wizard do that. Is it a skill the druids learn?"

"No," said the Seer. "I will tell you a secret only known to the Elderborn. Not even your father knows it. It should have been told to you long ago, but the High Druid refused."

"What secret?" said Romaria.

"The Elderborn are born with earth magic in their souls," said the Seer, "and exist in harmony with it. And this harmony manifests in the ability to change forms, to take the shape of birds and beasts."

"The Tribe of the Wolf," said Mazael, understanding. He remembered the rumors Lucan had told him about the ability of the Elderborn druids to change their shapes. "Or the Tribe of the Bear. That's why the Elderborn tribes take those names. It's their...chosen animal, no? They have the ability to change their forms to a wolf or a bear."

The Seer nodded. "The Seer is of all tribes. But before I became Seer, long ago, I was of the Tribe of the Raven. And this ability, Romaria, you have inherited from your mother, and it is killing you. It is unbalanced, uncontrollable, and killing you slowly."

"I know," said Romaria. "Is that why you've come? To tell me how I'm going to die? I already know that. I don't have much time left. So I'm going to spend it well, and take as many Malrags with me as I can. And Ultorin, if I have a clear shot to his throat."

"No," said the Seer. "You are the key. This I have foreseen. You were destined to save Mazael from himself. This has happened. Mazael was destined to save you from yourself. This, too, has happened. And I have foreseen that you have the power to save Deepforest Keep."

"How?" said Romaria.

"I did not know," said the Seer, "until last night. I entered the caverns below the mountain, and meditated, and a vision came to me."

"So," said Mazael, "how is Romaria to save Deepforest Keep?"

"She must face herself, and overcome herself," said the Seer, "in the Ritual of Rulership."

"The trial that the lords of Deepforest Keep must face," said Mazael, remembering what Romaria had told him, "before becoming the Champion and Defender."

The Seer nodded.

"Why must I do this?" said Romaria. "The Ritual is dangerous. Half of those who undertake the Ritual never return."

"Your brother Rhodemar undertook the Ritual and survived," said the Seer. "Your father insisted, so that he could serve as the Champion if Athaelin fell in battle. And you must undertake the Ritual, as well, to face yourself..."

"No," said Romaria.

The Seer said nothing.

"Why not?" said Mazael.

"Because they have no right to ask this of me," said Romaria.

"You said Deepforest Keep was your home," said the Seer.

"It is!" said Romaria, voice rising. "At least, I thought it was, for all those years. And then I came back, and I saw my mother again, what she thinks of me. What she still thinks of me. Do all the Elderborn think that way about me? And my father. He would do nothing about her. Nothing!" Her voice climbed to a shout. "He chided her, and scolded her, and did not lift a finger to help me!"

She paced to the balcony, shaking with anger. Mazael followed her, put a hand on her shoulder.

"I will fight for Deepforest Keep," said Romaria. "Even to the death. But this...I will not do this."

"So be it," said the Seer.

Romaria glared at him. "Why? What have you seen?"

"You will do as you will," said the Seer.

Romaria scowled, pushing the hair away from her eyes. "Don't tell me that nonsense. You tell us your visions, and we all dance upon your strings. So what strings do you want to tie around my arms and legs?"

The Seer sighed and closed his silver eyes, resting his forehead upon the staff. "The Seer's vision is more of a curse than a blessing, far more of a curse. For the future is not fixed. Did you not know this? It is a shadow, cast by the weight of the past and present. Shadows are changeable. And yet...so very often the shadow does not change. A man continues in his folly, when he might change his ways, and the shadow of destruction becomes a reality."

"And so what visions have you seen?" said Romaria. "What shadows?"

"I see the Elderborn destroyed, slain to the last man, woman, and child," said the Seer. "I see Deepforest Keep in flames. I see a child murdered atop an altar, and I see a god of blood and death rising in power from Mount Tynagis. All these shadows I see before me...if you do not enter the caverns and endure the Ritual of Rulership."

For a long time Romaria said nothing.

"And what shadows do you see," said Romaria, "if I undertake the Ritual?"

"The shadows are uncertain, tangled," said the Seer. "Anything could happen."

"But if I do not perform the Ritual," said Romaria, "then Deepforest Keep will certainly be destroyed." Mazael felt her tense. "Everyone will die. Mazael will die. My father and brother will die."

"Those shadows," said the Seer, "will become reality."

"If I do not perform the Ritual," said Romaria. She closed her eyes and gave a bitter little laugh. "Trying strings around my arms and legs."

"I told you," said the Seer, still leaning against his staff, "that foresight is often more of a curse than a blessing."

"Very well," said Romaria. She closed her eyes, took a deep breath, opened them again. "I will face the Ritual of Rulership."

The Seer nodded. "We must go now."

"Are you sure about this?" said Mazael.

"I am not," said Romaria.

"Do you need my help?" said Mazael.

"She must face herself," said the Seer. "And that is something every man and woman of mortal kind must do alone."

"I would like your help," said Romaria, "but if I am to face this...it seems I must do so alone." She gazed at his face. "Just as you did...when your time of trial came."

Mazael remembered Romaria lying dead upon the chapel floor, remembered Rachel unconscious upon the chapel.

"That wasn't your fault," said Romaria. Even in her troubled mood, she still knew him so well. "I've told you that." Her crooked grin flashed across her face. "And there's no Old Demon this time."

Mazael nodded. "I love you."

She leaned up and kissed him. "I love you, too."

She squeezed his hands, then turned and followed the Seer from the tower.

Mazael stared after them for a moment. Then he paced to the balcony and leaned against the railing, staring at nothing. Watching her go, letting her go, had been so much harder than he had expected. He knew that she might die in the upcoming battle, that he might die. But watching her walk away with the Seer, knowing that he might never return...that had been almost more than he could bear.

He would have helped her, if he could. He would have died for her. But she had to face this battle herself. Just he had faced the Old Demon alone, in the chapel, at the end.

Romaria's fate was in her hands now. And Mazael had work to do.

He took a deep breath, donned his armor, and went to find Athaelin and Rhodemar.

※

ROMARIA FOLLOWED the Seer through the heart of Deepforest Keep. She looked back at the Champion's Tower. Leaving Mazael to fight the Malrags had been harder than she had thought. But if any man could lead the defenders and kill Ultorin, it was him. And if the Seer was right, if she did not do this, then Mazael and every man, woman, and child in Deepforest Keep would die.

And the Seer had always been right so far.

The Seer led her to the center of the city. A huge circular garden lay there, the Garden of the Temple, surrounded by a ring of enormous oak trees. Traigs dotted the garden, covered in vines and flowers. In the center of the garden yawned a stone well, spiral stairs sinking to the earth.

The entrance of the caverns that led to the crown of Mount Tynagis, to the sacred temple at its crown.

And the caverns where she would face the Ritual of Rulership.

"Come," said the Seer, and she followed him into the caverns.

THE MALRAGS MARCHED through the night.

Sykhana rode in the heart of the Malrag host, encircled by the bodyguard of Ogrags that Malavost insisted Ultorin use. She was surrounded by tens of thousands of Malrags, Malrags that would kill any Elderborn they saw, Malrags that killed any deer or rabbit or wild pig they encountered, simply for the pleasure of it.

Yet she still lived in terror of an Elderborn arrow. Not for herself, but for the baby cradled in her arms. All it would take was one arrow, one stray arrow to sink into Aldane's unprotected flesh. And Elderborn scouting parties raided the more distant Malrag warbands. The scouts brought reports to Ultorin, and Ultorin flew into a rage every time he heard them, killing two or three Malrags before Malavost calmed him down.

Sykhana shivered. Very often Ultorin frightened her more than the Elderborn. There was not much sanity left in Ultorin.

And less that was even still human.

But only a little longer, Malavost told her in his calm voice. They only need Ultorin and his bloodsword a little while longer. Then they would gain the Door of Souls atop the mountain, and Aldane would become a god and live in splendor forevermore.

And she would be his loving mother, forever.

Sykhana wanted that so badly that it hurt.

The sun rose, and she saw Deepforest Keep standing atop its mountain spur, the walls lined with men in mail.

24

THE SIEGE

Mazael stood atop Deepforest Keep's wall, Athaelin, Rhodemar, Gerald, and Lucan at his side, watching the Malrag horde fill the hills below the city. He wore his armor, plate and chain beneath a black Cravenlock surcoat, Lion riding in its scabbard at his hip, a shield slung over his shoulder.

"There's so many of them," murmured Rhodemar.

Gerald shrugged. "It will merely make it harder for the archers to miss."

"Are all scouts in?" said Athaelin.

"Aye," said Mazael. "The last ones came in less than an hour ago. The Elderborn thinned the Malrags' ranks somewhat, along with the attacks of my men."

"How many are left?" said Athaelin.

"At least a hundred and thirty-five thousand," said Mazael. "Maybe more. Probably more."

"The old rule is that every man atop the wall is worth ten below it," said Athaelin. "And we have three thousand men of the Keep and fifteen hundred Elderborn. Ultorin has three times as many Malrags as he needs to assault us." He took a deep breath. "What do you suggest, Lord Mazael?"

"Put the Elderborn on the western wall," said Mazael. "Ultorin will send a strong force up the road to attack the gates. If the Elderborn aim well, perhaps we can keep them from reaching the gate. Keep the spearmen upon the southern wall, with a reserve by the gates and in the Garden of the Temple."

"Why the southern wall?" said Rhodemar. "The bluffs there are steep."

"But not steep enough," said Mazael. "The scouts reported that the Malrags were felling trees. They could construct ladders able to scale the bluffs and the walls. Or raise an earthwork ramp, and roll siege towers up to the wall."

"And we lack siege engines to counter any the Malrags might construct," said Gerald.

Mazael grinned. "But we have Ardanna and her druids. They can loose earthquakes, and blasts of ice, and command the roots to rise up and destroy any siege engines the Malrags might employ."

"And what about the Malrag shamans?" said Gerald. "If they loose a concentrated barrage of those lightning bolts, they might bring down a section of the wall."

Lucan gave a nasty little laugh. "No, they won't." He squinted over the battlements. "I wonder, in fact, when one of them will get bold enough to try it. Probably...ah, here we go."

No sooner had he spoken than a blast of green lightning screamed out of the sky. But even as it did, sigils of ghostly blue-white fire flickered across the stone wall. The lightning bolt slammed into an invisible barrier a dozen yards above their heads and dissolved into sparks. A heartbeat later another bolt thundered down, and this time it ricocheted from the barrier, ripping into the Malrag ranks.

Lucan laughed through the entire thing.

"The wards upon the walls are most potent," said Lucan. "I doubt even Malavost could send a spell past them. But if the shamans break into the city, they will be able to use their spells unhindered. And both the shamans and Malavost might counter any spells the druids employ against the Malrags."

"The best we can hope for, I think," said Mazael, "is that Ardanna and her druids will nullify Malavost and the Malrag shamans. So it will come down to steel, in the end. Man and Elderborn against Malrag." Mazael shook his head. "Remember, all of you. Our only hope of victory is to kill Ultorin. We must kill him, whatever the price, even at the cost of our own lives."

The other men nodded. They all might well die before the day was out, Mazael knew. They might die before noon.

At least Romaria was safe from the battle. Though she possibly faced a greater danger.

Then the growling voice rang over the walls.

SYKHANA GAZED at the walls of Deepforest Keep. The city was not as grand as Knightcastle, or as fortified as Castle Cravenlock. Yet the towers and walls stood tall and strong, and men and Elderborn waited atop the battlements, weapons in hand. Deepforest Keep would not yield without a sharp fight.

How would they ever get inside?

One arrow, that was all it would take. One stray arrow sinking into Aldane's flesh, and all of Sykhana's hopes would turn to ashes.

She steered her horse past the looming Ogrags, to where Malavost and Skaloban conferred with Ultorin.

"Our numbers are insufficient!" said Skaloban, head swaying back and forth in alarm. "There are more defenders that we anticipated! And I can sense the gathered power of the Elderborn druids. They are most potent."

"Our numbers are sufficient," said Malavost, calm as ever. "Your forget our goal, honored Skaloban. Our goal is not to destroy Deepforest Keep, or build an empire for the Malrags. Our goal is to take the Vessel to the Door of Souls atop Mount Tynagis. True, we may lose nine out of ten Malrags by the time the battle is done. But what of that? The Malrags are expendable tools. Even the Malrags themselves think so – they'll be reborn again in a few decades, after all.

And once the Vessel has fulfilled his purpose, once Sepharivaim has been born, we shall have no further need of Malrags."

"I will," said Ultorin, "speak to them. Now! I will speak to them now!"

Sykhana looked at the Dominiar knight, trying to hide her fear.

Ultorin's deterioration had accelerated over the last few days. His eyes had turned a sulfurous yellow, stark against his waxy skin. Black veins threaded their way through his hands and temples, and he stank of rotting blood. Strange gnarled tumors of twisted gray flesh bulged from his jaw and forehead. He held his bloodsword constantly now, the blade veiled in swirling darkness, and sometimes he talked to the weapon, muttering in a crooning voice.

Either the bloodsword itself was destroying him, or the sheer amount of Malrag life force had stolen through the blade was corrupting him into a monster. But even as his mind crumbled and his body warped, Ultorin had grown stronger and faster. She had seen him cut through an Elderborn scouting party, butchering a dozen Elderborn in as many heartbeats, laughing all the while.

As soon as Aldane achieved godhood, Sykhana decided, she would kill Ultorin.

"Speak with them, Grand Master?" said Malavost.

"Are you deaf?" bellowed Ultorin. "I will speak with them! Use your magic, wizard. Let them hear me! I will tell them their fates, how they will perish upon my blade. Let them know me and despair!"

"A sound strategy," said Malavost, and he cast a spell. The air in front of Ultorin rippled, and the wizard nodded. "They can hear you now."

Ultorin began to speak.

RACHEL STOOD in her guest room in the Champion's Tower, staring at the Malrag host.

She had seen the great battle near Castle Cravenlock, watching as the men of the Grim Marches strove against the Malrags. But this was worse. Barely five thousand men defended Deepforest Keep.

Her hands tightened into fists.

Aldane was out there, somewhere, in the middle of those Malrags.

A voice like thunder boomed over the city.

MAZAEL RECOGNIZED Ultorin's voice at once.

"Men of Deepforest Keep!" boomed the Dominiar knight. "I am Ultorin, Grand Master of the Dominiar Order!"

"A spell," muttered Lucan. "To amplify his voice."

"You cannot stop me!" said Ultorin. "I have Malrags and Ogrags beyond count. My shamans will butcher your precious druids. My Ogrags will tear down your walls. My Malrags will swarm through your gates, and butcher your women and children before your eyes, butcher them like hogs! Only then, only after you drown in your tears and choke upon the blood of your families, only then will I permit you the gift of death!"

Silence answered his pronouncement.

"But there is no need for unnecessary suffering," said Ultorin, his voice almost purring. "Lay down your arms, and depart the city, and I shall slay you quickly and without pain. Your lives are at an end, either way. The only choice left to you is whether you shall die quickly, or whether you shall linger to hear your children scream for mercy."

"He cannot possibly be serious," said Rhodemar.

"He's not," said Mazael. "Ultorin may be human, but he has a Malrag's heart. He's only toying with us. Go outside those walls and he'll torture and butcher you – you'll only have saved him the trouble of breaking through the walls first. But two can play at this game. Lucan! Can you use a spell to magnify our voices?"

"Certainly," said Lucan, and he gestured and muttered. The air rippled before Athaelin, and Lucan nodded.

Athaelin sprang upon the battlements, sword in hand. "Hear me!" His voice rumbled over the hills and the sides of the mountain like thunder. "I am Athaelin, the Greenshield, Champion of Deepforest Keep and Defender of the Mountain! I see you for what you are, Ultorin of the Dominiar Knights. You are a craven and a weakling, hiding behind your Malrags, relying upon stolen sorcery in lieu of true valor."

Silence answered his pronouncement.

"You want our lives?" said Athaelin. "Then come, craven! Come and face us! Come and face men with hearts of valor, with spear and sword and bow in hand! The Malrags may be reborn, Ultorin of the Dominiar Knights, but you will not! Come, and we shall send you screaming down to the hell you so richly deserve! Come and face the men of Deepforest Keep!"

A roar answered his pronouncement as the men and Elderborn upon the walls shouted their defiance, shaking their weapons in the air. On and on the cry went, the side of the mountain ringing with it.

It must have enraged Ultorin. And their one hope of victory lay in enraging Ultorin beyond all reason.

"Lucan," said Mazael.

Lucan nodded, gestured, and the air in front of Mazael rippled.

He sprang up onto the battlements besides Athaelin. "Ultorin!"

His voice thundered over the armies, enhanced by Lucan's magic.

"Do you remember me, Ultorin?" said Mazael. "Do you remember how you brought fire and sword into my lands? Do you remember how you swore vengeance upon me for the destruction of the Dominiar Order?" He drew Lion, and the Malrags were close enough that the sword burst into snarling azure flame. "I am still here, Ultorin! What are you waiting for? I am Mazael, Lord of Castle Cravenlock, and I defy you! Come and die, you coward, you murderer of children, you..."

Ultorin's howl of fury screamed over them like a dark wind.

∾

Sʏᴋʜᴀɴᴀ ʙᴀᴄᴋᴇᴅ ᴀᴡᴀʏ as Ultorin raged, lashing about with his blood-sword. The ashes of a half-dozen Malrags lay upon the ground, and even as she watched, Ultorin killed another, the bloody light of his blade burning ever brighter.

"Grand Master," said Malavost. How did he remain so calm? "We..."

"Kill them!" screamed Ultorin. "Kill them all! Attack!"

And around Sykhana, the Malrag host moved.

Tʜᴇ Mᴀʟʀᴀɢs ʙᴇʟʟᴏᴡᴇᴅ their war cries, and the combined noise was louder than Mazael's voice, louder than Ultorin's, louder than the thunder itself.

"I think," said Lucan, "you made him angry."

Mazael nodded.

The Malrag horde surged forward like a black tide, covering the foothills below the city, and still more and more surged out of the Forest. Yet there was organization in the chaos, and Mazael saw the Malrag attack splitting into two groups. One veered to the west, moving towards the road the climbed below the city's walls and led to the gate. The second surged towards the base of the bluff and the southern wall. Mazael wondered what they intended to accomplish, but then he saw the enormous ladders carried by the Ogrags, a hundred feet long, topped by spiked grapnels. They would only need to scramble halfway up the bluff, and let the ladders cover the rest of the way.

The Malrags would take horrendous losses...but Ultorin could afford to spend Malrag blood like water.

"Gerald," said Mazael, keeping his voice calm. "Go take command of the reserve. If the gates are breached, or if the Malrags make the walls, I'll need you to fill in the gaps. Rhodemar. Take command of the archers on the western wall. Make sure the Malrags don't reach the gates. Also, focus your fire on any Ogrags. They might be strong enough to batter through the gates by themselves."

Rhodemar nodded and ran off.

"Lucan, Athaelin, stay with me," said Mazael. "We shall go where we are needed. Lucan. If you see Ultorin, if he's within range of your spells, do not hold back. Hit him with everything you have."

For some reason, Lucan cast a nervous look at the black staff in his hand, but gave a sharp nod.

Around them, arrows hissed through the air as the Elderborn on the walls began to fire at the Malrags.

SYKHANA WATCHED the assaults surge towards Deepforest Keep, watched arrows fall from the walls. The Malrags heading up the road changed formation, raising their shields over their heads like overlapping scales. A tortoise formation, she had heard it called. The Elderborn arrows fell upon the tortoise in a storm, and some got through, but most did not.

Bit by bit the tortoise crawled its way up the road, towards the gates.

Ultorin paced back and forth before Sykhana, still snarling and cursing. He had killed his horse in his fury, the beast's withered carcass lying beneath an oak. Now Ultorin stalked through the ranks of the Malrags, gesturing with his bloodsword.

Sykhana held Aldane close...and kept her hand near her poisoned dagger.

"Ah," said Malavost.

The Ogrags at the base of the bluff moved. Their huge ladders, assembled from the trees of the Great Southern Forest, rose up. Each ladder weighed over a ton, yet the Ogrags' strength lifted them like delicate branches. A dozen ladders crashed against the city's walls, their spiked grapnels digging into the stones.

Hundreds of Malrags surged up the wide ladders, shields raised over their heads to ward off arrows.

MAZAEL CURSED as the spiked grapnels dug into the battlements. The huge ladders were hundreds of feet tall, and a dozen wide. The things were enormous, and too heavy to simply push away from the wall.

And hundreds of Malrags scrambled up the ladders, shields raised. From time to time an Elderborn arrow hissed through, sent a Malrag tumbling down the bluff to its death. But there were too many Malrags scrambling up too many ladders.

He risked a glance to the west. The Elderborn fared better there, pouring volleys of murderous arrow fire into the Malrag tortoise. The front ranks disintegrated, and soon dead Malrags paved the road, the survivors trying to protect themselves with their shields.

Another ladder crashed against the battlements, the spiked grapnels digging into the gray stone. Athaelin shouted orders, and the spearmen rushed forward and set themselves, shields raised, spears at the ready.

"Lucan!" said Mazael.

~

LUCAN SWEPT a glance over the ladders.

Too many of them. Far too many. If enough Malrags reached the battlements, they could establish a beachhead and pour into the city. If he did not act quickly, Deepforest Keep would find itself overrun.

Fortunately, Lucan had come prepared.

He reached into his coat and withdrew one of the copper tubes that Timothy had made. He removed the cork, tossed it over the wall, and whispered the spell. Magic stirred in response to his summons, and the end of the tube began to glow.

Lucan did not point the tube down, of course. The flames would only erupt upwards, into his face, and he had no wish to burn to death. Instead he tossed the tube over the battlements, watching it bounce of the rungs and Malrag armor.

And then it erupted.

Orange-yellow flames exploded from the copper tube, cloaking a dozen Malrags in snarling flames. The tube spun as it fell, spraying flame in all directions, and soon scores more Malrags and two of the ladders burned. The burning Malrags lost their grips and fell, sending dozens of other tumbling to the ground, while the two burning ladders collapsed in a pile of debris.

Hundreds of Malrags fell with the wreckage.

But ten ladders still leaned against the walls.

He needed more power.

Lucan sent his will in the bloodstaff. He yearned to open himself to it, to let the power fill him with strength and vitality. But he dared not. The druid's blood already marked his hands, and he might spill more innocent blood, if he drew too deeply upon the staff's Demon-souled might.

Instead he summoned a surge of power, enough to enhance a single spell, even as his body and heart screamed for more, more. Lucan leveled the bloodstaff, pointing at the ladders, and shouted the final phrase of his spell. Invisible force ripped from his staff, crashing into two of the ladders like giant fists. One fell backwards, the Malrags clinging to the ladder roaring as they plummeted to their doom. The second wobbled to the side, falling into another ladder. For a moment both tottered, the Ogrags fighting to keep the ladders upright, but too many Malrags had climbed upon them.

The ladders fell, shedding Malrags as they did so.

A wave of nausea surged through Lucan as the spell's power drained from him, but he gripped the battlements and stayed upright, preparing another attack.

And even as he did, the roots of trees erupted from the base of the bluff like writing brown serpents, wrapping around the bases of the ladders and tearing them to splinters.

ULTORIN CURSED in fury when the seventh ladder fell to the ground in a rain of splinters.

Sykhana shied away from him.

"How are they doing that?" he said, pointing with the bloodsword.

A thin line of drool slithered down his chin. He had begun growing fangs, misshapen spikes of twisted yellow bone.

"Magic, of course," said Malavost. "The druids are summoning the roots, and...ah. Yes. The Dragon's Shadow is using his little staff to rip down the ladders." He grinned, pale eyes flashing. "The little fool. He's going to regret that. Do you not agree, Grand Master?"

For some reason Malavost smiled, as if at a private joke.

"I don't care how they're doing it!" said Ultorin, yellow eyes narrowed. "Stop them! Mazael Cravenlock is in there, and I want his head."

"As you wish, Grand Master," said Malavost, unruffled. "If you will but order the shamans to follow my direction."

Ultorin growled and jerked his head, and a dozen Malrag shamans moved to Malavost's side, their tattered leather robes rustling. Malavost lifted his hands and began to chant, a cold breezing stirring around him, and the shamans did the same, their growling voices echoing inside Sykhana's head.

Then Malavost's fingers blazed with green light, and he thrust out his hands.

～

LUCAN STAGGERED.

A pulse of green light washed over Deepforest Keep. For a moment the warding sigils upon the walls crackled in blue-white radiance, and then faded. But the animated roots at the base of the bluff went still, their magic dispelled by the power of the shamans.

No. Not just the shamans. The Malrag shamans had the raw power, but it had been Malavost's subtle skill that guided the spell.

And still three ladders leaned against the wall.

"Lucan," said Mazael, Lion a bar of sky-colored flame in his fist.

Lucan gave a shake of his head. "That is the best we can do for now. Malavost will counter anything else we cast at him. And the spell to animate the roots took a great deal of power. It will take the druids a few moments to recover themselves."

Mazael cursed, looked at the courtyard below the Great Traig, where Ardanna and the druids stood, chanting as they cast spells.

"Then three ladders it is," said Mazael. "We shall have to fight."

Athaelin nodded. "Men of Deepforest Keep! Brace yourselves!"

The men shouted and raced to the remaining three ladders, shields raised, spears extended.

"And I," said Lucan, "will see if I can distract Malavost."

Mazael nodded and ran to join the spearmen, Athaelin at his right hand.

Lucan opened his mind to the bloodstaff, and the raging power flooded through him. He wanted to lash out around him with his magic, butchering human and Elderborn and Malrag alike. But some part of his mind held control, and instead he loosed the staff's full might at Malavost.

Vaguely, he realized that Aldane Roland might be with Malavost, but he did not care. The death of one infant was a small price to pay to keep Sepharivaim from rising once more.

THE GREEN LIGHT FADED, and Sykhana saw the living roots at the base of the bluff go still. Three of the massive ladders remained against the wall, and a steady torrent of Malrags poured up them.

"Well enough for now," said Malavost, flexing his fingers. "I suggest, Grand Master, that you order more ladders constructed, and..."

His eyes widened.

A flare of blood-colored light blazed atop the walls of Deepforest Keep, and a ribbon of crimson flame leap out, weaving back and forth like a drunken bird.

It was heading right for them.

Malavost moved faster than she had ever seen him move. One moment he stood among the Malrag shamans. The next he stood by the side of her horse, left hand closing about her ankle, his right coming up in a magical gesture.

"What..." began Sykhana.

Malavost barked a spell, and a shimmering globe of blue light surrounded them.

An instant later the ribbon of crimson flame slammed into the globe. There was a deafening roar, and a flash of fiery light. A blast of hot wind washed over them, almost throwing Sykhana from the saddle, sending Malavost's long coat flapping behind him like black wings. She closed her eyes and clung to Aldane, trying to keep from falling to the ground.

Then the light cleared, and Malavost's blue glow vanished.

Sykhana blinked the afterimage from her eyes. Around them, a half-dozen trees burned, reduced to smoldering ruin. A score of Malrags lay scattered on the ground, their armor half-melted, the air heavy with the stench of their scorched flesh. Ultorin stood some distance away, still bellowing at the Malrags. Sykhana doubted that he had even noticed the magical attack.

"Ah," said Malavost at last. "It seems that the Dragon's Shadow can hit harder than I expected." He smiled. "I underestimated him. Though not by very much."

"He almost killed Aldane!" said Sykhana. Some part of her mind realized that Lucan Mandragon had almost killed her as well, but she hardly cared. Aldane was all that mattered. "You promised, wizard! You said Aldane would live forever in power and splendor. He can't do that if the Dragon's Shadow kills him!"

"I told you that Aldane would reach the summit of Mount Tynagis," said Malavost, "and I keep my word. I have not brought Aldane Roland all this way only to see him die within sight of his destiny." His pale blue eyes fixed on her, his white hair stirring in the hot breeze rising from the burned ground. "But do not fear, Sykhana. When the time comes, I shall break Lucan Mandragon as easily a child breaking a twig."

THE DRUIDS' magic and Lucan's spells had destroyed seven of the massive ladders, but three remained, scores of Malrags swarming up each one.

"This is the hour, men of Deepforest Keep!" bellowed Athaelin, bastard sword in his right hand, the ancient Greenshield upon his left arm. "Stand fast and fight! Your wives and children rely upon your arms, your sons and daughters look to you to keep the safe! Fight, and make the Malrags curse the day they ever dared to turn their filthy eyes towards Deepforest Keep!"

Mazael saw terror in the spearmen's eyes, saw the sweat dripping down their faces, but they lifted their spears and cheered the Champion of Deepforest Keep nonetheless. Mazael raised his own shield on his left arm, Lion burning in his fist.

No sooner had he done so then the Malrags leapt over the ladders, howling their dreadful war cries, black axes ready in their hands.

Mazael sprang to meet them, Lion trailing azure fire, and behind him the men of Deepforest Keep shouted and charged into the fray.

RACHEL GRIPPED the railing in white-knuckled hands, watching the melee rage along the walls. She saw Mazael in the midst of the bloody chaos. No Malrag could stand before his wrath, or against his sword's burning fires. Yet the battle swayed back and forth, and she saw the endless tide of Malrags pushing the spearmen back towards the Champion's Tower.

Towards her refuge.

Rachel grimaced. She was the wife of Sir Gerald Roland, the youngest in a long line of Roland kings, lords, and knights. She would not flee like a frightened peasant girl! And yet, she knew, if the Malrags overran the Champion's Tower, they would kill her. Gerald might have to watch her die.

And if she perished, she would never see Aldane again.

The druids in the circle of oaks below the Great Traig, she

decided. She could take refuge there, watch the battle upon the walls.

And she had heard some of the Elderborn. A well in the Garden of the Temple led to the caves, the caverns that climbed to the temple atop Mount Tynagis.

The temple where the San-keth wanted to turn her son into a monster.

If the battle went badly and the Malrags forced their way into the city, Sykhana would take Aldane to the caverns. To the well.

And Rachel would have her chance at last.

She snatched her dagger from the table and ran from the room.

MAZAEL TORE his way through the fight, striking down Malrags right and left. His blood thundered through his temples, his heart beating like a war drum. This was a worthy fight, a struggle to defend the people of Deepforest Keep against Ultorin's Malrags, and Mazael let the battle fury rise without fear. As he fought to defend Deepforest Keep, his Demonsouled rage rose under the command of his disciplined mind.

And with it he cut through the Malrags like a scythe.

A Malrag lunged at him with a spear. He caught the point on his shield, shoved the creature back, and lashed out with Lion. The sword ripped open the Malrag's throat, thick black blood sizzling across Lion's blade. Two more Malrags came at Mazael, attacking with axes. Mazael sidestepped the first blow and swung his shield, catching the first Malrag across the face, broken fangs and black blood flying from its mouth.

Before the creature could catch its balance, Athaelin was there, his bastard sword a blur. The Malrag fell, slumping against the battlements. The second Malrag slashed its axe at Athaelin, and he interposed his ancient bronze shield. The shield, Mazael realized, must truly be magical – the axe's black steel did not leave even a scratch on the tarnished bronze.

The Malrag stumbled, giving Mazael the opening he needed to take off its head.

All around him the spearmen of Deepforest Keep struggled against the Malrags, the battlements slick with blood, both crimson and black. Men screamed and killed and died, and the Malrags bellowed their horrible war cries, flinging themselves into the chaos with abandon. A spearman fell, his helm and head cloven by a Malrag axe, only for two other spearmen to run the victorious Malrag through.

The men of Deepforest Keep fought well, as well as Mazael had ever seen men fight. But there were just too many Malrags. If they did not get those damned ladders off the wall, the Malrags would overwhelm the defenders.

"The ladders!" shouted Mazael, killing another Malrag as he did so. Athaelin was at his side, sword whirling. "Drive them to the ladders!"

The spearmen shouted and pressed the attack, fighting over the top of dying and wounded Malrags and men.

Then Lucan appeared next to Mazael, lifting his staff, the runes cut in the black metal burning with sullen light. He made a throwing gesture, and the Malrags nearest the ladder staggered, as if struck by an invisible fist. Again Lucan gestured, and this time a dozen Malrags went flying backwards, tumbling over the walls to fall to their doom.

"Now, my lords!" shouted Lucan, his eyes wide with something like glee. "The ladders!"

~

LUCAN SAW Mazael and Athaelin race forward, leading the men towards the ladders. Mazael snatched up an axe and began hammering at one side of the ladder. The ladder had been built out of tree trunks, but Mazael dug the axe deeper and deeper into the wood. Besides him two of the spearmen seized Malrag axes and joined in the effort.

Lucan grinned. If he tried to simply destroy the ladders, Malavost could counter his efforts. But here, on the battlements, he was safely behind the ward spells woven into the stones of the walls. Malavost could not touch him here.

For a moment Lucan wanted to lash out with his spells, to destroy every Malrag and human within sight. It would be so very easy to send Mazael tumbling over the wall, screaming to his death...

No. Discipline.

Lucan drew on the bloodstaff's power, just a little bit of it, and flung a psychokinetic blast into the Malrags. Two of them tumbled over the battlements, falling to their deaths, while the other tumbled back, staggered.

And Mazael and the spearmen cut through the first ladder, breaking it free from the spiked grapnels. For a moment the ladder wobbled, the broken ends scraping against the stone walls. Then it tottered and fell to the side, pulling down hundreds of Malrags with it.

Lucan turned to face the Malrags swarming up the other two ladders, summoning more power for a spell.

SYKHANA WATCHED another ladder tumble down the bluff, killing hundreds of Malrags in its fall, killing dozens more as jagged wooden debris crashed into the Malrag lines.

She looked at the attack below the western wall, making its way up the road to the gates of the city. It, too, had not gone well. The Elderborn archers manned the western wall in force, and sent an unending rain of arrows into the Malrags. The tortoise formation had first frayed and then disintegrated into chaos. Dead Malrags carpeted the road with torn gray flesh and thick black blood.

"Patience, Grand Master," said Malavost. He had insisted that Sykhana dismount, and stood besides her, as if to guard her and Aldane from any stray Elderborn arrows.

Or from Ultorin's rage.

"They are holding!" screamed Ultorin. Between his rage and the strange tumors growing from his jaw, his face looked like an inhuman thing, like some Demonsouled from a jongleur's song. "They are holding, wizard! Mazael Cravenlock is in there, and my vengeance will not be denied!"

"They have slain, perhaps, a thousand of your Malrags," said Malavost with his unflappable calm. "Tens of thousands more await your command. For every Malrag the defenders kill, ten more can take its place. Bit by bit, we will wear them down. Then the city, and the Door of Souls, shall be ours."

Ultorin growled, but did not answer.

The final ladder crashed in ruin at the base of the bluff.

MAZAEL PULLED OFF HIS HELM, wiped the sweat from his brow. All around him the spearmen milled with activity. Some cheered and shouted taunts at the Malrags. Others tended to wounded comrades, or sharpened their weapons. Athaelin strode among them, offering encouragements and praising their valor.

But the battle was far from over.

Mazael looked over the battlements, at the black sea of Malrags filling the foothills.

An Elderborn messenger ran up, breathing hard.

"What news?" said Mazael.

"Rhodemar the Greenshield's son sends news. The western wall holds," said the Elderborn. "For now. Some Malrags have reached the gates, but not many, and the tribes shoot them with ease."

Mazael nodded. "Any sign of Ultorin?"

"None."

Mazael frowned. "What about any Ogrags?"

"None, either."

Why was Ultorin holding them back? Each Ograg was worth a score of Malrags in a fight. Mazael doubted that the Elderborn arrows could penetrate the Ogrags' thick armor, and if enough Ogrags made it past the western wall, they could simply smash the gates and pour into the city.

And Ultorin. They needed to lure Ultorin into the open. Deepforest Keep could not stand against the Malrag storm, not for long. Their only hope of victory was to find Ultorin and kill him.

He had to draw Ultorin out.

"Lucan," said Mazael.

Lucan stepped forward, leaning on the black staff. He looked terrible, his face pale and waxy, sweat dripping down his forehead. Yet his black eyes glittered, and he looked at the Malrags with something like mad glee.

"Let Ultorin hear me," said Mazael.

Lucan grinned, nodded, and waved his hand. The air in front of Mazael rippled, and he sprang onto the battlement, holding Lion over his head.

"Ultorin!" he roared, and his voice thundered over the Malrag host. "I'm still here, Ultorin! Is that the best you can do? Fling your wretched creatures against our walls? Are you too unmanned to face me yourself? Or will you hide behind the Malrags and their spells until I come for you?"

~

It took the deaths of a dozen Malrags to calm Ultorin down.

"Mere words, Grand Master," said Malavost. Sykhana stood behind him, Aldane held against her chest. "Will you let mere words override your control? Victory is yours, if you will but choose patience..."

"No more," said Ultorin, his voice calm. Somehow, his calmness was even more terrifying than his rage. "I am going to take Deepforest Keep, wizard. I am going to butcher the men. I am going to rape the women, and then kill their children in front of them. And I will make Mazael Cravenlock scream for mercy, scream as I cut him apart inch by inch."

"Once we reach the Door of Souls," said Malavost, "you shall have all the vengeance you desire. And so much more, besides."

"I care not!" said Ultorin. "I will have Mazael's head. I will have it now!"

"But..." said Malavost.

"Ogrags!" roared Ultorin. "With me! All of you!" The massive plate-armored forms of the Ogrags gathered, towering over Ultorin and Malavost and Sykhana. "The rest of you, keep building ladders, and throwing them against the southern wall! I will have Deepforest Keep! I will raze it to the ground!"

Another bloodcurdling cheer went up from the Malrags.

"Ultorin!" shouted Malavost.

Ultorin turned, yellow eyes narrowed. "What did you say, wizard? Did you dare speak my name?"

"Forgive me, Grand Master," said Malavost. "I ask only that you leave me command of a dozen shamans and a thousand Malrags. So I might contribute in your glorious vengeance against Mazael Cravenlock."

Ultorin snorted. "As you will." He barked one more command, and then Ogrags followed him.

The rest of the host surged towards Deepforest Keep, a half-dozen newly-built ladders carried forward.

"At last," hissed Skaloban. "Victory shall be ours."

"Sykhana," said Malavost, voice urgent. "We need to act quickly."

"What?" said Sykhana.

"Ultorin is going to get himself killed, the fool," said Malavost, "and probably before he can break into Deepforest Keep. If he is slain before we can reach the Door of Souls, all of this will have been for nothing. Give me the Vessel."

"What?" repeated Sykhana. "Why..."

Before she could react, Malavost plucked Aldane from her arms, cradling the baby in the crook of his elbow. Sykhana almost attacked him, almost plunged her fangs into his neck.

Only the sure and certain knowledge that Malavost's magic would crush her like an insect kept her in check.

"This is what you shall do," said Malavost. "Take command of the thousand Malrags and the dozen shamans. There is a secret tunnel that leads into Deepforest Keep, near the large tower in the southern wall. Unleash the Malrags and create as much havoc as you can. The shamans will be useful – once inside the walls, the wards will no longer hinder their spells. Between the chaos inside the walls, Ultorin's assault upon the gate, and the attack on the southern wall, Deepforest Keep will fall." His smile returned. "And the Vessel shall be immortal, as I promised you."

"A secret tunnel?" said Sykhana. "How do you even know about this?"

"Through study." Malavost glanced at the walls. "Deepforest Keep was once a stronghold of the High Elderborn, built to guard their temple atop Mount Tynagis. And the High Elderborn always constructed a hidden tunnel in their strongholds, in case they needed to escape. Deepforest Keep is no exception. I performed a divination while Ultorin was busy posturing, and learned that the tunnel still remains."

"Why didn't you tell Ultorin?" said Sykhana.

Malavost's smile sharpened. "Ultorin...has almost outlived his usefulness to us. We still need him alive, but only for a little while longer. And once we have reached the Door of Souls, we shall have no further use for him at all." He looked at the battle. "Go, now. The timing for your attack could not be better. The entrance to the caverns is a well in the heart of the city. I will meet you there."

"Your plan is sound, wizard," said Skaloban. "Go forth and obey, calibah."

Sykhana hesitated, staring at Aldane, asleep on Malavost's arm.

"Do not fear for the Vessel," said Malavost. "His destiny is almost upon him. And where could he be safer than with me?"

At last Sykhana tore herself away and marched in the direction of the waiting Malrag shamans. It hurt terribly to leave Aldane. But it was for his sake. For his future.

To make him immortal, she would kill every living thing in Deepforest Keep, if necessary.

"Come," said Sykhana, and the Malrags obeyed.

SHE FOUND the secret entrance in the foothills, just as Malavost promised, and led the Malrags inside. Built of ancient white stone, the tunnel twisted and turned, climbing ever higher, and Sykhana's calibah eyes let her see in the darkness without trouble.

A pity the forgotten tunnel did not link with the mountain's caverns - they could have bypassed Deepforest Keep entirely.

At last the tunnel ended in a doorway. Sykhana pushed it open, poisoned daggers in either hand. The door opened into a vaulted stone cellar, crates and barrels stacked against the wall. Dim sunlight filtered through narrow windows.

"Silence," Sykhana ordered the Malrags. "Do not make any noise until we attack."

She crossed the cellar, a half-dozen shamans and a score of Malrags following her, and ascended a stone staircase. The cellar's door opened at the base of a house. From it she had a view of the high tower in the southern wall. Below the tower stood a grove of massive oak trees, surrounding one of those massive white statues of an Elderborn warrior. Elderborn women stood in the ring of statues, brandishing oak staffs.

The druids.

Behind her the cellar filled with Malrags.

"Attack," said Sykhana.

No sooner had she spoken then green lightning came ripping down from the sky.

RACHEL HURRIED down the steps of the Champion's Tower, and froze.

She saw dark shapes pouring from a house across from the courtyard, black spears and axes in their hands.

~

"BRACE YOURSELVES!" said Athaelin lifting his sword. "By the gods of tree and stone, men, we've beat these devils away once before, and we can do so again!"

Eight more ladders moved closer to the base of the bluffs, carried by straining Ogrags. Mazael waited, Lion ready in his hand. If Lucan or the druids tried to knock down the ladders, Malavost and the shamans would counter the spells. But once the Malrags gained the walls, Lucan and the druids could unleash their magic, and Mazael, Athaelin, and the spearmen could destroy the grapnels anchoring the ladders to the walls.

And send the Malrags tumbling to their deaths again...

"Champion!"

An Elderborn messenger raced up to the rampart.

"What is it?" said Athaelin.

"Dozens of Ogrags," said the Elderborn. "Heading up the western road. Our arrows cannot penetrate their armor. And a warrior in black armor leads them, a sword of darkness and flame in his hand."

"Ultorin," said Mazael, hand tightening around Lion's grip. It had worked. They had drawn out Ultorin. Now Mazael only had to kill him...

Green lightning ripped down from the sky, driving into the earth near the Great Traig.

"What?" said Athaelin.

Mazael turned, saw black forms racing through the streets, heard women and children screaming.

The Malrags had gotten inside the city.

25

RITUAL OF RULERSHIP

Romaria expected to find darkness within the caverns, but instead there was light.

Pale, faint light, but light nonetheless. Patches of moss dotted the walls and ceiling of the caverns, throwing off a pale white glow. It gave the caverns a surreal, ghostly air, as if Romaria had left the world of mortals behind and instead entered the realm of spirits.

Watching the Seer walk before her, the tip of his staff scraping against the floor, Romaria did not think that seemed far wrong.

"The moss," said Romaria. "What is it?"

"Starglow, the High Elderborn called it," answered the Seer, his voice echoing off the stone walls. "They bred it with their magic, to provide light in the galleries and vaults below their temples. The High Elderborn have passed from the world, but starglow lingers, here beneath the mountain."

The tunnel widened into a large chamber, lit by patches of starglow on the ceiling and floor. At one end Romaria saw a broad staircase of white stone, rising out of sight. At the other end yawned another cave entrance, like the jagged mouth of a predator, the tunnel beyond vanishing into darkness.

"The stairs lead to the summit of Mount Tynagis," said the Seer, "and the ruins of the sacred temple." He pointed at the darkened entrance. "But you must go there. Through there, you will undergo the Ritual of Rulership, and you must face yourself."

"What does that even mean?" said Romaria. "What must I do? Climb the mountain? Kill a dozen Malrags? What does that mean, to face myself?"

"You will face your past, your present, and your future," said the Seer, leaning upon his staff. "It is not too late to turn back."

Romaria hesitated. For a moment she almost agreed, almost turned and left the cavern. No doubt the Malrags were attacking Deepforest Keep even now, and she should be fighting alongside the others, not sulking through these ancient caves.

But Deepforest Keep would die, if she did not undergo the Ritual.

Mazael would die.

"Let's get this over with," said Romaria, and strode towards the entrance.

The tunnel beyond the jagged mouth sloped down, deeper into the mountain's depths. At first Romaria could see with the faint white glow still coming from the entrance. But even that light faded, and she used her bow as a staff to feel for pits along the floor of the tunnel.

She cursed herself for neglecting to bring a torch or a lantern, and then she saw the faint blue glow coming ahead. She made her way towards it, still feeling the ground with her staff, until the eerie blue glow grew bright enough to illuminate the passageway.

Mist swirled along the floor, curling around her boots.

She felt magical power stirring in the air, like the tension before a storm.

Romaria stepped into another chamber, smaller than the first. A placid pool filled perhaps half of the floor, reflecting the stalactites of the ceiling. The strange blue glow illuminated the chamber, coming from everywhere and nowhere at once. A hooded figured stood next to the pool, gazing down into it.

"Who are you?" said Romaria.

The hooded figure turned, and Romaria found herself looking into her mother's golden eyes.

"Useless abomination," said Ardanna. "You dare to defile this sacred place with your filth?"

Rage surged through Romaria, and her hands curled into fists.

But fear, as well. Perhaps her mother was right. Perhaps Romaria was indeed an abomination. She would lose control of herself, sooner or later, and become a ravening beast forever. The gods alone knew what she might do then, the innocents she might kill.

"I am ashamed that I ever bore you," said Ardanna, stalking closer. "I am ashamed that I did not purge my womb of you, as I should have done. I am ashamed that I did not leave you in the Forest to die. And I am ashamed that I let your miserable father bring you back to Deepforest Keep!"

Still Romaria said nothing.

"It would have been better," hissed Ardanna, "if you had never been born! If I had never laid eyes upon your..."

"Shut up!" said Romaria.

The High Druid flinched as if slapped.

"I've known hardship and pain in my life – a lot of it from you – but I would not give it up," said Romaria. "And I am not an abomination, I have done good things, I have saved people! Those villagers in the Old Kingdom. Ultorin's Dominiars would have killed them, if I had not stopped him." Her anger grew, spilling out of her in a torrent. "And I've saved more people than that. I've fought the San-keth. I've fought Malrags! And I saved Mazael from himself!"

"Useless vermin," said Ardanna, her eyes ablaze with rage. "Every breath you take pollutes the world further. Lie down and die. Lie down and die!"

"No!" said Romaria. "I will not! My life means more than you think, you arrogant and stupid woman."

Ardanna shrieked in fury, and an obsidian-tipped hunting spear appeared in her hand. She leapt forward, still howling in rage, and thrust the spear at Romaria's face. But Romaria jumped back, yanking her bastard sword from its shoulder scabbard, and parried.

The obsidian spearhead shattered against her steel blade, and Romaria shoved, sent her mother sprawling to the ground.

And Ardanna dissolved into mist, her body blurring into nothingness.

Romaria turned in confusion. There was no sign of Ardanna. Had that really been her mother? No – as much as the High Druid hated her, Ardanna would not abandon the defense of Deepforest Keep. Had it been an illusion, then? A spirit conjured out of the netherworld?

Or an illusion in her own mind?

You will face yourself, the Seer had said.

What did that mean?

The mist swirled past her ankles, eerie in the blue light. Romaria looked up, saw it flowing into another tunnel on the far side of the chamber. She followed the mist, circling around the placid pool, and entered another tunnel.

This tunnel was far narrower, the walls cold and clammy. It grew colder as she walked, until her breath steamed in the air, and she pulled her cloak closer for warmth. She had been in caves before, and they had never been this cold.

She kept her bastard sword raised.

At last the tunnel opened into another chamber. This chamber looked like an amphitheater, with the stone floor sloping down to a sand-covered hollow. The light in here was the color of blood. The same color, Romaria realized with unease, that shone from the sigils upon Lucan Mandragon's staff of black metal.

A man in black plate armor stood in the center of the chamber, his back to her. It was the same sort of ornate black plate armor worn by the commanders of the Dominiar Order.

"Ultorin!" shouted Romaria, both hands on her sword hilt. "You murderous dog! Turn around face me."

The black-armored man turned to look at her.

It was Mazael.

Not Mazael as she knew him, tall and strong and gray-eyed. This Mazael had eyes the color of burning blood, his face locked in a gleeful, cruel grin. He looked strong and powerful and terrible, a living god of war, a beautiful avatar of destruction.

This was what Mazael would have become, she realized, if he had succumbed to his Demonsouled nature. If he had embraced the darkness within him to become the Destroyer, the Demonsouled prophesied to destroy the kingdoms of men.

"Romaria," said Mazael, his voice deeper and colder than she had ever heard it. "Bow before me and worship me. You are mine, heart and soul."

She felt, for a moment, the overwhelming compulsion to kneel before him, to please him, to let him do whatever he wanted to her. She loved him, heart and soul, and she wanted him...

"No," said Romaria with an effort.

Mazael laughed. "You want this, as much as I do. I am a killer, Romaria. I am the Destroyer! I have embraced my strength, become what I was born to be! Now kneel before me, and give yourself to me. I will be the lord of the earth, and I shall trample empires beneath my feet. And you shall be my queen, and sit at my right hand in power and glory. Kneel!"

The visions flashed before her eyes, each more intense than the last. She had always been drawn to Mazael's strength, had she not? He was a warrior without peer, and a mighty captain of men. How his strength stirred her heart! What would it be like, she wondered, if he embraced his Demonsouled power? How strong he would become! He would become...

She frowned. He would become just like Amalric Galbraith, who had embraced his Demonsouled nature, and butchered innocents across the Old Kingdoms.

"No," repeated Romaria, louder this time.

Mazael's hellish eyes narrowed.

"I don't want the Destroyer," said Romaria. "I want Mazael Cravenlock. I want the man who saved the children from Mitor's thugs in the square of Cravenlock Town. I want the man who spared his sister's life, even if she deserved to die. I want the man who fought like a lion to defend his people and his lands from Ultorin and his Malrags."

For a moment pain flashed over Mazael's face, and the red glare dimmed in his eyes.

"Then die!" he roared, pulling his sword from its scabbard. It was not Lion he held. This sword was red gold, its pommel carved in the shape of a roaring demon.

The sword of the Destroyer.

Mazael leapt at her, snarling in fury, and the Destroyer's sword burst into blazing crimson flames.

Romaria had her bastard sword up to meet his blow, and their blades met and met again a dozen times in as many heartbeats. She circled around him, trying to stay out of his reach. He was stronger than she was, far stronger, but she was faster, and they were evenly matched. Yet his stamina was superhuman, fueled by his Demon-souled nature, and she would tire long before he did.

Still roaring, he brought the burning sword in an overhand chop for her head, and she only just deflected it. She remembered fighting with him in the garden atop Castle Cravenlock, when his Demon-souled rage almost consumed him...

And she remembered how she had defeated him then.

"You saw me die," said Romaria, and Mazael's face tightened in rage. "You saw the Old Demon strike me down." Pain flickered across his expression. "And you saw me lie dead upon the chapel floor, you saw them bury me in the crypt. And you will do the same to me now?"

She stepped back and lowered her sword, leaving herself open.

"Go ahead," she said. "Watch me die again. I won't stop you."

Mazael lifted the sword, his hand trembling. The sword's fires sputtered and dimmed. He stared at her for a long time. The hellish light drained him his eyes.

And at last he fell to his knees with a cry of anguish. The sword of the Destroyer shattered in his hand, crumbling into ash.

And then Mazael vanished, dissolving into the strange mist that swirled through the chamber.

Romaria looked around, but there was no sign of Mazael.

Another trick of the caverns' magic, she supposed. Or another illusion in her own mind.

The mist flowed past her, pouring into another tunnel on the far side of the chamber. Romaria shrugged to herself, and followed the mist, bastard sword still in hand. It was obviously magical, and it even seemed like something alive. Was it the defensive magic laid over the walls of Deepforest Keep, she wondered? A spell cast over the caverns? Or something even older, something the High Elderborn had left behind?

For some reason she could see the mist more clearly now. In fact, everything around her looked clearer, as if her eyes could make better use of the cavern's dim light.

Then she entered the third and final chamber, and all such thoughts fled from her mind.

This chamber was huge and domed, the ceiling of rough rock vanishing into darkness high overhead. Halfway across, the floor ended in an enormous yawning chasm, its depths vanishing into darkness. A woman stood gazing into the chasm, a tall, lean woman in leather armor, black hair pulled into a braid, a bastard sword strapped to her back.

Then the woman turned, and Romaria found herself gazing into an exact copy of her face.

The Seer had been right. She would indeed face herself here.

"Who are you?" said Romaria.

The double grinned, white fangs curling over her lips. "I am you." Claws sprouted from her fingers, black fur rising to cover her hands and face. "I am what you will become."

"No," said Romaria. "No. I will fight you to the end."

"Fight as you will," said the double, her voice now a bestial growl. "It does not matter. I am you, and you are me. And I am what you will become in the end, whether you embrace it or not."

The double became a great black wolf with eyes like blue ice and fangs and teeth the color of fresh-fallen snow. The wolf sprang forward, fangs bared, and Romaria leapt to meet it.

She would not succumb. She would fight as long as she had the strength. She would not yield!

They fought through the chamber, one moment teetering near the edge of the chasm, the next against the hard rock walls. The wolf's jaws snapped like a steel trap, its claws slashing like swords. Yet Romaria wielded her bastard sword with skill and power, and blocked or dodged every one of the wolf's attacks, giving her opportunity to launch attacks of her own.

Yet, somehow, no matter what she did, the wolf always anticipated it. No matter what combination of moves she tried, no matter how well she feinted, the wolf always knew what she planned. And the strange understanding went both ways. She knew that the wolf would bite at her a few heartbeats before it happened, and she knew moments before the tried to rake her with its claws.

They whirled through the chamber in their mad dance, neither Romaria nor the wolf able to land a blow upon the other. This battle would go on forever, she realized, with neither of them able to win, two halves struggling against each other for eternity.

Two halves...

She realized the truth then, the truth she had fought against her entire life, a truth she had resisted ever since Ardanna had spat it at her in tones of the deepest contempt.

She stopped, lowering her sword, and the wolf came to a halt.

"I am you," said Romaria.

The Elderborn half of her soul would always be a part of her, no matter how hard she struggled against it.

"And I am you," growled the wolf. "I have always been you."

Romaria closed her eyes, dropped her sword. The clangs echoed off the stone walls.

"Let's get it over with," she whispered.

The wolf tensed, and then sprang upon her.

But it did not knock her over. The wolf flew into her, somehow, sinking into the flesh of her chest. Pain erupted through Romaria, pain beyond anything she had known, and she screamed, falling to her knees.

Blackness fell over her, and the world vanished.

AFTER SOME TIME, Romaria awoke.

She lay on her side, her flanks heaving, her muzzle resting upon her paws. She blinked, and scrambled to her feet, all four of them. Even as dim as the cavern was, she saw everything clearly, and a amazing symphony of smells filled her wet nose. She felt her fangs resting in her mouth, her claws scrabbling against the cold stone floor, her fur bristling as her panic and fear rose.

She had become the wolf once more. The earth magic in the Elderborn half of her soul had overwhelmed her at last. She had become the beast, and...

Romaria blinked, tongue lolling over her teeth.

She had become the beast...yet she still had control of her own will. She could still think. Before, when the human half of her soul had been trapped inside Mazael, the beast had overwhelmed her entirely, her reason lost to its animal urges.

But not this time. Romaria's mind and will were still her own, even in the flesh of the great black wolf. She felt the instincts of the beast within her, its lust for meat and its fierce eagerness for the hunt. Yet she was still in control.

The beast was part of her...yet it did not dominate her.

Her ears pricked up as she heard the hard tap of wood against stone.

She waited, and the Seer hobbled into the chamber. Her eyes saw the power of the earth magic filling him, as strong and deep as the roots of the mountain. Her ears heard the slow, steady beast of his heart, the rush of the blood in his veins. And her nose smelled the power surrounding him, crackling like the charged air of a thunderstorm.

The Seer looked at her, and smiled.

"So you have faced yourself, and mastered yourself," he said. "Your soul is your own now, and even your flesh will obey you."

Romaria understood, and concentrated. Her flesh flowed and rippled, her muscles reshaping themselves, her bones shifting and moving. In a moment, the transformation was complete, and she stood in her own form, her own body, before the Seer.

Even her clothes and weapons were still with her, no doubt a function of the earth magic in her soul.

A wild urge seized her, and she reached for the power. Again her body changed, and she became the great wolf once more, and still her reason remained with her. She concentrated again, and took her own shape once more.

There were tears in her eyes. For so long, she had feared the day when her Elderborn soul would overwhelm her flesh, transforming her forever into a ravening beast. And now, to have control over the transformation, to move between the different forms at will...

"How?" she said at last.

"You have faced yourself," said the Seer. "Many half-bloods do not. They refuse to acknowledge the truth, or try to fight themselves until it is too late. You did not. You now know the truth. You are both human and Elderborn, and the power of both heritages is yours to command. Now, come. War rages against the walls of Deepforest Keep, and we are needed."

Romaria's elation vanished as she remembered the grim battle outside the city.

She nodded, picked up her sword, and followed the Seer from the caverns.

26

THE RALLY

B lack-armored shapes raced across the courtyard below the Champion's Tower, killing and slaying as screams rose from the houses of Deepforest Keep. Another green lightning bolt ripped down from the sky and exploded somewhere over the city, the thunder rumbling against the walls.

Mazael stared at the chaos, his mind racing. How the devil had the Malrags gotten into the city? Some trick of Malavost's magic? Or had they scaled the walls, unnoticed by the defenders? Or had they come through some hidden tunnel, some secret entrance long-forgotten by both the Elderborn and the men of Deepforest Keep alike?

He could figure it out later. Right now there were bigger problems. Ultorin himself advanced up the road below the western wall, accompanied by a hundred Ogrags, while the Malrags had just launched another attack at the southern wall with their ladders.

Combined with the sudden chaos inside the walls, the city might very well fall.

Unless Mazael took immediate action.

"What do we do?" murmured Athaelin, his voice low so the spearmen would not hear him.

Mazael made up his mind.

"We attack," said Mazael. "Leave half the men here under some captain you trust. We'll take the other half and join with Gerald's reserve." Odds were that Gerald, seeing the danger, had already attacked the Malrags inside the city. "Then we'll find out how the Malrags got into the city and seal off that entrance, wherever it is."

"And then we can take the fight to Ultorin at the gates," said Athaelin.

"Aye," said Mazael. But it would be a very close thing. It would not take the Ogrags long to smash through the gates. If they did not sweep the Malrags from the streets in time, if Ultorin broke through the gates before they could reach him...

Either way, Mazael realized, the battle for the city would be decided in the next hour.

"Athaelin," said Mazael. "Send a runner to Rhodemar. Tell him to shift some of the Elderborn to the northern wall, to slow down the Ogrags until we get there. Lucan!"

Lucan approached, fiery light flickering in the carved sigils of his staff.

"Stay here," said Mazael, "and help the spearmen to throw down the ladders. If the Malrags gain a foothold on the wall we're..."

Lucan stepped forward and thrust out his hand. For a moment Mazael thought Lucan was going to attack him. But then another blast of green lightning tore out of the sky, thundering towards the battlements. Lucan made a twisting motion with his hand, the staff burning ever brighter, and the lightning bolt twisted aside to rip a crater in the street below the wall.

"Good timing," said Mazael.

Lucan nodded, face twitching in something between a grimace and a grin. "I will aid the spearmen on the battlements. No Malrags will gain the walls. You should hasten, my lord."

"Let's go," said Mazael, and he raced down the stairs, Athaelin at his side, the men following.

∾

RACHEL RAN AS FAST as she could, panting. Three Malrags chased her, howling their terrible war cries, black axes in their hands. She was fit enough, for a noblewoman, but her legs burned and her chest heaved with her frantic breaths.

She had to get away. If the Malrags killed her, if they slew her, she would never see Aldane again...

A narrow alley between two houses of gray stone appeared on her left, and Rachel dodged into it. The alley led to the Garden of the Temple, if she remembered correctly. Gerald and the reserve would be there, and he could keep her safe.

The Malrags followed her into the alley, still howling.

An instant later a bolt of emerald lightning smashed into the roof of the house on her right. The thunder shook the ground, and the shock knocked Rachel onto her hands and knees. Cracks spread through the wall, and Rachel realized that it would collapse.

Onto her.

She threw herself forward, praying that she would see her son again.

The wall fell behind her, its thunder louder than the lightning bolt. Dust billowed through the alley, and Rachel scrambled forward on her hands and knees, coughing. Any moment she expected to feel the massive stones fall upon her, crushing her to pulp.

But the sounds of falling stone faded, and soon she heard nothing but the distant sounds of fighting men and roaring Malrags.

At last she rose to her feet and turned around. Rubble choked the alley, and she saw no sign of the Malrags. No doubt they had been buried in the collapse of the wall. Rachel turned to go, and heard snarls and roars and the tramp of steel-shod boots coming from the other end of the alley.

More Malrags.

She was trapped.

Frantic, Rachel looked at the damaged wall. The rubble formed a ramp to the upper floors of the house, to a place where she could hide. She scrambled up the rubble and ducked into the house's upper floor. Once the room had been a bedchamber, the walls hung with woven tapestries, the table adorned with wooden Elderborn statues. Now the tapestries burned, and heaps of broken stone lay upon the floor. Rachel hurried from the bedchamber, down a narrow hallway, and into another room. She ducked behind the bed, trying to keep quiet.

Noise streamed through the window, and she realized that she had a view of the Garden of the Temple and the stone well at the city's heart. Gerald and the reserve spearmen waited there, and she saw them moving to meet the Malrags.

Rachel swallowed, her heart hammering.

She and Gerald might get to see each other die after all.

~

"FOR DEEPFOREST KEEP!" bellowed Athaelin, racing to meet the Malrag charge.

Lion blazed in Mazael's fist, and he attacked the Malrags besides Athaelin. He dodged, caught a spear thrust on his shield, and twisted to the side, Lion blurring in a sideways slash. A Malrag fell dead, and then another, as Mazael cut his way through them.

Behind him the line of spearmen fought the Malrags, shields raised, spears extended. The Malrags fought viciously, without mercy, without scruple, but the men of Deepforest Keep fought to defend their homes and wives and children, and bit by bit they drove the Malrags back.

Green light snarled and snapped overhead.

~

LUCAN STOOD UPON THE BATTLEMENTS, struggling with all his might.

The bloodstaff's power thundered through him, filling him with strength, but even it was not enough. There were at least a dozen Malrag shamans in the city, summoning their green lightning, and it took every scrap of the staff's power and Lucan's magic to block their attacks. Lucan yearned to give himself to the staff's rage, to start killing Malrags and humans alike with his wrath, but he dared not. He retained enough sanity to realize that if he stopped casting wards, the Malrag shamans would slaughter the city's defenders.

And if that happened, Lucan would die. Even with all his skill, even with the bloodstaff to augment him, he could not possibly defeat Ultorin, Malavost, the shamans, and a hundred thousand Malrags.

Another lightning bolt thundered down from the sky, and Lucan screamed in exertion as he cast the ward to deflect it.

And still the bloodstaff's power surged through him, seeming to turn his bones and blood to fire.

~

SYKHANA CUT down a fleeing man with a slash of her poisoned daggers, and then another.

She grimaced, fangs curling over her lips, and looked around for fresh victims. Once, she would have rejoiced in the slaughter. But now she did not care. She only wanted to be reunited with Aldane, with her son, and be his mother as he ascended to godhood. Killing these people was a chore, nothing more.

But if she had to kill everyone in Deepforest Keep with her own hands to make Aldane safe, she would do it.

A noise from a side street caught her attention, and she saw a dark shape duck into a doorway. Sykhana slid into the alley, blood and venom dripping from her daggers and she lifted them. One quick slash, one kiss from her daggers, and another life would end...

She looked into the doorway.

Or two lives.

A woman of no more than twenty huddled in the doorway, weeping, clutching a child in her arms. An infant. No more than six months old. No older than Aldane.

Again Sykhana remembered the dead woman lying in the ruined village's street, the hand of the infant reaching from beneath the corpse.

Sykhana shivered, and for a terrible instant it seemed as if Aldane lay in the terrified woman's arms. Her hands trembled, and she almost dropped the poisoned daggers.

The young woman stared at her, red-eyed, waiting for the blow.

Sykhana turned and fled.

～

ROMARIA MARVELED as she followed the Seer through the caverns.

Her senses had become so much sharper. She heard the rustle of the Seer's cloak, the faint drip of water in the caverns. She smelled the oil upon the blade of her sword, the leather of her boots, the acrid smell of the starglow moss. And her vision had changed, as well. Even in the dim glow of the moss, she saw clearly.

And she saw the magical power, as well.

She could see the concentration of magical force in the Seer, earth magic ancient and strong. She saw the spells laid over the caverns, the work of the High Elderborn. And she saw the faint whispers of magic echoing over the entire mountain, the outer edges of a great vortex of power that waited atop the mountain.

The ruined temple, and the Door of Souls that Malavost and the San-keth wanted so badly.

Romaria now shared the senses that belonged to the beast. But that did not trouble her. All of her life, she had regarded the beast as an enemy, something she to overcome and defeat. But the beast was part of her. She was the beast, and the beast was her.

And at last, she was at peace with herself.

Daylight shone ahead, and she followed the Seer up the stone stairs of the well.

And then the Seer stopped.

Romaria heard the sounds of battle, the cries of men and the howls of Malrags.

She shoved past the Seer.

The first thing she saw was the light of the traigs.

A half-dozen traigs stood around the stone well, images of ancient

Elderborn warriors wrought in white stone. She saw magical power within them, far older and far stronger than even the Seer's power, akin to the spells laid over the caverns. All her life she had believed the traigs to be nothing more than statues, but somehow they were linked to the power of the caverns.

The second thing she saw was a troop of spearmen, led by Gerald Roland, charging to attack a band of Malrags.

~

MAZAEL STRUCK LEFT AND RIGHT, killing more Malrags.

Dead and dying Malrags and men covered the street. Ardanna and the druids had entered the fray, unleashing their powers. Giant shards of ice appeared in the air, driven by freezing winds to pierce Malrag flesh. Great fists of stone, supple as living flesh, rose from the earth to crush Malrags, or flocks of ravens plunged from the sky, ripping and tearing. Step by bloody step, they drove the Malrags down the city's central street, towards the Garden of the Temple.

The shout of men rose over the clamor, and Mazael saw Gerald and the reserve rushing into the fray.

Yet more Malrags poured into the streets, more and more, and green lighting still snarled and crackled overhead.

And to the north he saw the Elderborn archers upon the wall, and heard the roar as the Ogrags attacked the gate.

~

LUCAN DROPPED TO ONE KNEE, exhausted, the bloodstaff a pillar of flame in his hand.

Its power surged through him like a storm of burning rain. Yet even that power was not enough to beat back the concerted attack of a dozen Malrag shamans. Lucan knew he needed to launch an attack of his own, to strike down the shamans before they killed him. Yet it took very scrap of his strength to stave off their lightning bolts, and he had no power left to counterattack.

He warded aside another lightning bolt, black spots swimming through his vision.

~

"No," said the Seer, lifting his staff.

Romaria saw the currents of magical power surrounding the Seer blaze with sudden strength, like a river exploding in a flash flood. A dozen Malrag shamans stood in the Garden of the Temple, and as one they turned to face the Seer, sparks of green light crackling and snarling around their fingers.

The Malrags began the spell to summon lighting, and she shouted a warning.

And as she did, the Seer unleashed his wrath.

Emerald lightning fell from the skies, and the Seer made a hooking motion with his free hand. White mist swirled, and a shield of ice five feet thick appeared over their heads. The lightning smashed into the ice, blasting it to a thousand glittering shards. The Seer thrust his staff, and the storm of razor-edged shards hurtled towards the Malrags. The shamans summoned wards, surrounding themselves in shields of shimmering green light, but the spray of jagged ice ripped two of the shamans to bloody shreds.

Again the shamans began to cast, and the Seer slammed the tip of his staff into the ground. The earth heaved and bucked, knocking the shamans over and disrupting their spells. The currents of magical power surrounding the Seer brightened even further, and giant hands of earth and stone rose from the ground, reaching for the Malrags. One of the hands closed about a shaman, and the creature exploded like an insect crushed beneath a boot. Another Malrag turned to run, and twisting roots erupted from the ground, curling around the creature, and ripped off its arms and head.

In the space of thirty heartbeats, the Seer slaughtered all twelve of the Malrag shamans. Romaria had never seen such a display of magical prowess. Not from her mother, not from any of the wizards she had met from her travels, not from the San-keth, not from Lucan Mandragon.

But from what Mazael had said, Malavost might have that kind of power.

The Seer grunted and limped forward, leaning on his staff, and looked around.

"Go," he bade her. "Our men are fighting valiantly, but Ultorin himself is coming to the gate. If we do not first secure the city, he will overwhelm us easily.

Romaria nodded, shifted into wolf form, and raced from the Garden.

~

LUCAN BLINKED, sweat pouring off his face.

One moment the shamans had been pounding on his collapsing wards. Then he felt a vast surge of earth magic from the heart of the city, and the green lightning simply...stopped. Someone had destroyed the shamans. The druids? No, they hadn't commanded that level of power. The Seer, most likely.

Which meant that Lucan was now free to turn his powers against the rest of the Malrags.

He reduced the amount of power surging from the bloodstaff, and the fiery sigils dimmed. Nausea twisted his stomach, and his head swam, but his mind was clearer. He dared not release the power entirely. He had drawn too much Demonsouled power through the staff, and if he released it now, he would collapse.

Behind him one of the massive ladders thumped against the battlements. A dozen Malrags scrambled over, and Lucan blasted them from the ramparts with a burst of psychokinetic force.

The spearmen fell upon the ladder's grapnels, axes rising and falling.

~

MAZAEL KILLED ANOTHER MALRAG. Black blood caked his surcoat, and Lion's blade smoldered and sizzled with it. He had lost count of how many of the creatures had fallen to his sword.

Ardanna and the druids had found the tunnel, the secret entrance in the city, and used their powers to seal it, ripping down the house and burying its cellar. Now Mazael, Athaelin, and the spearmen drove the Malrags back, step by bloody step, until the battle raged in the Garden of the Temple at the city's heart.

Then a howl rang out, so fierce and terrible that even the Malrags froze for a moment.

A black wolf the size of a small horse, her eyes like blazing chunks of sapphire, raced from around one of the massive oak trees. The wolf moved fast, a gale of black fur and flashing white fangs and claws, hamstringing three Malrags as she ran past them.

Mazael stared at the beast, horrified.

Romaria. She had lost control of herself. Whatever test she had faced in the Ritual of Rulership, she had failed it. Now the beast had taken control of her, and she was lost to him...

Even as the pain ripped through his mind, the great black wolf blurred and changed, and became Romaria once more, bastard sword in hand. She cut down a Malrag from behind, took the hand from another, and gutted still a third in a vicious sideways cut.

A half-dozen Malrags turned to face her, and Romaria shimmered into the great black wolf once more. Her jaws ripped open a Malrag throat, black blood spraying into the ground. Her claws hamstrung another, and she tore her way free of them, snapping and snarling.

Then she blurred again, and returned to her own form.

Somehow, Romaria had gained control of herself, subdued the Elderborn half of her soul. No - she had merged with it, become one with it, and was now even more capable of a fighter than before.

"Fight!" roared Mazael, cutting down another Malrag. "Drive these monsters back!"

The men of Deepforest Keep bellowed in answer, and the druids called down shards of ice.

~

SYKHANA DUCKED BEHIND A TREE, breathing hard, her hands still trembling.

Her emotions had become a snarled tangle of grief and fear. Why hadn't she killed that woman and her child? They were nothing to her, only obstacles to sweep from her path, only human...

Human was Aldane was human.

Again she thought of the dead child in the burned village.

She shoved her poisoned daggers into their sheaths and pressed the heels of her hands into her eyes, trying to calm herself. She should have killed both the woman and her child. But the thought of losing Aldane, of seeing him die, was horrible beyond anything she could imagine.

Even thinking about it was like a dagger buried in her chest.

She stilled her shaking hands and took a deep breath. The battle still raged nearby. The druids might have collapsed the tunnel, but that didn't matter. Ultorin had tens of thousands of Malrags left. Sooner or later he would break through the walls and destroy Deepforest Keep.

She need only hide herself until that happened, until Malavost entered the city. Then they would take Aldane to the Door of Souls, and he would live in splendor forevermore.

Sykhana concealed herself in some bushes and settled down to wait.

~

BETWEEN THE SPEARMEN, the Seer's spells, and Romaria's fury, they cleared the Garden of the Temple of Malrags in short order.

Mazael stopped at the edge of the stone well, breathing hard, Lion burning in his fist. Dead Malrags lay everywhere, hundreds of them. He was sure that some had escaped, had concealed themselves in the lightning-damaged buildings and the cellars.

But right now they had to deal with Ultorin.

He heard the roaring from the northern wall and the gate.

Romaria approached him, followed by the Seer.

"Romaria," said Mazael, and he pulled her to him. "Gods...you're, you're..."

"Alive?" suggested Romaria.

"Yes," said Mazael. "And the beast. It's...you're in control of it?"

She smiled. "I am the beast. It is part of me. I never understood that before, but I do now."

Mazael did not understand, but he nodded. Right now, more urgent problems demanded their attention.

Athaelin hurried over, followed by Gerald, his silver armor splattered with Malrag blood, and Lucan, leaning hard upon his staff.

"We hold the city, for now," said Athaelin, cleaning Malrag blood from the blade of his bastard sword.

"The spearmen destroyed the ladders on the southern wall," said Lucan. He looked exhausted, and the sigils upon his staff sputtered and flickered with sullen light. Romaria gave him a hard look, her hand twitching towards her sword. "The Malrags are building more, but it will take at least another hour, I think."

"And the Ograds are at the gate," said Gerald. "Rhodemar sent a messenger. They are holding, for now, but not for much longer. The Elderborn archers are skilled enough to hit the gaps in the Ograds' armor, and they've managed to keep the Ograds away from the gate." He shook his head. "But sooner or later the enemy will charge the gate in enough numbers to break through."

"Is Ultorin with them?" said Mazael.

"Aye," said Gerald. "The messenger said he's stayed out of arrow range, so far."

Mazael made a fist. "Then this is our chance to finish this. Gerald! Send one of your men to Rhodemar. Tell him to send every Elderborn from the Tribe of the Bear to the gate."

Romaria gave him a sharp look, and then she grinned. The Seer gave him a grave nod.

"Why the Tribe of the Bear?" said Gerald.

"Because," said Mazael. "We can't cut through a hundred Ogrags on our own. But the Elderborn have a secret that will help us."

"What's that?" said Gerald.

"They're in harmony with themselves," said Mazael.

"You have a plan?" said Athaelin.

"Aye," said Mazael. "We're going to open the gate, go out there, and kill Ultorin."

Gerald snorted. "Simplicity itself. What could go wrong?"

"I shall remain here," said the Seer, "and guard the entrance to the caverns. The San-keth may try to slip into the city with the child, while you are distracted with the battle. The death of Ultorin would mean nothing, if the San-keth can open the Door of Souls and return Sepharivaim to the flesh."

"If you see my son," said Gerald, "will you..."

"Fear not, Gerald son of Malden," said the Seer. "If it is in my power to save your son from the San-keth and Malavost, then I shall do so."

"Let's finish this," said Mazael.

He ran for the gates, Romaria, Athaelin, Gerald, and Lucan following after him. Lucan stumbled as he ran, sweat dripping from his face, his dark eyes feverish and bright. The staff in his hand flickered with blood-colored light.

"Perhaps you should rest," Mazael told him.

Lucan gave a sharp shake of his head. "No. I will see this through to the end. A little more, and I can rest, I can...I can be rid of some things."

Mazael started to ask what that meant, and then they reached the plaza below the gates. Hundreds of Elderborn archers stood upon the battlements, loosing endless volleys of arrows over the walls. The ear-splitting roars of the Ogrags rose over the twang of the bows. About a hundred and fifty Elderborn, all clad in cloaks fashioned from bearskins, waited before the gates.

The Tribe of the Bear.

Mazael stopped before them.

"I know," he said, "that you like to keep the truth of your natures secret from humans, to keep your people safe from those who would seek power at any cost. But there is a greater threat outside the walls now. Our only chance to save your people has come, if we can kill Ultorin. Will you aid me?"

The ardmorgan of the Tribe of the Bear, a tall Elderborn man with a gaunt face and bright golden eyes, stared at Mazael for a long moment.

Then he nodded, and the Tribe of the Bear changed.

One moment they were Elderborn men and women. In the next they were bears, huge bears thrice the size of oxen, with claws like swords and coats of brown fur thicker than armor.

Bears that might prove a match for the Ogrags in hand-to-hand combat.

"The gods have mercy," said Gerald, stunned.

Mazael looked at the battlements, saw Rhodemar staring down at him, bow in hand.

"Open the gates!" shouted Mazael.

Rhodemar nodded and gave the order.

Spearmen hurried forward, pulling on chains, and the massive gates swung open with a groan.

Mazael strode out to face Ultorin.

27

THE SORTIE

Deepforest Keep occupied most of its mountain spur, but perhaps fifty acres of level, open ground lay between the city's gates and the rising flank of the mountain, dotted with worn boulders. North of the gates the slopes of Mount Tynagis rose sharply, crowned with the white ruins of the High Elderborn temple.

Ogrags and Malrags filled the ground below the gates of Deepforest Keep.

Four Ogrags lay dead beneath the walls, the gaps in their black armor bristling with Elderborn arrows. The rest of the Ogrags stayed out of bowshot, snarling and howling.

Mazael saw no sign of Ultorin.

He lifted Lion, the sword's azure flame blazing brighter, and walked to face the Ogrags.

The Ogrags stared at him for a moment, as if astonished that he would dare to approach them. Behind him walked Gerald and Athaelin, swords ready, and Romaria, her bow in hand.

Mazael stopped.

The Ogrags stared for a moment longer, and then sprang forward with a roar, the ground thundering beneath their feet.

~

LUCAN DRAGGED himself to the ramparts over the gate, leaning on his metal staff.

The Elderborn glanced at him, but made no comment. Rhodemar walked over, bow in hand, his eyes remaining on his father and sister.

"Will you aid us, wizard?" said Rhodemar.

"Not directly," said Lucan. "I am almost exhausted. When I see Ultorin, I will strike him with everything I have left."

Hopefully it would be enough.

The Ogrags roared and charged for the opened gate.

~

THE OGRAGS LOOKED like an advancing wall of black steel, or perhaps an avalanche tumbling down the side of Mount Tynagis.

Romaria set an arrow to her bow and drew back the string. To her enhanced vision, Mazael's burning sword looked like a weapon forged from light. And to her surprise, the ancient bronze shield upon her father's arm and the diadem on his brow likewise glowed with magical power. The same kind of power she had seen in the caverns, and burning in the hearts of the traigs.

Then the Ogrags were within range, and she had no more time for contemplation.

Romaria released her arrow. The steel-pointed shaft sped forward and buried itself in an Ograg's eye. The Ograg stumbled with a bellow of rage, lifting a deformed hand to its hideous face.

The rest came on.

"Now!" shouted Mazael, and ran to meet them.

~

MAZAEL SPRINTED FOR THE OGRAGS, Romaria, Athaelin, and Gerald following. The Ogrags showed no fear, no hesitation. And why should they? The gates to the city were open, and only four humans stood between them and Deepforest Keep.

Then the Tribe of the Bear surged through the gates, their enraged roars even louder than the Ogrags' terrible battle cries. The huge bears surged past Mazael and the others, moving with terrific speed, and leapt upon the Ogrags. The Ogrags were taller, but the bears were larger, with greater muscle mass, and flung the Ogrags to the ground, ripping into the knotted gray flesh with fang and claw.

Mazael raced into the chaos. He barely came to the Ogrags's bellies, but the enraged Tribe of the Bear held the creatures' undivided attention. An Ograg lifted its spiked mace in a two-handed blow, and Mazael thrust, arm extended over his head. Lion's blazing blade plunged a foot into the Ograg's unarmored armpit, and the creature bellowed in fury.

It turned to face Mazael, distracted...and one of the shapechanged Elderborn slammed into its side, ripping the Ograg to shreds. He risked a quick look around, and saw that the bears were winning. The Ogrags were strong, but the Tribe of the Bear was stronger. And the Elderborn archers upon the wall continued their accurate barrages, sending volleys of missiles into the gaps of Ograg armor whenever an opening presented itself.

Mazael scrambled atop the chest of a dead Ograg and lifted Lion over his head.

"Ultorin!" he bellowed. "Come and face me, you dog! Come and die!"

A roar of fury answered him, and bloody light flashed through the ranks of the Ogrags.

LUCAN FELT ULTORIN'S APPROACH, sensed the vortex of corrupted power surrounding the former Dominiar knight. No doubt Ultorin had used so much of the bloodsword's Demonsouled power, had stolen the life force so many Malrags, that it had...changed him. Made him into something less than human.

Something less than human, and much more dangerous.

The same fate might yet await Lucan. He felt the bloodstaff throb in his hand, reacting to the power of Ultorin's bloodsword. Lucan might resist for much, much longer, but in the end, the bloodstaff would transform him the way the bloodsword had transformed Ultorin.

It had already begun.

But it didn't matter. Once Ultorin was dead and the Malrags defeated, Lucan would destroy the bloodstaff. Its great power carried too many risks, caused too much damage to his mind. He would lose control again, kill more innocents as he had killed that druid in the Great Southern Forest. And the staff would change him as it had changed Ultorin.

One last time.

Lucan lifted the staff, let the maddening power flood through him, and prepared to unleash destruction upon Ultorin.

Only to find his magic blocked.

He frowned, probing the barrier. The Malrag shamans' spells could not pass the warded walls of Deepforest Keep. The shamans must have raised a similar ward around the battlefield north of the gates, a ward strong and potent. But to raise a ward like that, dozens of shamans would have to work together...

"Sir!"

A spearman ran up to Rhodemar. "Thousands of Malrags advance up the western road! The archers cannot kill them all! Every Malrag outside the walls is making for the western road and the gates!"

Ultorin had summoned aid.

～

THE BATTLE STOPPED. The Ogrags wrenched away, stepping back from the great bears. The Tribe of the Bear halted, still snarling. Between them lay the bodies of slain Ogrags and slain bears, their corpses slowly shrinking back into Elderborn form.

The sudden silence was shocking.

The Ogrags parted, and Ultorin came forward.

Or, rather, the thing that had once been Ultorin.

His features remained recognizable. But the Dominiar knight had grown, and now stood nine feet tall, the bloodsword wreathed in flame and darkness in his right hand. His skin had turned the cold, pallid gray of Malrag flesh, and a maze of pulsing black veins covered his face. His arms and legs and chest bugled with huge, misshapen muscles. His ornate black plate armor no longer fit him, so he had augmented it with Malrag chain mail and plate, making him look like a half-melted statue of black steel.

His eyes had turned yellow, like liquid sulfur.

"Mazael Cravenlock!" roared Ultorin, his voice distorted. His teeth had become yellowed fangs, jagged and broken.

In one smooth motion, Romaria raised her bow and fired.

Her arrow buried itself in Ultorin's throat. Her second arrow landed next to the second, and the third plunged into his left eye. Ultorin showed no sign of pain, no sign of annoyance. He reached to his face with a clawed hand and ripped free the arrows one by one. Black blood, smoking and sizzling, splashed across his gray flesh, and the wounds vanished in short order.

It seemed Ultorin had absorbed enough stolen life force that he could heal wounds quickly.

Romaria lowered her bow.

"I remember you," said Ultorin. "The little brigand from the hills of the Old Kingdoms." He laughed, high and wild. "Today I shall have my vengeance upon you as well."

"No," said Romaria. "Today you shall pay for your crimes."

"For the fire and sword you brought to Deepforest Keep," said Athaelin.

"For turning my son over the San-keth," said Gerald.

"For the murder and bloodshed you brought to the Grim Marches," said Mazael.

"I shall pay?" said Ultorin, still laughing. "You shall pay, Lord Mazael!" He pointed the bloodsword at Mazael. "You slew Amalric

Galbraith, the noblest man who ever lived! He would have remade the world, fashioned it into a paradise of order! Instead, you slew him. But he forged this sword in his own blood, and with it I shall kill you!"

"Amalric Galbraith was a monster and a murderer," said Mazael, "and his blood has made you into something even worse. He was Demonsouled – it was his nature to kill, even if he was too weak to defy his own blood. But you...you are nothing, a leech gorged on stolen power. I slew Amalric Galbraith with my own hands, and I will kill you too."

Ultorin's misshapen nostrils flared, and his eyes crackled with rage. "Aye? You shall? Is the brigand your woman, my lord Mazael? Maybe I'll kill her in front of you first. Or I'll slay you first, and cut your carcass to pieces and make her eat them, one by one." His eyes shifted to Gerald. "And the San-keth bitch's screaming brat is yours? Ha! I'll kill the brat in front of you, I'll bite off his head and lick up his blood."

"Like a rabid dog," said Gerald, voice colder than Mazael had ever heard it before. "And like a rabid dog, I will put you down."

Ultorin's yellow eyes widened, until they seemed like pits of yellow flame in his face. "Kill them! Kill them! All of you, kill them!"

The Ogrags howled and surged forward, and the great bears bellowed and charged to the battle. Ultorin came at Mazael in a run, bloodsword whirling over his head. And as he did, Mazael heard Malrag war cries coming from the road below the city's western wall.

Ultorin had summoned reinforcements.

LUCAN CURSED as he saw the black tide of Malrags swarm up the road. The Elderborn remaining on the western wall poured arrows in the horde, but there were simply too many Malrags. They reached the flat ground before the gate, racing to join the colossal melee between the Ogrags and the Tribe of the Bear. And the shape-changed Elderborn were struggling to hold their own against the Ogrags.

If Mazael did not kill Ultorin soon, they would lose. It was as simple as that.

Lucan ground his teeth in frustration, slamming his staff against the ramparts. If only he could unleash his powers to aid Mazael! If...

He heard footsteps, and saw the druids crowding onto the ramparts behind the Elderborn archers, who loosed a steady stream of arrows at any Ograg that came within range. Ardanna stood at the druids' head, her golden eyes fixed upon Lucan.

"Tainted one," said the High Druid, and Lucan felt a frisson of fear. How much did she know about him? About the bloodstaff? Even with the staff's power, he could not hope to fight off the combined power of the Keep's druids.

Especially if the Seer took a hand.

"The hour of victory or defeat is at hand," said Ardanna. "We must throw our efforts into the battle. Even your power, corrupted as it is, cannot be turned away. Lend us your aid to break the shamans' wards, and we shall loose our power at Ultorin himself."

Lucan nodded. The druids began to cast spells, blue-white light shining around their staffs, and Lucan joined with a spell of his own.

CHAOS REIGNED below the walls of Deepforest Keep, as the Tribe of the Bear struggled against the Ogrags, and sheets of arrows fell from the walls, landing with uncanny accuracy among the gray-skinned giants.

But Mazael saw nothing but Ultorin's bloodsword.

They met in the midst of the chaos, Lion's azure flame straining against the bloodsword's dark glow. Ultorin had grown hideously strong and terribly fast, his sword a storm of darkness and flame. But Mazael met him blow for blow, meeting and blocking his attacks and launching one of his own. Ultorin twisted aside, but not before Lion's cut a smoking line upon the gray flesh of his jaw. Mazael swept Lion sideways, hoping to reach Ultorin's throat, and but his foe leapt out of reach, snarling all the while.

The smoking line upon Ultorin's law faded...but not quickly, not nearly as quickly as the wounds from Romaria's arrows. Lion's power wounded things of dark magic, and Ultorin had abandoned his humanity to become a creature of Demonsouled power.

Lion could kill him.

Ultorin glared, eyes narrowed to yellow slits, and then raced forward with a roar, the bloodsword flying. The sheer fury of his attack drove Mazael back, Lion flashing up and down to beat aside Ultorin's blows. Ultorin's bloodsword ripped across his side, the magical blade parting plate mail like cloth. It did not reach his skin, but the blow still threw Mazael off balance.

Ultorin surged forward for the kill, and then an arrow plunged into his side, and then another, the force of the impacts knocking him to the side. Mazael recovered his balance, and saw Romaria standing twenty paces away, her bow in hand, Gerald keeping watch over her with his shield and sword. Even as Mazael saw her, she fired two more arrows into Ultorin's side in quick succession. Both impacts staggered Ultorin, and Mazael attacked, all his strength and weight behind Lion's blade. Ultorin twisted aside at the last moment, but Lion opened a vicious gash across his shoulder.

Ultorin snarled and stumbled out of reach, black blood smoking and sizzling against his armor.

But Romaria gave him no chance to recover, and sent another arrow plunging into his side. Her arrows could not kill him, could not even hurt him very much. But every hit from her powerful bow staggered him, gave Mazael a chance to carve another wound in Ultorin's flank.

He stabbed, his sword slipping past Ultorin's guard to open a smoking gash across his hip. Then Athaelin was at Mazael's side, his bastard sword blurring. Ultorin chopped at Athaelin, bloodsword in both hands, but the ancient Greenshield absorbed the blow without even a scratch. Mazael seized the moment and opened another wound across Ultorin's right forearm.

Ultorin staggered back, bloodsword raised in guard, a hint of fear on his misshapen face.

~

ROMARIA FIRED AGAIN, and again, shooting another arrow into Ultorin every time the opportunity presented itself.

To her enhanced vision, Ultorin has become a thing of nightmares, his misshapen limbs filled with the stolen lives of slain Malrags, his tattered soul burning in the stolen Demonsouled power of his bloodsword. He looked like a creature of darkness and filth.

Much the way Lucan Mandragon was beginning to look to her sight.

But the blazing light in Lion's blade drove back the darkness, made the shadows within Ultorin shrivel and die. And Ultorin was weakening. He could heal the wounds from her arrows, but not the gashes Lion carved in his gray flesh. Already she saw the darkness within him starting to flickering, shattered by the magic of Mazael's sword.

They were winning.

Romaria felt a surge of exultation and sent another arrow into Ultorin.

Then she saw the black tide of Malrags storming up from the road, spears and axes in hand.

~

"AID ME!" screamed Ultorin, stumbling back another step. "Aid me, now, I command it!"

The nearest Ograg shuddered, its enormous white eyes blinking.

And then, as one, every Ograg upon the field turned to look at Mazael.

He raced forward, hoping to catch Ultorin, but the Ogrags were faster. Mazael twisted, ducking under the blow of a massive spiked mace, and stabbed with Lion. The blade bit into the towering creature's knees, and the Ograg fell with a bellow, snarling and roaring. Mazael ripped Lion across the Ograg's throat and wheeled, seeking for Ultorin.

Ultorin raised his bloodsword and stabbed into the back of the nearest Ograg, burying the weapon to its hilt. Fiery light devoured the Ograg, crumbling the massive creature into ash and bones. Ultorin screamed in ecstasy and agony, his wounds vanishing in a surge of stolen life energy. Then he stepped back, laughing wildly, another pair of Ogrags racing past him.

Mazael hamstrung one and dodged past another. He looked around for the Tribe of the Bear, hoping the shapechanged Elderborn could hold back the Ogrags. But the Tribe of the Bear was losing. Mazael saw a dozen of them lying slain across the rocky ground, while the survivors faced two or even three Ogrags at a time. And more and more Malrags appeared, swarming the great bears. One of the shapechanged Elderborn could face a dozen Malrags at once. But hundreds, thousands of Malrags streamed up the road, despite the unending arrow fire from the walls. The sheer press of Ogrags and Malrags would drive the Tribe of the Bear back, perhaps even force through the gates.

Ultorin, it seemed, had kept at least a part of his wits.

Time to fall back. With the druids' aid, they could hold the walls, and goad Ultorin into making another mistake. He had exposed himself to danger once - if he became angry enough, he would do so again...

Athaelin grabbed Mazael's arm. "After him!"

"We have to fall back," said Mazael, "before..."

"No!" said Athaelin. "This is our chance to end this, to save my people! Now, kill him, before it's too late!"

Before Mazael could answer, Athaelin sprinted forward. In the space of two heartbeats he had killed one Malrag and sent another one sprawling to the ground with a blow from the Greenshield.

Mazael cursed and ran after him, Lion blazing brighter as he drew closer to Ultorin.

~

LUCAN SHUDDERED, panting for breath.

The Malrag shamans were too strong. Ardanna and the druids, even with Lucan's aid, had only managed to open small holes in the shamans' wards, not even enough to...

"High Druid!" said one of the Elderborn druids. "The Greenshield!"

She pointed, and Lucan saw Athaelin Greenshield fling himself into the Malrag ranks, hacking left and right, in pursuit of Ultorin. Mazael followed, Lion burning like a brand, while Romaria and Sir Gerald followed.

Ardanna hissed through her teeth. "The fool man! If he falls, we are lost! Aid him, now! Cast whatever spells you can muster through the Malrag wards!"

Lucan drew on the bloodstaff's power, letting the raging strength of Demonsouled magic flood through his veins. For a wild moment he wanted to blast Ardanna right over the wall, to butcher the druids and the Elderborn and the spearmen of Deepforest Keep where they stood.

But he mastered himself, and flung the most powerful spell he could manage.

~

"FATHER!" shouted Romaria.

For a moment Mazael thought they were finished. The Malrags closed tight around them, a half-dozen Ogrags following. Athaelin hacked and slashed through them in a whirl of masterful swordplay, the Greenshield turning aside their thrusts and swings, but more and more Malrags appeared to replace those he slew. Mazael tried to cut his way to Athaelin's side, but there were simply too many Malrags.

Once the Ogrags closed, it was over.

Then green light flashed, and the ground erupted.

Giant hands of stone erupted from the earth, reaching up to crush both Malrags and Ogrags in their implacable grip. Swirls of white mist hardened into knives of glittering ice, ripping Malrag flesh into shredded pulp. A ribbon of blood-colored fire screamed from the walls of Deepforest Keep and scythed through the enemy, cutting a score of Malrags and a half-dozen of Ogrags in half. The barrage of spells killed hundreds of Malrags in the space of a few heartbeats.

And the path was open to Ultorin.

Athaelin charged Ultorin with a yell, his bastard sword flying. Ultorin growled, tried to attack, but found himself driven back. Even with Ultorin's superior strength and speed, Athaelin's skill with the sword drove him back. The steel of the bastard sword could not kill Ultorin, but it still had the power to cause him pain, and he flinched from its blows.

Mazael sprinted to Athaelin's side, stabbing at Ultorin. The Dominiar knight stepped back, whipping the bloodsword back and forth in great arcs to keep his opponents at bay. Neither Mazael nor Athaelin could match the reach of the huge bloodsword, so they spread out, Mazael to Ultorin's left, Athaelin to his right. Ultorin kept backing away, trying to keep both Mazael and Athaelin in front of him.

Then one of Romaria's arrows slammed into Ultorin's belly, doubling him over. Mazael raced into the opening, swinging Lion in an overhand slash, and tore a smoking gash down Ultorin's back. The Dominiar screamed in pain, stumbling, his yellow eyes bulging and wide. Romaria put another arrow into Ultorin's hip, and a second into his thigh. Athaelin's bastard sword drew a line of black blood down Ultorin's jaw and neck, the battered black armor falling aside. Ultorin screamed in rage, but fear filled his yellow eyes as he raised the bloodsword.

He was beaten, and he knew it. Mazael lined up Lion for a killing blow...

The Malrags crashed into them like a black wave, and Ultorin's fear turned to glee.

Mazael ducked an axe blow, and a spear point struck his hip, crunching through the armor to dig into his flesh. He pivoted and killed the Malrag that had wounded him, trying to ignore the pain in his wounded leg. Still more Malrags came at him. Mazael killed two more, and Romaria three, as she turned her attention from Ultorin to the Malrags, her hands a blur as she fired again and again.

The Malrags ducked behind their shields, hoping to avoid the barrage, and Mazael had his chance. He raced past one of the great bears, locked in battle with an Ograg, and ripped Lion across the Ograg's leg in passing. The creature stumbled, the great bear's jaws locking about its throat, and Mazael kept running.

Athaelin dueled Ultorin, driving him back step by step, Ultorin panting as he tried to keep up with the older man's attacks. Mazael ran faster. If he could just reach Ultorin now, Mazael could land a killing blow and end this fight.

A Malrag leapt into his path, and Mazael beheaded the creature and kept running.

Athaelin twisted, pushed past a two-handed block of the bloodsword, and shoved. Ultorin staggered, and Athaelin reversed his sword, locked both hands around the hilt, and plunged the blade into Ultorin's belly. Ultorin's eyes bulged, and he shrieked, spittle and black blood flying over his jagged fangs.

Athaelin twisted the sword.

Ultorin seized the crosspiece of Athaelin's sword and used it to pull himself closer, the blade sliding deeper into his guts. The wound, no doubt, caused him excruciating pain. But Athaelin's sword could not kill him.

And Ultorin, Mazael suddenly understood, realized that.

And even as the thought came to him, Ultorin brought the edge of his bloodsword crashing into Athaelin's shoulder. The Champion of Deepforest Keep staggered, his face going gray as the bloodsword's edge sank into his chest. The darkness-masked sigils upon the blade burned hotter, and Athaelin withered before Mazael's eyes.

"Father!" shouted Romaria.

Her next arrow hammered into Ultorin, but the wound vanished even as the arrowhead penetrated his flesh, healed by her father's stolen life force.

Mazael flung himself forward, both hands around Lion's hilt. Ultorin saw him coming at the last minute and kicked Athaelin off his sword, but too late. Mazael stabbed the sword into Ultorin's side, flames pulsing from the blade and into the wound Ultorin wailed and wrenched free from Lion, staggering, hand clutched to his side. Mazael stalked after him, raising his sword to finish the fight.

The Ograg came out of nowhere, its massive spike mace swinging for Mazael's chest. He ducked, but the edge of a spike clipped his armored shoulder, and the force of the blow sent him sprawling. He scrambled back to his feet, intent on following Ultorin, but it was too late. Ultorin retreated behind a wall of Malrags and Ogrags, bloodsword in hand.

"Mazael!" It was Gerald's voice. "We must go! Now! Before they overwhelm us."

Mazael looked around, saw the Tribe of the Bear in full retreat before the Ogrags and the Malrags, saw Gerald and Romaria backing towards the gate, Romaria shooting any Malrag that drew too near.

He cursed, slung Romaria's father over his shoulders, and ran for the gate.

The Malrag horde pursued him.

LUCAN WATCHED Ultorin retreat into the ranks of Malrags, a bitter taste in his mouth. They had come so close! Another few heartbeats and Mazael would have killed Ultorin. And now they would not have another chance. Ultorin could not be foolish enough to expose himself again, and the Malrags had gained a strong foothold below the gates.

Mazael sprinted through the gates, the last one through, Athaelin over his shoulders. The gates began to swing close, but too slowly, too ponderously. The advancing tide of Ogrags and Malrags would make it through before the gates shut.

"Quickly!" shouted Ardanna, lifting her staff. "Before it is too late!"

The druids followed her lead and cast their spells.

Great stone hands reached from the earth, wrapping around the gates and the stone archway above them. The hands clenched, and the gates of Deepforest Keep fell in ruin, rubble and broken stone collapsing with a mighty roar. For a moment Lucan thought that Ardanna had betrayed them, or that she had gone mad. But then the stone hands themselves disintegrated, even as more rock and stone rose from the earth. Within seconds the gates had been sealed beneath tons of broken rock.

But not for long, Lucan suspected. Thousands of Malrags and Ogrags had gained the ground before the gates, with thousands more streaming up the road below the walls, despite the Elderborn archers. Ultorin need only launch one massive assault to gain the walls, backed by the magic of the shamans and Malavost. He would lose thousands of Malrags, but he had tens of thousand to spare.

Deepforest Keep would fall. They had lost.

~

MAZAEL DROPPED TO ONE KNEE, breathing hard, and lowered Athaelin to the ground.

Chaos filled the plaza below the ruined gate. Barely half of the Tribe of the Bear had returned from the attack on the Ogrags. Dust rose from the mountain of rubble choking the gates. The surviving members of the Tribe of the Bear shifted back into their Elderborn forms, tending to their wounds.

The triumphant roars of the Malrags outside the walls echoed over the plaza.

"Father," said Romaria, pushing to Mazael's side. "Father!"

Athaelin Greenshield, his shredded armor wet with blood, his face withered from Ultorin's bloodsword, did not answer.

A moment later his eyes closed, and did not open again.

28

RETREAT

"Father," repeated Romaria once more, bowing her head over Athaelin's corpse.

Rhodemar hurried down from the ramparts, a stricken expression on his face. Behind came Lucan, breathing hard, leaning upon his staff with its glowing symbols. Ardanna followed them both, her face expressionless as she gazed upon the dead Champion of Deepforest Keep.

"What...what do we do now?" said Rhodemar.

For a moment no one answered.

Mazael grimaced, rose to his feet. With Athaelin dead, it seemed that he had indeed taken command of Deepforest Keep's final defense.

"Get back to the walls," said Mazael. Everyone turned to look at him. "All of you! Every Elderborn able to hold a bow, and every man of Deepforest Keep still able to hold a spear."

They stared at him.

"Go!" said Mazael. "As soon as Ultorin can get the Malrags and Ogrags organized, he's going to throw everything he has at us. If we don't stop him, he'll be over the walls and into the city before the hour is past." Not to mention what Malavost and the Malrag shamans might do.

"Why bother?" said one of the spearmen, bleeding from a cut across his brow. "It's over. The Greenshield is slain. We are lost. We..."

Mazael backhanded the spearman, sent him sprawling to the flagstones. "It's not finished until we are dead, and we still live."

"You heard him," said Romaria, looking at the spearmen and the Elderborn. "My father gave his life to defend this city! Can we do any less?"

"Do," said Ardanna, her voice quiet, "as the Greenshield says. To the walls!"

The spearmen and the Elderborn turned and ran to the ramparts.

"What did you call me?" said Romaria.

"Athaelin is dead," said Ardanna, her face twisting with rage and loathing. "And you are the eldest of his blood. You passed the Ritual of Rulership, if only hours ago. So you are the new Greenshield, the Champion of Deepforest Keep and the Defender of the Mountain." Her golden eyes blazed. "As loathsome as it is that a half-blood abomination should ever become the Defender of Mount Tynagis."

Romaria gave a mirthless smile, her eyes red with unshed tears. "Oh, fear not. I will not be the Greenshield of Deepforest Keep for long. Nor will Deepforest Keep itself endure for much longer. So you will not have to endure this shame overlong, will you?"

Ardanna said nothing, her hands tight against the oak of her staff.

"Go to the walls," said Romaria. "With the other druids. Perhaps your magic will hold off the Malrags for a little longer."

"As the Greenshield wishes," said Ardanna, her voice ice. She marched away, the other druids following.

"I will go to the walls, as well," said Lucan. "Perhaps if Ultorin makes an error, I can strike him down."

"And I, as well," said Gerald, his face grim. "If we are to die here, then I will do so fighting. Maybe, if the gods are good, I...will have a chance to win my son free from the San-keth, before we fall."

"Do you want to go back into the city?" said Mazael. "To find

Rachel?" He didn't know where she was. The Champion's Tower, he hoped – the Malrags had not broken into that.

Gerald took a deep breath. "No. She is safe, for now. And if the city does fall...I would rather not see her die."

"Go," said Mazael. "I will join you shortly."

He left, leaving Mazael alone with Romaria.

And with the corpse of her father.

"I'm sorry," said Mazael. "I tried to reach him, but..."

"Shut up," said Romaria, blinking. She wiped at her eyes. "You always blame yourself for things that are not your fault. Ultorin killed Father. Not you." She shook her head, her hands clenching and unclenching. "The fool. The damned fool. If he hadn't...he knew his sword couldn't hurt Ultorin, the thing Ultorin had become. Why did he fight Ultorin alone? The fool. The damned fool." Her voice broke on the last word, tears running down her cheeks.

Mazael heard the rumbling outside the walls, the voices of thousands of Malrags joined together as they prepared to charge. They needed him on the battlements. Rhodemar could hold things together, but demoralized by the death of their Champion, the men of Deepforest Keep needed Mazael. More, they needed Romaria, their new Champion.

But he stood over Athaelin's body and put his hand on her shoulder.

"I should go to the walls," said Romaria. "Do you think we can still win?"

"If Ultorin makes another mistake," said Mazael. "If he's foolish enough to expose himself. Then we can take him, and make him pay for everything he's done."

But deep down, he did not believe Ultorin would make that mistake again, despite his obvious madness.

Romaria closed her eyes. "You are a terrible liar."

"You know me too well," said Mazael. "But you are the Champion of Deepforest Keep, Romaria, their liege lady. They must look to you and see confidence, see determination, and they must know that you will never stop fighting for them. Otherwise they will break and flee even before the Malrags reach the walls."

"You're right." Romaria took a deep breath. "We're going to die, aren't we?"

"Probably," said Mazael. "But everyone dies. Better to face it with sword in hand than to hide in a cellar, waiting for the end." His hand tightened about hers. "And I saw you die, once before. This time we shall die together, side by side."

Romaria nodded. "Then let us meet our fates." A faint shadow of her wicked grin flashed across her lips. "And perhaps take that murdering bastard Ultorin with us."

"The Greenshield," said Mazael. "And the diadem. You should take them with you. To show the men of Deepforest Keep that they still have a Champion."

Romaria nodded and reached for the Greenshield.

Then she froze, her blue eyes going wide.

~

MALAVOST STOOD some distance from the gates, watching the Malrags and Ogrags prepare for the final attack.

Aldane Roland rested in the crook of his left arm, asleep. The little brat cried constantly, so Malavost silenced him with a spell that kept the child in a trance. Aldane didn't need to be awake for what Malavost had in mind, after all.

Skaloban stood besides him, head swaying back and forth atop his undead carrier, tongue flicking at the air.

Gods and devils, but Malavost was tired of listening to the Sanketh cleric's endless complaints.

But no matter. He'd be rid of Skaloban, soon enough.

"The Vessel is in danger here!" said Skaloban. "If the druids sense our presence, they will strike us down."

"The danger is an acceptable one," said Malavost. He had wrapped them both in a spell of cloaking and obscuring, one that made them invisible to the eye and difficult to detect via magical means. "The fighting men and Elderborn are focused upon the Malrags and Ogrags. And the full attention of the druids will be turned upon the shamans. We are safe enough here."

"You are too accepting of risk!" said Skaloban.

Malavost favored the San-keth cleric with a bland look. "Life is risk, honored Skaloban. And if you dare the ultimate power, then you must dare the ultimate risks."

Skaloban hissed. "It is risky for Ultorin to lead from the front like this."

Malavost shrugged. "True. But an irrelevant risk. Once the Malrags get into the city, we have no further need of Ultorin. If he lives, no doubt he will lead the remaining Malrags to the Grim Marches and resume his war with Lord Richard. And if he dies, the Malrags will turn upon each other. Either way, it is of no importance. We shall have access to far greater power than Ultorin's Malrags."

Far greater power. For long years Malavost had plotted and schemed and studied.

And now, within hours, his labors would bear fruit.

He felt the weight of Aldane in his arm, his smile widening.

"Look!" said Skaloban. "It begins!"

Thousands of Malrags and hundreds of Ogrags charged the walls. Many of the Malrags carried ropes with grappling hooks, while the Ogrags were tall enough to simply climb up the wall.

Very soon now, Deepforest Keep would fall.

And Malavost's long-sought goal would be in reach.

"ROMARIA?" said Mazael. "What is it?"

She only half-heard him.

The light coming from the diadem upon her father's brow and the ancient shield on his arm held her attention. With her enhanced senses, she had seen the power worked into the ancient bronze, power somehow akin to the magical forces within the traigs.

But now the power had...changed, somehow. As if it had been awakened, perhaps.

"What is it?" repeated Mazael.

The sounds of battle washed over them as the Malrags charged the wall.

"You can't see it," murmured Romaria.

She knelt, took the diadem from Athaelin's head, and lifted up the Greenshield.

The power within pulsed at her touch, its tendrils sinking into her arm. The magic recognized her, acknowledged her as its rightful master. More tendrils ran off from the diadem, hundreds of them, thousands of them spinning in all directions.

Each one touching a traig, the magic within the traigs.

Magic that, like the power in the diadem, seemed to be waiting.

Romaria placed the diadem on her head, and the bronze circlet rested upon her black hair as if it had been made for her.

As if it had been waiting for her.

Just as the power within the traigs had been waiting for someone like her. Someone who was human, and therefore able to serve as Champion of Deepforest Keep. And someone who was Elderborn, who had the enhanced senses of the beast, the sight to see the power stirring in the diadem and the Greenshield and the traigs.

The power that had been waiting for so long.

Until it was needed...

Romaria's eyes opened wide as she understood at last.

LUCAN BRACED himself upon his staff, watching the Malrags charge at the ruined gate.

He was utterly exhausted. Only a steady trickle of Demonsouled power from the bloodstaff kept him on his feet. Besides him the Elderborn archers, the druids, and the spearmen of Deepforest Keep looked just as weary. It would not take much effort to sweep them all aside.

"Release!" bellowed Rhodemar, lifting his bow.

As one the Elderborn archers released their obsidian-tipped arrows, firing with superhuman skill. The arrows screamed out, and hundreds of Malrags fell, pierced by the shafts. But the dead Malrags disappeared into the black mass of the charge.

The Malrags flung their grapnels.

Hundreds of black steel claws lodged in the stone battlements. The spearmen scrambled forward, trying to dislodge the claws, even as the Elderborn continued the rain of arrows. But scores of Malrags scrambled up the ropes dangling from the grapnels and dozens of them made it to the battlements, slaying with axe and spear.

The Ogrags shoved past the Malrags and jumped, grabbing the battlements in misshapen hands, and pulled themselves up. The spearmen swarmed the Ogrags, stabbing with their spears, while the Elderborn fired arrows at every Malrag in sight. Ardanna lifted her staff, white mist swirling around her fingers, and a barrage of ice shards stabbed into the nearest Ograg's face. The creature bellowed, losing its grip on the battlements, and fell to crush the Malrags beneath it.

But more Malrags swarmed up the ropes, and the horde filling the field before the gates and the steep road seemed without number. Lucan attacked with a psychokinetic blast, knocking a dozen Malrags from their ropes.

A dozen more scrambled to take their place.

"I UNDERSTAND," said Romaria.

Her eyes darted back and forth, looking at the bronze shield upon her arm, as if following threads that only she could see.

"Understand what?" said Mazael.

"The traigs," said Romaria, her eyelids fluttering. "The Elderborn and the humans built this city together. The Greenshield was meant to be a half-blood, not just a human or a full-blooded Elderborn. But...the tradition must have been forgotten. Only humans have been the Greenshield. Which means they don't know about the traigs. They don't know!"

"What are you talking about?" said Mazael, taking her shoulders.

She looked at him, at the wall, and back at him.

"The Great Traig!" she said. "We have to hurry! Come with me!"

She slipped from his grasp. Mazael opened his mouth to protest. Ultorin had thrown the full weight of his Malrag horde against the ruined gates. They had to go the walls, at once. And if the spearmen saw their Champion running into the city, they might break and run themselves.

But he trusted her, as he trusted no one else.

Mazael took a deep breath and ran after her.

29

CALL OF THE WOLF

M alavost stood hidden in his cloaking spell, Aldane resting his arm, watching the battle.

It was almost over. Wave after wave of Malrags rushed at the wall, driven by Ultorin's wrath, only to perish beneath the arrows of the Elderborn archers and the spells of the Elderborn druids. The Malrags that gained the wall fell to the spears of Deepforest Keep's militia. For every man or Elderborn slain, seven Malrags fell - but Ultorin could pay that price twice over and still have enough Malrags left to destroy the city.

"We are losing!" hissed Skaloban. "You must speak with Ultorin at once, wizard! If the Malrags are destroyed, we are lost!"

Malavost paused long enough to make certain his voice was calm when he answered.

"It does not matter, honored Skaloban," said Malavost. "The defenders could kill a hundred thousandMalrags, and it would not change the outcome. Deepforest Keep shall be destroyed. If we lose every last Malrag and still take the city, then our goals have been accomplished."

He was looking forward to ridding himself of Skaloban. He only needed one thing, just one more thing from the San-keth cleric, and then Malavost could dispose of Skaloban.

He smiled at the thought.

An Ograg gained the battlements, laying about with its spiked club.

Very soon now.

~

ROMARIA STOPPED in the circle of oak trees below the Champion's Tower, gazing at the white stone bulk of the Great Traig.

"Here," she said, touching the giant statue. "Right here. All the lines lead here."

"I don't understand," said Mazael, again.

But Romaria didn't hear him. It was almost as if she had fallen into a trance. For an uneasy moment Mazael wondered if she had gone mad, if the pain of her father's death and the Ritual of Rulership had unseated her reason.

No. She had saved him. He trusted her, even if he didn't understand was happening.

Romaria put her hand on the Great Traig's side.

~

THE STONE FELT warm beneath Romaria's fingers, as if it had awakened to her touch.

As if it were alive.

She saw power stirring beneath her fingers, great power. The traigs had been waiting for someone like her, someone with mixed Elderborn and human blood in her veins.

Someone to call them forth.

"I am of the blood of mortal man," said Romaria, sliding her dagger from its belt sheath and pricking her finger. She heard Mazael's questions, but kept speaking. "I am of the blood of the Elderborn." She let her blood fall upon the Great Traig, crimson spots spattering on the ancient white stone. "I am the Greenshield, the Champion of Deepforest Keep, the Defender of the Mountain, and by that right, I call you forth."

For a moment nothing happened.

And then the Great Traig's eyes opened, blazing with white light.

MAZAEL TOOK a step back in alarm, raising Lion.

But the blade did not erupt into blazing azure flame, as it did when confronting the Malrags. Whatever the Great Traig was, it was not a creature of dark magic.

The Great Traig shifted, stone moving like living flesh, its glowing eyes focusing upon Romaria.

"Who calls me forth?" said the traig, its voice like thunder booming in the mountains. "By what right to you awaken me?"

"I call you forth," said Romaria, lifting her chin, the bronze diadem glinting. "For I am Romaria, daughter of Athaelin, and I have faced myself in the Ritual of Rulership, and by that right I am the Greenshield, the Champion of Deepforest Keep and the Defender of the Mountain. My father was a mortal man and my mother was a woman of the Elderborn. By right of my title, by right of my blood, I call you forth."

"You have that right," said the Great Traig. "We have slept, my brothers and I, for many long centuries, in observance of the pact."

"What pact?" said Mazael.

"The pact of ancient days, laid down when humans fled here and settled in the ancient ruins," said the Great Traig. "Once my brothers and I were servants of the High Elderborn, but the High Elderborn passed from the earth, and we lingered to guard the mountain. Then the humans came, and the druids and the humans formed a covenant, to defend the holy mountain forevermore. The druids awakened us, and we agreed to continue our duty, to defend the mountain and Deepforest Keep, and to come forth when summoned, when the Keep was threatened."

"And Deepforest Keep is now threatened," said Romaria. "The Malrags assail the walls,, led by a man wielding a sword forged in Demonsouled blood. If we do not receive aid, the city will fall, and the pact shall be broken."

The Great Traig's glowing eyes narrowed.

"This cannot be allowed!" said the Great Traig. "The pact must not be broken. We shall go to war."

The Great Traig lifted a stone horn to its lips and blew, and that blast was louder than thunder, louder than the bellows of the Ogrags and the crash of steel and steel and the cries of dying men.

For a moment silence answered that horn call.

And then, across the city, the traigs began to move.

"There," murmured Malavost, craning his neck for a better view.

Three Ogrags had gained the walls, butchering the nearby spearmen and Elderborn, providing a safe beachhead for the Malrags to swarm up the ropes. Soon the Malrags would slaughter the defenders, and swarm into the city.

"You see?" said Malavost to Skaloban. "There was no cause for alarm. We only..."

A thunderous horn blast rang out, so loud that Malavost took a step back in astonishment, his free hand coming up in the beginning of a warding spell. For a moment a pause fell over the battle, as man and Malrag alike looked for the source of the horn.

The echoes died away, ringing off the sides of Mount Tynagis.

"What in the name of Sepharivaim was that?" said Skaloban.

A dozen paces away, one of the traigs straightened up and ripped the heads from two Malrags.

Lucan staggered, surprised by the horn blast.

The bloodstaff blazed in his white-knuckled hands. He suspected, most strongly, that he was beginning to go insane. He wanted to lose himself to the staff's rage, to lash out in all directions with killing spells, to butcher every last man, woman, child, and Malrag in Deepforest Keep, and then to march north and repay his father and brother for all the pain they had inflicted upon him.

Only sheer exhaustion, perhaps, kept some shred of his sanity preserved. He was going to die here, Lucan knew. So perhaps his impending madness did not matter at all.

He looked into the city, and saw the traigs, the statues of the Elderborn warriors, rising from the earth and marching to battle.

Ah! So he was going mad. Hallucinations.

No sooner had the thought passed his mind than the traigs leapt upon the wall, and began slaying Malrags right and left.

"We go to war, my brothers," said the Great Traig.

Mazael stared in astonishment. There were hundreds of traigs scattered throughout Deepforest Keep, and every last one of them had come alive, marching to the northern walls and the ruined gates. And how many thousands more dotted the hills around Deepforest Keep? If the stone warriors awakened all at once, if they attacked the Malrag host...

Mazael's wits returned.

"Ultorin," said Mazael, "we have to find Ultorin."

Romaria gave a sharp nod, her bastard sword in hand, her blue eyes blazing.

"We go to war," she said, and they followed the Great Traig to the gate.

30

BLOODSWORD

"Fall back!" yelled Rhodemar, his face bloody. "Fall back! The wall cannot hold! Fall back to the Champion's Tower!"

He was right. Five Ogrags had gained the wall, killing all the spearmen and Elderborn within reach, providing safe beachheads for the Malrags to scramble up the ropes and gain the battlements. Neither spell nor spear nor arrow had been enough to stem the tide.

"Rhodemar!" said Lucan, leaning upon his staff. Rhodemar ducked, slashed his sword, and killed one of the Malrags driving him back. Lucan worked a spell and threw the nearest Malrags back with a psychokinetic burst. "Rhodemar!"

Rhodemar gave him a quick nod and turned back to the battle.

"Damn it, Rhodemar!" said Lucan. "Look!"

He pointed, and Rhodemar's eyes widened.

A dozen traigs leapt upon the battlements, and even more ran up the stairs, moving with a grace and power that belied their solid bulk. The traigs ignored the Elderborn and the humans, but attacked the Malrags with terrifying force. The living statues wielded stone maces and swords, their enormous weapons crushing Malrag flesh. One of the Ogrags picked up a traig in both hands, bellowing, but two traigs stepped behind the Ograg and buried their swords in its legs. The creature shrieked and dropped the traig, crushing a pair of Malrags beneath it.

As Lucan watched, the entire Malrag attack collapsed, the traigs mowing through the Malrags and Ogrags like scythes through wheat. The Malrags were fierce foes, but their axes and spears of black steel were useless against creatures made of living stone.

"The traigs?" said Rhodemar, astonished. "But...they're only stone. How..."

"The ancient tongue of the High Elderborn," said Ardanna, and even she looked shocked. "The word 'traig' means guardian, and legends spoke of them rising up to slay the enemies of the High Elderborn. But I never dreamed the legends were true." She shook her head. "How is this possible? Who could have awakened..."

She fell silent, eyes narrowed.

Lucan saw Mazael and Romaria running towards the gates, the Great Traig following them, along with a hundred smaller traigs. Even from a distance, Lucan fell the power rolling off Romaria in waves, the tremendous magical force concentrated in her diadem and ancient bronze shield.

"It seems, High Druid," said Lucan, "that your daughter is not quite so useless as you imagined."

Ardanna gave him a venomous look.

And the traigs plowed into the Malrags like a storm of falling boulders.

"WHAT IS HAPPENING?" said Skaloban, his sibilant voice reedy with terror.

Malavost watched the carnage with interest. He'd felt the magical power in the traigs, of course, during the long march south to Deep-forest Keep. But he had assumed the power was nothing more than an echo, some long-forgotten relic of the High Elderborn.

Apparently, Malavost had been wrong.

A few yards away, a pair of traigs ripped the arm from an Ograg. Quite wrong.

"They will attack us!" said Skaloban. "We must flee!"

"Don't be absurd," said Malavost. "We are perfectly safe. The traigs will kill any Malrag they can find, but they will not harm a human or an Elderborn." He hesitated for a moment, considering. "Though they might kill a San-keth. The High Elderborn were mortal foes of the San-keth."

Skaloban's tongue flicked over his fangs in near panic.

"Do stay close, honored Skaloban," said Malavost. "Remain within my cloaking spell, and you should be safe. Step outside of it, however, and the traigs will sense your presence. The results of that would be...unpleasant."

Skaloban shied closer, the bones of his undead carrier clacking.

"Now, come," said Malavost. "Our goal is within reach."

He strode through the melee, Skaloban hurrying after.

They passed Ultorin. The Grand Master of the Dominiar Order raved and screamed, shaking his bloodsword in one misshapen fist, bellowing for the Malrags to attack, to destroy the traigs, to kill everyone in Deepforest Keep.

Fool.

But, then Malavost had no further need of him. Whether Ultorin lived or died in the next hour was of no consequence whatsoever.

Smiling, he walked towards the walls.

"OPEN THE WAY," said Romaria, pointing her sword.

Dead men and Malrags littered the ramparts, and even as Mazael watched, more traigs leapt from the battlements, wading into the Malrag horde below.

"By the ancient pact," said the Great Traig, raising an enormous stone sword, "we shall open the way, and slay until Deepforest Keep is safe from its foes."

The Great Traig surged forward, slamming into the ruined gate.

The mound of rubble exploded outwards, raining into the Malrags. When the dust thinned, the gate had been cleared, the Great Traig tearing into the Malrags, the lesser traigs pouring through the gate.

The men and Elderborn upon the walls gazed down in shock.

"Men of Deepforest Keep!" yelled Romaria, lifting her sword. "Now is the hour! Attack! Drive the Malrags from our home!"

She raced through the gates, Mazael at her side, his hand tight about Lion's hilt. Ultorin would not get away, he vowed. Not this time. Behind him he heard the shouts as the Elderborn and the men of Deepforest Keep poured from the gates, the flash and crackle as Lucan and the druids unleashed their spells upon the Malrags.

Then Mazael plunged into the Malrags, and he had no more time for thought.

A Malrag came at him, axe raised, and Mazael caught the blow on his shield. He shoved, knocking the Malrag off-balance, and ripped open its throat with a single slash from Lion's burning blade. Two more Malrags charged, and then two more, and Mazael dispatched them all, black Malrag blood sizzling upon his sword.

But most of the Malrags attacked the traigs, and without fail they died. Their weapons could not harm the stone of the traigs, and the guardians' stone maces and swords slew a Malrag with every blow. The animated statues strode through the horde, striking left and right.

"Ultorin!" roared Mazael. He leapt upon a boulder, raising Lion to let its glow fall over the battlefield. "Ultorin, you murderous dog! Ultorin, come and face me! Face me now, or let all men know that you are a craven! Ultorin!"

A roar of fury answered him, and Mazael saw the flare of blood-colored light through the teeming ranks of the Malrags.

And Ultorin came for him. The Dominiar knight raced through the Malrags, yellow eyes bulging with rage, cutting down any Malrag that got in his way. A traig reached for him, and Ultorin slashed his bloodsword, the Demonsouled-infused steel cutting through the traig like butter. The statue collapsed into rubble, and Ultorin ran to attack Mazael.

Mazael raced to meet him.

Lion met the bloodsword with a tremendous crash, blue fire straining against darkness and blood-colored flame. Again the swords met, and again, a dozen times in half as many heartbeats. One of Ultorin's blows ripped through the top third of Mazael's shield. He slipped the ruined thing from his arm and flung it, the jagged wood striking Ultorin's face. Ultorin flinched away, but Mazael still landed a smoking cut on his forehead.

Ultorin backed away with a snarl, the black veins in his face and neck pulsing and throbbing.

"This is it," said Mazael, Lion ready in both hands. "For all the blood upon your hands. Today, you will pay for it."

Ultorin laughed, wild and deep. "Fool! You cannot stop me!" He lifted his sword, the crimson light flickering within its halo of darkness. "This was forged in the blood of Amalric Galbraith! He was unconquerable, and his power belongs to me now!"

"I slew Amalric Galbraith, upon this very blade," said Mazael, "just as I will slay you."

Ultorin screamed in fury. "I will slay you and feast upon your heart! I will raze the walls of Deepforest Keep and bathe in the blood of the city's women! And then I will march, I will march until all the world is a charnel house!"

"Only if you kill me first," said Mazael.

Ultorin attacked, roaring.

Mazael twisted around the blow, giving himself into his battle rage, to the speed and strength it offered him. He dared not go too far, dared not give himself to the Demonsouled madness within his heart. But in this...in a struggle against a monster like Ultorin, a fight against a man who had butchered thousands of innocents, Mazael could put his Demonsouled nature to good use.

Ultorin swung, and Mazael parried, Lion straining against the bloodsword.

Ultorin brought the bloodsword around in a high two-handed sweep, and Mazael ducked, Lion digging a groove in Ultorin's hip.

The pain drove Ultorin into a rage, and he went into a frenzy, hacking and slashing as Mazael danced back. The bloodsword's tip scraped at Mazael's armor, digging grooves in the steel plate. But with every blow, Ultorin left himself open, and Lion lashed out, carving smoking cuts in gray flesh. Ultorin's momentum played out, and Mazael went on the offensive, Lion flying through a barrage of swings and thrusts. The bloodsword's carvings blazed, and Ultorin stumbled back, yellow eyes widening with panic.

Then he broke away, and Mazael knew what he intended. Ultorin planned to kill the nearest Malrag, use its tainted life force to restore his wounds.

Lion shivered in Mazael's hands.

But what if Ultorin drank something other than Malrag life force through the bloodsword?

Ultorin wheeled and buried his sword to the hilt in the belly of an Ograg. The bloodsword blazed, and the Ograg shriveled and shrank as the bloodsword drank its life.

Mazael raced forward and plunged Lion into the Ograg's thigh, the sword's azure flame pouring into the creature's flesh.

And the bloodsword drank Lion's blue fire, pulling it into Ultorin.

Ultorin wailed, screamed as Mazael had never heard anyone scream, his eyes wide with shocked agony. Cracks of blue light spread along the bloodsword's blade, and sapphire flames glowed within Ultorin's black veins. He stumbled back, shrieking, arms and legs jerking, both hands clenched around the bloodsword's hilt.

Mazael hammered Lion down with all his strength behind it. The blade sheared through Ultorin's wrists, and both Ultorin's hands fell to the earth, the bloodsword clanging to land a dozen feet away.

"No!" wailed Ultorin, falling to his knees, smoke rising from the charred stumps of his wrists. "No! Give it back! Give it back!" He looked up at Mazael, terror in his yellow eyes. "Mercy. Mercy!"

"I will give you," said Mazael, voice quiet, "the same mercy you promised the people of my lands."

Ultorin screamed.

Lion swung in a flash of blue flame, and Ultorin's head rolled to join his severed hands.

Mazael stepped over the black-armored corpse and stood over the bloodsword. Blue flame struggled against blood-colored light in the sword's sigils, the veil of darkness swirling and twisting.

He raised Lion and brought the point down onto the bloodsword. The black sword trembled, and shattered with a scream and a flash of crimson light. For a moment a towering black shadow reared over the broken sword, seeming to take the shape of Amalric Galbraith.

Then the shadow dissipated like smoke, and nothing but ash and twisted steel remained of the bloodsword.

At that moment a quiver went through the gathered Malrags. Even as Mazael watched, an Ograg turned, striking down two Malrags, howling with glee. The Malrags turned on each other, hacking and slashing with abandon, ignoring even the traigs in their midst. The power of Ultorin's bloodsword had kept them in line, but with Ultorin dead and the bloodsword shattered, the Malrags had returned to their usual impulses, and now preyed upon each other.

A hundred thousand Malrags, packed below the walls of Deep-forest Keep, more concerned with killing each other than the humans and the Elderborn...

Mazael grinned at the thought.

His smile faded. It was not over, he knew, until they found Malavost and the San-keth, and he hurried to find Romaria.

31

THE BETRAYAL

Rachel huddled behind the window, watching the Garden of the Temple in terror.

She watched Gerald and his men fight the Malrags. The air filled with screams and roars, and the earth shook and heaved as the Malrag shamans called down their bolts of emerald lightning. Then Mazael arrived, and Romaria and the Seer emerged from the well in the center of the Garden. The Seer's magical wrath ripped apart the shamans, and Romaria became a great black wolf, killing every Malrag in sight.

Then they left, racing away to the north. To the gates, Rachel guessed. They might have stopped the Malrag infiltrators, but the Malrags outside the walls continued their assault. For a moment she considered joining Gerald at the walls, or returning to the Champion's Tower, but rejected the idea. Mazael had killed most of the Malrags in the streets, but more might lurk in the alleys and the cellars. One lone woman, armed with only a dagger, would make for easy prey.

So she huddled behind the window, watching the Garden of the Temple, weeping as she listened to the distant sounds of the battle. How could Mazael and Gerald possibly prevail? Rachel knew that if

Mazael killed Ultorin, the Malrag host would turn on itself. But Ultorin had to know that as well, and surely he would not be so foolish to expose himself to risk.

And Aldane. Her son was with Sykhana, somewhere in that Malrag horde. What would happen to Aldane if Mazael killed Ultorin and the Malrags went berserk? She had heard the stories, back at Castle Cravenlock, how the Malrags enjoyed torturing children.

How could this day end in anything but despair and death?

The traigs in the Garden of the Temple started to move.

At first Rachel thought her eyes had failed her, or that the horrors of the day had driven her mad. But the traigs kept moving. Dozens of them, then hundreds, all moving north towards the gate. A moment later Mazael and Romaria raced through the Garden of the Temple, following the Great Traig, which moved faster than Rachel could have imagined.

They vanished from sight, and the sounds of the battle changed. She heard men cheering, heard the Malrag war cries dwindle. More traigs moved through the street, chasing down Malrags, crushing them with stone maces, or simply ripping them apart.

Rachel blinked, her heart hammering with sudden hope. She had seen hundreds of the traig statues scattered through Deepforest Keep, and hundreds more standing in the hills. If Romaria and Mazael had somehow found a way to awaken them, to bring them to life...then perhaps they might yet defeat Ultorin and the Malrags.

And perhaps Rachel might see her son again.

She got to her feet. If the traigs were tearing apart the Malrags, she would go in search of Aldane. Of course, she had to first find a way out of this house. The building had been damaged by the Malrag lightning blasts, and she might have to climb down a pile of rubble or a ruined wall first.

A flicker in the Garden caught her eye, and Rachel took one last look out the window.

She froze in terror.

A San-keth cleric stood in the garden, looking back and forth.

The creature rode on an undead human skeleton, like the other San-keth clerics Rachel had seen. Besides the cleric stood a tall man in the long black coat of a wizard, with pale blue eyes and a ragged shock of white hair. This must be Malavost, Rachel realized, the wizard who had aided Ultorin.

Malavost turned towards the well in the center of the Garden, and Rachel's hands flew to her throat.

Her son rested in the crook of the wizard's arm.

SYKHANA CROUCHED IN THE BUSHES, trying to focus through the terror.

She had every right to terror. She had seen hundreds the things, all moving with tremendous speed, killing any Malrags they could catch. No doubt they were some ancient magical defense of the Elderborn, awakened to fight off the Malrags.

Malavost had erred. Badly.

Sykhana had to get out of the city. The Malrags were terrifying fighters, and each Ograg was strong as a dozen normal men, but black axes were no use against living statues. Malavost's plan would fall apart when the traigs ripped off his head. Sykhana had to find Aldane and get away, get far away. True, Aldane would not live forever in power and glory. But she would raise him as a normal child, as her son, somewhere far from Deepforest Keep and Knightcastle.

That would not be so bad.

That thought alone gave her the courage to move forward, creeping from bush to bush.

Malavost's voice reached her ears.

Malavost? Here? How had he eluded the traigs?

Sykhana risked a glance around the trunk of a massive oak tree. A shaman's lightning had sundered the tree, and several of its heavy branches lay broken and smoking upon the ground. She saw Malavost standing at the edge of the wide stone well, Skaloban at his side, and her heart soared to see Aldane resting safe in the wizard's arm.

Sykhana almost called out to them, almost rose to join them.

But something in Malavost's icy eyes made her wait.

"As I promised," said Malavost, pointing to the well. "The entrance to the caverns, and the path to the temple. And the Door of Souls."

"You have done well, wizard," said Skaloban. The cleric stepped past Malavost, gazing into the well. "You shall be well-rewarded, when Sepharivaim is reborn and the new order arises."

"Of course," said Malavost, reaching for his belt. "Honored Skaloban, I promised to bring you here, did I not? You should have had more faith in my judgment."

"Perhaps I should have," said Skaloban. "You are wise and clever, for a human. Truly you have proven a worthy servant of Sepharivaim..."

In one smooth motion, Malavost drew a dagger from his belt and rammed it into the base of Skaloban's skull.

"You should have had more faith in my judgment," agreed Malavost, "but putting faith me personally...why, that was a dreadful mistake, honored Skaloban."

The San-keth writhed, smashing the undead skeleton to pieces, flopped upon the grass, and went motionless. Malavost stooped, filled a vial with the San-keth's blood, and straightened up.

He gazed at Skaloban's corpse for a moment, and then laughed.

"That's all I ever needed from you, Skaloban," said Malavost. "Just a vial of your blood. And enduring your whining was certainly a heavy price." He glanced at Aldane. "And that's all I ever needed from you, young lord. Just a vial of blood." His pleased smile got wider. "Or, rather, all of your blood."

The words struck Sykhana like a thunderbolt.

Malavost wasn't going to transform Aldane into Sepharivaim reborn. He wasn't going to make Aldane into a living god.

He was going to kill Aldane.

Sykhana gripped her poisoned daggers and straightened up.

~

THE BATTLE WAS all but over.

Lucan leaned against the battlements, the bloodstaff flickering in his hand. The traigs continued their slaughter, killing every Malrag in sight. Not that there were many Malrags left to slaughter any longer. Like the traigs, the Malrags were efficient killers. They had torn each other apart with enthusiasm, even as the traigs slew them. And if Lucan walked to the southern walls, he knew, he could watch the Malrag host upon the foothills tear itself apart.

The battle was all but over.

But what had happened to Malavost?

Lucan had expected the renegade wizard to throw his considerable strength into the fray, to intervene in the fight between Mazael and Ultorin. Yet Malavost had not appeared, had allowed Mazael to strike down Ultorin. Perhaps Malavost was already dead, killed when the traigs attack. Or maybe the wizard had seen no further use for Ultorin, and slipped into the city.

Impossible. Potent wards layered Deepforest Keep's walls. Malavost would not have been able to enter, not without the druids knowing, unless...

Lucan looked at the ruined gate.

Unless the wards had been damaged.

Unless Malavost was already in the city, abandoning Ultorin and the Malrags to distract the defenders.

Lucan cursed, looked around, but all the druids had left, joining the slaughter below the gates.

He ran for the Garden of the Temple as fast as his legs would carry him.

~

RACHEL SAW Sykhana step out from behind a damaged tree.

Anger exploded through her. If she had a bow, she would have shot the changeling dead. If she had been a wizard like Lucan and

Timothy, she would have thrown a blast of power to burn Sykhana to ashes, to make the changeling pay for having dared to touch Aldane...

Yet through her rage, something strange caught her expression.

Sykhana looked furious, her poisoned daggers in her hand.

∼

"MALAVOST!" called Sykhana.

The wizard turned to face her, white eyebrows lifted in an expression of polite surprise.

"Ah," he said. "You survived."

Sykhana paused. The rational part of her mind, the cold part of her mind, knew that she should dissemble. That she should feign ignorance, and steal Aldane away from Malavost at the first opportunity.

But the thought of Malavost harming Aldane filled her with such fury that she did not care.

"You killed Skaloban," said Sykhana.

Malavost's smile faded, his face settling into a cool mask.

"You saw that, did you?"

"I did," said Sykhana. "What are you going to do to Aldane?"

"You know the answer to that," said Malavost. "As I promised. Aldane will become a god, will..."

"Don't lie to me!" said Sykhana. "I heard what you said to Skaloban. What are you going to do to Aldane?"

Malavost sighed.

"Well, why not?" he said. "Why should you now know the truth, in the end? When I put this plan into Skaloban's head, years ago, I told him the spell would only work with a special child. The child of an apostate, the flesh and blood of one who had abandoned Sepharivaim. But that was only half true. Sepharivaim is dead, and the Sanketh worship an empty memory that cannot save them. Sepharivaim is dead...but his power remains, imprisoned in the spirit world. His power remains, and can be claimed by anyone with the boldness to take it."

"You," said Sykhana.

"Me," agreed Malavost. "I needed only three things. Someone to destroy Deepforest Keep, so I could reach the Door of Souls of safety. The blood of a San-keth, to open the Door and draw Sepharivaim's power to me." His smile took on a cruel edge. "And the blood of a child of a human apostate, under a year old, to draw the power into the world and into me. All of the blood, as it happens."

"You'll kill Aldane!" shouted Sykhana.

Malavost shrugged. "A small price to pay to become a living god, no?"

"I will not allow it!" said Sykhana.

Malavost laughed at her. "You will not allow it? How will you stop me, foolish child? I will give you one chance. Walk away, and you shall live. Or stay and serve me, and receive rich rewards once I come into my power. Decide now."

"You will never touch Aldane again!" said Sykhana.

She raced at Malavost, one arm drawn back to throw a poisoned dagger.

Malavost flicked a finger, just one.

And a wall of invisible force slammed into Sykhana with the force of an avalanche. She heard a dozen loud snaps, and realized that she was hearing her bones break. The spell threw her into the damaged oak tree with crushing force, and a fresh explosion of pain erupted through her. All the strength drained from her legs, yet she remained upright, somehow.

She looked down, saw three feet of jagged oak jutting from her stomach, thick as her arm.

"Aldane!" she cried, reaching for the baby, her precious one. "Aldane!"

Malavost turned away, Aldane still in his arm.

"Aldane," whispered Sykhana, and blackness swallowed her.

~

RACHEL WATCHED Malavost and Sykhana speak, saw Malavost strike down the changeling with a single spell.

Her hands clenched. Malavost was taking Aldane to the caves, and then to Mount Tynagis and the Door of Souls. And there he would kill her son and loose a horror upon the world.

She had to stop him. No one else was here. But what could she do against Malavost? Rachel knew nothing of fighting. Sykhana was a trained assassin, and Malavost had killed her without the slightest effort.

Malavost paused.

Rachel followed his gaze, saw the Elderborn in the fur cloak at the edge of the Garden, a staff in his hand.

The Seer.

~

LUCAN STOPPED at the edge of the Garden, breathing hard.

Malavost stood at the edge of the well, a baby in his arm. Aldane Roland, no doubt. The Seer walked towards Malavost, leaning on his staff, his cloak fluttering behind him.

"So," said Malavost, smiling. "The Dragon's Shadow and the Seer. What a lively combination. Come to kill me, I believe?"

Lucan let the bloodstaff's power flood through him, ready to cast a spell.

"Were you a Malrag, I would kill you without hesitation," said the Seer. "They are only slaves to their madness and bloodlust. But you are a mortal man, and you may choose freely. I therefore give you this choice. Lay down the child, unharmed, and leave Deepforest Keep, and I will let you go. Resist, and I will crush you."

Lucan readied himself to strike.

Malavost laughed. "A bold show of confidence. You assume, of course, that you can crush me."

"I can," said the Seer. "I am the stronger, and you cannot face me alone. And with Lucan Mandragon's assistance, you cannot overcome me. I wish no further blood spilled upon the earth. Surrender, and leave, while you still can."

"No," said Malavost, glancing at Lucan, and then returning his attention to the Seer.

But Malavost's voice echoed inside Lucan's head.

-Still using the bloodstaff? I warned you against it. You are a bigger fool than Ultorin-

Lucan began to cast a warding spell over himself, a defense against mental intrusion.

-Stop-

To Lucan's astonishment, he stopped the spell.

"Perhaps I will give you one final chance," said Malavost. "You do not know how close you are to death, druid. Leave, and I will let you live for a little longer."

Lucan tried to cast another ward.

-Remain still and do not speak-

And to his horror, he obeyed.

-You didn't realize it, did you? Demonsouled power corrodes sanity. The mind itself has natural defenses against magical intrusion, defenses that your use of the bloodstaff has destroyed. Which means I can invade your mind with ease-

"I will defend Deepforest Keep and slay you, if I must," said the Seer, silver-white light glimmering around his staff. "This is your last warning."

"No," said Malavost, still grinning.

Lucan fought against the mental intrusion, fought with every ounce of strength he could muster, but to no avail. Malavost's power was too strong, too overwhelming, and the bloodstaff had indeed destroyed the defenses of Lucan's mind. He could gain no traction to fight against Malavost.

"So be it!" said the Seer, lifting his staff.

-Kill him-

Lucan leveled the bloodstaff. The sigils burned with bloody light, and twisting ribbon of crimson flame erupted forth. The Seer had no time to raise a defense. The snarling flame sheared through his head and chest like a burning knife, and the Seer collapsed, dead before he even hit the ground.

Lucan screamed inside his head.

Malavost lifted a single white eyebrow.

"The Seer never saw his death coming," said Malavost. "Now, there's a rich irony."

His pale eyes focused on Lucan.

-As for you, troublesome child. You wanted to wield the power of the Demonsouled so badly? Then wield it! Draw on the staff's power, as much as you can-

Lucan had no choice to obey, and he opened himself to the bloodstaff's magic.

And the power flooded through him a blazing torrent, more than he had ever dared to draw, even when in the grip of madness. It filled him, making him stronger, augmenting his magic.

Changing him.

His hands turned gray, the veins beneath the skin growing black and rotten. He remembered the horrifying thing Ultorin had become and screamed inside his head, even as his hands began to shake, smoldering as the staff grew hotter.

-And now turn the power back upon yourself-

Lucan had no choice but to obey.

The bloodstaff exploded in his hands, the molten shards driving into his arms and chest. Crimson flames devoured Lucan's clothes, melting into his skin and flesh, and he shrieked through the pain, even as he felt his body deforming in the grip of the Demonsouled power.

His legs collapsed beneath him, and everything went black.

MALAVOST LOOKED at the smoking husk that had been Lucan Mandragon, at the Seer's vivisected corpse, at Sykhana impaled upon the branch of oak.

His lip curled in a sneer of contempt.

No doubt Lucan had viewed himself as some sort of tragic hero, nobly sacrificing himself upon the altar of dark magic to save the Grim Marches. The boy had been nothing more than a gnat. The Seer, though...the Seer had been formidable.

But the problem of the Seer and the problem of Lucan Mandragon had solved each other quite nicely.

Malavost walked to the stone well, ignoring the corpses of Skaloban and Sykhana. He had told them that he regarded Ultorin as a tool, and that had been true. What he had failed to mentioned was that he regarded Skaloban and Sykhana as nothing more than tools, as well. And when a tool outlived its usefulness, you simply discarded it.

He wondered vaguely if Ultorin was still alive, and decided that he did not care.

Malavost took the worn steps spiraling down the interior of the well. He entered the caves, making his way by the dim light of the starglow, until he came to a vast chamber. At the far end of the chamber, he saw white stairs rising, ascending into the mountain.

The way to the ruined temple and the Door of Souls, at long last.

Malavost put his foot upon the first step and stopped.

He felt the presence of the ward, like a warm breeze upon his face. Not powerful enough to do him harm, he judged. But it was too large for him to effectively dispel. Another step, he thought, and the ward would activate, warning Deepforest Keep's surviving druids of his intrusion.

He sneered. Not that any of the druids had the power to stop him. But the druids might bring Mazael Cravenlock with them, if he survived the fight with Ultorin. Which was a very real possibility. Ultorin, for all his madness and idiocy, had been a dangerous opponent, and yet had failed to kill Lord Mazael again and again. Certainly Malavost wanted no interference when he cast the spell to open the Door of Souls.

The answer came to him, and his sneer became a smile.

He turned, facing the cavern, and cast a spell of summoning magic. A pool of gray mist swirled at his feet for a moment, perhaps thirty feet across, and a huge shape rose out of the mist, higher and higher, until it blotted out the pale gleam coming from the starglow on the ceiling.

Malavost gazed at the huge dark form. He felt its hatred washing over him, but it did not attack him. It could not go against the power of his spell.

"Defend me," he commanded. "Stay here and guard these steps. If anyone enters this cavern, kill him. If anyone follows me, kill him. Am I understood?"

A growling, metallic buzz answered his question, a sound of pure hatred, but the dark shape did not move to attack him. It would obey.

Anyone who tried to follow Malavost would sorely regret it.

He turned and began climbing the stairs.

32

THE OPENING

Mazael climbed up the ruined wall, Lion in his hand.

The battle was over. Dead Malrags and Ogrags filled the ground and choked the road. The traigs had torn through Ultorin's host, ripping apart the Malrags, and neither axe nor spear nor shaman's lightning bolt had stopped them. And once Ultorin fell, the Malrags turned on each other, butchering themselves with the same glee they had shown while butchering humans.

Some of the warbands had escaped, Mazael knew. The ones at the outer edges of the host, the ones that defeated their neighbors and vanished into the trees. Malrag raiders would haunt the Great Southern Forest for years. But he guessed that a hundred and twenty thousand Malrags lay dead outside the walls of Deepforest Keep.

They had won. Against all odds, they had won.

But there were no signs of the San-keth or Gerald's son. He had sent parties of men to search the dead Malrags for Aldane Roland, but he doubted they would find anything. He hoped they found nothing.

Mazael did not relish the prospective of presenting Gerald and Rachel with the corpse of their son.

He heard the scrape of leather against stone, saw Romaria climbing up.

"The Seer was right," said Mazael. "You saved Deepforest Keep."

"You killed Ultorin," said Romaria.

"And you awakened the traigs," said Mazael. "How did you know to do that?"

"I don't know," said Romaria. "It...the Ritual of Rulership changed me, Mazael. I had always fought against the Elderborn half of my soul, the way you fought against your Demonsouled half. But the Elderborn are not tainted the way the Demonsouled are. The beast...the Elderborn half of my soul...wasn't some dark thing within me. It was me. I am the beast, and the beast is me. And when I accepted that, I gained control over it...and my senses changed. I can see magical force, now." She shook her head in wonder. "And I could see the power in the traigs, the diadem and the Greenshield, how they were all linked. I always wondered why the Greenshield had to lie with the High Druid. I thought it some foolish ancient ritual. But it was more than that. The Champion of Deepforest Keep was always meant to be half-human, half-Elderborn. Someone who could see what the traigs were, and awaken them."

"And the Seer was right and you saved Deepforest Keep," said Mazael. "Your mother must be furious."

Romaria barked a short laugh. "She is. If the druids allowed themselves to touch iron, she would be chewing nails." She closed her eyes. "I only wish...I only wish my father had been here to see this."

"I wish I had been able to save him," said Mazael.

"I know," said Romaria. "His death was not your fault. But I know."

They stood in silence for a moment.

"What will you do now?" said Mazael.

Romaria let out a long breath. " We have to tend to the wounded, and then to the dead. The walls need to be repaired. We'll have to rebuild from the lightning damage inside the city..."

She was planning to stay, Mazael realized. And why not? She was the new Greenshield, the Champion of Deepforest Keep and the Defender of the Mountain. This was her city, her home. Mazael's home was at Castle Cravenlock, hundreds of miles north, and he would have to return to it.

He realized that Romaria was lost to him, again.

"What is it?" said Romaria, frowning.

"Rachel and Gerald," said Mazael. He saw Gerald, looking through the heaps of dead Malrags for any trace of his son. "My nephew is almost certainly dead. " He shook his head. "I don't..."

"Champion!"

Ardanna stood at the foot of the wall, staring at Romaria. Mazael saw the usual loathing and contempt in the High Druid's golden eyes, along with fresh hatred and rage. Ardanna did not approve of a half-breed as the Champion, not at all. But there was something else on the High Druid's face, something new.

Fear.

"What is it?" said Romaria.

"Someone has entered the caverns!" said Ardanna.

"What?" said Mazael.

"The druids have laid wards over the caverns of Mount Tynagis," said Ardanna. "We can sense when someone enters. And someone has entered the caverns. A wizard of overwhelming might."

"Malavost," spat Mazael. But how the devil had Malavost gotten into the city? No doubt he had crept in, during the mad chaos of the battle. And that explained why Malavost had not intervened in the battle, not used his spells to save Ultorin.

Ultorin and the Malrags had been distractions, nothing more.

"Gerald!" he called over the wall. Gerald looked up, his surcoat tattered and stained with Malrag blood. "I know where to find Aldane!"

RACHEL STOOD FROZEN before the window, hating herself.

Malavost had her son. She had to stop him. She had to get Aldane back.

Yet she could not.

She had seen the Seer wield mighty magic, the very earth itself rising at his command to crush the Malrag shamans. She had seen Lucan unleash his spells in battle, mowing down both Malrags and humans alike. Both men had possessed power beyond anything Rachel would ever know.

And Malavost had crushed them both in a matter of seconds. Or he had tricked or lured Lucan into killing the Seer, and then disposed of the Dragon's Shadow afterward. And if Rachel tried to pursue him, Malavost would kill her as easily as he had killed Sykhana. Even more easily – Sykhana had been a skilled assassin, one who had escaped from Knightcastle itself. There was nothing, nothing at all, Rachel could do to stop Malavost.

But he had her son.

She took a shuddering breath. It didn't matter that Malavost was a wizard of great power. It didn't matter that he could kill her in the space between two breaths. Malavost had her son, and she would get him back.

Or die trying.

That seemed more likely.

She wondered if this was how men felt, when they went into battle, knowing that they would almost certainly die. Was this how Gerald had felt? He had gone into some hopeless battles, yet had come through victorious. Would that happen to her?

Doubtful.

But after so long, her son was within reach. And if she died trying to get Aldane back, so be it.

Rachel began searching for a way out of the damaged house.

THE FIRST THING Mazael saw was the Seer's corpse.

The Seer, the mightiest druid of the Elderborn tribes, lay sprawled at the edge of the Garden of the Temple. It looked as if his chest and his face had been opened by the tip of a burning sword, the edges of the wound charred black.

"What is that smell?" muttered Romaria, frowning. Gerald stood behind her, sword drawn. Ardanna gazed at the Seer, her face a mask. Mazael had never expected to see that woman shocked into silence.

And Mazael was stunned, as well. He had seen firsthand the strength of the Seer's magical power. For Malavost to have simply killed the most powerful druid of the Elderborn...

Gerald looked at the Seer and frowned. "Burnt flesh, perhaps?"

"No," said Romaria, shaking her head. "Something worse. Like...corruption."

"That San-keth?" said Mazael, pointing with Lion. A San-keth lay in loose coils near the edge of the well, its black-slit eyes staring into nothingness.

"This is worse," said Romaria, nostrils flaring. "Like...something rotten was locked in a vault, for years, and then left out to putrefy in the sun. Or an infected wound, gushing pus. It's like...there!"

A twisted corpse lay some distance from the Seer, its limbs black with char. Chunks of jagged metal lay on its chest and scattered around the nearby ground. At first Mazael thought the corpse was some strange sort of Malrag that he had never seen before. It had the grayish skin and deformed growths on its arms and legs as the Ogrags, though it was much smaller. Human-sized, in fact. And the creature's face...

"Gods," said Mazael. "That's Lucan."

"What the devil did Malavost do to him?" said Gerald.

"He reeks of corruption," said Ardanna, her cold voice just a touch unsteady. "Of tainted power. I sensed it upon him, when he entered the city, It has consumed him."

Mazael went to one knee besides Lucan, examining the wounds. His senses were not as potent as Romaria's, but even so, the stench was terrible.

"I don't think Malavost did this to him," said Romaria, voice quiet. "I think he did it to himself. His magic was much stronger than I remembered. I think he found another source of power, and it devoured him. That black staff of his, probably. The thing reeked of dark magic."

"He's still alive," said Mazael. There was the faintest pulse of the veins in Lucan's neck, the hint of breath over his bloody lips.

"You should kill him," said Romaria.

"What?" said Mazael, looking at her in astonishment. "He has saved my life time and time again. It was his spell that restored the human half of your soul. He has fought valiantly to defend this city. And you want me to kill him out of hand?"

"It might be a mercy," said Romaria, voice quiet. "Look at Lion."

"Why..."

"Just look at Lion."

Mazael drew the blade a foot from its scabbard. Pale blue flames flickered around the sword's razor edges, flames that grew brighter when he moved closer to Lucan.

And Lion only responded that way to creatures of dark magic.

"Do you see what he has become?" said Romaria. "You should kill him, now. Before you regret it later. And he might thank you for it. If there's anything left of his mind, he must know what he's become."

"No," said Mazael.

"Lucan is beyond our help, one way or another," said Gerald. "My son is not, but only if we act now."

Mazael straightened up. "You're right." He hesitated. What the devil had Lucan done to himself? Mazael hated to leave him here like this. But if Malavost reached the Door of Souls, Gerald's son, Mazael's nephew, would die.

And Malavost would unleash a new horror upon the world.

Something Lucan had fought to stop.

He crossed the Garden, making for the well, and the others followed him. The stone stairs spiraled down, opening into a tunnel lit by patches of white-glowing moss. After a short distance the tunnel widened into a large chamber perhaps the size of Castle Cravenlock's great hall, its ceiling lost in gloom. At the far end of the chamber of a broad set of white stone steps climbed up, rising into the mountain.

"The way to the sacred temple," said Ardanna, pointing with her staff, "and to the Door of Souls. Malavost would have gone this way..."

Mazael nodded. "Then let's..."

Lion jolted, the blade bursting into brilliant azure flames, enough light to illuminate the gloom of the cavern.

And enough light to reveal the misshapen thing hanging from the ceiling. It looked like a scorpion, but most scorpions didn't have three trails like braided whips, barbs glistening with poison. Or carapaces like plates of black iron, or great leathery wings, or the head of a beautiful woman, albeit a woman with jutting fangs the size of Mazael's arms.

And most scorpions were not the size of three warhorses put together.

The scorpion loosed a terrible screech and leapt from the ceiling, and Mazael threw himself to the side, only just avoiding the creature's black-armored bulk. It landed with a thump and spun to face Mazael, the three barbed tails rising back for a strike.

But Mazael had anticipated the scorpion's motion, and he whipped Lion around in a sideways cut. The blade sheared through one massive leg as if it were no more than a silken cord, carving a smoking gash into the spirit-creature's carapace. The scorpion's screech doubled in volume, and it lashed out with one of its serrated pincers. The edge caught him across his armored chest, and the strength of the blow knocked him from his feet.

The scorpion-thing wheeled, preparing to spring upon Mazael, only to catch one steel-tipped arrow in its flank, and then two more, in rapid succession. Romaria had her bow in hand, and she loosed arrow after arrow in the spirit-creature's side. It shrieked again and raced for her, pincers yawning wide. Romaria threw aside her bow, her form blurring, and became the great black wolf. She slipped past the pincers, her white fangs snapping, and the scorpion stumbled, another of its legs lamed. The creature spun, its tails cracking like whips, its two wounded legs dragging as it tried to pursue Romaria.

Ardanna lifted her staff, silver light flashing along its length, and gestured. White mist swirled, and a barrage of ice chunks, frozen harder than granite and sharper than razors, ripped into the scorpion. One of its tails fell to the ground, leaking black ichor, and the scorpion screamed. Gerald darted in close, hacked off a second tail. The remaining tail hammered down, but Gerald caught its spike upon his shield, and sliced off the stinger before the scorpion could tear its tail free.

It gave Mazael an opening. He sprang to his feet, ran forward, and leapt upon the scorpion's back. The creature screamed, its remaining tail lashing at him, but Gerald had severed the stinger, and Mazael's armor protected him from the lash. He drove Lion into the creature's neck, between the human head and the black carapace, and the scorpion's constant screaming became a sudden agonized gurgle. The blade pulsed with azure flame, and the scorpion went still with one final spastic twitch.

Then the scorpion vanished in a swirl of gray mist. Mazael landed hard upon one knee and climbed back to his feet. Romaria blurred back into her true form, retrieving her bow.

"What the devil was that thing?" said Gerald, looking at Ardanna. "Do many such creatures dwell in these caverns?"

"No," said Romaria, before her mother could speak. "It was a spirit-creature, a thing summoned from the netherworld."

"Malavost conjured it," said Ardanna, glaring at her daughter, "and set it to wait here for any pursuers."

Mazael nodded. If Lucan had been here, he could have dispelled the summoned scorpion, or conjured creatures of his own. But Lucan lay dying in the Garden above, and Mazael and the others were on their own.

"We'd best hasten," he said, and led them towards the white stairs.

Rachel stumbled down a pile of rubble.

It had taken her a while to find a way free from the ruined house. At last she located a pile of debris heaped against the wall, the remnants of a neighboring house, and she went out the window and picked her way down the pile, terrified that she would fall and snap her neck, or that the rest of the stone wall would collapse, burying her alive to choke out her final breaths in darkness.

But the rubble held, and Rachel found her way down to the alley, breathing hard, covered in dust. Again she cursed herself. Yes, she could certainly find Malavost and defeat him, if the simple effort of escaping from a house winded her!

But her own life did not matter.

She clutched her tattered skirts in one hand and hastened to the Garden of the Temple. The Seer's corpse had not moved, and Lucan's misshapen body lay where it had fallen. Up close, he looked even more grotesquely deformed. Rachel wondered what sort of vile magic Malavost had used upon him. Or had Lucan's own magic rebounded upon him? The feared Dragon's Shadow, no doubt, had dabbled in forbidden things.

Rachel stopped, and looked at the woman who had taken her baby.

Sykhana slumped against the lightning-damaged oak, the jagged branch jutting from her belly. Blood stained her dark clothing, head slumped against her chest, poisoned daggers still in their sheaths. Rachel stared at the corpse. She had dreamed of this moment, played it over a thousand times in her mind, thinking of what she would do if Sykhana was ever in her power. How she would make Sykhana beg for mercy, make her regret ever laying her filthy hands upon Aldane.

But the changeling looked like a small, pathetic thing. A broken tool, cast aside by Malavost. Rachel remembered the look of horror upon Sykhana's face before Malavost had killed her. What had the wizard told her?

She turned away, and Sykhana's eyes fluttered open.

Malavost had not killed her so easily after all.

Rachel stepped back in alarm, fearing a poisoned dagger. But Sykhana only coughed, blood trickling down her chin. Her eyes were yellow with vertical black slits, a serpent's eyes, and they focused upon Rachel.

"You," whispered Sykhana. "I killed you. A fever dream. Or this is hell, and you are waiting for me." She laughed, her voice despairing. "Yes, hell. I deserve hell, for my folly."

"You took my son!" said Rachel, stepping closer in her rage.

"Yes," said Sykhana.

"Why? Why? To spill his blood in some vile San-keth rite? To turn him into a living monster? Why? You will tell me why!"

"Because I love him," said Sykhana.

Rachel had no answer for that.

"The calibah cannot bear children," said Sykhana. "I looked upon Aldane...and I loved him from the first moment I saw him. I hated you. You were not worthy of such a son. But I could do more for him. Malavost...Malavost could turn him into Sepharivaim reborn, infuse him with the very soul of serpents. He would be a god, and reign forever in power and bliss. I believed...I was a fool. Malavost. Malavost!"

Sykhana shuddered, and for a moment Rachel through the calibah would tear free from the branch in fury. But Sykhana slumped, fresh blood trickling down her chin and her legs.

"Malavost lied," said Sykhana. Rachel had seen people die from wounds, men and women both, and she knew that Sykhana was very near death. "Oh, my Aldane. I didn't know. Malavost lied to me. He never wanted to make Aldane into Sepharivaim reborn. He wanted to steal Sepharivaim's power for himself. To use Aldane as a blood sacrifice, to open the Door of Souls. He lied to me. Malavost!" Sykhana clawed at the air, eyes open wide. "Aldane! Aldane!"

"This is your fault!" said Rachel. "You took Aldane from me, and handed him over to this butcher!"

"Save him!" shrieked Sykhana. Rachel didn't know if the changeling had heard her or not. "Don't let Malavost kill him! Save him! Please, if you are listening, save him, save him..."

Sykhana's cries ended in a burst of coughing, more blood dripping from her mouth. She shuddered once more, eyes bulging, and went limp. Rachel watched her for a moment, but Sykhana remained motionless. At last Rachel summoned the courage to step forward and tap Sykhana's shoulder. The changeling did not respond.

Sykhana was indeed dead.

Rachel's eyes strayed to the sheathed daggers at Sykhana's belt. She tugged one of the daggers an inch or so from its scabbard, the blade gleaming with grease. Changeling poison, lethal to any living man.

And Malavost, despite all his magical prowess, was still a living man.

The notion was absurd. She could not get close enough to use a normal dagger on Malavost, let alone a poisoned one. But if she did get close enough to only scratch him with the poisoned dagger...

Just one scratch would be enough to kill Malavost.

And to save Aldane.

Rachel took the belt and the sheathed daggers, and hurried towards the well at the Garden's center.

THE STAIRS ENDED, and Malavost stepped from the darkness of the caverns to the sunlight atop Mount Tynagis.

He stood in the vast courtyard of a half-ruined temple, soaring arches and mighty walls rising around him. The pillars has been carved in the shapes of High Elderborn warriors, like much larger versions of the traigs ripping apart the Malrag host - though these statues, thankfully, were free of defensive magic. Even in ruins, even with its roof and half the columns lying strewn across the courtyard, the temple stood in ancient splendor, and the view of the Great Southern Forest in all directions was magnificent.

Malavost felt the power in the air, the latent magic.

He walked through the temple's entrance. Once it would have opened into a vast, gloomy hall, its vaulted ceiling supported by a forest of white pillars. But the roof had collapsed long ago, and half of the pillars as well, their jagged crowns stark against the blue sky. At the far end of the ruined hall stood a large dais of white marble, built into the very side of the mountain itself, with a view of the foothills and the Great Southern Forest far below. A stone altar rested before the dais, carved with ancient reliefs.

And upon the dais stood the Door of Souls.

It looked like a delicate stone arch, ten feet wide and thirty high, its top coming to a point. Ornate sigils and carvings covered the arch's sides, and unlike the weathered stone of the rest of the temple, the arch looked as if it had been carved and built yesterday.

Which was not surprising. Even without using a spell, Malavost felt the potent magic waiting in the Door of Souls, more powerful that the wards upon the walls of Deepforest Keep, stronger than the magic within the traigs. Here was power enough to rip upon a passage to the spirit world, and pull the power of a dead god into this world.

Into Malavost.

At last, at long last, he had come to his goal.

Now to prepare. The Elderborn and Mazael, no doubt, would be too busy with the Malrags to pursue him. And even if anyone did pursue him, Malavost had no doubt that the spirit creature upon the stairs could handle any pursuers.

Still, he had not come this far by taking foolish chances, after all.

He set the unconscious child upon the altar and began to cast spells. First, a series of wards around his person, to protect him from physical attacks. Especially arrows, given the Elderborn penchant for archery.

Next, a series of summoning spells. Pools of gray mist swirled around the altar, and four huge shapes rose out of nothingness, creatures out of nightmare, covered in chitinous armor and barbed claws.

They snarled and snapped at him, but could not harm him, thanks to his spell.

"Guard me," commanded Malavost. "If anyone enters the temple, kill them without hesitation."

The spirit creatures moved away, settling among the piles of rubble to wait.

Malavost turned his back to them, faced the altar and the Door of Souls, took a deep breath, and began to cast a spell. Power thrummed and crackled in the air, and the sigils upon the Door of Souls burned with harsh silvery light. The air within the Door shimmered and flickered, sometimes showing the Great Southern Forest, and sometimes...elsewhere.

A dark place, a place of monsters and dark magic.

Where the power of Sepharivaim had laid unclaimed for long millennia.

Power that would soon belong to Malavost.

He continued the spell, and the Door of Souls began to open.

33

THE DOOR OF SOULS

A t last the stairs ended.

Mazael climbed into the courtyard of the temple, Romaria, Gerald, and Ardanna following him. Even ruined, the great walls and pillars of white stone were still impressive, still stern with splendor and ancient grandeur.

Through the temple's entrance Mazael saw a forest of columns, some half-crumbled, and piles of white stone, no doubt debris from the temple's long-collapsed roof.

And beyond the rubble, flickers of silver light, visible even in the daylight.

"There," said Ardanna. "The Door of Souls is there, in the old sanctuary."

"I can feel him," said Romaria, gazing through the archway. "Malavost. He's gathering power. He's preparing to open the Door of Souls."

"Then we have not come to late," said Ardanna.

Gerald drew his sword. "My son is in there."

"Then let's get him back," said Mazael, and he led them through the archway and into the ruined sanctuary.

MALAVOST CHANTED THE SPELL, drawing more power into himself, more and more, until he felt as if he would burst from it.

The air within the Door of Souls continued its strange flicker, giving Malavost glimpses of the dark place, the netherworld where Sepharivaim's power awaited him.

Soon, now. A little more power, and the Door would be primed. Then Malavost could use Skaloban's blood to pry it open all the way.

And Aldane Roland's blood to draw Sepharivaim's power into this world.

He heard a rasping noise, the sound of leather scraping against stone. For a moment he wondered if one of his spirit creatures had made the noise - but, no, they would remain soundless.

Someone had followed him up here.

Though the spell, he smiled to himself. Whoever it was would soon regret it, once the creatures from the spirit world made their move.

Malavost kept chanting, and the space within the Door grew darker.

IN ITS PRIME, the sanctuary must have been magnificent. For a moment Mazael wondered at the skill of the ancient High Elderborn. How had they built this place? Had they used magic to carve the stairs, to haul the white stones to the crown of Mount Tynagis? Or had their skill as builders simply surpassed the skill of any men living today?

Mazael pushed the thought aside. He could muse upon history later, once Aldane was safe and Malavost was dead.

Heaps of rubble stood between the pillars, but the central aisle was mostly clear. The silver light came from a dais at the far end of the great sanctuary.

Mazael walked around a pile of rubble, and saw the Door of Souls.

It stood upon the dais, a tall, pointed arch of white stone, the sigils carved into its sides flickering with silver-white light. Through the stone arch Mazael saw the endless green carpet of the Great Southern Forest. Or, at least, he should have. Instead darkness writhed within the Door, and through it Mazael caught glimpses of another place, a place of nightmares and horrors.

The source of the spirit creatures both Lucan and Malavost conjured up, no doubt.

A stone altar rested before the dais, and Malavost stood over the altar, gesturing, green light flaring around his fingertips, his long black coat dancing in the wind. And upon the altar lay an unconscious child no more than five or six months old.

For the first time, Mazael laid eyes upon his nephew.

Several things happened at once.

"My son!" said Gerald, stepping forward.

But Romaria was faster. Even before Gerald had begun to move, she had her bow in hand, her hands blurring. Before Mazael could blink she had an arrow in the air, and then another, and another, all streaking towards Malavost's back. The arrows slammed into Malavost, and shattered with flashes of green light, falling in harmless splinters to the ground.

Malavost turned, one eyebrow lifted, as if in amusement.

Then something black and misshapen moved atop one of the pillars.

MALAVOST PAUSED HIS SPELL, the power thrumming and snarling as it awaited his attention.

There were four of them. An Elderborn woman he did not recognize, holding an oaken staff. One of those annoying druids, no doubt. A tall woman with black hair and icy blue eyes, a bronze diadem on her brow and a bow in her hand. Romaria Greenshield, and it been most amusing to listen to Ultorin's endless rants about her. A knight in polished armor - Sir Gerald Roland. And Mazael Cravenlock himself, his ancient longsword burning with azure flame in his right hand.

Only four of them. He had expected more. Still, Mazael was the only one that was truly dangerous.

"You have my son," said Gerald, pointing his longsword, "and I..."

Malavost snorted. He had no reason to talk to any of them.

"Kill them all," he said. His summoned servants leapt into motion, and Malavost began casting one of the spells he had learned from the Malrag shamans. The spell upon the Door of Souls would start to unravel soon, but Malavost had more than enough time to first butcher his enemies.

~

ROMARIA SENT another arrow flying for Malavost's face, but she knew it was useless. The arrow shattered an inch from Malavost's eye, breaking apart against his wards. She saw the magical power gathered around the wizard - he was strong, stronger than Lucan Mandragon, far stronger than Ardanna, and at least as strong as the Seer had been.

And behind him she saw the immense vortex of magical power swirling around the Door of Souls. The Door would tear open the veil between the mortal world and the spirit world, allowing the power of the serpent god to enter.

And even as Malavost began casting a spell, emerald fire flickering around his hands, more of the giant human-headed scorpions appeared. One clung to a pillar near the dais. Another scrambled over a pile of rubble. Still a third perched atop another pillar, and a fourth raced around a fallen column, its legs clicking against the marble floor.

Four of them. One of the great scorpions had almost been enough to kill them upon the stairs, and now they faced four of the things, in addition to the might of Malavost's spells.

Romaria spun and loosed an arrow at the charging scorpion. The arrow caught the creature in its human face, and it reared back with a scream, black slime bubbling over the wound. But the remaining three scorpions charged forward, barbed tails waving.

She threw aside her bow and changed, her body blurring into the form of the great black wolf. Her senses, already sharp, became far keener, and she smelled the vile reek of the scorpions, the sweat upon Mazael's face, the sharp scent of Malavost's potent magic.

Gerald and Mazael ran to meet the scorpions, shields raised, but Romaria was faster. She darted past them, fangs snapping, her jaws closing about the base of the scorpion's first leg. The taste was unspeakably vile, but the scorpion lost its balance.

It was all the opening Mazael needed to bring Lion sweeping down, taking the scorpion's head from its neck, and the black-armored body went into a mad dance, tails lashing at the air.

Mazael spun from the dead scorpion, even as its body dissolved into gray mist, and turned to face the remaining three creatures.

The spirit beasts watched him warily, their tails twitching back and forth in preparation for a strike. Mazael kept his shield up, watching for an opportunity to land a telling blow. He had to act quickly. Malavost might kill Aldane at any moment, or loose his powers in the fight...

No sooner had the thought crossed Mazael's mind then Malavost raised his hand, ghostly fire crackling around his fingers.

A green lightning bolt screamed down from the sky. The blast slammed into the earth at Mazael's feet, shattering the marble flag-stones, the shock knocking him from his feet. Gerald crashed hard into the base of a broken column, armor clattering, and toppled to the ground.

He did not get up again.

Mazael scrambled backwards as the scorpions pursued him, their long tails snapping like whips. He caught five of the barbed tails on his shield, but two more bounced off his armor, leaving scratches in the steel.

And two more barbs penetrated the joints of his armor over his knee and shoulder, pumping their poison into his flesh. Mazael stumbled, felt a cold numbness begin to spread into his left arm and leg.

And still the scorpions kept coming, and Malavost began another spell.

∾

ROMARIA SAW the blast of Malavost's spell drive Gerald to the ground, saw Mazael stumble back, the scorpions pursuing him.

She howled and leapt into the fray, attacking the scorpion on Mazael's left. She sprang upon its back, claws scrabbling uselessly against its armored carapace, but her fangs sank into the soft flesh below its human neck. The scorpion reared back with a scream, its pincers and barbed tails lashing at the air, and Mazael got his feet under him, shield raised.

But the scorpions' poison had slowed him, she saw. His Demonsouled essence would purge the poison from his blood, but not fast enough, and a claw or a barb through the heart or brain would kill him as surely as any other man.

The scorpion shrieked, its entire body heaving, and threw Romaria to the ground. She rolled back to her feet, paws gaining purchase upon the white stone, and stood at Mazael's side, fangs bared as the scorpions advanced.

∾

MAZAEL TRIED to keep his balance, breathing hard.

A cold numbness spread through his left side, making it difficult to keep his grip on his shield. Or to keep his feet, for that matter. The world was beginning to spin around him, and from time to time his vision flickered. The scorpions' venom, no doubt, and soon his Demonsouled power would heal him.

But not before one of the scorpions ripped his head off.

The scorpions rushed him, tails cracking like whips. Mazael backed away, trying to catch the blows upon his shield. Romaria snapped and snarled, and the scorpions shied away in fear. But they were too fast and too strong, and they pushed forward, bit by bit. Sooner or later they would drive Mazael and Romaria against one of the pillars or piles of broken stone, and then the fight would be over.

Where the devil was Romaria's mother? Why had she not intervened in the fight?

No sooner had the thought crossed Mazael's mind than a barrage of razor-edged ice chunks slammed into the scorpion on his left, sending the creature crashing to the ground in a spray of black blood. Mazael risked a glance to the side, saw Ardanna standing atop one of the rubble heaps, staff thrust forth, fur cloak billowing in the wind rising from the Door of Souls. She cast a spell, launching another barrage of dagger-edged ice chunks at the scorpions.

On the dais, Malavost wheeled to face her, and green lightning fell from the sky.

Lucan had been able to deflect the lightning bolts with relative ease, despite the obvious cost in pain to him. Ardanna barely had the power to deflect one. She fell to her knees with a scream, staff clutched in both hands, and the lightning bolt rebounded to shatter one of the pillars. Ardanna remained on her knees, trembling, face white and drawn with exhaustion.

She was finished, Mazael realized. The battle at the walls of Deepforest Keep had taxed her, and deflecting the lightning bolt had taken the final scraps of her strength.

One of the scorpions surged forward, tails whipping. Mazael swept Lion in a blazing arc, managing to sever one of the barbs. But the second tail's spike bounced off his shield, and the third crunched deep into his side, the poison pumping into his blood.

≈

RACHEL STUMBLED up the final steps, breathing hard, Sykhana's sheathed daggers in her hands.

She stood in an ancient courtyard, a great temple, splendid even in its ruin, rising over her. Through the temple's doorway she saw flashes of light, heard the rumble of spells and the sounds of battle.

She hurried towards the arch, still clutching the poisoned daggers.

~

MALAVOST WATCHED the Elderborn druid collapse, watched his summoned spirit creatures drive Mazael and Romaria back. Behind him he felt the strain as his spell upon the Door started to unravel.

He turned his back on the melee and resumed the spell. At once the darkness within the Door's arch congealed, becoming thicker and blacker. Tendrils of shadow, like long serpents, reached out from the Door, feeling the dais and the nearby pillars like the questing fingers of a blind man.

Malavost reached into his coat, drew out of the vial of Skaloban's blood and threw it towards the Door of Souls. The blood spilled out in a crimson arc, and even before it reached the floor, one of the tendrils wrapped around it, sucking the blood into the arch.

The darkness within the Door roiled, an ominous green light shining in its depths. The sense of power emanating from the Door redoubled, and then doubled again, until the mountain itself seemed to vibrate with it.

The power of Sepharivaim, waiting for him to claim it.

Malavost's fingers trembled with excitement. One more spell, the blood of Aldane Roland spilled, and the power of a god would be his.

He began casting the final spell.

Malavost leaned over the altar. The green light in the Door of Souls grew brighter, the tendrils of shadow more agitated in their thrashing. He forgot the scorpions, forgot Mazael Cravenlock, forgot everything except the spell.

And the great power that awaited him.

He drew his dagger, ready to spill Aldane Roland's blood and draw the power into this world.

~

ROMARIA RIPPED at the injured scorpion's flank, tearing at the wounds Ardanna's spell had left in its side. The scorpion reared back, screaming, eyes narrowed in rage and pain, but its pincer lashed out. It caught her across the flank and knocked her from her feet, sending her rolling across the flagstone.

She righted herself, saw Mazael sink to one knee, blood streaming down his side.

~

RACHEL RAN INTO THE TEMPLE, uncaring of the danger.

Aldane, she had to find Aldane.

She saw Gerald, lying motionless against a pillar. But he was still breathing, and she had to find Aldane. Mazael and a great black wolf faced off against three creatures of nightmare, hideous hybrids of scorpion and human, but she did not see Aldane with them.

Then she saw the dais, and the darkness swirling atop of it, tendrils of shadow radiating from a pointed arch of white stone. The Door of Souls, no doubt. Before the door stood Malavost, a dagger in his hand, his arms and shoulders trembling with strain as he cast a mighty spell.

Aldane, her Aldane, lay motionless upon a stone altar, eyes closed.

Malavost's voice rose to a bellow, the dagger coming up.

Rachel screamed and ran for him.

~

MAZAEL DROPPED TO HIS KNEES, breathing hard, the world spinning around him.

He could not regain his feet. The poison was too potent. He felt it healing, felt it passing from his blood, but not quickly enough. Every blow from the scorpions' stingers sent another dose of venom coursing through his veins, and even his Demonsouled healing could not fight it off fast enough.

And the scorpions...he and Romaria had hurt them, but not enough.

He had failed, and they were going to die.

The scorpions drew closer, pincers snapping.

And then Mazael saw Rachel.

She ran at Malavost, shrieking. Malavost noticed her, hand coming up in a spell, and the scorpions whirled to aid their master, but too late. Rachel had a black dagger in her hand, and she buried it in Malavost's chest, once, twice, three times. The wizard staggered under the blows, his eyes wide with shock and pain. Blood burst from his wounds, spraying Rachel, the altar, the child upon it.

And some of the drops fell upon the writhing ropes of shadow.

"No!" shouted Malavost, voice hoarse.

One of the dark tendrils wrapped around him, drawn by the blood, then another, and another. Malavost fought and screamed, clawing at the tendrils, magical flames bursting from his fingers. Some of the shadowy cords vanished beneath his attack, but more wrapped around him, more and more.

Serpents, Mazael realized. The twisting cords of shadow looked like serpents.

And the serpents dragged Malavost back, screaming, into the Door of Souls, into the dark place within the arch. Mazael had one last glimpse of Malavost, face frantic, and then the wizard vanished into the darkness. There was a dazzling flash of silver light, and the darkness within the arch vanished, along with Malavost himself.

The Door of Souls had closed.

The scorpions shivered, and vanished into gray mists.

And silence hung over the ruined temple.

～

For a moment Rachel stood frozen, watching as the writhing serpents of shadow pulled Malavost into the netherworld, as the Door of Souls closed.

Then she flung aside the bloodstained dagger and scooped up Aldane with a cry.

Larger, he was so much larger than the last time she had held him.

He was warm, he was breathing, but his eyes were closed. What had Malavost and Sykhana done to him? Had they hurt him? Put him into an enspelled sleep from which he would never awake?

Then Aldane opened his eyes, took a deep breath, and began to wail at the top of his lungs.

Rachel sobbed and hugged him close.

Mazael dragged himself back to his feet. His wounds throbbed, but already he felt the cuts closing, the numbness beginning to fade away. His Demonsouled nature would heal him in short order.

It had been a close thing, though.

Besides him Romaria blurred back into human form and picked up her bow. She had bruises on her face, and walked with a limp, but seemed otherwise unhurt.

"How are you?" she said.

"I've been better," said Mazael, taking careful steps towards Gerald. "But I'll be well again, soon enough." He knelt, helped Gerald to his feet.

Gerald groaned, pulled off his helm, rubbed at his head. "Did we win?"

"We did," said Mazael.

Gerald nodded, then his eyes got wide. "My son..."

Romaria grinned. "Still alive."

Gerald pulled free of Mazael's grip and half-ran, half-staggered to the dais. Rachel stood there, weeping, Aldane cradled in her arms. Gerald put his hand on her shoulder, and she beamed up at him.

"She killed him," said Romaria, voice soft.

"She did," said Mazael.

Romaria shook her head. "Malavost was a wizard of power, so strong he killed the Seer and defeated Lucan. And your sister...your sister is not the kind of woman to face such a man. Yet she killed him. I can scarce believe it."

Rachel was laughing and crying at once, her face tight with joy and relief.

"She loves her son," said Mazael, voice quiet. "She followed Aldane all the way from Knightcastle. She would have followed him into hell, if Malavost had gone there."

Romaria looked at the rubble heap, where Ardanna climbed to her feet. She made no move to help her mother. "I wonder what that's like."

Mazael remembered his own mother, who had lain with the Old Demon. "I wouldn't know."

Ardanna hobbled down the pile of rubble, leaning on her staff. "You have done well, Lord Mazael. The temple is safe, and the power of Sepharivaim will not be loosed upon the world."

She did not look at her daughter.

"Rachel killed Malavost, not I," said Mazael. "And we could not have done it without Romaria's aid."

Ardanna said nothing, still refusing to look at her daughter, and Romaria's eyes narrowed.

"Mazael!" Rachel walked closer, smiling, Aldane cradled in her arms.

"My lord Mazael," said Gerald, his arm around Rachel's waist, "it is my honor and privilege to introduce you to your nephew, my first-born son, Aldane of the House of Roland."

"It is an honor," said Mazael, taking Rachel's hand, "and a long overdue one, at that."

"Thank you," whispered Rachel.

Mazael smiled, and kissed her forehead.

34

THE LADY OF CASTLE CRAVENLOCK

D eepforest Keep celebrated.

Six hundred men of the city had been slain, along with three hundred of the Elderborn, and many more wounded. But Deepforest Keep had survived. Ultorin had been slain at Mazael's hand, and Malavost devoured by the very power he had sought to conjure. At Romaria's command, the people of the city and the tribes of the Elderborn gathered in the Garden of the Temple for a great feast, to honor their dead, to praise the valiant, and to offer thanks for their victory.

And to the people gathered to eat and drink, to celebrate and weep. Singers from the Elderborn tribes wandered among the tables, singing both laments and songs of victory. Men and women wept, while others cheered and drank.

Mazael had seen such celebrations before, a mixture of joy and sorrow. So many had fallen...but they had survived.

"I have to stay," said Romaria.

"I know," said Mazael.

They stood at the edge of the Garden, watching the crowds. Rachel stood with Gerald, showing Aldane to Rhodemar and Sil Tarithyn and Sir Cavilion and Circan anyone else she could find.

Ardanna and the druids were absent, gathering in secret rites to select a new Seer.

"There's been so much damage," said Romaria. "So much needs to be rebuilt. There are still Malrags left to hunt down, and the Elderborn will not rest while a single Malrag lurks in the Great Southern Forest." She took a deep breath. "And the people need me. I can step down later, once the damage has been repaired."

"I know," said Mazael. "I thought you were dead, Romaria. This time with you...it has been a gift. Even if we spent most of it fighting for our lives. I will wait for you, however long it takes."

"Thank you," said Romaria, and then, "I love you."

"I love you," said Mazael.

Her eyes glimmered in the torchlight. "Come with me."

She took his hand, and led him to their rooms in the Champion's Tower.

~

THE NEXT DAY Mazael Cravenlock left Deepforest Keep, with Gerald, Rachel, and all his men.

Lucan Mandragon rested in a cot stretched between two horses. He remained alive, if barely, despite whatever Malavost had done to him. Sometimes Mazael looked at Lucan, at his twisted limbs, gray flesh, and black veins, and wondered if Romaria had been right, if it would have been kinder to simply kill him.

But, no. Lucan had stood by him through some dark times, and Mazael would not abandon him now.

Mazael took one last glance at Deepforest Keep, at the walls and towers, at the mighty oaks rising from within the city. Romaria was there, and his heart would remain with her as well.

Someday, she would return to him.

He returned his attention to his men. Ultorin was dead and his host shattered, but Malrag warbands still prowled the Forest, and he would be ready for them.

Mazael rode away from Deepforest Keep and did not look back.

ROMARIA STOOD atop the Champion's Tower, listening to the reports.

"Four months to rebuild the gate, I think," said the chief of the builders. "And the druids will have to repair the warding spells, of course."

Romaria nodded, the bronze diadem cool against her brow, and the builder left, leaving her alone with the High Druid.

"What about a new Seer?" said Romaria.

"A new Seer is born, not chosen by the druids," said Ardanna, her golden eyes cold, her voice tight. "When we find him, we shall know him. Until then, we shall have to do without the guidance of a Seer. You should know this, child, if you are to serve as the Greenshield."

"And how am I to know," said Romaria, "if you will not tell me?"

"You are an abomination," said Ardanna, anger flashing in her eyes, "and..."

"Still, mother?" said Romaria. She ought to feel hurt, she knew. Or angry. Instead, she only felt exasperation. "After all this? The founders of Deepforest Keep intended for the Greenshield to be a half-blood. Only a half-blood could awaken the traigs. And without the traigs, Ultorin would have razed the city to the ground."

"Then the founders of the city were mistaken," said Ardanna. "A half-blood is an abomination! It..."

And Romaria had heard enough. Deepforest Keep had been her home while Athaelin had lived, but her father had died defending it. And now home was wherever she made it. Wherever she wanted to go.

She looked north, towards Castle Cravenlock.

Towards home.

"You must let yourself be guided by me in all things," said Ardanna, "and..."

"Shut up," said Romaria, without rancor. "I am sick to death of your voice."

Ardanna fell silent, stunned, and Romaria walked away without another word.

~

ROMARIA FOUND her brother in his rooms, honing the edge of his sword.

"Romaria." Rhodemar smiled, though his eyes remained sad. Then he grinned. "Or my lady Greenshield, I should say. What..."

Romaria removed the diadem, placed it upon his head, and handed him the ancient Greenshield.

"What?" said Rhodemar, stunned. "What is this?"

"You passed the Ritual of Rulership yourself, did you not?" said Romaria.

Rhodemar managed to nod. "But you are Father's eldest child..."

"I have visited Deepforest Keep perhaps five times in the last fifteen years," said Romaria. "You lived here, Rhodemar. This is your home, your people. You would make a better Champion for them than I ever would."

"But you defeated the Malrags," said Rhodemar.

"And now the people need you to rebuild," said Romaria.

For a long moment Rhodemar stared at her. "Are you sure?"

"I am," said Romaria.

"Is there anything you would ask of me?" said Rhodemar. "Anything at all?"

"Yes," said Romaria. "Just a horse."

~

THREE DAYS FROM DEEPFOREST KEEP, Gerald looked at Rachel.

Rachel blinked. "What?"

"You're smiling," said Gerald.

"And why should I not smile?" said Rachel, lifting the baby in her arms. She had to put Aldane down from time to time, but she tried to avoid it as often as possible. She had lost too much time with her son already. "Our son is restored to us."

"This is different," said Gerald. "Like...you have a secret."

He knew her so well.

"I do," said Rachel. "I found out before I left, when I spoke to Romaria. She...said I smelled different, and I asked why."

"What's the secret?" said Gerald.

Rachel smiled. "I'm pregnant."

She had the great satisfaction of watching the surprise on his face change to a delighted smile.

~

"MY LORD!"

Mazael reined up. One of the scouts hurried over.

"What is it?"

"A rider," said the scout. "Just one, coming from the city."

Mazael frowned. A messenger?

The rider came into sight, mounted on a mare, face hidden beneath the cowl of a worn green cloak. The rider reined up, and threw back the green hood, and Mazael found himself looking into Romaria's brilliant blue eyes.

"My lord Mazael!" she said. "Do you have room for one more in your party?"

He grinned. "I think so."

~

THE COLUMN RODE NORTH, weaving its way around the massive trees.

The two horses carrying Lucan's cot stayed to the rear. Lucan himself lay upon the cot, still breathing, his eyes closed.

Though from time to time a glimmer of blood-colored light leaked through his eyelids.

THE END

ABOUT THE AUTHOR

Standing over six feet tall, Jonathan Moeller has the piercing blue eyes of a Conan of Cimmeria, the bronze-colored hair of a Visigothic warrior-king, and the stern visage of a captain of men, none of which are useful in his career as a computer repairman, alas.

He has written the DEMONSOULED series of sword-and-sorcery novels, and continues to write THE GHOSTS sequence about assassin and spy Caina Amalas, the COMPUTER BEGINNER'S GUIDE series of computer books, and numerous other works.

Visit his website at:

http://www.jonathanmoeller.com

Visit his technology blog at:

http://www.computerbeginnersguides.com

Contact him at:

jmcontact@jonathanmoeller.com

CPSIA information can be obtained
at www.ICGtesting.com
Printed in the USA
BVHW040246311218
536761BV00021B/918/P

9 781975 892906